The Weight of Love

The Weight of Love

Gawain Barker

bushbrother

Cover design and imprint
bushbrother

website
thecolourofshadows.com

for
the band

Contents

Two Kings

Cairns 1977

Seth loved his brother, but not right now. The bastard was dodging around like a willy-wagtail and that wasn't like Alex at all.

It was a bloody stupid idea – taking Mum up the Gillies Highway to Auntie Grace's with twenty pounds of dope stashed in the back of Alex's truck. Mum didn't even know they smoked marijuana – let alone grew and sold it.

The coppers, getting ever smarter, were stopping cars and finding stuff. A Mercedes got pulled over in Abbott Street last month; in the boot and back seat, two thousand nicely wrapped Buddha-sticks worth fifty grand. Crikey.

Back at the driver's joint the lucky boys in blue found more foils of the primo – and a loaded semi-auto; a Ruger .44 carbine. Obviously under a bit of pressure, the bloke escapes from the watchhouse on the Esplanade and does a runner through town and into the suburbs, dodging through back-yards and leaping drains.

Then out at Edge Hill, after ducking around washing-lines and sending dogs crazy, he gets surrounded, but is keen to fight on, and housewives, seniors and toddlers get ring-side seats at the ensuing punch-on. It's seven against one and Mr Buddha Sticks has to make a detour to Cairns Base for stitches before being re-booked.

Yep, dope could be a rough old world and he didn't want Mum anywhere near it. So, he got in Alex's face.

They were both big boys – fit and hard; Seth six two, Alex six and a bit. Evenly matched, they'd had their scraps in the past. Seth unfailingly came up the under-dog. Alex was two years older, always the leader, and maybe it was this big-brother edge that made him prevail. Or maybe it was something else.

The times when Seth had found himself on the ground with Alex's forearm hard on his throat, choking him for real. Or with his ribs aching from a punch that had too much beef in it. His brother was willing to cross a line that he wouldn't.

And that day in Kuranda a year ago when Alex had put him in hospital. It had been his own fault; he'd mucked up good. Things between them had changed after that.

But Mum in a vehicle with dope in it was worth crossing a line for. As expected, Alex didn't like it.

"Bugger off," he said, raising his hand in Seth's face as though to deliver a back-slap.

Seth stood his ground. "It's not happening."

Alex laughed loudly.

"You take Mum up to Auntie Grace's," said Seth. "Bring her back then move your twenty pounds of dope."

"Grow a brain, mate. Two birds with one stone – heard of that? I'm not wasting fuel on two trips."

"Then you're not doing it."

Alex grinned and shook his head. Seth steeled himself, the idea of fighting his brother making him light-headed.

"What you gonna do? Tell Mum?" smirked Alex.

"Yeah . . . yeah, I will. That's a bloody good idea!"

It was a dob-in like no other, but Alex instantly knew he meant it, and the cunning bastard slid an arm around his shoulder and pulled them both backwards into the couch, nearly breaking it. Seth tried to get up, but his brother held him down and leant in; forehead to forehead.

"There'll be no cops," he promised. "It's a Sunday. With Mum in the truck and how I look, no one's going to take a second look at us. I'll drop her off, do the deed, pick her up later and be back before Countdown. It'll be tickety-boo, mate."

His brother's wheedling was a soothing and infuriating thing he'd heard his whole life. Sure, everything probably would go fine – but that wasn't the point. He was right about this and Alex was wrong.

And couldn't his brother trust him after all they'd done? Seth smarted at being side-lined; it locked him out.

"Delivery to who, Alex? Why won't you tell me?"

His brother, sensing victory, released him.

"That's what this is about," he said. "You're acting like a little girl because you're not in on it."

In a last-ditch effort, Seth pressed on.

"Nah, where did the dope come from?"

"It's booty, Seth. Spoils of war and all that."

"It's . . ."

"Yeah, it's nicked."

"Jesus, Alex – from who?"

"I trust you, you know that, but it's just me today, mate. Listen, I'll give you three thousand dollars tonight if you give me a smile now and forget about it. How about that?"

Alex gave him time like he was being respectful, but he already knew the answer, and when Seth's sullen silence confirmed it, he squeezed his brother right in close. It was a big consoling hug and Seth shook him off, feeling shame and relief – and endless resentment.

"Why do you think Dad named us Seth and Alexander?" crooned Alex.

"He read about ancient history at Uni. I know all that."

"Yes, but who were they?"

"I know all that too."

"They were kings, mate. And so are we. Don't forget it. We can take whatever we want."

It was bunkum, but Alex laughed his big laugh like you knew what he meant, but were too scared to admit it. Seth hated it and loved it at the same time.

His brother had an irresistible way of making you feel special, like you were included in grand mysteries he'd already solved. If you were up for knowing of course, and brave enough to jump right in with him.

A lot of times he didn't make logical sense, but seeking an explanation felt unworthy; revealing you as a junior at best, or as just another Cairns meathead at worst. Seth usually played along, Alex's encompassing laughter and overwhelming confidence hard to resist. But what really rubbed your nose in it was the glint of cheek in his eyes, like knew he was full of it and was just daring you to call his bluff.

"Seth wasn't a king," said Seth.

"Yes, he was – like Alexander the Great was a king."

"No, Seth was the brother of Cain and Abel."

"Aye? Didn't Cain kill his brother?"

"Yep."

"Abel yeah? Not Seth."

"Yep."

"What did Seth do to Cain – kill him?"

"No, it wasn't like that."

"I'd have done something."

"What, like kill your brother for killing your brother?"

"Piss off."

"Y'know, Seth lived nine hundred-and thirteen-years."

"True? How long did Alexander live for?"

"Thirty-two years."

"Bugger that – I'm gonna live to a thousand!"

Between God and the Army

King Reefs 1981

The ocean was warm, limpid and clear, and from out of its aquamarine vastness a tiger shark glided into view.

Wow, that's a big girl, thought Seth. At least four metres long and just the perfect predator. He looked around for Pep and Henry – they had to see this magnificent animal.

Ten metres behind him; the multi-coloured slope of the reef faded into indigo darkness; its top glittering with the metallic flash of waves – but no sign of his mates.

Surfacing, he scanned for heads and snorkels along the reef and nearby coral bommies; listening for air and water being expelled. Forty metres away from the exposed coral shelf of the low-tide reef, Henry's boat sat at anchor. They're going to miss out, thought Seth.

Just before he ducked back under, he took a second to dig the view – on the edge of King Reefs with the grey-green domes of the South Barnards a few kilometres further out into the Coral Sea, and over on the mainland, the primeval massif of the jungle-covered range capped with cloud. Catching painted crayfish with Pep and Henry was a great excuse to spend time out here. Eyes peeled for long spikey antenna; he'd bagged two, the yummy things now hanging off his belt in a mesh bag.

Back underwater, Seth got a surprise. The tiger shark wasn't swimming along lazily anymore – sunlight and water reflections were now strobing along its long body as it barrelled in. Adrenaline exploded through him; his ears went hot and his fingers tingled. The shark was having a go at him!

Kicking out hard with his fins, he swam backwards at the reef; but he knew the massive fish was faster than him. Over his pumping legs he watched it come tearing in.

The tiger's eyes turned white and its big square mouth opened. The exposed rows of big saw-edged teeth made Seth raise his Turnbull spear-gun. He'd shot a swag of fish with it, but nothing like this big creature – not even close.

He might be able to fire the steel spear into the shark's great maw, the double floppers tearing deep, but that's all he'd be able to do, and whether he escaped injury or not, the spear would bring the animal endless pain, and be a major, if not terminal impediment to its feeding. From its great size and faint stripes, he knew the shark was a good deal older than him.

If he pulled the trigger, this epic elasmobranch would die pathetically before her time. And for what – a story for the boys in the pub? He couldn't do that.

Hearing muffled shouting, he snatched a look and saw Johnny Pep; the silver oval of his mask looking around a bommie, incredulous bubbles bursting from his mouth.

With no chance of getting up onto the long shelf of reef in time, he turned to the slope of coral. There was the dark indentation of a cavity a few metres below him, and he swam to it at full speed. Flipping around, he centred up and back-pedalled into the space – trying not to look at the monster mouth full of teeth rushing towards him.

Coral branches jammed in, breaking against his back and shoulders. No blood, he prayed; and no moray eel in here. Rubber-covered heels and pumping fins broke off coral, and very damn lucky – he just squeezed in, turning his head sideways so it wouldn't stick out. Frozen like a fly beneath a swatter, he watched the water go dark around him.

The tiger shark barged in, turning to one side at the last metre, and an endless rasp of saw-edged teeth appeared centimetres from Seth's mask. Needing all the air in his lungs, he didn't yell – but he sure heard it in his head.

Water buffeted his ears and face, broken coral tinkled dully, and coral fragments swirled in the passing shock wave. He turned his head to look and saw the immense beast pull a ninety-degree turn with amazing speed then calmly swim off the way it had come. In outright disbelief, he crouched in the bosom of the reef, making out he was a big, blonde coral head.

Twenty long seconds went by before he burst out of his sanctuary and went like blue buggery up the reef wall. He surfaced at the edge, looking back as he gasped down air. Leaping out, he tore his mask off and kept looking in the water for the shark – and his mates. Behind him, somebody started screaming.

Christ, no – the big shark must have got stuck into Pep! Spinning around on his arse, he saw Johnny Pep climb up on the reef not far from him. With his mask off, he was screaming alright – with laughter. Now Henry popped up five metres away, alerted by the howling, and he pulled his mask up. "Henry – get out of the water!" yelled Seth, and Henry quickly swam in and hopped up onto the coral.

"What happened?" he said. "Pep! You right mate?"

Pep kept up his racket, his muscled shoulders jumping with mirth, his eyes streaming with tears. Seth felt shaky now and he began laughing fit to piss himself.

"What? What happened?" Henry's grin was huge.

"Oh, man!" Pep finally spoke. "This bastard, he's . . ."

His voice, all high and squeaky, dissolved into laughter again. Laughing his guts out, Seth couldn't speak either. Around him the ocean and sky vibrated diamond-sharp. He was as high as a kite.

Henry chuckled in anticipation, he knew it was a good one, and after another mis-start, Pep finally got it out.

"This bastard," he said, pointing at Seth. "Just got bush-whacked by a big tiger shark! Over four metres long!"

"True!" Henry, just like Pep, was delighted. Tough nuts through and through, they'd both spent a lifetime on the ocean. Any narrow escape was to be celebrated. Loudly.

Laughter now claimed Henry, and on the shimmering expanse of reef they bawled like crazy men.

The sunset was a corker, sets of rain clouds to the north swimming like dark purple whales behind Mt. Marquette and across the high jungle ranges. They were anchored by the channel, and in the good-sized galley Seth knocked them up a feed; dunking the crays they'd caught in boiling seawater then dishing them up with Malanda butter and slices of crusty bread from the Italian bakery in Innisfail.

On the side – a tomato, capsicum and red-onion salad, a thing he'd learnt from Sunny, his hippy lady-friend who lived up from his place at Machans Beach.

They ate in a silence punctuated by the slap and gurgle of water on the hull, the cracking of cray shells and legs, and the occasional happy grunt or sigh.

After that, they had a good shot of Bundy rum, blew a joint, grabbed beers, and began casting and drop-lining over the side. Drinking quietly, lazy from the day's sun, they slowly caught some fish – a couple of nannygais, a nice trevally, and a bonza golden-band jobbie going on five kilos.

Henry's boat, the Maria, was a little beauty: a Norman Wright cruiser; forty-five foot, four berths, Oregon timber on hardwood frames, a well set-up galley, and a hundred-and-forty litres of freezer space; nothing by commercial standards, but that wasn't the point.

The sweet looking boat was Henry's home and base of operations, not a serious instrument of commerce. When chasing real money, he would work hard on company or private boats as a sought-after gun for hire in the prawn, barramundi and marlin seasons. Then a favourite nephew or cousin would care-take the Maria in Chinaman Creek.

Seth reckoned that Henry had saltwater running in his veins. There had always been fishermen and seafarers in his Torres Straits family and he'd caught his first fish as a toddler. Over the last decade or so he'd basically lived on the water, either fishing or thinking about fishing.

From the Sir Edward Pellews in the Gulf of Carpentaria, to the Capricorn Islands off Gladstone: it was all Henry's country – infinite, everchanging, every square kilometre brimming with life. In this boundless place he'd seen things: dark ghosts of centuries-old shipwrecks caught in the silvered reef, the Pompey blue holes, and the white-sand glare of coral keys steaming with migratory birds. He'd outrun tropical storms, their frozen tops blotting out the sun and stars for five hundred kilometres around, and he'd gazed upon the winged and bird-beaked wonder of the sunfish, weighing a tonne or more, basking on the surface in solar-induced bliss.

To his sprawling family's disappointment, he was still a single man without kids for his mum and sisters, aunties and grandmas to fuss over. But they knew why – he was married to the big blue.

Living on the Maria, Henry kept it, and his life, ship-shape. Sure, he liked a beer and all that, but he diligently saved money and used it well; buying his boat for one, and helping out the family with operations and school fees. He was a well-respected man on his way to becoming a well-respected elder, and Seth felt honoured being his mate.

If there was one bloke who knew as much as Henry about fishing then it was the laughing, blue-eyed pirate sitting next to him. Johnny Pep was Greek Australian and all fisherman, and as young blokes, he and Henry had crewed on trawlers and fishing boats together. Unlike the master of the Maria, money never stayed in Pep's net very long; somehow wriggling free. But he'd have a damn good time while it was his – romancing the ladies and living large, all while slaking an insatiable appetite for the best food, drink and smoke.

Fortunately, Pep was a bloody good fisherman and his net never stayed empty for long. Sixteen years on the sea had given him an unerring eye for the unexpected. Alert, quick and relaxed, he was also reliably good for a laugh, and who couldn't like that on a small crew?

Digging the simple pleasures – fishing after a good feed with good mates, Seth grinned at the sea and stars. It was quiet out here and the night stretched all around them in warm silence. Aside from the electric glow of Kurrimine Beach and someone's beach fire at Murdering Point, there were just a couple of boats glimmering in the dark a few kilometres to the north.

The sea was flat, the wind a gentle knot or two from the south-east, and as Seth cleaned the trevally, two bright flashes came from the north; then one after the other, two lights zipped across the night sky before exploding with far-off booms out near the Barnards.

"Bloody hell, it's not Guy Fawkes night, is it?" said Seth.

"Army," said Henry. "Up the top of Cowley Beach. They got a firing range there."

"Those are bloody big guns."

"Nah, I reckon that's rockets," said Henry. "Sixty sixes or Redeyes, hey."

"Is that right?"

"Yep. You don't want to get too close. Restricted area."

They watched the dark mass of the northern shore and

after a few minutes, saw two more lights flash out to sea, quickly followed by two distant detonations.

"That's crazy," said Seth.

Henry stared intently towards Cowley Beach.

"Whatcha see, Henry?" said Pep.

"One of those boats up there – it's moving now."

"Not surprised with World War Three going on."

Their lines hung listlessly in the water, the tide on the turn. Seth reeled his in and ditched the bait.

"Reckon we've had enough?"

When the boys nodded, he got a bucket of seawater and cleaned down the bait table and his fishy hands. The boys put away their rods and cleaned up, the pump running as Henry hosed down the deck with sea water. As he stowed the hose around the side, he stopped and looked north again, and Seth and Pep followed his gaze.

In the darkness there was a moving light, and over the chuckle of water on the Maria's hull there came the faint growl of an engine.

"Oh-oh, watch out skipper," said Pep. "Army's coming! Whatcha got? Three-o-three? Shotgun?"

Henry smiled, his eyes on the incoming boat. The light altered course for a bit, moving back and forth like a lost star before sticking to the one line, and they watched in silence until it changed direction again.

"They're coming this way," said Henry.

Within twenty minutes the boat was close enough for Seth to see the shapes of three blokes in the wheelhouse light. A few hundred metres out it slowed and came in, slowing again as it puttered up to them.

It was a tidy little cabin cruiser, and in the light from the Maria, Seth saw the name Syracuse in red script on its bow. The lanky bloke at the wheel cut the engine and let the boat nose in.

"Hey, Henry," he yelled. "How ya doing, mate?"

"Who's that there?" said Henry. "Tallie?"

"Yeah, it's Tallie! Fishing with a couple of mates here from Innisfail. We were having a beer off Cowley when the army started throwing crackers around."

"Hey, good to see you. You blokes wanna come aboard and have a beer?" said Henry. "Might even find a nip of rum."

"Yeah?" said Tallie to his two mates and they nodded.

Seth sat drinking his beer, watching the Syracuse gently bump alongside. Pep grabbed the gunwale and took a rope from a big, black-haired bloke and tied it off. In the light of the two boats the bloke looked familiar.

The three men came on board, everyone grabbing a seat and getting a beer. Seth recognized the black-haired bloke as he sat down next to him.

"Hey, Vinnie Sabbotini," said Seth.

"Seth Kelly. Well, this is a surprise," said Vinnie. "But I guess not if you like fishing, hey?"

Seth laughed, uneasy at seeing him.

Tallie and his mate introduced themselves and it wasn't long before Pep brought up the tiger shark. That got some laughs and the rum was poured. Now the sea stories came out, each bloke trying to outdo Seth's misadventure.

While this contest went on, Vinnie Sabbotini leaned in.

"You've haven't heard about my brother, hey? Gerry."

Gerry Sabbotini, known as Sabbo, was Seth's friend – not his big brother Vinnie. The Sabbotinis were a proud family of staunch Catholics who worked as hard at sugar-cane farming as they did in following the word of God. Sabbo was the youngest and he'd been the rebel; defiantly unmarried and into boxing and customising cars.

He'd also grown a crop of dope with Seth that had gone like green clockwork. After that, they'd had some raucous times together, the well-spoken and curly-haired Sabbo a great partner in chasing women. And a few times they'd worked together as a team; buying and selling dope, or smuggling it interstate for other blokes.

Like his family, Vinnie Sabbotini was super-straight. He abhorred any sort of coarse language, hedonistic fun or illegal activity, and Seth knew that Vinnie had mightily disapproved of him as his little brother's friend.

"No, how's he doing?" said Seth.

"He's in jail. Stuart Creek. He's been assaulted, but no-one's fucked him up the arse yet."

Seth nearly dropped his beer.

The other blokes were roaring with laughter; something about a dolphin using its old fella to hook onto the arm of a marine scientist it had taken a shine to.

"Aye? What's he in jail for?" said Seth.

"According to him – nothing. I believe him, but he's too scared to tell us the truth. He got ten years. They wanted an attempted murder charge. Sound like Gerry to you?"

"No. No, that's not Gerry."

"Looks like he was mixed up with some drug-dealing mates of yours. Know anything about that?"

There was a fish scale in Vinnie Sabbotini's hair. His big raw-knuckled hand tightly clutched his undrunk beer.

"I was down in Sydney for three years," said Seth. "Been back for nearly two, but I've only seen Gerry once in all that time. Our paths went different ways."

"Yeah?" said Vinnie. "Well, you certainly put him on the wrong path first."

"Hey c'mon mate, I'm a different bloke now. Four and a half years is a long time."

"So is ten."

Seth took it back a few notches and looked around. Pep gave him a 'you right?' look. He nodded and turned back to Vinnie Sabbotini.

"I'm shocked, mate. I can't believe it. That's not Gerry."

"Yet somehow he's in prison."

"You haven't talked to him about it? Found out what the real story is? Could he appeal?"

"Like I said, we tried all of that, but he's frightened of somebody, and with good reason – ashamed."

"I should go see him."

"That's right – you should. Maybe he'll talk to someone he doesn't feel ashamed with. Someone who has got down in the dirt like he has."

Seth smothered a frown. This stuck-up churchie was pushing it now; he had no right judging him, and no right making him feel guilty. With the timber deck warm under his feet, Seth drank some more beer. Well, here's a rotten way to end a great day, he thought.

But Sabbo's big brother was right – he should go and visit his old mate; see if there was something he could do.

"Yeah, I'll go talk to him," he said.

Vinnie Sabbotini nodded grimly.

"You do that. See – between God and the army, that's the reason why we've met here tonight."

Stuart Creek

Back home at Machans Beach, a few kilometres north of Cairns, the meeting with Sabbo's brother at King Reefs simmered away in Seth's head. Nearly five years down the track and he couldn't help feeling some responsibility for where Sabbo was now. Vinnie Sabbotini had pushed a few buttons alright. Still, it all boiled down to the one thing — he had to go and see his mate.

With Christmas coming up there wasn't much on. Make that nothing on, so he had time to make the three hundred and seventy km drive south to the prison just outside of Townsville; a military town, and Cairns' erstwhile rival for big smoke of the far north.

The next day he joined everyone going in to work under overcast skies, and was soon south of Cairns and passing Mt. Sheridan. On the forested hillsides there were fresh red-dirt scars; blocks carved out for houses. Everyone had a right to a home, but it gave Seth a funny feeling.

In Edmonton, there were virtual car-parks of muddy, rutted grass on either side of Mill Road turn-off. By lunch time, the pubs on both corners, The Hambledon and The Grafton, would be chockablock with cheerful drinkers all basically on holiday now, the major work of the year done.

It was sugar country, the harvest over, with the cut cane at the mill and the narrow-gauge trains back in their big tin sheds awaiting next year's season. Beyond Edmonton, the kilometres of cane fields alongside the highway were now stubble, and scores of white cattle egrets worked the great expanses of rippled ochre dirt.

Soon he was clear of what passed for populated areas, and he let the Pig, his customised FJ55 Land Cruiser, go hard down the Bruce Highway; the 1,800-kilometre-long road down the east coast to the state capital Brisbane.

The Bruce was a long rough ride; pretty much two lanes of dust and stones that rattled cars apart or to a standstill, and jokers called it the Crystal Highway for all the broken windscreen glass along its edges. At this time of the year it didn't look too bad, with the usual number of crumbling shoulders and wheel-pounding potholes. After the wet it would be another story.

Traffic was light, aside from a trio of semi-trailers north of Innisfail which he overtook one after another; the last one blaring its airhorn in salute. There was some roadkill; a few bloated wallabies and squashed birds, and near the Bingil Bay turnoff – a good-sized python smeared across the tarmac. It was a bloody shame.

Still, he felt the thoroughly modern fella with the air-con going full-bore and the Marantz car-stereo playing cassettes. The one he had on now was from some Sydney boys, and though more pop than rock, it was bloody great.

bjorn is just a viking.
he is very handy with a sword.
he loves nothing better
than to cut and slash right through a horde.
mutilation, jubilation.
friendly muscles in a tussle.

In the cool of the Pig's cabin, he grooved along to the chugging acoustic strum of the beat, digging the zany, shivery guitar chords, and getting a kick out of the lyrics. Mental as anything alright.

The low cloud had cleared by the time he ascended the Cardwell Range, and he pulled over at the top to check out the view of the enormous island that hugged the coast. It was bloody humid outside the air-con chill of the Pig as he looked at the prehistoric vista. Several hundred metres below, the Seymour River snaked out through a hundred acres of mangrove swamps into the channel. Beyond the channel; the island, its jagged central spine of mountains more than a kilometre high in parts. Rising up from the sea, it looked like a dinosaur.

A jungle peak on the island had claimed over a dozen lives one stormy morning during the war; a Yank bomber flew into it, the plane exploding with no survivors. The payroll for the Iron Range heavy-bomber air-strips got scattered across the jungle. Two tin-miners, fellas from a clan of locals, were working the creeks up there and they struck it lucky. A few days later, the blokes and their families were buying all sorts of good stuff in Halifax with greenbacks courtesy of Uncle Sam. Seth could dig that. He liked manifestations of the rebel spirit.

The Murri people called the jungle island Pouandai and the whitefellas called it Hinchinbrook, and nearly fifty years ago it had become a National Park. Seth reckoned that a great idea – he loved the place.

Moments of mind-bending beauty and skull-cracking weirdness filled his head. He'd have to go back there one day and try and work out which memories were real.

In Townsville, he parked on Palmer Street amongst a dusty array of Holdens, Fords and Toyotas. It looked like the rain hadn't made it here this week, or the week before. Brownsville was living up to its nickname.

In The Australian Hotel he turned on the charm with a sweaty young barmaid and got her to bribe the cook with a five dollar note. This tickle-up resulted in the pub's first counter-lunch of the day.

Wolfing down a T-bone, chips, gravy, and garden salad, he avoided the disgruntled gaze of locals wondering how this blow-in was getting a feed half an hour before official kick-off. As feeds go it did the job, and he washed it down with a pot of NQ Lager.

He wondered if there was steak on the menu at Stuart Creek. There sure as hell were no beers. Sabbo liked a beer and he'd surely have a big thirst when he got out. Seven years from now.

Seth couldn't think of anything worse than doing time. It scared him stupid. Separated from life, but still in it. No bush, no ocean, no beaches. No family, no friends, no fun. No sex, no grog, no dope. No rock'n'roll. No way.

It was no wonder that Murri blokes killed themselves in jail. Cut-off from their families and country, buried deep in concrete and steel, they died before their bodies did. Locking those blokes up was like chopping out their souls. Truth was – Seth wasn't altogether sure he wouldn't do the same.

His grim state of mind fed a deepening unease. When he parked outside the prison and put on an ironed shirt, dread started wrestling with lunch in his guts. Looking at the big colonial edifice – its entrance framed by cream-coloured bricks and topped by a great fanlight of iron – gave him the chills. This was a hell on earth; one with demons aplenty.

It had been humid outside, but the air inside the prison got thicker and thicker the further he went in; a psychic fug soaked with blood, sweat and tears, and the stink of brutal incarceration. Oh man, he thought – how could a fella's life go arse-up so badly?

In the visitor's room the smell of cheap disinfectant was strong, and a dozen prisoners sat behind glass talking to visitors on hand-sets. Sabbo was already seated behind the greasy window, and for a second, he looked surprised. Then a hard smile sealed his face and he flicked a look to his left, as if checking on someone sitting there.

Sabbo didn't look too bad, but his chick-bait curls were now a number two, and when he held the phone, Seth saw fresh scabs on his knuckles.

"Seth Kelly. Surprised you even know I'm here."

"I saw Vinnie the other day."

"Yeah, good old Vinnie. Surprised he even knew who you were. I'm having a hard time remembering myself."

"It's been a while," said Seth, hating the bitter tone in

his friend's voice. "But we caught up last year, right? I saw you in the front bar at Hides with . . ."

His memory sharpened and he saw the men who'd been sitting with Sabbo that day. Now he got it. Now he knew why his mate was in here.

". . . Gordy and Liam Mac," he finished.

Sabbo's tough smile disappeared.

"They dropped you in this."

Sabbo looked away, but Seth caught the impotent rage gutting his eyes.

"Sabbo, mate! What did they do?"

His friend's face was a mess of self-loathing and Seth's heart went out to him.

"Listen, I can help you," he said. "What happened?"

Sabbo, head down, shook it slowly like he was listening to Pink Floyd.

"Come on Sab. What happened?"

Wary as a dingo, Sabbo flashed another look to his left. Whoever was sitting there was holding his tongue. Ten, twenty seconds went by, but he wasn't saying nothing.

Seth laughed. Sabbo looked up with razorblade eyes.

"What are you laughing about?"

Seth hardly recognized his friend now. It wasn't just the prison hair-cut and uniform – he looked like a beast; the charming mug that had ladies swooning now a hard fist.

"I'm happy," said Seth.

"Happy? You right there?"

"Yeah, I'm happy because I didn't think you'd bash a bloke half to death. With the dirty Macs involved, I know for sure now it wasn't you."

"Still doesn't help me."

"You're right there."

Sabbo stared at him.

"I know you're scared of them," said Seth. "And I don't blame you. They're real bad news, but now you're stuck like a parrot up a drainpipe. It's a real shame."

Seth, receiver in hand, began to get up. Sabbo's eyes wilted.

"You going already?"

"Yep. I mean what else is there to say? You've decided to roll over to protect two bastards who never thought you were much more than dogshit from day one. Of course, you don't want to be crippled or knocked in here on Gordy Mac's say-so – I understand that. But there's no way I'd put myself through this. I'd rather fight and die. Or win."

Sabbo looked like a lost kid.

"When you're ready – Kelly Investigations in the Yellow Pages," said Seth. "You're in a big hole, mate. If you want a ladder to get out – you're going to have to help me build one."

Minder

He should have stopped at Dad's on the way home, but he didn't want to make up a story about why he was in the area. Later that evening he rang him for a chat.

Dad was on the farm near Gordonvale. He'd spent a few months living with Seth at Machans last year, getting his head together. And helping me get my head together too, he thought. They'd both gone through a few years in their own private hells, but now they were as tight as – a team in fact.

Dad was like his secretary and tax-agent rolled into one. Seth had checked out a three hundred and eighty-dollar answering machine in town, but in the end, he got a new phone number. The old one was now Dad's, and he'd field Kelly Investigations calls, his precise and educated voice impressing potential clients. And the old man loved it.

A master of tax, Dad kept the business records tighter than a mouse's clacker, and his trained scientist's mind and sharp logic had already helped Seth close one case.

"Kelly Investigations," said a melliferous voice.

"Hey Dad, how you going?"

"I'm going very well, thank you, Seth. Just put in three rows of sweet potato crowns and the taro is flourishing. You'll have to get some before I sell it all."

"Nice one, Dad. Maybe on the weekend."

"I look forward to it. Now listen, we finally have some business. I got a call from a friend of yours in Sydney who wants to hire you. A Mr David Silver."

"You're kidding me."

"No, I'm not. Is this . . . positive news?"

"Yeah, yeah, Davey's a good mate. What did he want?"

"All he told me was his new phone number. Got a pen?"

When they'd finished talking, Seth looked at the Rolex Submariner on his wrist. It was pushing five o'clock, but Davey might still be home.

Seth had spent nearly three years in Sydney working as an armoured-car guard in the day, and providing security for rock bands at night. In this role of muso's minder, he'd made good friends with the motor-mouthed dynamo that was Davey Silver.

Seth pictured him in his little flat off Oxford Street: the city hum outside, the stereo full-on inside; choofing away on a Camel and typing furiously on his typewriter. Seth could hear that manic voice too – talking about music and bands. Davey lived and breathed the scene, and was hell-bent on making himself a name in it. And a fair bit of cash too.

With gold and glory beckoning like bikini girls on a yacht, Davey did whatever it took to turn a buck and get a little further up the ladder. From noon to sunset, he'd be writing ads, flyers and press releases while listening to all the new singles and albums. When night fell, he'd do the rounds of the venues: holding impromptu meetings with musicians, agents and managers; standing at the bar, out on the street, or in the toilets – wherever, always going balls-out promoting the scene.

Perhaps Davey's most career-enhancing skill was his uncanny ability to source and deliver musical gear, and other essential items and services to those who worked in the industry. A particular amplifier was needed by a name guitarist for a gig in two hours. Davey would find one and have it onstage before the guitar-roadie knew. An up-and-coming singer had mislaid the photographer tasked with capturing her showcase performance. Davey would find a shit-hot replacement. The edgy drummer of the headline band needed a calming smoke – preferably Queensland heads. Davey would find that calming smoke . . . and it would be Queensland heads.

Seth readied his head and dialled. His mate answered the phone running.

"For the love of God, it's Seth Kelly, the Jungle Jim of the north! You're ringing to tell me you're coming back, right? If it wasn't for the sweet little hippie chicks, giant lobsters, dynamite dope and eternal sunshine, you'd have seen the sense of it earlier. And your timing is perfecto because things are exploding here at the moment. Ex-plo-ding! This kid I saw Friday night would give Moss, Ross, Lobby *and* Jeff Beck a run for their money. I swear he had six fingers on each hand!"

Seth put his feet up.

"I've been busy of course. I've got a nice office now and a secretary. Remember Janice Eaton – smart no-bullshit girl doing promo for EMI? Well, she's learning to be even smarter and more no-bullshit with me. And Cold Chisel – I'm angling for work with them. They're about to record a new album that's gonna blow up bigger than East. So how were their gigs up there in jungleville last year? Did you say hello? You caught both of their shows at . . . Up the Hill – what's the venue called?"

"House on the Hill."

"So, how were they?"

"I didn't go."

"What! Were you sick?"

"No – I went fishing."

"What? Did you say fishing?"

"Yeah. I caught some nice fish."

There was silence then real concern.

"Seth, you have got to get out of there! The humidity is rotting your brain, man. You went fishing! Look there's a hundred opportunities here in Sydney just swimming by. I'm serious and you know how serious? Tah – dahhh! I'm the new manager of The Tygers! Howzat!"

Seth knew what was coming now. The Tygers were the band he'd worked the most with in Sydney; as security, and twice as de facto tour manager. He'd spent a good chunk of time with them in '79 and '80.

They were a good band who were flat-out brilliant live. With an audience they ignited, generating dozens of fresh ideas from the templates of their songs. Their two albums were well-crafted, too well-crafted, and outside of a string of chart-busting singles, sales were a little soft. The band's rock'n'roll splinters had been sanded down and polished by a name, but not very intuitive, producer. They should have got Opitz to produce, Seth had told Hugh, the band's brilliant lead-guitarist.

He'd also suggested the band record their live gigs with a good sound-engineer at the desk; cherry-pick the best songs for a live album and really show people what they were all about. Hugh and Patrick, the bass player, thought it was a wonderful idea. As usual, Charlie and Marko were stoned and indifferent. Richie the lead singer and their sleazy prick of a manager had shot Seth a shut-your-hired-mouth look – and that was that.

"Seth, listen! An amazing opportunity awaits you," said Davey. "The Tygers need you! I need you!"

"Stop, stop," said Seth, his intimation vindicated. "I'm not coming back to Sydney. I've got a business here now."

"What, as a private investigator? In a sweaty, dead-end town chasing up kids better left lost and spying on poor sods whose marriages are screwed anyway? You can do better than that, man. It's boring! It's straight! Even the guy answering your phone sounded like someone's dad."

"He is my dad," said Seth.

Davey loved his parents and Seth quickly hopped into the guilty silence.

"Look, thanks a million for the thought, mate, but I'm happy here. Really."

Sorry Davey, he thought. Cairns might be a sweaty little dead-end town, but it'll do me for the moment.

"Do you charge by the week?" said Davey.

"Aye? What for?"

"For being on the ball and keeping someone in line."

"The bass-bins must be making you deaf, Davey. I told you I'm not coming back to Sydney."

"I mean looking after someone up there in that tropical wonderland of yours."

"Up here? In Cairns?"

"Yes – up there, deafboy – in Cairns."

"Who?"

"Hugh."

Seth stared through the louvre windows, cries of, 'hello, hello?' coming from the receiver. Hugh bloody Christie, he thought. What unbelievable mess was he in now?

"C'mon man!" Davey was yelling now.

"OK, OK," said Seth, "What's the story?"

"I thought you'd hung up on me!"

"Give me time. So, why me? Why Cairns?"

"Well, he's screwed up again. With his family this time. We know he's a beast with the booze, smoke and whiffy, but it's got out of control. His family want him out of town to calm down, and wait for whatever he's done to blow over. They want a minder for him too, so I thought of you up there in little old Cairns."

"Are you serious?"

"I sure am. You guys always got on, and he loves you, man! He's always telling some story about you and him and it always ends with – I miss him, I fucking miss him."

"Hah – is he playing the violin now?"

"All you gotta do is talk to his father. You want me to set this up or what?"

"His father?"

"Yeah, even Hugh's got one. Michael Christie, Order of Australia, architectural genius, land developer and multi fucking millionaire."

"Is that right?"

"Got your attention now? Play it right and you'll end up with a big handful of shekels."

"How long?"

"A month? Depends on what's gone down I guess."

"When?"

"Like next week."

"Next week? It's the holidays. Don't you have gigs?"

"Ah . . . the band's currently taking a well-deserved hiatus from playing live."

Seth didn't like the sound of that. Bands taking a hiatus often never came back from it.

"You have no idea what's up with Hugh and his family?"

"Nope. He's said nothing and his father is . . . well . . . I didn't feel like asking him."

"Why not?"

"You ask him."

"Sounds like he put the wind up you, Davey boy."

"Up yours, Seth. Dealing with one Christie is enough for me and, yeah – Hugh's father is an uptight old prick. He probably got thoroughly caned at a posh private school. God knows Hugh could have done with some of that – he's as loose as the proverbial goose right now."

Outside the window, dirty rotten mynah birds started screaming at a bird that wasn't a dirty rotten mynah bird.

"What in God's name is that noise?" said Davey.

"Birds," said Seth, thinking hard.

"What? In the house!" Davey was a resolute inner-city boy; the only animals he knew about were the ones he'd seen on TV – Skippy, Kermit the Frog, Agro.

"They're outside, you big nong," said Seth, coming to a decision. "OK – give daddy Christie my number."

"Seth, you're a mensch! Thank you, thank you, thank you! You are helping Hugh and me, and The Tygers, in a major way. You will not regret this."

Seth mused that last line. The promise of a good little fee soothed his trepidation, but when it came to booze and drug-soaked lead-guitarists in the league of Hugh Christie – all bets were off.

"One more thing," said Davey. "And it's very important. Hugh needs to write some songs, for the Tygers – and for himself. A few things depend upon that happening."

After the call, Seth did some bits and pieces around the house before taking a beer and going to check out the sky.

A line of rain-swollen clouds was blowing across Trinity Bay, and where the back of his garden turned into beach, the sand was pocked with tiny craters from the last downpour. With his ears turned up for the phone, Seth slowly drank his beer. As the clouds billowed in, spits of rain began to fall, and he went back in.

Finishing his beer, he wondered what he'd have for tea – and when Hugh Christie's father would ring.

It felt undignified waiting for a phone-call; it was what the knee-socks did. Still, it was part of the job, and it had been a long time between drinks. With his bank-book out of temptation's way in the pipe stash in the back garden, he was living off a dwindling roll of fifties and twenties.

The business had been a gamble – set up with two big chunks of cash earnt from an old flame, and her friends. He'd applied for, and got, an investigator's licence, printed up business cards and took out ads in the papers. His fifty bucks a day fee, plus expenses, was proving a bit rich for the far north, but it wasn't such a bad thing as it kept the feuding neighbours, fruit-cake pensioners and missing-pet owners away.

It hadn't taken long for his hometown to find out he was for hire and he'd knocked back lucrative offers for strong-arm stuff; fifteen thousand dollars to help rip off a semi-trailer full of dope; five hundred bucks for the few seconds it would take to bash a recalcitrant crim back into line; seventy per cent of what he could get debt-collecting from rough-neck miners and crazy cow-cockies out west – the sort of blokes you'd have to knock out cold to get even a sniff of a wallet.

He'd been muscle on the door, run concert security, and prowled venues as a bouncer, but monstering blokes for money wasn't him. Sure, he could knock heads if he had to, but he was a private investigator now, a man who used his brains, connections, and a bit of cash to get things done.

Now and then he'd get a glow on his knuckles thumping someone who needed it – but not for money. Only to help out a friend.

Like the time he helped out his taxi-driver mate, Harry Spinks. The wayward son of one of the old cabbie's friends kept dodging his fare when Harry took him from his piss-ups in town out to his shack at Holloways Beach.

Cruising on his father's friendship with the old cabbie, he booked the fares up, promising to make good on payday. But payday never came, and finally jack of the bull, Harry refused to budge without cash up front. The little shit had grabbed the old cabbie's ear and twisted hard.

Seth more than bristled at that. Not only was Harry an absolute gem, he'd also gone toe-to-toe with the Japanese in the Owen Stanley Range, where he'd seen and done things that would make young fellas today fill their jocks. It fair made Seth's blood boil.

So, when it came to frighteners time, he slipped into full bone-cracking mode, and instead of a growling and a few slaps, he punched the grub right through the fibro wall of the rotting beach shack. On the deck outside he picked the prick up and banged his head against a row of hanging pot-plants – breaking them all apart. Only soil and dead roots tumbled out, and that was lucky, because Seth liked plants.

Helping people was second-nature to him, but it was a bit of a struggle doing it professionally. He wasn't looking for jobs in the paper just yet, but he'd started thinking seriously about a couple of plan Bs.

The main thing was, he wasn't going hungry or missing out on life's little luxuries. Like the stash of mango Weis bars in the freezer. He grabbed one, and as he got down to the end of the wrapper, the phone rang. He answered and heard a thousand bucks in every syllable of the voice on the other end.

Impeccably correct, diction spot-on, it resonated with a perfectly calibrated timbre, speaking the Queen's English as taught in the most exclusive schools in the country. The voice also contained a steely seam of command, redolent of important decisions made by important men. This hard underlying tone spoke of money, and the things money could do.

"This is Michael Christie, Mr Kelly. Mr Silver has told you I would call."

"Hello Mr Christie. Yes, he did," said Seth.

"Are you available to work for me there in . . . ah . . ."

"Cairns."

"Yes, up there. I understand that you have previously worked for my son in a personal security role."

"That's right."

"It's in that same role that I will employ you."

"Is he in trouble?"

"In what way do you mean?"

"Do you have fears for his safety?"

Silence. Seth sensed Michael Christie was finding this a bit irksome. Tough luck, chum – you called me.

"The only threat to his safety is from himself," said Christie. "I'm sure you're aware of that."

"Ah, I'm not sure I can comment Mr Christie. I haven't seen Hugh in nearly two years."

"Do you use drugs Mr Kelly?"

"I'm sorry?"

"Please don't play coy with me. I'll get someone else the minute after I put down the phone."

"I smoke the occasional joint, probably drink too much beer, enjoy rum in moderation, and I can drink cocktails when I'm with a lady. That's it really."

"I appreciate your honesty," said Christie, sounding like he appreciated bugger-all.

"My son has addictions – alcohol, cocaine, marijuana."

"I'm not a counsellor Mr Christie."

"I'm aware of that," snapped Christie. "No, I want you to curtail his intake of drugs and alcohol. Take him fishing or whatever it is you do up there that's healthy. Can you do that?"

"I can do that."

"What is your fee?"

"What sort of time-frame are you thinking of?"

"Let's say a month."

"Well, I do have some other jobs on, so . . ."

"Spare me Mr Kelly. How much?"

"Five thousand dollars and expenses." Yeah, bung it on, thought Seth.

"Expenses?"

"Yes, like hiring a boat to go fishing, and scuba gear and rods and reels – all that healthy stuff we do up here."

"I will expect invoices and receipts."

"Kelly Investigations is a professional business."

"You have a bank account then."

"Yes, we operate with all the latest mod-cons."

"Mr Kelly, I'm enjoying this conversation as much as you are. Your bank account details and postal address?"

"Please phone this number, Mr. Christie – 613027, and a Mr Kelly will take care of those details. He's my father and business partner."

Seth grinned meanly. Yeah mate, I get on with my dad.

"Alright," said Michael Christie. "I'll send you a contract

by today's express post. You read it, sign it, and send it back immediately. It will have a confidentiality clause. I will transfer half the money on receipt of the contract, the other half upon my son's return."

Holy bloody dooley, thought Seth. Five grand and he didn't even blink.

"Now, Mr Kelly, I need to make the penalties related to the confidentiality clause clear. Any failure to comply will result in full retention of the second part of the fee, and comprehensive legal action." Michael Christie's voice was all steel now.

"I do not care about the previous relationship you had with my son. You are working for me now, so you will do as I say. Whatever my son says about this family will be ignored and forgotten. Do you understand?"

"Clear as a bell."

"Good. Now, if you'll excuse me." Christie hung up.

Still not believing it, Seth slowly put the receiver down. That was weird – but it was five bloody grand's worth of weird! He air-punched a victorious left-right combination, before cheerfully opening another NQ Lager.

Being in the money again made the beer taste even better, and Dad was going to be over the moon, and . . . he put the beer down.

It's Hugh Christie, thought Seth. How much weird am I going to get for five grand?

Dad rang twenty minutes later, very impressed.

"How about that? Michael Christie, the architect. And five thousand dollars! Well done, son. Now, Mr Christie wants his son to stay with you – not at a hotel."

Aye? thought Seth. Dad read his silence.

"It's quiet at Machans Beach. No hotel bars or night-clubs. I understand his son needs some rest."

That made sense, thought Seth. It would be a lot easier to keep an eye on Hugh. Was this babysitting or what?

"Yeah, that's fine Dad."

"Good. He'll send the contract to me, I'll read through it and we'll have a chat before I send it off."

Seth smiled. Dad was in control – the perfect secretary. With decades at CSIRO working for the government, and a stint with the sugar giant CSR, his father had signed off on a hundred thousand bits of paper.

It wasn't really Seth's thing – the written word. Aside from music magazines like Ram, Rolling Stone and Juke, the occasional thriller or blockbuster, and boat engine or car manuals, he didn't read an awful lot.

Dad had been disappointed. He'd left real classics out for him; fellas like Xavier Herbert, Ion Idriess and Ernest Hemingway; men who had lived full-on outdoor lives in nature and in war. But the sea and the bush, the cars and girls, not to mention the drugs and rock'n'roll, had been much more interesting than books.

"Aw, thanks Dad," he said.

His father would read the contract, they'd talk over the phone and he'd know exactly what he was liable for. Dad would forge his signature, send it off, and then tell him when the money hit the business account.

"I'm so lucky having you," he said. His father chuckled, and after what they'd been through, it had to be one of the best sounds in the whole world.

Things ticked along nicely after that; the contract came and went, and three days later Michael Christie's office rang Dad to confirm that the first two and half grand had been deposited. The day after that, the man himself rang.

"Hey, Seth, it's Hugh here."

"Mate, how ya doing?"

"I'm doing fine but no one else seems to think so. I'm being sent on holiday, but you already know that."

"Yep. I got a call from Davey."

"Yeah, Davey. Who else?"

"Your father."

"That's right," said Hugh. "Look Seth, thanks for being honest about talking to him. You might be my only real friend right now."

Seth didn't mind that.

"I'll be honest with you too. Things aren't so good with The Tygers. I brought in three songs – lyrics and all, and Richie flipped. I didn't back down and it's all got stupid. Richie still lives in the sixties. I mean, who wants to hear 'baby, baby' in a song anymore! When I become king, I'm going to ban it – on pain of execution.

"I arrive next Friday and apparently I'm staying at your place. But the real point of this little jaunt is to write, write, write. I'll have the Hummingbird, the National, and a Phillips recorder to capture some lightning in a bottle.

"Now, up there there's real people living real lives and doing real things. Canecutters and lumberjacks, right? And fishermen and truckies – and Aboriginals! They're all fucking real, unlike the pale imitations of life here. *That's* what I want to write about."

That would be bloody cool, thought Seth. A musician of Hugh's calibre writing songs at my place.

"Yeah, the real people with their little wins and broken dreams," continued Hugh. "Hard men and strong women teeming with raw emotions in a . . . epic, unforgiving landscape! So has the rainy season started there yet?"

"Yeah, sort of – still clearing its throat."

"I've got to see that! The primeval forces of nature, the flooding, the destruction. And hurricanes! Is it hurricane season too?"

"Yep. Cyclones too."

"Any around?"

"We had a little one in the Gulf last week but she pissed off over Darwin way."

"In the Gulf . . . oh wow. Listen, Seth," said Hugh, his voice dropping to a thrilled whisper. "I want to meet some outlaws, and desperados."

"You've got no worries there," said Seth. "We get 'em all year round up here."

Hook, Line and Sinker

A bloke was shouting; the voice echoing off the prison walls filled with . . . Seth couldn't place it. Not pain or fear or anger, it was the loud declaration of an emotion he was sure he'd never felt. Following the prison guard down the hallway, he recognised it now – boredom.

The guard turned down another long corridor; halfway along it, he opened a door, and they went into a small room with a bolted down metal table and two chairs. Seth gave the guard three hundred dollars and he pocketed it.

"Keep it quiet in here," said the screw. He went out and Seth heard the deeply unpleasant sound of the door being locked.

It hadn't taken long. Sabbo must have written the letter the day after his visit. It was business-like; running to a single sentence. Seth then spent seven hours across two days on the telephone, before speaking to an old and very influential mate, a bloke who had fingers in pies all over the north – including Her Majesty's Prison Stuart Creek.

Seth had told him he needed to meet Sabbo away from the prison flies who buzzed for Gordy Mac.

There was something else he needed, but his mate had become like royalty nowadays and you didn't ask the king for too much in the one go. That would take a face-to face meeting, and some kind of payment. He'd also sounded distant on the phone, maybe a little dark that Seth hadn't visited him in nearly a year.

He'd got it sorted out though; Seth now had his covert meeting place and the screw had his three hundred bucks.

When Sabbo came in, he looked calm but fragile, as though a storm had passed through him. Looking around the room, Seth threw out his arms like a side-show magician, and Sabbo acknowledged their privacy with a nod. Seth gave him a big smile and was chuffed to see his mate dust off one of his own.

Sabbo was a good bloke; brought up right with two big brothers and three older sisters as role models. From an early age he'd fallen in love with cars, tractors and trucks; anything with four wheels really, and by his late teens he'd established a garage on his Uncle Carlo's farm. The whole Sabbotini clan had been proud of the family mechanic, and very pleased he was making a living already.

He also drove like the devil himself, attending and often winning illegal car races held on night-time roads.

But when Sabbo got into sticky heads and rock'n'roll, he moved out of his family's steady orbit into Seth's wild one. They'd been a couple of real tearaways together and it had been fun and games. Except for that one road trip; a non-stop hallucinatory nightmare to Sydney and back.

It was a paid job for someone and someone had yapped about it, and a gang of mongrels had followed them with nearly 200 pounds of primo dope in their car as the prize. They'd lost the last car in the outer north of Sydney, Sabbo driving like Steve McQueen until the city swallowed them up.

What dropped them in poo was that they had to drive the same car back; the payment for the load now packed into the hidden compartments they'd brought the dope in. Sticking to their plan, they went back the same way they'd come; the Burnett Highway having a good deal fewer cops than the Bruce. The bastards must have sat there waiting for them.

In that one minute of madness at the Monto roadhouse, Sabbo proved no chocolate soldier. He saved us, thought Seth. When it all went down, he'd come through big-time. Now Seth felt awful regret; he'd badly neglected a mate, a true brother. Maybe if he'd said something a year ago at Hides Hotel?

But that was all chewed bones now, and Sabbo had been royally screwed by the worst bastards in the far north. The crims who'd chased them to Sydney and back had been straight-up ruthless, ready to maim and murder to get what they wanted – but the fellas who had put Sabbo in prison were a whole different level of nasty.

Gordy MacIntyre and his evil younger brother Liam were criminals not just content with the plunder. They liked hurting people, with Liam often throwing in some nasty degradation too. Terrorising the non-straight world of the far north, they gate-crashed parties on bush blocks and barged into fishing camps – bashing and humiliating blokes in front of their mates, women and kids; totally power-tripping on the fear they created.

Though muscled-up, agile and fit, they were work-shy bastards who ripped off dope, cars and money, or hooked into other crims' activities to monster them for control, or a hefty cut of the action.

The Mac's awful legend grew in proportion to the acts of bastardry they committed. Consummate biff-artists, they badly bashed blokes and vanished a few. They raped out-of-it strays at parties and played sicko mind-games. Totally bush-savvy, they were spooky night-creepers – the stuff of nightmares. Midnight fires burnt out sheds and cars, and fresh turds appeared on dawn verandas. They even shot people's dogs.

Masters of confusion, the Mac brothers took delight in the unexpected, using criminally-minded fools as decoys and cut-outs then throwing them to the cops as necessary. Extremely cunning, they avoided arrest, and with a couple of cops and a magistrate rumoured to be on-side, neither of them had been inside since their early twenties.

When some of what they did made them too hot, they'd hide away at remote properties and on lost beaches. In pubs from Innisfail to Cooktown, the lesser devils would drink a little easier.

Sabbo had foolishly swum with these sharks and they'd ripped him apart; leaving him in pieces for the shitfish of Stuart Creek.

"So, how the hell did you get in with Macs?" said Seth.

But Sabbo had a question of his own first.

"What happened to you in '77, man? You just vanished. I was really worried. I thought you'd gone off the rails. Wasn't until I met Mick, like six months after you'd gone, that I found out you were living in Sydney."

Hearing his wounded tone, Seth felt shame. I was a big influence on him and a good mate too, he thought. They'd had a friendship made of good times, some hard work, and moments of serious strife; a bond that just hanging out at pubs and parties drinking and talking bullshit could never produce.

"I know what happened must have gutted you, Seth. I don't even know what to say about it after all these years, and I thought about it often enough. Yeah . . . I'm so sorry, man."

"I'm sorry too, Sab," said Seth "All I could do was run. It was like Cairns didn't exist for me anymore."

Sabbo nodded in sad acceptance then looked relieved. Seth felt relief too. A whole lot of water had just gone under the bridge, and the old vibe between them felt like it had returned. They were still mates.

"So, what happened with the Macs?" said Seth.

Sabbo sighed, and then laid out the whole sorry story.

In '78, he'd gotten real busy; his reputation as a crackerjack mechanic attracting blokes eager to have their cars rebuilt or tricked-up. Fifteen-hour days became common and he dug every minute of it. He was doing what he loved and making good money too. Then Uncle Carlo got wind of his nephew's dalliance with marijuana and the garage on his farm was declared off-limits.

Now Sabbo's whole family – the good Lord and all the

saints too – brought the full-force of the straight world to bear on him. It was time for him to change, to get married and settle down. It was his chance for redemption. A line had been drawn and all he had to do was step over it.

But Sabbo couldn't, and he collected his tools and the few car bodies he couldn't bear to part with, and moved up to Cairns.

With his automotive talent he could have got a job at Chellingworth's at Edge Hill, even driven their souped-up Cortinas at the races – but he went his own way.

He set up at a fella's orchard off the highway at Clifton Beach. There were two big concrete-floored sheds up the back, and he negotiated a reasonable rent and share of the power. Then he fixed up the long driveway with a grader and a few loads of blue metal. It was a great spot. And it was good finally getting out of Innisfail.

It took a few months to get established, but as word got out on the rev-head grapevine, the work flowed in. It was cash only, and the occasional invoice made out to the odd customer who wanted one, came from books the tax office never saw. In between jobs he worked on cars he'd found; rough diamonds that he rebuilt, polished to a sexy sheen then sold for good profit.

After a year, things were going so well he began to think about going legit and getting a proper garage in town with the Sabbotini name right across the front of it. Yeah, he'd love to hear what the family would say about that.

He had twenty grand stashed, so he set up a meeting with Rollie Scaddon, an accountant who knew about the shades between black and red. Rollie, who also knew real talent and dedication when he saw it, knocked together a five-year financial plan that made Sabbo smile every time he read it. Now he started looking for a place to rent.

But Cairns was a small town, and though he kept things on the quiet, he began to attract mongrels; dodgy blokes with stolen cars and insurance-scams. When he told them that the cops watched his place, they usually lost interest, but it was a continuing hassle he didn't need.

There was even a bastard who ran in and tried to extort him; a prick with a cock-eye that bulged when he yelled. Sabbo was doing oxyacetylene work and he re-lit the jet and thrust the hot blue flame at that eye. The bastard reared back in shock then ran back out again. This made Sabbo feel like a tough guy.

The real tough guys turned up a week later; two pairs of boots appearing by the orange and black Monaro GTS he was working under. Where's your manners? he thought. You should sing out coming into a bloke's garage.

He slid out and jumped up into a seriously bad vibe. He didn't recognize the two blokes standing there at first, but he knew what they were.

"G'day mate," said the one with the rocker sideburns and well-trimmed moustache. "Nice little garage. Never even knew it was here."

"How's this?" said the other fella. "A Monaro. Always wanted one."

This bloke was clean-shaven, the younger of the two – actually, they looked like brothers – and he'd picked up one of Sabbo's old baseball caps and was wearing it.

"Hey," said Sabbo. "That's not yours."

The prick smiled like he'd got a compliment.

"A few cars in here," said the other bloke. "You must be doing well, aye?"

"Hold on," said Sabbo, glaring at the idiot in his cap. "What do you blokes want?"

"To provide you with some security," said the older one. "There's lots of cars in here and lots of idiots out there."

"I got security," Sabbo lied. "The owner of the orchard and two workers live here. They're around all the time."

The older one smiled indulgently like he knew it was bullshit. A pheasant coucal went off in the bush near the shed, and from out on the highway came the passing roar of a semi-trailer; the sound fading into the buzz of insects.

A loud metallic bang made Sabbo jump. A piece of steel pipe rattled into stillness by the younger brother's boots. He picked it up and held it in his hands like a police baton.

"This isn't yours – is it?" he said.

Sabbo, confused, peered at the length of pipe. The older brother snorted with amusement.

"No – this is mine," said the younger brother, his eyes flat and cold. Sabbo felt like pissing now.

"Is your security any good?" said the older one.

Sabbo couldn't speak. He knew who they were now.

The MacIntyre brothers grinned, giving him the time to work out a way to welcome them onboard without looking like a little girl. Nah, bugger you, thought Sabbo.

"Yeah, it's great," he said. The younger Mac threw his brother a horrible, eager look, that was thankfully ignored.

"OK . . . Gerry," said the older Mac. "We'll see you round the ridges, mate."

A few days after their visitation the Monaro developed several deep scratches in its glossy paintwork. Sabbo got proper padlocks. The next morning there was a tin full of petrol against the locked wooden doors and a Bic lighter tucked into the chain by the padlock.

Sabbo was renting on the esplanade at Clifton Beach, living with his very sexy girlfriend, so he didn't want to sit in the garage at night. Besides, what was he going to do – use his face to smash the Mac's knuckles and boots? Fear and anger now competed to steal his sleep, and his girl began pouting in frustration at his failing libido.

Then one morning in Bransford's tackle shop across the highway from the orchard, Sabbo was getting milk from the chiller, when a pleasant voice said, "What do you think now?" He turned and saw Gordy Mac.

Rage flooded him. He saw himself punching the bastard into the racks of fishing rods then smashing his head on the metal corner of the bait freezer. Instead, he gave his tormentor a *vaffanculo* glare.

"You called it, mate," said Gordy Mac.

The next day two cops came into the garage, followed by his worried landlord. The cops had a heap of questions regarding the unlicensed operation of a garage and the possibility of stolen cars on the premises.

License plates were recorded and when the boys in blue left, Sabbo placated his landlord and rushed home. It took many phone calls before every car owner agreed to lie on his behalf. Tell any government bastard who asks, that you're paying me in beer and rum, he pleaded.

He needed a beer himself after that, but it worked. No

government bastard turned up looking for paperwork. The Mac brothers did though, and now feeling worn down by their assault – Sabbo asked the question.

"How much?"

"What were you paying your security fellas?"

Sabbo said nothing while the brothers laughed.

"What about a hundred bucks a week?" said Gordy Mac.

Sabbo was very surprised. All that grief over a hundred dollars a week? His expression made the Macs laugh some more, and Sabbo, with much-needed relief, found himself laughing too. Gordy Mac slapped him on the back.

"Mate, we've heard you're the best at what you do – so you need the best of what we do."

Sabbo began paying and the intimidation stopped. So did the fellas looking for a chop shop, or an accomplice in an insurance scam, and no-one, cock-eyed or not, tried to put the bite on him again. It was like the brothers had put up a force-field around the place, and Sabbo actually felt safer. The hundred bucks a week now seemed like a pretty good deal.

And the brothers had mates who needed work done on their cars, blokes who paid well and appreciated the work they got. Best of all, his debilitating fear had gone, and his girlfriend was very happy about that.

Gordy dropped over to the garage a bit and they talked about cars and dope. He knew about a lot of stuff and was funny too, and before long, Sabbo was drinking with the Macs at pubs and going to parties with them. He was now recognised as a serious mate of theirs, and when the fear and respect they enjoyed began to rub off on him – Sabbo was pleasantly surprised to find that he didn't mind seeing the deference in fellas' eyes.

Rollie Scaddon was a bit upset when the business plan got put on the back-burner. Sabbo felt bad too, but with the Macs around now it wouldn't be a hundred bucks a week at a nice new place. Besides, Gordy thought he had a top spot at Clifton Beach – just off the highway but not in the limelight. "Don't ever move," he said.

Soon enough, Sabbo understood why.

From the start, Gordy had seen how the garage was a great transit point between the Cape, the west and Cairns. With no close neighbours it was totally discreet. Vehicles could appear from the driveway and go north or south.

When a three-ton truck caked in red dust rendezvoused with two vans at the garage, the brothers supervising the transfer of plastic-wrapped bales of what had to be dope, Sabbo had kept his head down under the bonnet of the car he was working on. He felt edgy seeing all this, but when Gordy brought a cold beer over to him and asked if he was cool with it – he just nodded his head like a pro. With a smile of approval, Gordy put a lipstick sized roll of fifties in his hand, and over time, Sabbo saw more examples of marijuana industry logistics go down at the garage; each one netting him a roll of fifties.

One morning his landlord said there'd been trouble last night. A small truck and a ute had gone up to the garage, and sometime later two shots had been fired.

"Shots?" said Sabbo. "You sure?"

"I was in the reserves, mate," said his landlord.

And furthermore, he'd found four fifties on his kitchen

table this morning. Gordy was already paying him a few bucks a week to mind his own business, so he didn't know what was expected of him.

"You gonna keep the money?" said Sabbo.

"Yeah, I reckon. Two hundred bucks, hey."

"Keep your mouth shut then," Sabbo growled, feeling a real thrill at the fear he'd put on his landlord's face.

Bit by bit, more of the Macs' business happened at the garage. One morning, Liam used a vice and a hacksaw to cut down a pump-action shotgun. A few days later, Gordy rocked up with two heavy looking bastards, and they sat at the lunch table by the shed, where a big blue tarp strung up between two flame trees provided shade.

The murmur of their voices stopped with an oath and the sound of things rattling on the plastic tabletop. Sabbo peeked through a rip in the shed's tin wall. One bloke was holding a black revolver in his hand; all of them gathering spilled bullets and slotting them back into the foam slots of an ammo box.

Then one day Gordy said to forget about the hundred bucks a week – they were mates now – and that was cool. But when he brought in a nice red Mercedes Benz without number plates, Sabbo, in a joshing sort of a way, put his foot down.

"Hey c'mon Gordy, that's a no-no. You know I . . ."

Something flashed through his vision, hit the side of his face, and he fell down next to the Mercedes. His head rang and his cheekbone bloomed with pain. What in the hell? Something must have slipped and fallen from the storage racks above.

But when he sat up and looked at Gordy, he realised the bastard had just punched him in the face.

"Don't you talk back to me," said Gordy Mac.

After a year of hanging with the Macs, getting on the grog and partying with them, it was an absolute shocker to realise how he'd been taken – hook, line and sinker; Gordy just reeling him in like an undersized whiting.

"I've got no problem at all, taking you up the back there and putting a bullet in your head," said Gordy Mac. "And remember – I'm the nice one."

The Ladder

"And all those cars of Gordy's mates I worked on? They were mostly stolen." Sabbo shook his head sadly. "Made me an accessory. The bastard really played me."

"I reckon," said Seth. But how many times have I seen this happen? he thought. Good blokes sucked in by the fantasy of violence and the respect it got. The silly buggers got as dizzy as flies at a barbie.

"I was a real donkey," said Sabbo. "I got in deep."

"How did you end up in here?"

Sabbo bit his lip and looked away.

"C'mon Sab. You're getting out of here, you know that."

Sabbo looked at him, wanting to believe, and Seth put that belief into his own eyes and gave his friend a big serve of hope. Sabbo's smile was all pain, but he went on.

Now he began to witness, and participate in, things far dodgier than stolen cars, bulk dope and a shotgun getting a hair-cut. He helped Liam wrap two select-fire rifles in plastic and tape and hide them in the body of the Dodge truck outside; the one he was going to fix up to perfection.

The guns were gone the next day, and the truck became a criminal's post-box where God knows what was deposited and collected.

He built clever stash places into cars and vans and filled them with packages of dope; sometimes cash, and once, a couple of handguns. He changed number plates on cars, swapping them for ones that Gordy Mac supplied.

Then his driving skills were brought into play and he became one of the Macs' wheel-men in crop rip-offs out west, navigating rutted tracks, his heart wildly pounding as he waited for a shotgun blast to cave in the windscreen.

One night he sat in a ute in a cold sweat, as Gordy and Liam vanished onto a property at Silver Valley. Minutes passed like hours, the lights of a dwelling glinting through trees. Then a long howl of pain pierced the dark. Sabbo cringed and squirmed as the howling went on for a week it seemed. Ten minutes after it stopped, grins appeared in the darkness and the Mac brothers packed onto the bench seat beside him.

Gordy had a large, stuffed-full manila envelope and he reached in, pulled something out and threw it on Sabbo's lap. It was a wad of fifties as thick as a truckie's sanga.

"There you go, mate," said Gordy. "Bit of petrol money."

Sabbo tried not to witness the beatings at the garage; blind-folded blokes getting taught brutal lessons by Liam and an evil druggy bastard called Fuckinkev, who was the Mac's back-up muscle. When the workman-like grunts, frantic pleading and shouts of pain ended, the bleeding victims would get forced, or chucked onto cardboard laid in the back seat of Fuckinkev's car – then driven off.

A couple of times Fuckinkev's car drove past the garage as some poor bastard was taken into the big trees up the back for special tutoring. Sabbo scarcely dared look to see if they came back.

Real deep now; a real crim and with real money, Sabbo socked away the dough. Between the garage work and the cash that Gordy Mac continued to give him to do jobs, he saved fifty grand. The money became his escape hatch. If the shit really hit the fan, or if it all got too much to handle – he'd just pull the pin, drive south and disappear into Australia.

It almost made him feel sorry for a broke, drug-addict, crim like Fuckinkev – a doomed loser with the future of a cow in an abattoir. Almost. No, Sabbo could never sink that low or become that vulnerable. The take-it-to-the-bank truth was – when the bolt-gun went off, he wouldn't be there. Then it all unravelled like the guts of a horse ripped open by a mickey bull.

Not long after Seth had seen Sabbo at Hides, the Macs had apparently mixed business with pleasure, and the result was an absolute disaster for Sabbo. He didn't do a thing – but he ended up wearing it all.

Taking a legit customer's car to a house at Aeroglen, Liam Mac had turned a meeting into near murder. Maybe there was bad blood between him and the bloke he bashed – some infamous old criminal hard-case gone straight, or maybe Liam wanted to take down a legend for the story he could tell in the pub.

Seth knew all about that. He'd had glory-hunters try it on with him. None of them had got the story they wanted.

Whatever his motive, Liam used a piece of steel pipe to smash the bloke's face and head. It was touch and go, and Liam had to hit him heaps. Sabbo knew all this because Fuckinkev, who was there, had told him.

The car was quietly returned and Sabbo hadn't noticed it gone. The next day at the garage, a troupe of cops rocked up, yelling and pointing their guns at him. At the words 'attempted murder', he just about fell over in shock.

It was bad luck for Sabbo that some eagle-eyed, old bird at Aeroglen had noted the make, colour and licence plate number of the car. Worse luck, he had no alibi: he'd been working alone at the garage when the bashing went down.

It went quickly after that, as though it was the natural way of things. First, he was refused bail then his shocked family came to see him; Dad, Vinnie and Gio, cold-faced and tight-lipped; his mother bawling like he was going to be hung at dawn. Rollie Scaddon knew a good lawyer, a sharp bloke who managed to get the charge reduced down to GBH with intent.

The evidence was compelling; the car was at his garage, its owner verifying it was there for work; the piece of steel pipe found in the car had one end smeared with the blood and hair of the victim; the other end wiped clean of prints.

The prosecutor and the cops side-stepped the complete absence of motive, describing the bashed bloke and Sabbo as hardened criminals – 'men who clash, often violently.'

The final nail in his coffin was being identified as the attacker by the victim himself. Outraged, Sabbo had been aggressively commanded by the judge to keep silent. The victim's girlfriend gave an articulate account of coming home to find her man near-dead, and her angry testimony set the nail-head flush to the wood.

The prosecution wanted fourteen years. The judge took into account Sabbo's clean record and the dozen character references from upstanding citizens of Innisfail, and gave him ten; seven of them non-parole.

Seth now realised why this was all news to him; he'd been out of Cairns working, and he didn't mix with dodgy old mates anymore in the kind of circles where news of Sabbo's downfall would have been readily broadcast.

"So, what did the Macs do?" said Seth.

"When I got charged, I said I didn't do it. Then on the second night in remand I was asleep when someone came into the cell and grabbed me by the throat."

Sabbo gulped madly as he throttled back tears, his face scrunched up with rage and shame. It tore Seth up, and a pilot-light of deep anger lit inside him.

"This bloke said I'd be shut up permanently if I told the truth," Sabbo finally said. "Then . . . then he said this address. My sister Connie's address."

"Ah, shit, mate. So, who do you reckon the bloke was?"

"Not a prisoner or a guard. Must have been a cop."

"Sounds about right. He say anything else?"

"There'd be a lot of petrol money for me when I got out."

The fella who'd been bashed must have been offered the same sweet incentive, thought Seth.

"So, the fella Liam nearly killed," he said. "You know anything about him?"

"Wouldn't know him from Adam. The bastard wouldn't look at me in court. I felt happy his face was smashed up."

Sabbo buzzed with acrimony, his fists balling up.

"Tell me about this Fuckinkev fella," said Seth.

"He's from Bowen, got no mates up here except for some bikers living at Wonga Beach. Been nearly two years with the Macs. He's a druggie who likes his heroin. The Macs don't use or deal it, but Gordy always has some for him. Keeps him on a nice short leash. Yeah, he really didn't like Liam nearly killing the bloke while he was with them. Reckoned it was too public and he wasn't wrong. When he complained about it, Liam threatened to bash him, and that pissed him off even more."

That's good, thought Seth. A wedge I can tap on.

"You know where he lives?"

"Last I knew he was at the railway end of Scott Street. Old wooden cottage – white and pale green."

"Car?"

"Red EH Holden. What are you thinking?"

"An appeal."

"An appeal? How?"

"I'll get this Fuckinkev, and the bloke who got bashed, to tell the truth. Make them sign proper statements. Get your trial lawyer on the case."

"How you gonna do that?"

Everything pointed to money – a lot of money. Enough to get Fuckinkev to stand witness in court. Same with the bashed fella.

"You still got that fifty grand?" said Seth.

Doubt clouded Sabbo's face and Seth didn't blame him. Handing over his nest-egg to a friend who'd disappeared on him before wasn't a top-shelf choice.

"Look, we'll bring Vinnie in on this and your father too. They'll dole out money on your say-so."

Sabbo shook his head.

"No, man. Vinnie's likely to give it to the church and let me take my punishment. You reckon Alex was hard on you, but Vinnie has it all over him."

From somewhere in the gaol came the muted sound of metal like an evil cog turning.

"That money, it's . . . everything I worked for, all the shit I put up with. It's what keeps me going in here."

"But if it gets you out of this place you can make more dough, you know that. You're a bloody auto wizard, Sab. Brisbane, Sydney – anywhere. The best garages will snap you up."

Seth zipped his lip, an encouraging expression masking quiet elation. His mate's reluctance at handing over the money had nothing to do with not trusting him.

Sabbo's right knee vibrated, idling like a 426 Hemi. His face was statue-still; frozen in thought. Then he looked up and there was some fire in his eyes.

"Zia Ademina," said Sabbo.

"Mate, the only Italian I know is pizza, vino and 'ti amo donna', and your sister slapped me for saying that to her."

"Zia means aunt and Aunt Ademina is my Mum's older sister. Like nineteen years older."

"Where's she live then?"

"You catch on real fast, Kelly." Sabbo's smile was great.

"That's why you've got me on the case."

"You got yourself on the case."

"Couldn't help myself."

Sabbo nodded, eyes shining with emotion.

"So, the money," Seth continued helpfully. "It's at your auntie's place, right? Tell me about her."

"Ah, yeah. She's nearly eighty, lives in Innisfail. Uncle Joe died two years ago, so the family drop by to do the shopping, cleaning and keep her company. She doesn't go out and she doesn't drive."

"Could you write to her, tell her I'm coming?"

Sabbo sniffed a couple of times then shook his head.

"Not only do the family collect her mail, they also read it out to her."

Seth let his mate think about the other options.

"Yeah, you'd have to break a bit of glass to get in," said Sabbo. "But I don't want my old *zia* scared. Her hearing's still good, aye. The house is high-set, you'd need a ladder, and with the neighbours and the road right there. . . nah."

"I'll knock on the front door then," said Seth.

Sabbo grimaced. "See, the problem is, she's not keen on strangers; especially blokes, and especially blokes who don't have an Italiano background. She's told the meter-reader to clear off before."

"So, the money is inside the house."

"Up in the roof of the back bedroom."

"There's a manhole in the roof there?"

"Yeah – with a push-up lid. The cash can't be more than a foot from the edge. It's like a brick, wrapped and taped in plastic."

Seth pulled out his notepad and sterling silver Parker pen, and Sabbo gave him his auntie's address and the name of his lawyer from the trial.

"Listen Seth, my old *zia* really loves me. We've always got on. She thinks I'm working in Melbourne. I even write her letters that Vinnie takes to her."

"I get ya, mate."

"You're a real brother," said Sabbo.

Now memory took Seth back to that manic Sydney dope run – and those dreadful seconds in the men's room at the Monto roadhouse.

At the urinal. The sudden scuff of shoes making him look over his shoulder. A skinny chick sailing in. Terrible, speed-glittering eyes. One hand holding her t-shirt up to expose small, pointed breasts. His bouncer's eyes seeing the other hand holding the knife, its blade flush against her leg.

Outside – "Seth!" Sabbo yelling in alarm. The thump of a body against a car.

Cutting off hours of held-in piss, stupidly trying to zip up. Slipping on the wet trough edge, bouncing off the reeking urinal wall and falling to the floor. The woman scampering right in, fully jacked up on fear, drugs, greed and adrenaline. And a chance to make a fella pay for all the shit she'd taken from them.

Rolling across sticky white tiles, kicking his boots up. The chick swearing in frustration, hopping and jumping, trying for his jugular or eyes. Rolling and jerking like a headless chook, the row of cubicle doors now above him, boxing him in. By the time he got to his feet, the little horror would be mounted on his back, cutting his throat.

Sensing victory, murder girl picking the pace right up, slashing and slashing, missing his face by an eyelash.

Now the rapid squeak of shoes, a masculine grunt and the dull thump of a fist hitting flesh and bone. The ting, ting, ting of the knife on the floor. The thump and flop of a body on tiles.

Sabbo standing there, right fist cocked, the scrawny assassin laid out on the floor. Running with Sabbo out to the car – an unconscious man next to it, knocked out in the dust. Sabbo was punching like Rocky Mattioli today.

Leaping into the car and roaring off up the highway. Shocked silence as they collected their thoughts. Sabbo sniffing the air then saying with perfect cheek – 'I think you pissed yourself, mate.'

"You saved my life," said Seth.

"Couldn't help myself," said Sabbo.

Seth took a deep breath to contain what he felt.

"So, my Auntie Ademina," said Sabbo kindly. "The big problem is getting her to let you in. She loves a chat, but she's got paranoid since Uncle Joe died – on her own and all, so the only stranger I reckon she'd take to would be another old bird like herself."

"No way," said Seth.

Sabbo looked alarmed. "What do you mean?"

"I'm not putting on make-up and a dress."

King of Rock & Roll

The next day Seth went through his back garden onto the beach and walked north, splashing across Redden Creek to O'Shea Esplanade, where he climbed up the rock wall and walked bare-foot along the quiet seaside street.

The ocean was pretty flat. Clouds clustered over on the range and there was even some sunshine. Not far from the sea-wall, the streamlined head of a cormorant popped up.

Above the bay, a Bush Pilots Trislander was starting its final descent. The old Bushies, hey. Seth's first time on a plane had been with them. Just last week they'd changed the name to Air Queensland, everyone keen on getting hip and with-it nowadays. Bushies sounded better, but.

In less than an hour, Hugh Christie's plane would start making its own descent, and with the airport just across the Barron River from Machans Beach, Seth had time for a quick look in on his friend Sunny.

She was a recent Machans arrival like him, and they'd become friends last year. Ten or fifteen years older than him, she looked like a hippy, but was more of a bushie. Capable, self-sufficient, sun-brown and fit, she'd lived in Darwin and Wyndham, and across the border in Northern Rivers and Byron Bay. Though she worked as a teacher's aide at the Machans school and baby-sat her neighbour's kids, she had no children of her own.

There didn't seem to be a man in her life either, not that it was any of his business, and she seemed pretty content living alone; perennially amused, a nice lazy smile never far from her lips.

Flirtation went on between them at times, but as a joke. Hopping into bed wasn't on the cards. They'd settled that wordlessly a while back.

And there she was, sitting in shorts and a tank-top on the pot-plant-screened veranda of her timber cottage. The rust blistered front gate creaked when he came in and she gave him one of those rolling sunshine smiles.

"Hi, Seth. Whatcha up to?" A teapot and cup sat on the salt and sun-bleached timber floor by her chair. On a small cane table, a half-smoked joint perched on a cut-glass ashtray. Seth came up the steps and sat down in the other woven lawyer-cane armchair.

"Just going for a wander before going to the airport. Got a mate from Sydney coming to stay. He's the lead guitarist in The Tygers."

Sunny shrugged and smiled, her bells unrung. She liked gypsy music and reggae and didn't own a TV.

"Nice one. It's great when friends come to stay."

"Yeahh . . . I've got to keep an eye on him, though."

"Got to?"

"It's sort of a job."

"Friendship can be like that sometimes."

An image of Sabbo banged-up in Stuart flashed through his head.

"No overtime, pay-rises or sickies either," said Sunny.

"Aw, that's a bit hard."

"Or realistic."

Seth needed to think about that, but his thoughts were scattered as Sunny yawned and stretched voluptuously, her smooth arms arching back, her small fingers splaying out. With a sigh of contentment, she blissfully closed her eyes, and dishevelled auburn curls fell from her head to nestle in the dark hair of her armpits.

Seth stared at her; all unfolded like a succulent flower, fully alert to the points of her nipples inside her top, the fine hair on her forearms. Drinking her in like a teenage boy, he quickly snatched his eyes away when she opened hers. Looking across the esplanade, he strived to appear intrigued by something that might have just jumped out of the ocean.

"So, party-time at your house," said Sunny.

"Yeah, sorta, but I'm not supposed to encourage any, ah . . . dissolute behaviour."

Sunny laughed like honey flows, her eyes twinkling and her belly shaking. Though she looked supremely relaxed, she felt kind of vulnerable – like she was younger and not so self-assured. Seth breathed deeply, inhaling her body perfume.

Silence buzzed between them. Something had changed. For the tiniest moment, Seth had seen desire in her eyes.

This was unexpected, almost disconcerting, and he looked at his watch. "I better go. It's later than I thought."

With a goofy grin, he got up, Sunny's eyes right on him. She gave him a lazy wave goodbye and he managed one in return. Walking back down the esplanade, the ocean felt absolutely immense there beside him, as though scarcely held back by the big rocks of the seawall.

Sunny's pheromones had soaked him through, and he wondered about the smell and softness of her skin, and how she'd feel pressed close to him, luscious and warm. I'd love to butt my face like a cat right into her, he thought. Anywhere she'd let me.

Totally sex-tipsy, he went home and had a cold shower. Driving over to the airport, he saw Hugh's plane coming in, and while he found a park, it taxied up to the terminal. As he walked through the car-park, the infernal jet noise ceased. Then he saw the three cops by their car – watching the terminal doors.

He automatically wove through vehicles; staying out of sight, and an unloading bus gave him cover as he slipped into the tin shed that was Cairns Airport. A few minutes later he was pleased to see the guitarist coming in off the tarmac; a black guitar-case in each hand. Wow, thought Seth. He must have bought an extra seat just for them. A DC-9 started moving up the runway, so they wordlessly hugged and slapped backs. While the guitarist went to the gents, Seth waited for the baggage trolleys to get wheeled in. It didn't take long and they soon had his bags.

"You've got to be kidding me!" laughed Hugh Christie as they walked towards the exit. A big black marlin hung over the doorway, its mouth open in surprise at finding itself wrenched from the ocean and mounted on a wall.

"What in the sweet Julie Andrews is that?"

Christie's urban drawl drew the ears of two local blokes, and the expressions on their faces was easy to read. Seth could just about hear it – Check this ignorant southerner out. He's got no idea that Cairns is the black marlin capital of the world and that rich Yanks, Aussies and Europeans fly in. Famous bastards too, like the Golden Bear, Ernest Whatshisname and Lee fuckin' Marvin. Even bloody Bob and Dolly Dyer from Pick-a-Box.

Seth winked at the boys, and one nodded sympathetically.

"That's a grander," he said, leading Hugh out of the hot shed. "A thousand plus pounds of fish, mate."

"Pounds?"

"Yeah, important things like dope, wild-pigs and black marlin still come in pounds up here."

"Hey Seth, speaking of dope . . ."

"Hold on," interrupted Seth. The boys in blue were still outside watching the world go by, and – here we go – their heads swivelled towards Seth and Hugh.

Seth instinctively groaned. Though short-haired, clean-shaven and looking straight enough in ironed slacks and short-sleeved shirt, he was carrying two sticker-encrusted guitar cases, and Hugh . . . well Hugh was wearing big freaky sunnies, tight and fuzzy crimson flares, a pair of tooled-leather fat-heeled boots, and an orange waist-coat over a crumpled black floral shirt. His hair was half-way down his back and bangles jingled on his wrists. Living in the 70s indeed.

It was like a red flag to the Queensland bulls. Staring hard at Hugh and Seth, they began walking over.

It wasn't easy explaining it to anybody who lived south of the border. All across the country, rock'n'roll sound-tracked ads and movies. Hippy boutiques and head-shops flourished on main streets, and there was heavy-metal, reggae, even new-wave and punk in the charts. Lots of people, young and old, were looking like the musicians they liked, and dressing however they damn well pleased.

But in Queensland, the majority of the population had problems dealing with such sartorial rebels in the flesh. Outside of the university campuses and nightclubs, most Queenslanders looked, and pretty much were, straight.

Any individualism was seen as an indicator of a God-forsaken lifestyle that included weird sex, drug use, pinko politics, bludging, and dangerously loose morals.

In the pubs, bigots and meatheads would seethe with outrage, their loud observations getting coarser as they gave the weirdos stick. Outside, it was heavier still. On any street on any night in Queensland, carloads of horrible bastards might gleefully jump out and do serious damage to anyone who looked different.

Seth numbered a few colourful looking people among his friends, but he'd never felt the need to stand out in the crowd. He still didn't like it – the hate directed at people. Who cared how you looked? It was you and your mum's bloody business.

People got bashed, a few killed, but it was far worse for the Murri people. Changing clothes and hair-styles made no difference to the mountain of shit they copped.

Hugh saw the cops bearing down on them now.

"Just keep quiet, OK?" said Seth. "I'll do the talking."

"Why?" said Hugh. "I haven't done anything."

"That means nothing. You're in Queensland now."

The lead cop was a sergeant, and with an unfriendly nod he blocked the way. As his mates closed up the flanks, the Sarge looked Hugh up and down with the professional eye of a primate keeper at the zoo.

"Where you fellas off to?" he said, the insinuation being that something had just gone down and that the Sarge and his boys were on the look-out for suspects. It was typical cop bullshit.

"I've just picked up my mate," said Seth.

"Is that right. Where's he come from?"

"Sydney."

"Sydney," said the Sarge, like it was a final confirmation of his suspicions.

"What are you doing up here?" he said to Hugh.

"I'm on holiday," said Hugh.

"Yeah? Looks to me like you're always on holiday. You got a job?"

"Yes, I do."

The Sarge waited but Hugh wasn't playing their game.

"Don't make me crack the shits here. What do you do?"

Hugh nodded at the guitar cases in Seth's hands.

"I'm a guitarist."

"I can see that, but I'm asking you if you have a job."

"I'm a professional musician."

"In Sydney?"

"Yeah, and all over the country when we tour."

"When you tour?"

"Yeah, I'm in The Tygers."

Recognition lit up the face of the youngest cop.

"The Tygers?" he said. "I've got an album. My missus likes you fellas too."

The Sarge turned to him. "Is that right, Daniels?"

"Yes sir, they're top musos," said the young cop. "A lotta blokes like 'em."

"What about you Norm – you heard of them?" said the Sarge to the other cop.

"Yes sir, the kids seen them on Countdown. Not my cup of tea though."

"Countdown, hey? So, what do you like Norm?

"I like country, sir. Slim, Smokey – Suzanne Prentice."

"Waylon?" said Hugh.

"For sure. I like Waylon."

"Are you the guitarist?" said the young cop to Hugh. "I recognise you now."

"Yeah – Hugh Christie," said Hugh and he stuck out his hand. The cop's face reddened as he shook it.

"Mike Daniels. Never thought I'd see you up here."

Seth coughed and changed grip on the guitar cases. The Sarge regarded his boys with bemusement; then raised a hand at Seth and Hugh in dismissal.

"Alright then, you gents have a nice day," he said, before adding a warning for Hugh.

"Oh yeah, Mister Guitarist. Enjoy yourself in Cairns, but be careful – what with the way you look. You should be right around town and up with the hippies in Kuranda, but there'll be blokes who won't like it."

"Thank you, officer." Hugh's sarcasm was buried deep.

Seth walked briskly across the car-park, the guitar-case handles sweaty in his hands. He opened the back door of the Pig and carefully placed the guitars inside. Leaving it open, he got into the driver's seat. Relax, he told himself.

Hugh chortled as he put his bags in the back. When he got in, he sported a smug grin. Seth busied himself with his seat-belt.

"You got all paranoid for nothing," laughed Hugh, and he punched Seth on the arm. "Relax, man! You're with the King of Rock'n'Roll now."

Seth had made up a bed in the spare room of his two-bedroom house, and even though Hugh complimented him on what a cool pad he had – Seth knew he didn't like it. Sharing a small place with another bloke was definitely not his style.

In Sydney, Hugh lived in a three-story terrace-house in Paddington that belonged to his family. The top floor was all bedrooms and from the landing on the stairs you could smell a hypnotizing mix of incense, hashish and expensive perfume up there. It was legendary in Sydney muso and rich-kid circles, a rock'n'roll Eden where Hugh's gorgeous girlfriends and super-cool mates would repair for . . . yeah, you could only imagine.

Seth had never been invited up to find out. A couple of Hugh's girlfriends had given him the come-on though. One loud and raucous night, a total knock-out, kohl-eyed and jingling with bangles, had stood at the top of the stairs beckoning him up like the Queen of Sheba. Though sorely tempted, Seth really didn't want to muck-up any potential friendship with Hugh. Graciously declining, he'd politely flirted with her, but when she lifted her dress, revealing not panties, but sleek thighs and a dark bush of hair, he had stumbled back down to where he belonged – on the second-floor with all the other plebs.

Here the regulars partied; a nice mix of chicks and fellas who smoked, drank and snorted while the musos jammed on a small PA. Come morning there would be a sprawl of snoozing bodies with the occasional muffled sounds of furtive sex in other rooms as a low-budget reminder of the elite coupling that was surely taking place upstairs.

Now and then, drunks, rough-neck musos, and dealers with second-rate gear would attempt to invite themselves up to the third floor. That's when Seth and a Maori friend of Hugh's called Tiny came in. On that hallowed landing Seth body-blocked wayward wankers back down to where they belonged, even frog-marched a few outside. And now and then he'd had to bring the biff, and for his pains he'd received cheers from the party, and shots of strange booze and hits of opiated dope from the host.

It was around his sixth party at Hugh's terrace that he realised he'd never met this fella, Tiny. Everyone had told him what a great guy he was – a big tough fella with a wonderful smile, who was brilliant at stopping fights and defusing trouble. Just like you, Seth.

Now he realised why he got invited to Hugh's parties. The smart bastard was hip to making it work two ways.

Hugh's guitars went in the lounge, the bags in his room. They ditched shirts and sat on the back porch table with cold beers. The guitarist was reasonably well-built – good genes, not exercise or physical work, but he'd lost weight. Worry, stress, and a fair bit of candle-burning had etched his handsome face.

"Nice place, man. Nice and private," said Hugh. "You got a cigarette?"

Seth shook his head.

"Yeah, that's right – you don't smoke. You got some of that famous north Queensland dope though?"

Seth sure did, and after a three-papery, they had a few more beers. It took over an hour of the latest Sydney rock-scene stories before Hugh got around to it.

"So, my father's paying you?"

"Yeah. To keep an eye on you. Get you healthy and keep you away from booze and drugs."

Hugh gave him an appraising look over the top of his stubbie as he finished it.

"Look, we'll just take it easy – north Queensland style," said Seth. "Beers, bit of choof, some rum now and then. But that's it."

"No coke?"

"Sure – if you like it cold and fizzy."

"Dear God." Hugh looked around as if he'd just landed on the moon.

"Hugh, this is north Queensland. Ten years ago, nobody even knew what marijuana was."

"This is hellish. I've been banished. An exile of desire."

"Whatcha do?"

Hugh laughed bitterly then held up his empty stubbie like he was a customer in a restaurant.

"You know where the fridge is," said Seth.

"Aren't you getting paid?"

"Yeah, to keep you away from it."

Hugh hoisted himself up as though breaking through thick chains and went into the house.

"Hey, grab us one while you're there," called Seth.

He laughed at the inevitable expletive but was happy to see two stubbies accompany Hugh back to the table. Seth knew he needed to show this wilful bugger who the boss was here. Otherwise, he'd get steam-rolled.

"So, what are we doing tonight?" said Hugh. "Hit some bars and clubs? If the music's good enough I might sit in. Give the locals a bit of quality they must so sorely crave."

"I was thinking of cooking some snapper. We can have a nice feed, a few beers, listen to some records – settle in a bit. I just got Borderline – Ry Cooder."

"That came out last year."

They drank in silence for a minute until Seth relented.

"OK, I'll get a Cairns Post – see who's on. Maybe Wayne MacIntosh is playing. You'll dig him."

Hugh gave him a blinding smile.

"Look, Seth I'm in a bit of a spot."

"Yeah – that's why you're here."

"It's not that. Can you lend me some money?"

You've got to be pulling my pencil, thought Seth. Old mate here was notorious when it came to dough. He'd got the drum from Davey, and within a week of working with The Tygers he saw how drinks got paid for when ordered, no tabs. Cigarette packs stayed in pockets too, and drugs were never offered when Hugh was around.

Slap-up dinners with mates and hangers-on never felt the sting of his wallet either. The King of Rock'n'Roll paid for nothing; his fame, wit and prodigious talent were a fair bargain for everything he consumed. Generous even.

But he pushed it right over the line by not paying back money he'd borrowed. Looking incredulous at even being asked, he'd airily dodge restitution – offering a plus-four at the next Tygers show, or a joint of good dope instead. People then realised they hadn't lent him money – he'd lent them his stardom.

"Wait a sec, The Tygers sold *some* albums, didn't they?" said Seth.

"Yeah, yeah – everybody thinks that, but by the time everything gets paid for – my weekly expenses too, it all gets chewed up."

"You must have saved something."

"Yeah, I did, but . . . I went into a business."

"Drugs?" said Seth, remembering how impressed Hugh was with the roadies who'd cleaned up smuggling hash inside speaker cabinets.

"I should have. No, it was a chauffeur-driven limousine business."

"Really? What do you know about that?"

"I like them. I use them."

Seth flashed on a son trying to impress his father that he could do something more than just play rock'n'roll for teenage girls and long-haired wastrels.

"Why don't you ask your dad for a loan?" he said.

"Not happening right now. I'm being punished."

Seth now saw the hook Daddy Christie had his son on.

"Nah, mate," he said. "I'm paying for food, drinks and smoke, and whatever else you need or want to do, but I'm not lending you any money."

"Bullshit!" Hugh put some grit into it, slapping a long pale hand on the table. "My father's paying you heaps. It's practically my money."

Seth wrestled with a smile. Hugh getting tough was like a bilby in a balaclava.

"What's he paying you?"

Seth said nothing.

"Thousands? How many thousands?"

Seth gave up and smiled.

"Fuck you, man!" Hugh leapt up and ran angry fingers through his dark hair. "I'll just fucking take off! You won't get paid if I'm not around."

Unfortunately, that's true, thought Seth. I won't get the next instalment.

"Yeah, but you'll get cut off for a lot longer. Maybe forever," he said. "The Tygers sound a bit shaky right now and it takes money to kick-start a solo career. It might be wine-bars and noisy restaurants for a year or two. Covers. John Farnham. Billy Field."

"Fuck you, man."

"You're repeating yourself."

"Just five hundred! I can't keep putting my hand out. I need something if I wanna have a look around."

"Mate, forget being a tourist. I'll take you around, OK? You're here to unwind and get into writing songs. You've got a month away from everything – including being in The Tygers. You've got the time, your guitars, and God knows you've got the talent. This is it, man! You could write some of the best songs of your life here."

Seth couldn't think of anything cooler, but did this silly bugger have the sense to see how good his here-and-now could be?

"Fuck you, man," said Hugh.

Looking as though he'd just been knifed in the back, the guitarist got up and went inside. Seth blinked in surprise. This must be the sort of stuff managers do, he thought.

He waited for a minute then went into the house. The door to Hugh's room was closed.

"Hey, you wanna sandwich?" he called, getting a ratty 'no thanks,' in reply.

"We'll go get a paper in a bit. Check out the beach too."

Silence. Seth shrugged then went into the kitchen and made himself three rounds of toasted cheese and tomato sangers, all spiked with basil and parsley from his garden, and topped with black pepper cracked fresh in the long peppermill; just like in an Italian restaurant.

He ate outside on the back porch, washed up and went to Hugh's door again.

"Hey, let's go out, man."

Seth waited a tick, called again. Then he knocked. Don't tell me he's gone all weird, he thought. Davey said he was hitting it hard, maybe harder than anyone knows.

He opened the door and woah! – copped an eyeful. Hugh, stark naked, was spread-eagled asleep on the bed.

Seth quietly closed the door. It hadn't been something he'd wanted to see, but there'd be at least fifty thousand Australian women who'd have swapped places with him.

Instead of going to the shop at Machans for the paper, he drove over to Redlynch to see if his mate Jeffyman was in the pub there. He was up on Christmas holidays from his electrical apprenticeship in Brisbane, and Seth hadn't clapped eyes on him yet.

Last week he'd popped over to Jeffyman's uncle's place. After he got through the mob of sparky kids pestering him with sparky kid questions, he'd found Uncle Owen sitting in a comfy chair on the back lawn, freshly showered and relaxing after a hard day's work on the railway.

"I don't know where he is," Uncle Owen had said. "Got back on Friday. He's seen his mum, my mum, his brothers and sisters – then he took off. I didn't get a look in. But a little birdie tells me he's with a woman in that town up the hill near Barron Falls. If ya track him down – tell him his uncle wants a word."

When Seth got to the Redlynch pub it began to rain and he ran from the Pig to the front bar. It was half full with blokes, none Jeffyman, so he popped into the newsagent for the paper. Back in the pub he scanned it for decent live music while fitting a quick schooner in. Outside of discos, cover bands and the touristy shit, there didn't seem to be so much on. It was looking like a quiet one after all.

When he returned home, Hugh's door was still closed. Well, that's cool, thought Seth. The peace and tranquillity of my place here by the sea will give him some proper rest.

He went for a walk on the beach, and then pottered around in the back garden, and at five-thirty, put a few beers in the freezer. Just after six, he knocked on Hugh's door. Outside in the dusk, birds were calling. Behind the door nothing stirred. A pang of worry went through him again and he knocked louder. Bracing himself for more nudity, Seth swung open the door. The room was empty.

The gear Hugh had been wearing was gone. His guitars were still in the lounge, but Seth just knew he'd gone to get shit-faced, play music, and give the world all the Hugh Christie it had been missing out on. In the kitchen he saw the Yellow Pages were upside down under the phone. The silly bastard had called a cab and done a runner.

The Barbary Coast

Seth moved the beer back into the fridge and pulled on clothes. He grabbed the newspaper and got moving.

Going across the Redden Creek bridge, its big wooden planks rattling under the weight of his truck, he looked at the creek mouth open to the grey of the sea and sky, and saw a seabird skimming along above the water.

He drove down Marshall Street faster than he should; eyes peeled for errant kids and dogs. Calmly looking at the Submariner, he calculated that Hugh had a head start of at least two hours. His brain filed that away because he had to work now, appraising possibilities and weighing up options and – you selfish prick, Christie!

At the Cook Highway he'd settled down enough to start appraising possibilities and weighing up options. Against the darkening mountains in the west, he pulled over by the cane-stubble and rechecked the music listings in the paper. He saw three possibilities, all happening later, and there'd be a couple of other gigs not advertised. Mentally gridding-up town, he got to it.

Down Sheridan Street and then along the Esplanade, he swiftly checked out the chintzy tourist bars. In town he went through the pubs like a dose of salts. At Hides Hotel, Cable, his old fisherman mate, grabbed him in a sea-gull grip, insisting he have a beer, and he did, listening with a fixed smile to an acrimonious rave about the Taiwanese stripping Australian seas then escaping on their boats with the Navy in pursuit. Seth had heard all about it in the news, but he gave the old bloke a respectful eight minutes before extracting himself.

At the Great Northern he parked in the undercover car-park and looked in on a sound-check in the Tudor Room. A band was banging out a song, but no Hugh. The Marlin Bar was right there, the sound of Bonnie playing piano drifting out into the airless landing. He popped his head in and a few faces snapped around to look.

Yeah, blokes were still a bit nervy at what had happened here some months ago and Seth didn't blame them. He'd been there and it had been hairy alright.

Enjoying a first beer with Johnny Pep and a couple of his fishermen mates around eight o'clock one night, he'd been jolted from this happy task by a ka-bloody-boom out front and a sudden bright hole appearing in the glass front door. Some bastard had just fired a gun into the Marlin Bar.

The door flew open and the bastard himself, shirtless and heavily-built, ran in, pointing a Lee Enfield .303 rifle at the crowd. Shit! thought Seth – the bullets in that thing are full-power military rounds.

"Which one of you bastards started the blue?" screamed

the rifleman into sudden silence. Blokes slid under tables, drew back against each other, and from the bar came the rush and jingle of coins as the barmaid grabbed the till and ran it through the doorway into the Homestead Bar.

Bang! The bastard fired again, just above everybody's heads, and the noise of it in the crowded room was like being punched in the ear. There was a sudden bad smell and Seth hoped it was a fart.

"You bastards stand there!" yelled the crazy man, and he used the rifle barrel to line some blokes up. "Which one of you started it? Who hit me?"

"You fuckin' idiot!" yelled a voice and the rifle swung towards it and bang! – another big round went into a wall, shattering a framed picture on its way. Blokes yelled and women screamed.

The gunman rounded on some more fellas, shouting, "Line up you dogs! Who started it! Who went me?"

With gritted teeth and scared eyes, men formed a line, cringing as the rifle muzzle passed in front of their chests.

"They chucked him out earlier," Pep muttered in Seth's ear. "He's going to kill someone at this rate."

Seth had looked at Pep and it was a yes, and he looked around and saw a couple of blokes nod at him, and it was on. The bare-chested idiot was standing half-on to them, and Seth, Pep and the two blokes rushed him.

It was mad scramble; the crazy bastard strong, but Seth and one of the blokes forced the barrel down and bang! – it went off – and the gunman jerked back in shock then bolted through the bar and right out the door. There was silence and then a roar of voices, and Seth and Pep and a mob of blokes had run out after him, all slowing at the top of the steps outside.

Right there on Abbott Street, a grey HQ Holden was double parked; three blokes helping the limping gunman to it – one shirtless bloke laughing at the blood spurting out of his mate's left thigh. Seth saw the fresh splashes of gore on the wide sidewalk, and a great shout of laughter rang out. The idiot had shot himself in the leg!

The gunman got bundled into the Holden, and with a screech of rubber and a blare of angry car-horns it took off up the street. More blokes piled out of the Marlin Bar, and as word of the own-goal spread, everybody cracked up, the brightly-lit sidewalk echoing with great guffaws and shouts of astonished delight.

Yep, thought Seth, looking fruitlessly around the noisy but placid Marlin Bar, Cairns could be a rough old place at times. But this joint was up-market compared to where he knew he had to go now. It was the last place left to look – the Barbary Coast.

Down on Wharf Street, he pulled over and parked by the big grass verge next to the harbour board workshops, a couple of palms throwing moving shadows onto their tin roofs. A light wind off the inlet brought the stink of brine and diesel. Through the chain-link fence, the warehouses were night-time still, the cargo-cranes of a ship poking up above their low-pitched orange roofs. There wasn't much lighting, but enough to see a big rat doing its rounds.

A whole lot of everything had gone down on this strip of waterfront over the years. Fortunes made and lives lost.

He'd had his own kak-your-daks moment here one wet

night back in '72; the rain so full-on it had washed away his blood squirting onto the wharf. Leaving no trail for his assailant to follow probably saved his life, but the force of the rainfall had really hurt the knife wound.

The main entrance was closed, and a line of red cargo containers waited on the railway track by the street for tomorrow's locomotive. The shrill squabbling of fruit bats in a tree overhead mixed with the basso rumble of many hundreds of drinkers, all quenching their thirst in the tin-roofed hotels across the road. There were a couple more hotels around the corner in Abbott Street, and this clutch of waterside pubs was known as the Barbary Coast.

They offered no-star accommodation, basic pub meals and endless beer. The cheap and cheerless rooms, sweaty batten-roofed boxes off creaky hallways, had provided shelter for working men, and some hard-as-nails women, for more than sixty years. You name 'em – RAAF and navy boys, wharfies, fishermen and sailors; cane-cutters and truckies; salesmen, cooks and hookers – they'd all been through here.

In recent times this hard-drinking clientele had been joined by the Murri people, finally allowed to drink next to whitefellas, and in the last few years – the drug dealers, their customers, and their respective entourages.

Every town had its wild part and this was Cairns' own corner of depravity; a bubbling slurry of working-class people, local and itinerant, and desperadoes from all over and everywhere in-between. It was as rough as guts here, and seedier than a badly grown head, the wide pavements stained with decades of involuntarily spilled bodily fluids.

You watched your wallet and your mouth. Getting bashed here was as easy as taking a slash in the nearby long grass.

Seth looked across the road to the corner of Wharf and Lake Streets. Next to The Oceanic was a grassy vacant lot. There'd been a real old pub there – The Royal. Built in the twenties, the two-storied timber edifice had been a Pacific legend. Its long verandas had looked onto the maritime traffic on Chinaman Creek in the early days, and over the decades in the hard front bar on the corner, unbelievably tough blokes had kept the pub's reputation as an all-out blood-bucket going; night after bloody night. The Royal had been the Port of Cairns' wild brawling soul; now it was gone, demolished earlier in the year.

He walked across Wharf Street; the parking strip down the centre full of vehicles, and though empty of traffic, the street rang with voices. The Oceanic was packed, probably since mid-day, with fellas talking and smoking on the footpath; The Barrier Reef on the other corner just the same.

When he'd first started drinking in pubs, the Barbary Coast had been on the skids; the wharfies and canecutters a dying breed. Mechanisation, the sugar terminal, and new truck and transport depots slowly tore the guts out of it. Derelict souls haunted half-empty front bars; world-beaten blokes died forgotten in sundrenched rooms. Men and women expired in the street, taken by violence, or ground down by excess. It grew ramshackle and scabby; even more than before. Only the roughest and the dirtiest drank there; fishermen too, and blokes gathered at the Fighting Tree on Abbot Street to bash each other.

Those waterfront pubs had reeked of desperation and decay. It was a raw eye-sore, and the Council, the cops and publicans finally cleaned it up, a bit, and enforced rules and regulations. Over the last few years, especially with new development, a hardy new generation of hellions and party animals had joined the old bastards still left.

Seth hardly ever drank here for fun, but he'd always felt a bit of pride in the old strip. It was hairy arsed, true blue, take-it-or-fuck-off uncompromising, and this attitude epitomised the rugged physicality and individuality of the far north to him.

On the pub side of the street, Seth walked past blokes; a mob of muscled-up Torres Strait Islanders in well used work boots; a grubby chancer with no shoes but lots of scars; loud fellas in shorts and thongs, and it made him smile. Cairns might be changing, but in these old hotels rugged history was still alive and kicking.

The air here had always rung with tales of hardship and wonder, of miracles and disasters; with stories from the great blue sea, the high green mountains, and the hot red west, and whoops! – a bloke emptied his guts onto the sidewalk and Seth had to quickly side-step the splash.

On the corner he looked up Abbott Street. The meridian strip was thick with trees; murmuring shadows loitering in the darkness beneath them, and down the side of The Barrier Reef, a fella lay insensible against the wall.

Across Wharf Street was the peaked white roof of the Cairns yacht club; inside it a dancehall – The Aquatic. He'd seen some great rock'n'roll in there. And met a few full-speed women.

A loud mix of accents coming out of The Barrier Reef made him turn; a couple of working-girls, one black, one white, were sharing gap-toothed laughter with two stocky Taiwanese fishermen; everyone looking pretty happy with how the business at hand was turning out.

He walked down Abbott Street to the two hotels there, the beer advertisement festooned buildings side-by-side, their second floor verandas making a wide roof over the sidewalk. Drunken men and women stood beneath it, everybody talking loudly over the sonic uproar of music coming from The Australian.

A fast blues-rock was going down; standard fare around here, but riding the swamp boogie was a guitar soloing its arse off. The virtuosity of the playing sent a tingle through Seth. It was pure sinuous electricity; the solo repeatedly turning in on itself like a snake made of quicksilver. He'd found Hugh.

Seth listened for a minute then went in. As he pushed slowly through the crush, his bouncer's eyes looked for trouble makers. There were a few who fitted the bill, and in here that was saying something. No-one gave him a second look; no one gave a shit. Until they did that is.

About a third of the crowd were turned towards the bar, drinking and talking loudly over the music. Everybody else faced the stage with expressions of joy on their faces. There were a fair few women in the place, and most were at the front, throwing around hair, hips and bosoms as they danced with real abandon. Some of them, even the skinny ones, looked like they could eat a man whole and just spit out the bones.

"Who's that poof bastard making all that noise?" yelled a bloke at the bar to his mates. He had a long chin-beard and Seth felt like yanking the ridiculous thing and saying, "Just one of the best fucking guitarists in the country."

Instead, he got a couple of beers and found a spot closer to the stage. It was probably thirty degrees outside and the jam-packed front room sweltered with the crush of bodies. Gratefully guzzling half a schooner, he cheerfully checked it out – Hugh Christie, tearing up a room on the Barbary Coast.

The rhythm section wasn't bad, the drummer a lean and sweat-soaked machine in a cut-off shirt; the bass player trading any flashiness for raw power and timing. The two other guitarists – one was blonde, it was Johno of course – supplied the endless boogie. Knocking out the chords and changes, even as they expertly laid down supple patterns of countrified funky blues, these two players didn't need to watch their fingers. It was more fun watching the blow-in lead guitarist in flight.

And he was flying. Seth had seen Hugh play quite a few times, but without rehearsed songs and the structure of a band chasing a career – this was different. Different too, to the hip-as-fuck jam sessions that Hugh sometimes deigned to join; the vibe edgy and fragile with the peer-group pressure of name musos, the air cloying and sticky with the adulation of groupies and hangers-on.

Here in the front bar of The Australian, Hugh was like Atlas unbound. With closed eyes, and fingers blurring on the fretboard – he was free – spinning the wildest web of notes exactly as his heart and soul wanted.

The band's energy built to a climax, and with a sound like Hendrix, Clapton and Page colliding on speedboats in a mangrove creek – the song finished.

The room erupted with rebel yells, jungle howls and unhinged screams. Women roundly hugged each other, and blokes spun about yelling gleefully at their mates. A woman up the front bent over and joyously waggled her arse at the crowd. Ripples of riotous energy criss-crossed the room, the excited audience like fish jumping on the surface of the ocean.

The ear-splitting roar of approval now subsided to an ear-splitting babble of intoxicated voices. It was turning into a top night.

Seth had to laugh. Nobody here gave a tiny fraction of a fart about how they looked or acted. For raw, unconscious hedonism, this mob left the city for dead.

In all their sweaty, scarred and stained glory, everyone was guts-effort real. Blokes who smashed through hard physical labour in the relentless humidity, the working-girls doing just the same; grimy-fingered mechanics and engineers, women trawler cooks, commune rejects and wild young things; drunks and druggies of every sex and colour.

And skittering at the edges; the desperates who hustled a living between scams, a pension or the dole; hard-luck, nothing-to-losers, living in fetid old boarding houses, run-down Queenslanders, on leaking boats in the inlet, or on cardboard carton beds in the long grass.

People stunk of diesel, booze, tobacco and dope, cheap perfume and sweat. Nobody gave a good goddamn. Aside from a few of the ladies, no one here was even remotely close to the concept of dressing up. For what? In case Jesus or Bo Derek walked through the door?

Hugh, ignoring some very graphic entreaties from two very drunk women, picked up a jug of beer at his feet and poured himself a glass of beer. That's funny, thought Seth. He wouldn't be caught dead drinking a jug in Sydney.

Hugh guzzled the pot, refilled it and did the same again. As he drank, a scrawny fella in jeans and an AC/DC t-shirt reverently placed a second jug of beer at his feet. The band also took a quick drink, the bass player vacantly sucking a schooner of Coke through a straw. One guitarist had a few puffs on a cigarette, stubbing it out in an ashtray atop a speaker. Contemplative, bright-eyed and sweating, they all looked like they were having a big night.

Then Hugh and the band conferred, and everyone took their positions. At the front, a lanky Murri bloke started dancing, his knees and elbows flying. With a wild yell he stopped and pointed a dramatic finger at Hugh. The noise level dropped a tad as the sweating audience re-focused on the band. Some bloke screamed. A few women up front screamed back, and there was general laughter.

At the mike, Hugh smiled out over the room. He looked nicely drunk and stoned. Seth looked at his watch. It was nearly eight. Our boy doesn't waste any time, he thought.

"Uh, hi there, Cairns," said Hugh in a deep drawl. "It's great to be . . ."

"Shut up and play guitar," someone yelled. The crowd cheered in affirmation, and as that died down, a woman yelled, "Yeah, come on you big spunk – fuck us!"

With knowing grins at this serendipitous request, the band launched into a libidinous slow groove that sounded like a chugging steam-train full of naked men and women all sliding around in warm coconut oil. It was sex on a stick and the crowd ate it up.

At the front, the ladies slid into the rhythm, turning into sex goddesses, and the triple row of women; young and old, black and white, big and small, now laid out the oldest story in the world as graphically as their sweat-soaked dresses, blouses and pants would allow.

Blokes staggered, eyes blinking and popping at this display, beer spilling unnoticed down their fronts. At the bar, the uninterested shut up and turned, craning heads to get a load of this. Fellas started doing things with their hips they would have been ashamed to do a minute earlier; shimmying, wriggling, popping open buttons and bumping into other blokes.

No-one talked as the hypnotic beat palpitated through the room. An islander lady, dark skinned and afro haired, gyrated in close to a pale, freckled gypsy style woman. In the groove, they smiled blissfully at each other, and men swayed, open-mouthed at this wonderous vision.

The insistent erotic throb filled every pore and groin in the room. A young woman, big boned, long haired and country strong, turned and danced facing the audience. With her eyes closed and her lips open, her breasts, belly and hips were a rippling locus of primeval power.

Now blokes were looking like Jesus or Bo Derek had come into the room, their faces slack with something like religious ecstasy. The tumescence was going off the dial.

As the tension reached an unbearable peak, with every man and woman in the room feeling like their libidos had been polished to a throbbing sheen – the most eloquently filthy guitar solo Seth had ever heard came spurting out of the speakers.

The shock and release were palpable, and an immense groan erupted. Eyes rolled and faces twisted as though in orgasm. Country Girl raised her arms like a preacher, her mouth wide open in a yell of deliverance. Behind the bar a stack of glasses crashed to the floor. At the door, a bloke toppled out backwards into the street.

The solo didn't stop at eight or sixteen bars; it caressed, stroked and cajoled like an inspired lover on a really dirty weekend. Teasing then satisfying then teasing again, it found every nook and cranny possible – and licked them all clean.

Then the solo ended with a delirious squeal, the band vamping nice and greasy on the groove, and an explosive roar of appreciation just about tore the roof of the joint. Hugh Christie, as requested, had fucked them.

When the song ground to its end, the charged-up room blew up in paroxysms of manic delight. From the stage, a perspiring Hugh slyly surveyed the room like a king done dispensing manna. This is gold, thought Seth with wild hilarity. Davey Silver should see this.

Then they did a Chain cover, and with the band just killing it behind him, Hugh proceeded to blow minds even further with an inventive guitar solo. After another couple of loudly received songs, the band called a break.

Seth went for more refreshments at the chock-a-block

bar. Waiting in the steaming crush, he looked out through the doorway and saw Liam and Gordy Mac walking past. He waited a few moments then went outside.

The brothers, in heavy boots, black jeans and t-shirts, were walking towards Wharf Street. Seth followed slowly, using blokes on the sidewalk outside as cover. When they turned onto the street, he hurried up to The Barrier Reef and carefully looked around the corner. He watched them go past the brick wedge of the Jack and Newell store and come to a halt outside The Oceanic. They started talking, Gordy Mac looking into the pub. After a minute he went in; his brother walking on before turning into the grassy vacant lot where The Royal used to be.

Seth went up the street, passing The Oceanic with his face averted then peeked down the side of the pub. Liam was moving through shadows and grass, and when he got to Lake Street and turned right, Seth followed him. He kept close to pub; its wall only recently exposed by The Royal's demolition. A dark second floor veranda loomed above him. Rubble and broken glass crunched underfoot. It smelt old, the shadows infinitely deep, and Seth felt a disquieting accumulation of time around him.

At Lake Street, he slowed and moved cautiously to look up the street. Ten metres away in the sepia wash of the street lights, Liam Mac was walking up to an orange Datsun SSS coupe, car keys jingling in his hand. With his loping stride and well-muscled shoulders, he looked like an animal – something deadly and implacable come down from the jungles of the Lamb Range to hunt in the streets of Cairns.

As he opened the car door, headlights appeared further up on Lake Street, a car screeching in from Spence Street, its engine gunning flat-out; revheads doing blockies.

I'm sticking out like the proverbial dog's here, thought Seth, so he nipped back through the vacant lot. As he got closer to Wharf Street, he saw someone standing on the grassy corner looking right at him. Gordy Mac.

Looking weak was not something he wanted to do, so he went over. "Hey, how's it going?"

Gordy Mac, his arms loose at his sides, said nothing; his face expressionless.

Seth cranked up a smile. "You right there, mate?"

But Gordy Mac kept up the silent vibe. Well, bugger you then, thought Seth. I'm not hanging about.

From behind him on Lake Street came the furious roar of the rapidly approaching car. Liam Mac appeared by his shoulder. A supercharger fired up in his chest. Fight juice squirted through his veins.

"Mate," said Liam, his tone of voice stunning Seth. Gordy, with a warm smile, reached out and squeezed his shoulder. The car came around the corner and screeched to shockie-rocking stop.

"Look at these poofs!" yelled a stupendously agro voice, and an empty longneck flew through the air, bounced once then burst. Five country boys, fit as stallions, stared from the car. In the back seat sat an absolute giant of a bloke. For the love of Larry, thought Seth, these bastards are going around town unleashing their big dog onto whoever takes their fancy.

"Ooo, he's a big one," said Gordy.

Liam laughed then yelled at the boys. "Up your arse!" As the car's doors flew open, he made a noise of delight and bounded forward. With battle cries and yells of rage, the car began to empty.

Seth wanted to run away. He had less than an ant's dick of interest in fighting these bastards from whatever cane-farm crossroads they came from. But like a rip on a beach, he was being pulled towards the impending violence; the Macs just the same. The moment the car had stopped, the three of them had started moving towards it.

On what had been the toughest corner in town, soaked with a hundred years of grog, sweat and blood, Seth felt the ground at his feet dissolving into dark swamp mud. An undertow inexorably sucked him towards the coming violence – and he ran at the car.

A fella sprung out from the back, a stumble saving him from a fist to the jaw. As Seth recovered from his mis-hit, the fella threw his arms around him like a girl wanting a pash and tried to trip him to the ground. The foreplay was to get him ready for the giant, now emerging with his big feet settling onto the road; just seconds away from launching himself up and into it.

Using the weight of the fool holding him, Seth pivoted, and stamped sledge-hammer hard on the giant's ankle. Something snapped and screaming started. Seth held his dance partner by the shoulders, rammed his knee up into the family jewels, and the bloke's eyes popped out of his head like Wile E. Coyote in a Looney Tunes cartoon.

Seth shook him off, leapt back and looked around. A sun-browned, thick-browed bastard was throwing a big-knuckled doozey into Liam's head. It was a match-winner, but his target danced sideways, and in a blur, locked his hands onto the bumpkin's wrist. With his biceps suddenly rock hard, Liam snapped it. Then he stepped back, lined up, and floored the bloke.

Seth flashed on the only fight he'd ever had with Liam. The bastard kicked him so hard in the leg he'd fallen down in agony. Then Liam had grabbed him by the hair, lifting his head, and delivered a single knock-out punch.

From the other side of the car, the last back-seat boy was yelling, but the anger in his voice was rapidly turning to fear. Even as Seth guessed he'd take the ball and run, he did, pelting off up Lake Street.

The other two farm boys were fighting off Gordy Mac, punching, ducking and weaving, but not doing too good. As Liam bopped in, Gordy dropped one fella with a knock-out hit that would make his knuckles hum for sure then stamped hard on the bloke's right hand.

The last man standing had hands like mallets. Jumping over his decked mate, he swung a mallet. Gordy had to move bloody quick as it was a blow to knock him out.

This son of the cane had style and he didn't seem that drunk either, but Gordy went low, hitting him in the guts hard enough to bring him down on one knee. With an exultant roar, Gordy swarmed over him, his arms blurring machine-fast, and the last contender hit the ground.

Gordy looked at Liam and Seth. It was a glorious look – like they were kings; three absolute monsters who could bring brutal, overpowering violence to whoever the fuck they wanted to – and Seth loved it.

He turned and ran from the brothers, and that haunted corner alive with the ghosts of drinkers, brawlers and lost souls; hard sons of the sea and soil, drunk on the violence of the ages. Over the timeless mayhem of the screaming bone-shattered country boys – Gordy yelled, "Wait! Seth! Mate! Wait!"

On Wharf Street, Seth slowed to a walk. The blokes outside The Oceanic were silent; listening to the hideous racket coming from the corner; everyone watching Seth. He nodded pleasantly as he passed, a bloke murmuring at him, "By Christ, you boys can blue."

Passing the Jack and Newell store – memory took hold.

The Macs had been Alex's mates since high school, and he'd only hung out with them with his brother. In his late teens, he learnt to drink with them, struggling to keep up in long sessions at the pub: always the junior, listening at the edges and doggedly shaking off their attempts to make him fight other blokes; Alex riding him the hardest.

He kept up with his boxing and worked as a bouncer to show them he was no weak sister. They'd cheered him at boxing comps and were pleased to shake his hand when he was working a door. Mr. Niceguy was Gordy and Alex's nickname for him; always said with piss-take cheer.

Then marijuana had come along and he got paid good money when they needed someone they trusted. He took his orders from Alex and that was cool. There'd also been times when they'd fronted up to intimidate or fight rivals. But he'd basically done it to help his brother.

He might have had a few beers with the Macs over the years, but he'd never gone fishing with them.

Gordy Mac knew lots of stuff and could be a real laugh, but Liam was a bastard; a cunning, mean bastard. When the nasty stuff started, not the usual punch-ons with other rough-nuts and players, it had put Seth right off.

Liam grabbed hats off old blokes in pubs and walked out wearing them. He broke a kid's hand at Ellis Beach in a game of touch and raped a young woman at a party. Gordy got rougher like he had to keep up – chasing and bashing motorists who cut him off, shooting some fella at Archer Point in the leg just to make the boys laugh, and kicking the shit out of blokes already down.

When the Macs went from being dinkum scrappers to sick puppies, Liam's mongrel streak turned rabid. It was like he was permanently troppo: crazy-weird all the time, and his brother used the fear he created to dominate blokes and situations. It had taken Alex a bit longer to break with the bastards, but he eventually did.

In pubs and at parties all over, the Macs loudly declared that Alex and his poof brother were as hard as chalk; little girls who'd got their reps riding on the Mac's true outlaw power. Alex had acted like he didn't give a damn – but Seth knew.

It had freaked him out a bit. That his brother was scared of nobody had always been a given; a dependable source of strength, and pride.

One evening at Alex's house at Palm Cove, the two of them had been sitting stoned and reflective out the back, his brother cradling his sleeping daughter Sophie in his lap. Seth brought the Mac brothers up, and at the word 'scared', Alex had gone totally Krakatoa. His face flushed with rage and he turned his head away from Sophie and coughed oddly for a few seconds, his chest moving deeply. Seth cringed, waiting as his brother stretched out his neck and spat out on to the grass. When he turned back to Seth, his face was demonic.

"Don't you ever think or speak that shit to me. *Ever!*"

Seth, demolished, looked down at his beer.

Sophie cried out in her sleep, and her mother came to the back door, both disturbed by the raw menace they'd heard. After that, Seth and Alex never talked about the Macs again. To anybody.

In hindsight, it was the smart thing to do. Soon enough, any bloke caught running them down ended up spitting teeth and pissing blood.

But what had just happened then? Seth wondered, as he walked under the old tin roof of The Barrier Reef. The two of them had come onto him like old mates; Liam sounding pleased to see him, and Gordy reaching out to hold his shoulder. It was weirder than rocking-horse shit.

On the corner he mentally checked himself out – no busted knuckles or aching ribs, and his foot and knee felt just fine. Savouring the last of the fight's rush, he turned into Abbott Street and sauntered back to The Australian. Coming up to the drive-in entrance of the Liquor Barn, he saw something happening just ahead.

Against the brick wall of the row of old shops, a group of chuckling men were watching someone get a smacking. Two blokes held a man against the wall while another one slapped his face. Nothing unusual around here. Then Seth did a double-take and broke into a run.

It was Hugh getting the smacking – one arm held by a happy shit in greasy engineer-grey overalls, the other by some streak of piss Seth vaguely recognised from around the traps. The fella doing the slapping was a stocky, jowly, ginger-stubbled prick, looking like a young boar – porky, but fast with it, and he was playing up to the boys.

"If it walks like a girl and talks like a girl – then it gets slapped like one."

The laughter died as Seth elbowed through.

"What the fuck are you doing?" he yelled.

The streak of piss evaporated. The happy shit went sad, letting go of Hugh and sliding away along the wall. Porky, surprised at Seth's appearance, took a second to re-group.

"Well, looky here. The poofs are getting bigger," he said, stepping back against the wall next to Hugh.

Seth now saw that the drunken fool was going to have a go at him; there must be blokes that he wanted to impress. Seth got between him and Hugh.

"What the fuck are you doing?" he asked, this time in a dangerously reasonable tone.

"I'm just giving your root a slap," said Porky.

"That's not a slap – this is a slap," said Seth, and his hand flashed into Porky's head, knocking him against the wall. Stepping in, he delivered another mighty slap, and the idiot's head made a double bone-meets-brick sound, bouncing from wall to hand and back again. The crowd groaned appreciatively, and Porky slid down the wall into an unconscious heap.

Seth felt like kicking him in the head, but he didn't. He wasn't Liam Mac.

He turned to the semi-circle of men, ready for trouble. Everyone stared at him, some blokes looking amused, and Seth reckoned they might be thinking the wrong thing.

"What? You wanna fucking kiss?" he roared.

A few blokes flinched, and with some laughter, the men wandered back to the pubs. Against the brick wall, Hugh swayed, frowning at nothing in particular.

You absolute bloody fool, thought Seth. Those bastards would have rearranged your face, broken your fingers too. You'd never play guitar properly again.

He got right into the guitarist's face and gave him a big serve of his anger – but didn't say a thing. Staring white-hot burning daggers, Seth put as much exasperation and fury into it as he could.

"Fuck you, man," mumbled Hugh.

The Good News

The morning was grey and wet, an easterly blowing in from the Coral Sea. Rain pattered, sometimes drummed on the tin roof. Hugh was in his room: asleep or awake Seth didn't much care. After a shower and breakfast, he dawdled over a second cuppa and considered the man he was being paid to play nanny to.

Basically, Hugh was spoilt. With no thought for anyone else, he knew that money always pulled him out of the shit – then paid for it to be cleaned up after him.

With that headspace, he probably didn't have any real mates – mates whose respect and appreciation had been earned by sharing hard times or hard work. Mates who took up the slack when you were broke or ill. Mates who came through with zero fuss, never big-noting their help or expecting anything in return. True brothers. It must be easy to ignore all that when you're rich, thought Seth. And bloody lonely too.

Eventually Hugh got up and shuffled to the toilet. As he came out, Seth said, "Can you flush it, please?"

Hugh ignored him, so Seth leapt up and used his size and height to monster him back the way he'd come.

"Are you serious?" said Hugh in disbelief.

"Sure am," said Seth pleasantly.

The guitarist went and flushed.

"Thanks mate! You're a champ," called Seth.

Hugh frumped back in, tossing his hair like a huffy go-go dancer, and began looking in cupboards. Seth sneaked over, grabbed him by his shoulders, and the poor thing actually screamed in shock.

Seth spun him around. "Guess what I got for you?"

"Fuck you, man – you scared me!"

"Da-dah." Seth put a coffee-maker and a bag of coffee on the orange Formica countertop.

"I remembered you drink this stuff, so I popped into Andre's Deli yesterday."

"Oh, coffee," sniffed Hugh, as he scrutinized the bag of ground beans. "Local coffee."

"From Mareeba. Supposed to be the tomcat's nuts."

With his eyes averted from Seth, Hugh measured out coffee. Seth had to laugh at this performance.

"C'mon you big sook – you survived the Barbary Coast, didn't you? And you got coffee."

Hugh cast him a surly look.

"That was diabolical last night," he said.

"Aw yeah, pretty tame by local standards."

"Oh, hark at the provincial. He's actually proud of those clapped-out fire hazards. They'll be gone in twenty years."

"Maybe, but it's . . . real down there. Not all dollied up."

"You're not wrong. I bet the rats have the clap."

"Mate, the ghosts have the clap."

This exchange made Seth laugh again, but Hugh turned away and got busy with the coffee maker. Seth pulled a face at him then sat down at the kitchen table and started a shopping list. With his coffee made, Hugh went sat on the lounge, drinking it while watching the canna lilies outside the windows shiver and bounce in the rain.

Seth surreptitiously watched him. *I can't babysit him every hour of the day. I have to set an appeal into motion.*

"There's toast, bacon, eggs and tomatoes," he said. "Or Corn Flakes, bananas and red pawpaw."

Hugh didn't respond, the lines on his face prominent. Seth's eyelids momentarily drooped with exasperation.

"Listen, I'm gonna go out for a few hours," he said. "Set yourself up in the lounge and play as loud as you like. Just go for it. I'll do a bit of shopping in town. Anything you like to eat or drink?"

Hugh remained silent.

"Cool. I'll get that then."

Gathering his keys and wallet, Seth headed out, not super sure that Hugh wouldn't take off again. Hopefully the inclement weather would keep him home, and the things that he liked: live music, wild women and partying, were unlikely to be happening in daylight hours.

But groceries weren't the first thing on his list. In town he drove past the railway workshops and depot on Bunda Street, turned into Scott Street, and immediately saw the place where Fuckinkev, the Mac's muscle lived. There was no red Holden in the driveway, so five houses down, he did a U-turn and parked diagonally across the street. With raindrops freckling the windscreen, he sat and watched the place.

The area around here had always had a vibe. Notorious, Mum had called it. Three hundred metres from the Cairns railway station, five blocks from the waterfront, and right where the Bruce Highway hit town; the area had always buzzed with illicit activity. For eighty years, day and night, the worker's cottages and boarding houses here had been where a fella could find working-girls, after-hours grog, gambling and drugs – even opium back in the day. Old blokes had told him how busy it was here during the war, with Yank and Aussie troops by the tens of thousands: all eager to root, drink, dance and gamble.

It was the wrong side of the tracks alright, and as a kid he was told to keep away. But he'd cycled around: seeing broken glass and single shoes in gutters, empty wallets and used condoms in front gardens; women drinking and laughing in back yards, sunning themselves bare-legged and bra-less; shirtless, hard looking fellas smoking and yarning on front steps, sometimes drinking too.

Later still, he'd gone to parties here, but it always felt edgy and transient – a place where strangers came and went without a trace. There were surely upright, hard-working citizens living here now, but it was still less than salubrious. Short term, low rent, and in walking distance of the pubs, bars and hotels – the area was a handy abode for itinerant labourers, hookers and musicians, chefs, dealers and waitresses.

It also looked bloody shabby. Trucks splashed through big corner pot-holes, and old rusty roofed timber cottages perched exhausted on their timber poles; one rotten old box of a place crowned with a gutter full of seedlings. Clots of faded old rubbish clogged the rusty wire mesh of front-fences, and kerbs crumbled into muddy rubble and eager weeds.

High-rises might be going up at the Esplanade now, but this back-water by the Bruce was stagnant; its glory days gone. What remained was deeply stained with decades of raw unfiltered pleasure and hard-scrabble pain. Not eight hundred yards from the Town Hall, this was the Cairns the tourists never saw.

Stretching a crack from his back, Seth dug through his memory, conjuring up a picture of Fuckinkev. He'd seen him at Hides Hotel with the Macs and Sabbo just over a year ago. Though not so big, he looked strong and hard; probably from physical work growing up in his hometown Bowen. But his choices up here had left him lean and pinched – and marked with the classic druggie, desperado look of furtive eyes, worn greasy jeans and scuffed boots, flannelette shirt with cut down sleeves, eternal stubble and busted knuckles.

Actually, a lot of law-abiding hardworking fellas fitted that description, their clothes stained with honest sweat, engine oil, and God's good earth. The exception was their eyes. The eyes were the give-away.

Working as security in pubs and clubs from Parap to Potts Point meant Seth could quickly pick out villains by watching where their eyes settled. Blokes usually looked at women, the band onstage, who they were yakking to, at nice cars and bikes, or the floor if they'd fallen down.

The blokes who looked all over the shop – at pockets and wallets, windows and back doors – were the nefarious ones. Maybe even undercover cops.

Seth shifted irritably in his seat; conscious he was going to have his work cut out turning Fuckinkev. Getting a crim to dob in his mates wasn't easy, even if their mates weren't top-flight predators like the Mac brothers. It wasn't any honour among thieves' bullshit either. It was survival. The far north was big, but its criminal world was small. Sooner or later, dogs got punished; maybe even put down.

Now Seth deeply sighed, acknowledging the dread that had settled over him the last few days. Winning the appeal wouldn't be the end of it. From prison, the Macs could put a bloke in a midnight bedroom, or in the shadows of a pub carpark at closing time, and the bloke would put a bullet in his head. Prison would slow them, but only death could truly snuff out their power.

His thoughts went there. Make it look accidental; a car off a cliff or something. The only thing was – he'd never murdered blokes in cold blood before, and he wasn't about to start now. No, when the appeal succeeded, he'd just have to be on his guard. All the time. Or maybe leave town again for a spell. It would be worth it, but.

When the drizzle stopped, Seth locked the Pig, crossed the road, and slipped down the fence line of the house into the backyard; his eyes watching windows. Over the trucks and cars on Bunda Street, he could hear the clangourous din of the railway yards and workshops.

A garden shed by the house looked like it might be good to watch from; its door ajar and sagging from one hinge, and Seth snuck inside. The shed was a home-made jobbie knocked together with scavenged offcuts. Tarnished tools and crusty old paint tins slept in corners; a cracked, cob-webbed window looked out to the house. Not bad.

He gave it a go, but mosquitoes soon materialised and began buzz-bombing his head, so he went back along the fence-line to the street. In the Pig he pondered the nut he needed to crack. It was more like a bloody ball bearing.

Money and violence were the nutcrackers, but he wasn't going to put the frighteners into Fuckinkev by bashing him. He didn't do that. And even if he did, he wouldn't go to the extremes that the Macs would, and he had a pretty good idea Fuckinkev would know that. It really was going to require Sabbo's money.

A battered red EH Holden with new tyres pulled up out front of the house. Seth slid down in his seat, making the lowest profile possible and watched two men get out.

One of them was the man he'd seen at Hides Hotel last year – Fuckinkev, and from the way he glanced around then went up the front stairs two at a time, Seth knew he had something illegal on him. The other fella, some gaunt sickly bastard he'd never seen before, followed, missing a step and nearly falling.

Thirty seconds after the front door closed, Seth hopped out, nipped across the road and went down the side of the house. Below window height, he ran to the garden shed, hearing boots clumping on the wooden floor in the house.

Inside the shed, he went over to the window and froze.

Fuckinkev was outside already and scurrying across the lawn to a gnarly old frangipani tree. At the tree he felt around in a hole at the base of a big branch, and then pulled out a plastic packet the size of a half-burnt candle.

Seth made a camera sound; ker-chik, ker-chik. Gotcha, he thought. It was odds-on the packet contains the works: hypodermic syringes and flame blackened teaspoons. With his prize held against his chest, Fuckinkev went back into the house.

Well, this could be alright, thought Seth. It wasn't real nice thinking this way, but addiction was weakness, and it could help him dominate this junkie crim.

He swatted mozzies; giving the boys a few minutes to cook up, blast up and go goo-goo. Then he went around the front and climbed the shaky old stairs.

As he knocked on the door, the sonorous metallic clang of a shunting rail-car hammered the air. He waited for the sound to fade and knocked again – hard. Two minutes went by and he knew that the stash in the frangipani tree was being refilled. He gave the door some more knuckle.

"Kev! Kev mate!"

"Yeah? Who's that?" said a voice behind the door.

"Kev, it's a mate of Gordy's."

The door opened a sliver. A stunned looking eye peered out. Seth held up a fifty-dollar bill and the eye widened.

"G'day, mate. Gordy says you're a good bloke, so I'm wondering if you can help me. Make it worth your while."

If Fuckinkev was wrapped up in white-powder cotton wool he certainly reacted quickly.

"How fuckin' worth my while?"

Seth shook the fifty. Fuckinkev laughed. Seth took out another fifty. "I'll come in, aye? Bit more private."

"If that's for what you're thinking – then it's nowhere even fuckin' close."

"What am I thinking?"

"That your mate Sabbotini shouldn't be fuckin' banged up in fuckin' Stuart Creek."

This bloke wasn't totally stupid, thought Seth.

"I'm not totally fuckin' stupid," said Fuckinkev. "And I remember you, what you did at Hides – fuckin' funny too. And Sabbo told me about you."

"Let's talk, mate."

"Not for two fifties."

"This money is just for you to listen to me. That's all."

"Add two more and I'll let you in."

Seth hated doing it, but he handed the money over.

Inside they sat around a visibly shocked kitchen table sticky with . . . stickiness, and dusted with cigarette ash. An unrealistically coloured Samantha Fox pin-up sagged on a wall. Next to the fridge, a creased Harley Low Rider poster provided yang energy. By the sink, grotty in excelsis, a greasy black frypan, a dozen empty longnecks, and a slew of unwashed mugs completed the picture of domestic bliss.

Seth, still pissed off about the two hundred, didn't want to seem too eager, so he took a copy of Easyriders from a dog-eared stack of magazines on the floor and began idly leafing through it.

The junkie crim also played hard-to-get, taking his time rolling a smoke; a gold chain bracelet swinging lazily from his wrist. Seth browsed the bikie magazine. It was full of useful tips and advice. Plant Growin' Problems was about problems growing marijuana plants. How to Roast a Pig was about roasting a pig. Swapping the Ol' Lady was about . . . he threw the magazine back on the pile.

On the floor and up through the hallway was a scree of rubbish: newspapers, empty bottles and cans, a snapped thong, balled-up fish'n'chips wrappings, and brown paper pie-bags caked with dried sauce. The boys were disgusting drug pigs, and this was their pigsty.

"Fuckinkev, aye," said Seth.

"Yeah?"

"Everybody calls you that and I can see why, but it's . . . demeaning."

"De meaning? It just means fuckin' Kev."

"Yeah, right," said Seth absently. Steel suddenly bashed into steel at the rail depot, but neither of them jumped. Seth waited. So did Fuckinkev. The non-verbal Mexican stand-off was easy for him; he was in a big bliss-bomb of smack, his ciggie and eyelids sagging.

The cards were on the table; they both knew what the other wanted, but Seth wanted to hear, unprompted, what price this bastard thought his testimony, and probably his life, was worth. Name your price, he thought.

The stagger of footsteps made the old cottage shake. A clinking of bottles and rustle of paper came down the hall and a festy mess of a man tottered into the kitchen. It was the stickman who'd come with Fuckinkev; totally wasted, unshaven and slack-mouthed, smelling of antique sweat and unwashed arse. His hands were graffitied with crappy jail tattoos and there were infected scabs on his forearms.

A cherry-red sore lit up a corner of his mouth. He looked grey and deathly; a skeletal streak of shit a long way down Scag Highway – maybe in sight of his final destination.

"Wessels, fuck off willya!" exploded Fuckinkev. "I'm fuckin' busy!"

It took a moment, but Seth recognised the name and his hands turned into fists. This Wessels bastard was Class A filth; a human cockroach who'd preyed on young women, getting them hooked on free heroin – then making them sell themselves to pay for their habits. I'd love to shoot this shit, he thought. Blow his tiny brains out.

"Kev, mate, I need another taste, aye" slurred Wessels. "That was like . . . nothing."

"You fuckin' kidding? You got the tolerance of a fuckin' gorilla. You had twice what I had. As fuckin' usual. Nah."

"Bum a bit of baccy then, mate? I'm out."

"You didn't pay for all your gear, now you're sponging me smokes!"

"Thursday, mate – cheque day."

Seth wanted to break an empty longneck over this slimy bottom-feeders' head, but he didn't. Not yet.

It was grub city in here; a dirty, sordid sewer-pipe slap-bang downtown. Not far away, normal people were doing normal things; clerks, shop assistants, railway workers and mechanics, all just getting on with it. He felt filthy just sitting there.

"Give him some White Ox and fuck him off," said Seth. "You're not short of a quid now – are you?"

"Who's this bastard?" said Wessels, turning to Seth, his eyelids sagging like a pair of worn out jocks.

Fuckinkev, wanting to keep his four new fifties a secret, hurriedly thrust a wodge of tobacco at the swaying man.

"Aww thanks, aye." said Wessels, his hands cupped to catch his prize. "You're a real mate, mate. I'll pay ya back Thursday."

Fuckinkev, puffing furiously on his rollie, looked at the table. Wessels turned his idiot gaze onto Seth again.

"What you looking at?" he said.

"I swear to God . . ." Seth muttered, his anger re-erupting. If it wasn't for Sabbo's appeal.

"Wessels – fuck off now!" yelled Fuckinkev.

"Yeah, yeah, you don't have to shout," said Wessels and he staggered back down the hall.

Seth leaned in and spoke low and slow.

"A signed statement, witnessed by a lawyer – that's the bottom line. Then you in court as a witness."

"Mate, you don't know how fuckin' crazy the Macs are."

"I do."

"Yeah, that's right, you used to be in with them."

"How much?"

"I'll have to leave town. They'll be gunning for me."

"How much?"

Fuckinkev looked at him with stoned speculation.

Seth's lips drew back in a silent snarl.

"Ten fuckin' grand," said Fuckinkev.

Seth let nothing show, but it wasn't too bad. If the bloke who'd been bashed wanted a similar amount, there'd be enough to pay the lawyer and get protection for Sabbo in Stuart Creek.

"You're fuckin' kidding," he said.

"It's ten grand or nothing."

"Fuckin' cheeky," said Seth and he spat on the floor.

"Hey!" Fuckinkev attempted outrage.

Seth stood up.

"Where you going?" said Fuckinkev.

"To rob a fuckin' bank."

"Nah, c'mon! It's my fuckin' life on the line."

"At least we know what it's worth."

"Fuck you, man! You just fuckin' walk in here and ask me to dob on the two heaviest fuckers in the north."

"OK, OK! Ten grand. You got it, OK?"

Fuckinkev stared in stupefied realisation.

Seth watched the pinhead's brain work. A few minutes ago, his life had been grim routine; scoring and shooting up in this stinking house, running at Gordy's command, menacing and hurting blokes. Now he had a choice.

And maybe he'd heard the good news about Seth Kelly, that he was a straight-shooter, maybe a bloke you could trust. Maybe, thought Seth. But if things go off the rails, you'll be the first one thrown to the Macs.

"Ten thousand fuckin' dollars," drawled Fuckinkev, as he lounged back in his chair. The moron thought he was starring in a movie. Posing-up something rotten, he blew out a plume of smoke, and aired tobacco-stained teeth.

Yeah, the money, thought Seth. It's still in the roof of a house in Innisfail. But he had the hook in the mouth now – he just needed to set it. Time to dig out the bankbook.

"I'll have two thousand for you this arvie," he said. "I'll come back here in the next day or two and we'll go to the lawyer's office. You talk and sign – then you get the rest."

"You said ten."

"Yeah, I did."

"Well, I want to see it first. Fuckin' ten, not two. Then I'll go see this fuckin' lawyer."

The hook was being spat.

"Yeah, fuck! I'm a busy man at the moment, so you have my fuckin' ten thousand bucks in your fuckin' hand before you come knocking on my fuckin' door again."

Fuckinkev was revelling in his unexpected moment of power and it gave Seth the shits. It would be too easy to punch the supercilious bastard's nose into his head – but he refrained, scowling in exasperation instead.

Digging the umbrage he'd given, the rotten prick smiled broadly; the stench of his mouth forcing Seth to his feet. Battling the urge to stand over him and deliver a cast-iron warning as to what would happen if he talked about this, Seth spat on the floor instead.

This time Fuckinkev laughed. "Pleasure doing business with ya, mate."

Nothing Like Ryan

Seth had a good mate, Les, who'd been eight years in the army, four years of that service in the war in S. E. Asia where he'd been a long-range reconnaissance specialist. Les also studied the history of weapons and warfare, and with a dry smile, he'd sometimes drop an apt quote into a conversation or situation.

'No battle plan survives first contact with the enemy,' was one of them, coined by a Prussian general back in the day, and like just about everything that Les came out with, Seth found the concept eminently practical.

Improvising when things slid off-plan, and discarding stratagems that weren't cutting it had saved his arse, and the arses of others in some fraught times. The unexpected was to be expected when confronting a foe, but it was a bit of a shock coming from an ally.

In the morning post was a message of surrender from Sabbo. 'All good, mate – I'll be doing the seven,' was the first sentence. The second one explained why. Sabbo had been warned not to talk to Seth Kelly anymore. Otherwise, he'd be seriously bashed, or worse.

That's about the first visit, Sab, thought Seth. Not the second one. I'm getting you some hard bastards to keep an eye on you in there, and I've got a first witness lined up, and I'm going to ring the trial lawyer now. I won't visit again, but I'm not giving up just yet, mate.

The Yellow Pages yielded the lawyer's details. With the receiver between his shoulder and cheek, he wrote down the phone number and address in his notebook as the ring tone began. The lawyer, a Mr Bob Loftus, was brisk, but when Seth mentioned Sabbo's name, the bloke told him to come to his office in an hour's time.

After a shower and shave, he ironed a shirt and a pair of trousers and slipped them on. Hugh was sitting in the lounge drinking coffee and Seth ignored him; just like the ungrateful bugger had ignored him last night. Oh – except for the top spaghetti marinara he'd made and the two nice joints he'd rolled. He'd noticed them.

After fuelling up the Pig in Portsmith, he briskly applied knife and fork to a big breakfast at the trucker's café there. Outside, a fishing eagle soared way up in the grey sky, its eyes searching the swampy channels of Chinaman Creek.

I bet you can see it all from up there, thought Seth. Little old Cairns surrounded by the mountains and the sea – a speck of sweaty humanity in God's pristine eye.

At the lawyer's Lake Street office, a serene but steely secretary took him through. Bob Loftus was standing and they shook hands. Seth took a seat and Loftus sat down behind his desk. He had Sabbo's trial transcripts laid out across its polished timber top, and as Seth explained the situation, he went through them, underlining a few names and addresses with pink Magic Marker.

Although he remained professionally impassive, Loftus didn't look like a fella who believed in second chances. His face was grimly pragmatic as Seth laid out the Macs part in it, like he knew how things were done in the far north. Maybe this is a waste of time, thought Seth. But Loftus was still bitter about Sabbo's conviction.

"It was unbelievable. I knew Gerry was innocent and his family did too. I believe the police also knew, but it made not an iota of difference. Justice was not done. I can see now that the paralysing fear these two brothers command just silenced the truth."

"Mr Loftus, I'm confident that this criminal associate of the MacIntyres – Fuc . . . Kevin, will make a statement."

"Why?"

"Apparently he wasn't too thrilled to be at the scene and he piped right up about it. Liam MacIntyre didn't like that and threatened him. He's getting a bit of money too."

"How much?"

Seth couldn't bullshit this bloke.

"Ten thousand dollars."

"Whose money?"

"Gerry's."

"I see. If the victim, Peter Neary, recants his testimony as you've indicated he may – will he be paid too?"

"Yes, but don't worry – there's money for you."

Bob Loftus's flinty grey eyes sharpened. A tough little nugget of a bloke, sun-browned and fit, he looked like he mastered whatever the physical world threw at him. Seth had a flash of him young, in tattered army green, firing a Bren gun and shouting defiance in the face of death. He looked old enough for that.

Loftus smiled, but it was a cold hard thing.

"Tell Gerry that I will take on his appeal – pro bono."

Shit, thought Seth, that sounds expensive.

"Pro bono?"

"Yes. I don't want to be paid. I want justice."

Aye? This was like no lawyer Seth had ever heard of.

Bob Loftus had real malignancy in his eyes now. Yep, thought Seth, he probably topped a few banzai boys.

"But most of all," said Loftus. "I want to see that piece of excremental vermin; that walking pox on humanity – the younger MacIntyre brother – go to jail. This time he will."

With that stirring declaration, the lawyer then laid out the plan of action. Because his office had an alarm system and contained a hefty safe, Fuckinkev's money would be kept there, along with a co-signed receipt for it, witnessed by Loftus's secretary.

Two thousand dollars would be used as bait, regardless of Fuckinkev's protestations. Loftus was adamant that the crim wasn't getting anything close to the full whack until he'd come to the office and made a signed statement.

Seth had to agree. He didn't trust the dodgy bastard any further than he'd like to kick him. Fuckinkev would get a further three thousand upon signing his statement, with the other five remaining in escrow until after the appeal.

Five thousand up front, the rest when it was done. It

wasn't a bad deal for a drop-kick loser. The same process would be applied to Neary – if and when he agreed.

"If we don't do it this way – signing for and witnessing the money – then I won't do it," said Bob Loftus. "It must be iron-clad, watertight. We want to be like a rock in the courtroom. Do you have a criminal record?"

Seth shook his head.

"But you know that world."

"I used to."

The lawyer stared at him impassively then nodded, his eyes telling Seth that it was on, and that they were on the road to court now. They stood, the lawyer coming around his desk, and firmly shook hands to seal their pact.

"Gerry has a very good mate in you," said Loftus.

"It works both ways," said Seth.

The lawyer's resolute assurance, not to mention the pro bono thing, was a tonic for the troops. Even the cardboard box of court transcripts and reports that Loftus gave him looked good. To get into the mood to read them, Seth tapped the chest freezer at the milk bar up the road for a mango Weis bar. He liked a little reward first.

The ice block did the trick, and after drying his hands, he sat in the Pig and started with the trial summary.

It was short but not even close to sweet. Prosecution rolled out seven witnesses – Sabbo had none. With no alibi and the victim identifying him in court, the case had opened and shut like a well-oiled dog trap.

Seth looked through the files for the bloke who'd been bashed; the rotten bastard who'd lied through his teeth. And lost a couple too, according to the medical report; an ugly rundown of multiple head and facial injuries. He'd had his bell rung, that's for sure. Leafing through the trial summary again, Seth found his full name and address.

Recognition fluttered around his head; this bloke had a rep, didn't he? He was a hard nut from a while back who must be getting on now. But further delving into memory came up with nothing more than that.

But there was someone close by who knew about the murky currents and colourful identities in the far north, and Seth went over to Little Spence Street where his mate Knoxie was working in a shed full of motorcycles.

In the warm, greasy space, intermittent rain zinged and pattered like snare-drums on the high tin roof. Knoxie, cleaning wheel nuts on a bench, stopped when Seth came in. With a pirate grin, he fired up a half-smoked rollie and gesticulated at the greasy, stainless sink-top on which sat a grease blackened electric jug. A jar of raw sugar, a tin of International Roast, and some mugs; everything stained with mechanic's black, made up the rest of the offer.

Seth shook his head and got to it.

"Peter Neary – you know anything about him?"

Knoxie puffed and nodded like the bloody caterpillar in Alice in Wonderland. Seth smiled benignly as he waited, but he was still a bit dark on the motorcycle mechanic. He'd asked him for info last year, paid him too, but had got sweet F.A.

"Yeahhh, old Pete Neary," pondered Knoxie. "They call him The Fossil. Prospected for gold and stones out west. A real bushie – hard as. A real crim too. The word is – he worked as an enforcer, bashing blokes who didn't pay up."

"Standover man?"

"Sorta."

"Debt collector?"

"Nah, a bit more specialised than that."

"Specialised?"

"Yeah, he doesn't get stuck into blokes behind on their payments, or fellas who reckon they won't pay. Nah, old mate deals with crims who rip off other crims. The Fossil undoes the hard nuts, even knocks them if he has to. He'd know where a few bodies are buried."

Knoxie blew out smoke and grinned through his beard. Seth still didn't feel like he'd got his money's worth.

"That's it?"

"Basically. I never met the bloke."

"Know anyone who has?"

"Mate, they'd all be dead or in prison. Or in Indonesia."

Seth thanked Knoxie and headed off, his sense of Neary now sharpened a little more. The bastard was an enforcer, a sledgehammer for knocking apart real blockheads. And a prospector and bushie. Those blokes were a breed apart. Liam must have moved very bloody fast, bashing him long and hard to keep him down.

Neary and his girlfriend lived in Aeroglen, a leafy blink-and-you'll-miss-it suburb tucked between Mt. Whitfield and the airport. It felt like the wild man had been tamed.

Seth motored slowly up the Mt. Whitfield end of McGee Street, parked down from Neary's and wandered up. The house, a low-set, mouldy white, Besser-block job, backed onto a scrub-covered slope. No vehicle was in evidence, and a knock on the door confirmed no one was home.

Through louvre windows he scanned the contents of the tiled front room: black vinyl lounge, Asian sarong covered table, cheap JVC stereo, big television. A ceiling fan left on low rustled a TV guide on the table.

Neary had given gemstone cutter as his profession. He could be at a workbench somewhere putting in a day's work, as his eyes and hands had been spared in the assault.

Seth went out back to where an umbrella tree wrestled for space with an African tulip and some tatty palms. On a patch of unruly grass pretending to be lawn, a rusty Hills Hoist hosted a lone sock. Through a back window he saw a washing machine, drier, and a basket of rumpled clothes topped by a black bra.

The nearest neighbour was about fifteen metres away; an old wooden house in the shadow of a black bean tree. Set into the beginning of the slope, it had a long, lattice-screened veranda that looked onto Neary's place and over some of the street. The upkeep and gardening were a bit slack – leaves peeked from gutters and palm fonds hung from the empty garage's roof.

The place looked closed up, like no-one was home, so he went over and crossed through a long boundary line of finely patterned mother-in-law's tongue, careful not to crush the long green and yellow spikes. He moved across a carpet of wet leaves to the old Queenslander house and stopped. Somewhere a gutter dripped. The tic, tic, tic of a gecko sounded.

Seth looked back at Neary's place, wondering if he'd get the bastard to tell the truth in court, and a woman's voice close by said, "I've called the police."

Seth turned. She was standing behind the lattice screen in a floral dress and slippers; greying hair in a bun and eyes like shards of glass in the gloom. Of course – this was the sharp-eyed old girl who'd brought Sabbo undone.

"Oh, I'm very sorry, ma'am," said Seth. "Please don't be startled."

He took one of his business cards from his wallet.

"I'm not a thief," he smiled. "I'm working. I should have asked if I could come into your yard. It looked like no-one was home."

"You could have called out."

"Yes, you're right, I should have. I apologise. Look, can I show you my business card?"

She thought about this for a moment. "Alright then."

Turning up the power on his smile, Seth came up to the veranda and held up his card. From beneath the lattice-work frame, small fingers snatched it. With his smile at full wattage, he watched her read. She wasn't so old close up.

"Hmm – an investigator. Mr Kelly, is it?"

"Yes, ma'am and yourself?"

"Mrs Sampson."

"Mrs Sampson, I sincerely apologise for walking onto your property. It was most rude of me."

"Are you investigating?"

"Yes, I am."

"About what happened to the man next door?"

"Mrs Sampson," said Seth, like she was a well-informed pupil. Nodding authoritatively, she cast a dark look across the mother-in-law's tongue hedge.

"A terrible thing. A few minutes after two on a Tuesday

afternoon – the tenth it was. The sudden shouting like the devil himself had come to visit."

Little do you know, thought Seth.

"What did Mr Sampson have to say about it?"

"Mr Sampson didn't come back from the war."

"Oh, I'm so sorry for your loss. That's very sad."

"It was nearly forty years ago, Mr Kelly."

Yeah, he was laying it on a bit thick.

"Would you like a cup of tea?"

"What about the police?"

"I said that to make you run away. You didn't, so I know you're all right."

"Mrs Sampson," said Seth. This time she smiled.

She walked briskly down the veranda and a side door opened. Seth went in, took his boots off and respectfully followed her into the kitchen. He took a seat at a solid old timber table while Mrs Sampson, with little fuss, put on the kettle and made a pot of tea.

While the tea brewed, she got the lowdown on him. One of the advantages, and disadvantages, of growing up in a small town was that people usually knew something about you. Unless you were a recent blow-in, or you lived in the bush, it didn't take long for your bona fides, or the lack of them, to be established. Degrees of separation were few and somebody always knew someone who knew you, or had heard of you or your family.

Reputation was crucial, an immediately identifying mix of family background, school and work history, truth and gossip. It was hard to change once it had been established; a fact that Seth had worked out before he'd hit his teens.

So of course, Mrs Sampson knew of his family; that they were hardworking and educated, and upon hearing that Mum had passed, she put her hand on his, and said, "So young."

In the little kitchen, with its blue enamel and cast-iron gas stove and china cups hanging off hooks, the big man and the little woman sat in silence.

Mrs Sampson withdrew her hand and looked at Seth.

"What's this case about then?"

"Case?"

"I've seen Ryan, Mr Kelly. Why are you here?"

"Ryan? The TV show?"

"I watched every episode."

Well, how about that? Seth tried not to grin. Ryan was an Aussie private investigator who dressed flash, kicked arse and drove a Valiant Charger. He had an Italian mate, a bit like Sabbo if you thought about it, and his lovely blonde secretary was as sharp as a knife. Although the show had been on years ago, it wasn't the sort of thing he'd imagine Mrs Sampson enjoying.

"It's actually not a case. It's to do with a friend."

"Yes?" Mrs Sampson fixed him with the stare of a senior police detective.

"Well," he began hesitantly. Then to his surprise he told her about Sabbo, keeping it rated PG of course, and she listened intently, occasionally spluttering with outrage. When he finished, she thumped her fist on the table with enough force to make him jump.

"We have to get Mr Sabbotini out of jail," she declared.

We? thought Seth.

"I've got your phone number here, Mr Kelly," said Mrs Sampson, tapping her finger on his card. "I can ring you if something untoward happens again. I can be of help."

"Mrs Sampson," said Seth. "You don't have to do that."

"Nonsense. I'm home all the time."

"Does anyone visit you?"

"Of course. My son and Mary, my nieces, and Ethel and Rhonda. Are you worried about me?"

"I just didn't want to think you were all alone."

"That's very nice of you. You're a good boy."

Nowadays I am, thought Seth.

Then he had a brain wave.

"Actually, Mrs Sampson – there is something."

"Yes?"

"Would you come to Innisfail and talk to a lady?"

"Now?"

She sounded like a teenage boy asked if he wanted to fire a rifle.

"Well, if this is a . . ."

"I'll go put some proper shoes on."

As Mrs Sampson hurried from the kitchen, Seth heard a piano and guitar riff start in his head. He couldn't place it at first, but when the brass stabs and big beat joined in, he remembered – it was the theme from Ryan.

On the drive to Innisfail, he explained to Mrs. Sampson why he needed her help, and how he had to get something of Sabbo's from the back bedroom at his auntie's place, something vital to freeing him from jail; something that his aunt didn't need to know about. Sharp as a stingray, Mrs Sampson immediately guessed it was money.

He wondered if he should be telling her all this, but she was more than interested. It was as if she'd been waiting her whole life for something like this to happen.

It had been touch-and-go when they'd first knocked on the door; Sabbo's aunt frowning through her thick glasses at them. But Mrs Sampson had kicked in strong, playing a Country Women's Association rep from Cairns, keen to conduct an informal survey on the expectations of older women regarding the association. Sabbo's auntie looked enthused then, inviting them in for a pot of tea, and wasn't long in telling them about her beloved Joey.

"I feed the chooks, water the beans and tomatoes. Then when I check – he's gone! But still he's smiling, all tucked up in his bed."

Sabbo's Aunt Ademina was a talkative soul, gloriously plump, short-sighted, faintly whiskered and given to deep chuckles. Seth liked her. More importantly, she liked Mrs Sampson and her big blonde nephew.

"Oh gosh, that must have been such a shock for you Mrs Tamborello," said Mrs Sampson.

"Oh, we knew it will happen. He was sick for two years, in pain, too much pain. So, really, it was a blessed thing."

Seth nodded in respect then took another sip from the ridiculously fragile tea cup he was holding.

They were in the good room; a front parlour whose sole purpose was to receive visitors. Kept clean, and dusted, its use was forbidden to kids, dogs, courting teenagers, even dads and uncles. The furniture in here was all covered in transparent plastic sheets that kept everything fresh and dust free.

Shifting his thighs, Seth made the plastic squeak. When he finished his tea, he'd ask Sabbo's aunt if he could use the toilet – via the back bedroom.

"I miss Joey so much, 'specially to cuddle up in bed," said Sabbo's auntie plaintively.

"Oh, Mrs Tamborello," said Mrs Sampson

"And you? How is your husband?"

"He's passed on too."

"Oh, I'm so sorry for you. Ah, we are widows together. You must miss him."

"It was a long time ago. Nineteen forty-three."

"Oh Lord. You marry again?"

"No."

"Oh, my dear – it's a long time for no cuddle."

"I didn't marry again but I always get cuddles – don't you worry."

"Mrs Sampson!"

"And when I get sick of them, I kick 'em out and wait to see who's next."

Aunt Ademina nearly fell off her chair, admiration and awe shining through her tears of laughter. Mrs Sampson began whooping with hilarity, and Seth hid a wince, trying not to even think about it. Smiling faintly, he sipped his tea and turned his thoughts to his battle-plan.

When the Macs smelt the appeal, they'd unleash a slew of jailhouse mongrels onto Sabbo. Seth had to get some protection happening for him. He needed a sit-down with his mate with the connections in Stuart Creek.

"Mr Kelly. Mr Kelly."

The insistent voice broke into his thoughts, and he saw

the two women staring at him – Mrs Sampson in barely concealed excitement, Sabbo's auntie with a taskmaster's intent. What have I done? he thought.

"We must be making him bored," said Aunt Ademina. "He's a good nephew driving the car for you. I have a good nephew too, but he's in Melbourne working."

Mrs Sampson's eyes were urgent and prompting – he'd missed something important.

"Ask him again," she said to Aunt Ademina.

"You want to look in the roof of the back bedroom?"

Seth sat up in shock.

"In the roof of the back bedroom?"

"Yes, yes please, if you don' mind? So noisy."

Seth got up – amazed, but not about to ask questions. Mrs Sampson nodded grandly like a general overseeing a battlefield.

"Can you look?" said Auntie Ademina. "In the roof is the . . . what do you call it . . . the hole . . ."

"The manhole," said Seth.

Sabbo's Auntie screamed with laughter, and Seth was alarmed to see Mrs Sampson readily join in.

He carefully put the teacup on a clear-plastic covered side table, still unable to believe this stroke of luck.

"The back bedroom?" He pointed down the hall.

"Yes, yes, the last bedroom. I put the step-ladder there for Vinnie. You are a good boy. Like my nephew."

Listen to Sabbo's *zia*, thought Seth and he glided out the door. Behind him Aunt Ademina kept singing praises.

"My nephew writes letters to me every week. Beautiful letters. He's a good boy."

The hallway smelt of old lady perfume and mozzie coils. In the bedroom it was mothballs, scented disinfectant and something a bit rank, like a senile cat had repeatedly peed in a corner at some time.

The aluminium stepladder was against the wall and he used it to get up to the access panel. Popping it open, he put his head and one arm up into the darkness. From the street, he'd eyeballed the roof and guessed that the space up here was of reasonable size.

The bad smell assailed his nostrils stronger; animal and ammonic. That's what Aunt Ademina had been on about, he realised. That's why she'd asked him to look up here. Well, bugger that, thought Seth. I'm no bloody possum catcher. Vinnie can do that. I'm here for Sabbo's money.

Putting out his hand he began to feel around on the attic floor, most unexcited by the thought of ancient dust and mouse shit – and bingo – he encountered a fat book-sized package. As he took hold of it, something bumped and slid along the roof panel right by him.

The thump was big, shaking the frame of the man-hole, and the hair stood up on Seth's arms and neck. The sliding sound sped right up, rapidly getting louder and the panel vibrated with sudden weight. Then extremely bloody fast, a heavy coil of solid muscle spiralled around Seth's outstretched arm. The smell in the roof was python piss.

He immediately raised his arm, flexing hard to make his biceps bulge out. Snapping his chin down to his chest, he felt the pythons' head slam into his then bounce off a good inch of Kelly cranium, leaving a sting of pain where its teeth had stabbed through his scalp.

The weight of the snake enveloping his arm told him it was a big bastard. If this carnivorous reptile got a loop of its hefty body around his neck, or even dropped some of its length into the bedroom to hug around his chest – then he might just get crushed to death in a cane-farmer's house in Innisfail while two old girls discussed their love life in the good front room. It was nothing like Ryan.

Knowing he had a second before the snake brought all of its strength to play, trapping his arm, bursting blood vessels, and crushing muscle and bone – he relaxed his biceps, spun sideways and stepped off the ladder.

He yelled in pain, feeling his arm just about dislocate, but it worked; his weight and manic energy delivering him from the beast. He hit the floor hard, sprawling sideways. Something pa-tanged off the stepladder and thumped onto the floor. Sabbo's fifty grand.

Cries of alarm came from the front room. Seth rolled away, half expecting the big snake to come down through the man-hole at him. The sliding noise began again, the roof panels creaked, and the sound receded. Seth sat up and let shock blow through him.

Mrs Sampson came running into the room. Quick as a mouse she took in the scene, reaching down to pick up the packet of cash. As Auntie Ademina bustled up to the door, calling out excitedly in English and Italian, Mrs Sampson quickly moved aside; the money behind her back.

"Aw, what happen? You fall down? Where's the snake? You catch him?" Auntie Ademina wasn't happy.

Neither was Seth. His arm hurt. He felt ambushed too, and not just by the python.

"I'm sorry Mrs Tamborelli, it got away."

"Got away! You supposed to catch him."

"Believe me I tried, Mrs Tamborelli."

"My nephew Gerry would have caught him."

Smiling graciously, Seth massaged his aching arm while his heart pounded like a brace of conga drums. I'm going off her, he thought.

But Mrs Sampson was something else. Behind Sabbo's aunt, she held the money up for him to see, an exhilarated smile on her face, her eyes shining with admiration.

"Mr Kelly," she said with headmistress pride.

The Trifecta

Mrs Sampson's excitement continued all the way back to Cairns. Bopping along to the radio, she told him what a big fan of Johnny O'Keefe she was, and that she'd seen him twice with his band at The Pacific Hotel. When she said, "That boy knows how to rock and roll," Seth realised that his initial opinion of her had changed. Exactly to what, he wasn't quite sure.

All he knew was that Mrs Sampson thought on her feet and held up her end, and she had his full respect for that. Back at McGee Street, he regretfully declined her offer of tea and cake. With fifty grand on board, he needed to keep moving.

There was no vehicle yet at Neary's place, but he heard a woman singing that spooky Split Enz song that had been all over the radio last year; the odd one that pissed blokes off and made women go all mysterious.

This must be Neary's girlfriend, who'd pushed hard in court, describing the violence done to her man. Probably not a softie. It sounded like she was alone, and he quietly left – his priority now stashing Sabbo's money.

At Cinderella Street, he parked up from his place and slipped unnoticed through the garden; listening for Hugh. When he heard the chatter of the telly and saw the top of his head above the couch, he felt relief then frustration. Why doesn't he play his guitar? It was crazy.

In the back garden he put Sabbo's money into the stash, a sealed waterproof length of PVC pipe sunk into the earth behind a big hibiscus bush. After screwing the lid back on, and covering it with dirt, he took a look at his arm. It was still sore, but not much more than you'd get playing a hard game of footy. Good luck with that Vinnie, he thought.

Now he'd go back to McGee Street and see if he could get the trifecta. With Sabbo's lawyer and the cash secured, maybe he could finish the day by bagging Pete Neary as a witness.

There was five o'clock knock-off traffic on the roads, but nothing like Sydney where big traffic jams could develop at any time. Working as an armoured car guard he'd been stalled in six lanes of cars, unmoving and vulnerable, with up to half a million bucks onboard. Being caught like that made his skin crawl.

He and the driver had .38 specials, even enough bullets for reloads, but if serious thieves attacked; firing bigger guns, maybe letting off explosives or gas – then he'd have run like hell. Money wasn't worth dying for. Especially someone else's.

Back at Neary's place there was no car, and no singing either. Instead of waiting for Neary to come home, Seth reckoned he'd try his luck with his girlfriend first. Women could tell you things fellas couldn't.

He knocked on the front door and waited. From up the hillslope came the nagging cry of an orange-footed scrub fowl, but the house remained silent. Knowing that anyone inside could hear him, he knocked again.

"Hello, anyone home?" he said, loud but friendly. After a few seconds, he asked again, hearing only the sound of the whirling ceiling fan in reply. Oh well, he'd come back later. The Strattie was just around the hill and a cold beer would be good for his arm.

The carport was by the front door, its back wall made of breeze-blocks, and Seth walked a few curious paces into it. An unseen door squeaked open and the slap of feet on concrete rushed towards him.

"Hello?" He walked in a little further.

On the other side of the breezeblock wall, someone ran up and stopped. He went closer and through the mosaic of gaps, he saw a bare-foot young woman in t-shirt and jeans aiming a rifle at his head.

Barely a metre away, measured from the rifle's muzzle to his head, was intensely focused. The gun looked like a pump-action rifle; fast shooting in the right hands, and its barrel didn't waver a millimetre.

"Hey," said Seth, flat-out stock still. "How you doing?"

No reply. Her finger was scary white around the trigger and he didn't move even more. He tried to catch her eye, but the young woman didn't divert her gaze one bit, her total concentration fixed on drilling a bullet through the centre of his forehead.

Seth reflected on this angel of death in a carport. Man, he thought, it's been a day for it. First an arm-wrestle with a giant python – now a woman who not only knows what she's doing, but also looks capable of actually doing it. This mortal threat thrilled him.

"I just want to talk. I'll stand out here," he said.

"That's not in question," said the woman.

"Would you mind pointing that away from me?"

"I would mind."

"Can I show you my business card?"

Silence. The dark eye of the rifle watched him. As they waited, a twin-prop plane came off the airport runway five hundred metres away. When the ear piercing drone had subsided, Seth smiled at the gunwoman. For a second, her eyes took in his face; not just a bullseye on his forehead. Encouraged, he said, "I'll reach into this pocket here."

He slowly swivelled around, the back pocket of his jeans obviously containing nothing more than his wallet. When her eyes flicked down to look, he wiggled his bum at her. Hearing her snort, the sound not without humour, Seth smiled, took out his wallet and found a business card. Slowly, slowly, the card held out at full stretch, he went over and placed it in the breeze-block cut-out beneath the gun barrel.

Smelling nice perfume, he paused, moving his head to look at her face. The rifle barrel jabbed out at him and he moved back; hands in the air. The card vanished. She re-aimed one-handed at his head; the card now held up and being read. Wow, thought Seth. She's real cool.

A second later his card hit the concrete. More silence.

"You're scaring me, mate," he said.

"What's scary is I'm not. Who the fuck are you?"

"You just read my card."

"No, who the fuck are you to us?"

"Please, Wendy." Seth remembered her name from the court transcripts now. "I need to talk to Pete."

"Who are you to him?"

Seth resisted the urge to step closer.

"I'm a concerned friend of Gerry Sabbotini. Look, some of us know who really attacked Pete. Gerry's lawyer from the trial is working on it, so am I. Gerry didn't lay a finger on Pete. He was framed – setup with false statements so that the . . . "

"I know what framed means."

She lowered the gun, turned and went into the house. The door stayed open as Seth waited. It was crazy but he felt a real attraction to this woman he'd barely seen. She came back out, smoking a cigarette, the rifle held against her leg, her forefinger close to the trigger. He kept his trap shut as she smoked.

"I want to get out of here," she said after a bit. "It's too damn hot and too many crazies. I'd be happy going back to Victoria. He says he doesn't like winter, but I hate all the seasons up here. I'm managing a café, but I can do that down there. And the things I like."

"Like what?"

"Like going out on forest trails looking for mushrooms. Hunting rabbits and deer."

"He like doing that?

"He does."

Seth gave her his number one smile.

"You'll be doing it pretty soon Wendy – you know that."

"I'm not holding my breath."

"Well, I'm sure that . . . "

"You don't know him. He's changed."

"I can . . ."

The cigarette arced through a breeze block and landed in a somersault of sparks.

"OK, fuck off," she said, bringing the rifle up again. "I'll call the police if you don't. Or shoot you."

"Look, I'm going Wendy, but you have to tell Pete that he has to speak to me. An innocent man is in jail."

"I heard you before. Please – *go* away!"

Fully frustrated, he nodded genially and left. Bugger. He'd given it a bash, but there'd be no trifecta today.

Back at the house, Hugh was still on the couch, drinking an NQ and watching TV. Seth grabbed one himself, and got the telephone extension happening out on the back porch.

It was imperative he tee-up a meeting with his kingpin friend and get protection for Sabbo. But after the fourth call things felt a bit odd. Everybody was cagey; one stoned bloke trying to speak in a code that he made-up as he went along. Seth had to ring numbers back a few times, but no-one seemed to know where his mate was. With the final number rung, he despondently finished his beer. It felt like he'd been served up some bullshit.

After re-plugging the phone, he idly stood behind Hugh as he watched the ABC news. Some American general had been kidnapped in Italy by a mob of terrorists called the Red Brigades. "Hope they shoot the fascist pig," muttered Hugh.

Seth walked away. He'd seen the effects of gunfire on blokes; even felt it himself, and the world didn't need any more of it, that's for sure.

He was having his second beer outside when the phone rang. It was Tablelands Ross.

"Jeez, you're a hard bastard to track down."

"I'm on the phone ain't I?" said Seth.

Ross was an old mucker of his, a bit of a redneck who lived on a big block on the Atherton Tablelands. He made a buck growing potatoes and fixing tractors. And growing and selling dope.

"I'm having a party tomorrow night. Robbie the Bomb's been on my arse to make sure you come, so you better look sharp, mate."

Seth nearly smiled. *Robbie, you smart bastard. I get the run around for the last hour, and now Ross is telling me I'm allowed to come and see you at his party.*

"Henck's coming too, Freddie Eddie, the Armstrongs," yammered Ross. "I got kegs to start and there's a band."

"What band?"

"Little Greg's band."

Seth looked across the room at Hugh. Little Greg was a bloody good guitarist.

"Who's on drums and bass?"

"Fuck, I don't know. As long as they're loud, aye?"

Ross's tone was indicative of some of Seth's dumber mates who thought he'd gone soft in Sydney; mooning over long-haired musos and their wanky la-di-dah. Music to them was a loud backdrop to drinking, talking, playing pool, and fighting.

"I got this mate with me. He's a guitarist," said Seth. "I reckon Greg would dig a play with him."

"They can play with each other's old fellas for all I care. Just as long he's not some poof folk singer."

Hugh's massacre of the front bar of The Australian still resounded in his head, and Seth laughed loudly.

"This fella can blow the school pants off Angus Young!"

"Who?"

Sweet Jesus in a straightjacket, thought Seth.

"Yeah, yeah, bring him, but listen – bring some girls, right," said Ross. "You're good at that. Looks like there's gonna be a shortage of fluff. Gunna be mainly blokes."

Seth shot another look at Hugh, who was watching him now. Yeah, that was the downside to hearing Little Greg's band and seeing Robbie the Bomb – the local boys.

Up on the Tablelands, down winding dirt-roads, in tiny hamlets of timber and tin, and up hidden valleys, lived fellas, some born and bred, some more recent, who all who found Cairns busy. They could get pretty feral, and this breed of back country boy was often more familiar with the outlines of a rifle than with those of a woman.

Everybody had a dog, a chainsaw, and a gun, and they drank rum on Friday nights and weekends, and beer every day; sometimes sinking a carton before tea-time. This sort of intake combined with the inevitable joint or two, magic mushrooms, and some rough old speed, meant that their parties rapidly became unhinged and often violent.

Seth thanked Ross, told him they'd be there, and then hung up. Hugh shook his head at him.

"Blow the pants off Angus Young? That's a bit insulting.

What are you lining me up for?"

Seth gave him the lowdown, hyping up Little Greg and his band, while toning down the Tablelands ape-life and lack of ladies.

"How much?" said Hugh.

"Aye?"

"How much am I getting paid?"

"C'mon Hugh, this is just a mate's party. A chance to have a jam with some cool players."

"No money, no music."

What a chiseller, thought Seth, but he really wanted to hear him play with Little Greg. He took two fifties out of his wallet. Hugh laughed, shook his head, and Seth peeled off two more.

"Howzat?"

"Fuck you, man," said Hugh as he took the money.

When he put on a shirt and tucked a fifty in the pocket, Seth fronted him.

"Where are you going?"

"What is this – prison?"

Seth now realised his charge was barefoot.

"Cool out, for God's sake," said Hugh. "I'm going to the shop to buy cigarettes with the money I've earnt."

"You haven't earnt it yet."

"You don't know how wrong you are."

Bonecrunchers

In the morning while Hugh used all the hot water in the shower, Seth went into the garden and got Sabbo's money out. With his foldup knife he carefully slit open the top of the packet, counted out ten thousand dollars and put it in a paper bag. After resealing the packet with gaffers' tape, he stowed it back in the pipe. The paper bag went into the stash under the dash of the Pig.

Then he phoned Bob Loftus; the lawyer happy for him to come over. When Hugh slouched into the kitchen, Seth gave him an easy smile.

"Listen, Hugh, I'm popping out for a bit. Be a few hours. We'll go up the Tablelands to the party around five."

"OK, fine." With zero eye contact, Hugh got the coffee happening.

"You said you wanted to see outlaws and desperados."

"Yeah?" Hugh looked sideways at Seth.

"There'll be a few there at the party tonight."

"Wow." That perked him up.

"Yeah, wow," said Seth, pleased with the response, and with a farewell jingle of car keys, he headed off.

Coming up to the Cook Highway, he saw that the cloud cover had lifted in the east and the south. It felt more than sticky now; the sunshine drawing up moist heat from the land. Everything green looked glossy, and under leaves and branches, insects were breeding by their millions.

Alongside empty cane fields, drainage ditches glittered with standing water. At the Barron River bridge, the river roiled past, tumid and brown.

In Bob Loftus's office, his secretary witnessed and co-signed an invoice for eight thousand dollars. The money, and instructions for its use, went into the green monolith of his safe. Loftus watched Seth put the envelope with the remaining two grand in his shirt pocket.

"Interesting how money can make bad people do good things," he observed.

"I prefer to pay 'em not punch 'em now days," said Seth.

The lawyer nearly smiled then leaned forward.

"Change of subject here. Want some work in the future? I get clients from time to time who can't get access to the information they need. It's beyond my brief, but I could recommend you."

"Yes, please," said Seth, and he gave the lawyer half a dozen of his business cards.

"Nice one, Mr Loftus. I really appreciate that."

"Bob," said the lawyer. Then he nodded seriously.

"What you're doing for Gerry is not just applaudable, it's also what underpins a fair society. Justice cannot be suborned – it must out. In the prevailing political climate, especially in the far north, taking a stand is important."

You're not wrong, thought Seth. Things were getting so

bent around here, you'd be needing a corkscrew to open a bottle of beer soon.

When they shook hands, it was good and solid, and Seth welcomed the appreciation – and respect, in the lawyer's eyes. Then with two thousand dollars' worth of bait in his pocket, he went to see the rotten little fish he had to land.

In town, where the railway tracks and road intersected at Aplin and Water Streets, a four-door Morris stuffed full with bedding and clothing had just expired – the Crystal Highway claiming a victim right on the finish-line.

Two pale young fellas were pushing the car onto the no-man's land of the railway reserve, and a passing Kenworth truck pulling a jinker of chained-down logs blasted its air-horn at them. Welcome to Cairns, boys, thought Seth.

At Fuckinkev's place there was no red EH Holden in the driveway. He'd have to sit and wait. And he did. And did. And did. After three hours he went looking for lunch in all the wrong places and ended up scoffing toasted chicken and cheese sangas, followed by two slices of cake.

Back on Scott, he waited. Trucks thundered by and the saddest looking man in the world shuffled past, his face a frozen landslide of despair. Then more waiting. A near hit between a Datsun Bluebird and nervy VW Beetle was as close to a highlight as it got. He hung in until nearly four-thirty, watching clouds slowly swallow the Lamb Range.

Back home, the guitar cases were still by the wall in the lounge – and the house was empty. Keeping his cool, Seth went out the back and found Hugh sitting on the beach, smoking a cigarette and gazing out at the sea.

"Showtime, Mr Christie!"

Seth was pleased to see him jump up and quickly come across the sand; apparently keen to go to the party.

Getting ready, they squabbled over Hugh's appearance. If the far north coast of Queensland was a bit backward for a Sydney rock god then going west was going to be prehistoric. Seth reminded him of the police sergeant at the airport – specifically his warning.

"Mate, blokes will throw rocks at you. The touch-up you got down the Barbary Coast is nothing compared to how the country boys play."

"What is wrong with you people? It's like the land that time forgot!"

"You better believe it – even the punches are bigger up here. Oldest pair of jeans; no bangles, one ring."

With much whinging, Hugh toned down his look, even finding a plain red t-shirt to wear.

"Here," said Seth. "Some decent shoes. Try them on."

"Those are Kenny Rogers boots for God's sake."

"Nah, they're just a pair of old RM Williams. It's that or thongs and it gets cold up there."

The boots fitted well, and with his hair pulled back in a pony-tail, Hugh now looked like a bloke with a rock'n'roll hippie vibe, not an androgenous rock-dog from Mars via Paddington.

"You look like James Taylor," said Seth.

"Insults – that's all I get!"

We sound like an old married couple, thought Seth.

From Machans, winding up over the jungle mountain range to Kuranda and then west through the eucalyptus scrub to Mareeba, they listened to John McLaughlin, while Seth improvised a travel commentary full of freaky facts and bent yarns. Despite himself, Hugh managed to grin at this nonsense a few times.

When they entered the Tablelands proper, the country became lush again. Seth fell silent, the Marantz too, and Hugh wound down the window and watched the big view unfolding around them.

Across twenty-five kilometres of rich farmland, the top of the Lamb Range was hidden behind clouds. Up ahead rain was dumping on Baldy Mountain and the Herberton Range – the rugged hills and peaks that were the western edge of the Tablelands. Pretty nice huh, thought Seth.

But beyond the range was a hard landscape, a killer in summer; the valleys scattered with remote and suspicious communities outside places like Watsonville and Innot Hot Springs. Prospectors and growers, hippies, hermits, runaways, and crims were all attracted by the cheap land or rent, and the complete privacy. It was the wild west out there alright. The people out there would freak him right out, thought Seth, looking at Hugh.

Rain suddenly pelted down and the windscreen wipers jerked in squeaky rhythm. Then they were through it and Tolga rushed by, the main street glistening from the rain. Roadside gutters ran bubbling and foaming with run-off, and the great clumps of vivid green guinea grass alongside the road seemed to be growing by the second.

When they got into Atherton, the main town of the Tablelands, more rain fell, and the cheek-by-jowl shops along Main Street looked empty and dark. Rain rushed along gutters, and on street corners, storm-water drains frothed like filthy chocolate milk-shakes.

"Hey, the fella who did the Doctor Who theme was born here," said Seth, pleased to remember it.

"Ron Grainer," said Hugh, absentmindedly. "Steptoe and Son, The Prisoner – lots more."

Well, of course, Mr Music knew that.

On a rain-slick corner under the second-floor veranda of the Grand Hotel, a lonely cowboy stood, his swag by the wooden pub wall and his big hat pulled down against the spray. Through his rain-blurred window, Hugh watched him closely as they went by. You're gonna be in a song, cowboy, thought Seth.

Up around Evelyn Central where the roads were as high above sea level as it got in Queensland, the rain became drizzle, the windscreen wipers busy as they drove through luminous green hills; their steep sides etched with cattle runs. Visibility wasn't too good now – the air around them so saturated with water it was now misty cloud.

After the humidity of the coast, it was nice and cool up here, but in winter, icy black frosts of minus five or more, sometimes crept over these hills and valleys. In the chill brittle hours before dawn, farmers and locals would lose years of hard work, their crops and gardens left shattered by the hard dry cold.

Forty minutes later they were parking on the grass next to fifty or so utes, trucks and motorbikes. Some utes had barking mad pig-dogs in cages bolted to their trays. Other dogs ran about, occasionally breaking into snarling fights that called down booted feet and mass swearing.

A log fire was burning next to a big farm shed that had been mostly emptied. There were old chairs, tree stumps, logs and home-made benches to park your arse on in the shed. Partygoers were scattered around, mostly standing; a loud mob surrounding the beer kegs, around their feet a crushed windfall of paper cups.

Amongst blokes talking and wandering about, Seth saw Tablelands Ross – short, fat, red-faced and unshaven – and he led Hugh over.

"Hey onya Seth, you made it!" said Ross when he saw them. They mashed hands and Ross gestured expansively around the barn.

"Righty-o, kegs are over there, hunt out Stevo if ya need a smoke, but don't go into the house, aye. I want to keep it off limits. Don't want anything smashed or nicked."

Ross looked beyond Seth and scowled.

"The girls, mate? Where's the girls?"

"This is my mate Hugh, the guitarist I told you about."

Ross grunted in disgust and waddled off.

"Da girls? Where da girls?"

Hugh's voice was caveman primitive. It was funny, but Seth felt a jab of shame. Yep, this certainly wasn't the bar at the Sebel with super cool musos and gorgeous women holding court.

Up one end of the smoky shed was the stage; the tray of a truck. When Seth introduced Hugh to Little Greg and the band, he was pleased to see the recognition in their eyes. Typical musos, they didn't make a song and dance about it, everyone just mumbling hello – though Little Greg gave him a private nod of appreciation.

The pocket-sized guitarist was a good bloke and a top muso; a virtuoso veteran of many great nights and parties in the far north. If anyone would appreciate a top-flight player from down south, it would be him.

"Remember," said Seth to Hugh. "You just hang with the band. They'll get you drinks and a smoke. Keep your head down and your mouth shut."

Hugh looked over the crowd and nodded in agreement.

"No problems there, this lot make the Barbary Coast look like a Johnny Farnham concert."

The drummer laughed. "You'll be right," he said. "Play hard, play loud and nothing too fucking clever."

Little Greg held out an electric guitar, and Hugh, all smiles, took it from him with a bow. Done with this first bit of business, Seth went looking for his mate.

Robbie the Bomb got his name from footy and fighting. On the pitch he'd detonate any ruck, blowing up the knot of players; sending fellas flying like rocks in a mine blast. The same thing happened in punch-ons.

Sure, he was a big hard galoot; raw-boned and fast as a taipan, but when he went off – he really went off. Maybe he sweated gelignite and pissed ammonium nitrate, but the explosive power that Robbie the Bomb released was a thing to behold. Luckily, he didn't have a short fuse.

Seth found him amongst a group of likely looking lads, everyone smoking and sucking down beer. Robbie caught sight of him and let out a yell that made the blokes around him jump in shock.

"You've got a real fuckin' nerve turning up here!" he shouted at Seth.

Dozens of beer-marinated, dope-smoked, speed-jacked eyes fastened onto Seth. Within seconds the alarm turned to glee. Robbie the Bomb had some bad blood with this big blonde bastard. It was looking like a fight!

Their champion downed his stubbie and chucked it to the ground. His face suffused with anger and he pointed a finger at Seth.

"I'm gonna knock the living shit out of you!"

Pushing the excited fellas around him aside, he came striding towards Seth, his face set like a warrior's helmet, his fists like big sticks of dynamite ready to blow.

"Oi! Oi! Clarrie! Over here!" someone yelled across the shed. "It's a blue! Robbie the Bomb and fuckin' Seth Kelly!

Men scampered in towards the impending fight, eyes lit up like Christmas morning kids.

Seth cracked his knuckles and put up his fists. A rising masculine growl filled the air. Through the stink of beer, diesel and woodsmoke, came the reek of testosterone. The boys were fizzing at the bung.

Robbie the Bomb ran now, snarling like a tip dog, and as they closed, he grabbed Seth's head with his hands and planted a smacking kiss on his lips. Blokes reeled in shock and involuntary cries rang out. Robbie the Bomb stepped back and bellowed, "Seth Kelly – how the fuck are ya?"

Around them, men screamed with laughter, turning to their mates in joy at the prank Robbie had pulled on them. Others frowned darkly or looked away, either disgusted at the sight of two blokes going mouth to mouth, or let down that a good blue was not to be.

Robbie clapped his strong arm around Seth's shoulders

and threw back his head in loud hilarity. From the stage came a piercing noise; an electric guitar wolf-whistling. Seth looked across the shed and saw Hugh looking at him, his eyebrows raised in disbelief.

Ah bugger you, chum, thought Seth. It was a wind-up. Sometimes blokes are so tough they take the piss like this.

With a roll of the snare, the drummer started the count-in and the band let rip; a hard-rocking blues that swung with a tough loping bass-line; just the sort of thing for this mob. A few blokes cheered and raised their beers.

Seth sat down with Robbie and his boys, shaking hands with his lieutenants, two fellas from way back: Ray and Evil Simon. Neither of them looked particularly big or tough, but they were hard bastards who'd outwitted the cops and rivals – year in, year out. Long haired, unshaven and lean, Evil Simon looked . . . evil. Ray looked like the cool uncle he was. Along with Robbie the Bomb, they were stone-cold pros at growing and selling dope in the far north; the three of them tighter than most real brothers.

There were half a dozen other blokes, mostly younger, and they all reverently shook hands with Seth. The respect was a bit embarrassing, but he didn't mind it too much. It was sort of cool to be known amongst this lot – even if it was all history now.

Over a joint, he and Robbie had a catch-up, and while a young bloke kept up the icy, opened beers, Seth got all the news from all over. Henck was in hospital. He'd come off his bike near Mount Lewis, crawled nine kilometres with a broken leg to the road and then waited six bloody hours for someone to come along: crazy Dutchman that he was.

There'd been a big raid supported by a helicopter on a massive crop out of Irvinebank, the cops in full force. Seth nodded sympathetically at that. The very same thing had ruined his day five years ago.

And yeah, Robbie's big sister Kay, who Seth had really liked back in the day, was getting married – to a high-school teacher, can you believe it?

"Mate, you should have used your brains around her. Might have been you walking up the aisle," stirred Robbie, and Seth was pleased to hear a tinge of regret in his voice.

Then Robbie took it back to the days when they'd been wild boys in the first waves of dope growing; trailblazing and scrub busting; putting in crops way out the back of nowhere. They'd been outlaw kings on their customised Yammie YZs, toting semiauto Winchesters, their tough and up-for-it girlfriends riding pillion.

You'd fall asleep covered in dust under a million stars; awake to take a swim in the most beautiful billabong on the planet, before knocking back moonshine and choofing on a big fat joint for breakfast; while your strong-legged country girl danced naked in the sunshine.

It was pretty cool really, taking a time-trip with Robbie, everyone listening and nodding; the young blokes with something like awe in their eyes.

Yet he felt disconnected from the man being described. It was someone he used to be. It had been a time alright, but it was gone. And right here, right now, it was like being an old movie; one that jarred with its crudeness.

Just beyond the light thrown from the shed, men stood emptying their bladders, holding beers and drinking from them. Twenty metres away on the veranda at Ross's place, the few women here were watching the band, and some of the pissing men yelled foul things at them, waggling their dicks in the dark like the filthy monkeys they were. It was prehistoric alright.

Beyond the band, the only thing of interest here was the business he had to conduct. But Robbie had been accosted by a wild looking fella seeking some boon or advice, and Seth turned and looked sideways at the stage.

Little Greg and Hugh were keeping it tight, the boys in the rhythm section like double-bolted scaffolding beneath them. The two guitarists, heads down, played with steely intensity. They weren't dribbling fancy licks or spewing up complex solos: it was rhythm guitar on rhythm guitar, interlocked in a motor-roar of sound; the changes chisel-edged precise. It was a masterful display of power; full-bore, but without flash or decoration.

But being such good players, they just couldn't help themselves – the balls-out rock'n'roll they were playing also seethed with subtle and inventive melody.

Seth was impressed. Hugh with The Tygers was a show-pony, forever competing with singer Richie, and diligently spellbinding audiences with the brilliance and longevity of his solos. A lead guitarist's lead guitarist, he could play anything. But here, he was a machine-tooled cog meshing perfectly with Little Greg and the boys. Hugh was showing a restraint and a . . . maturity, that he hadn't expected.

Savvy to the vibe, the band played instrumentals. When they finished a song, a few blokes yelled in appreciation, while the knuckle-draggers kept rah-rah-rah-ing away.

Robbie was now explaining the best way to cure heads to the bare-footed, shirtless rough-neck, and with a nod to Evil Simon and Ray, Seth went looking for somewhere to sit where he could watch the music.

He needed a beer first, but the kegs were surrounded by bigmouths and meat-heads, roaring away to each other in a red-faced flurry of spittle. You'd want a hot shower after getting near that lot, so he raided someone's Eski and was chuffed to find a nice cold stubby of NQ Lager.

Up the back, he spied a truck bench-seat on concrete blocks, and he went and sat down. Knocking the crown off on the edge of a concrete block, took a good swig on the beer. It was good and the band was great, but it was hard to ignore the boasting aggressive voices all around.

Back then it would have been fun: the bluster and front as he checked out who was who, and who was harder than who; waiting for fights to break out then watching how well blokes did. Now it was as boring as batshit.

Someone sat down on the bench seat. Seth turned to see Robbie swigging on a longneck, his eyes on Hugh.

"Yeah, he's pretty good, your mate," said Robbie after a bit. "So, how'd you go down there in Stuart? See your mate Sabbotini?"

Seth nodded, took an envelope from his pocket and put it on the car seat between them. Robbie glanced at it.

"Ah, don't worry about that. You can owe me one."

Seth didn't want to owe his mate nothing. Robbie was a good bloke and all that, but Seth knew this debt would be called in as an act of violence someday, fighting Robbie's enemies or rivals, and he didn't do that anymore.

"Nah, I'd prefer to give you the bucks, Robbie. There's a grand there."

"Aye – a grand? It was a screw, mate, not the bloody governor."

"It's for some protection in there too. First instalment."

Robbie nodded, getting it now. Since the early days he'd done good, growing bigger crops and dealing dope from Townsville to Darwin. Now he had property all over, and his gang, once jokingly known as the Upper Barron Mob, had become a force to be reckoned with.

The secret to his success wasn't just that he treated everybody from the lowliest shit-kicker to the wealthiest farmer as an equal; he was also esteemed, even loved, because he made sure everyone made good money. This, and the respect he gave them, was more than a lot of them had ever had in their lives.

He also looked after families of his crew who'd been jailed; financially, even emotionally, being a generous and well-loved uncle to the kids without Dad around. He even did the right thing by some of the mums.

And by keeping up good connections with fellas serving long sentences, he had real influence inside Stuart Creek.

Beloved as he was, he was no push-over. Blokes who tried to cross him had either realised their mistake quick enough to make good, or they'd suddenly leave town, maybe even to vanish off the face of the earth.

Like his brothers in crime, Ray and Evil Simon, Robbie wasn't shy of knocking a bloke if he had to.

"Who's after your mate?" he said, like he didn't know.

"The Mac brothers."

"Yeah," said Robbie, transferring the envelope from the car seat to his pocket. "That will be a first instalment."

He raised the longneck and drank, his eyes on the band. Seth waited. Robbie lowered the bottle and nodded.

"Blokes willing to go up against the Macs aren't cheap," he said. "But I know a few boys inside Stuart who will."

"Yeah?" Seth felt relief. A big piece had fallen into place.

"Oh, yeah. Bonecrunchers."

"Bonecrunchers?"

Robbie the Bomb nodded, his smile shit-scary.

White Cliffs

Dawn cockatoos woke Seth. Woolly-headed but keen to catch Fuckinkev in bed, he drove across the Barron and into a slowly awakening Cairns. At Scott Street there was no car, no lights on, no nothing. The bastard must be out west or up the coast, terrorizing people with the Macs.

He drove listlessly through town. On Grafton Street, the garbos were going hard, leaping on and off the high truck, shirts taut over wide backs as they hefted and emptied full rubbish bins into the hopper's filthy maw. It looked like hard, dirty work, but at least they were getting a result.

On the Esplanade, he pulled over by Fogarty Park, and while a freshening wind rattled the palm fronds overhead, he looked at the towering edifice of the nearly completed Pacific International.

There'd never been a hotel this big in town before, the line of jungle-covered range to the west now truncated by the brutal rectangle of concrete. The scale of it felt wrong for little old Cairns – and for this classic, tropical, ocean-front road; a place he'd cycled up as a kid a million times, a place he'd thought would never change. Yeah, right.

Back at Cinderella Street, Hugh snored on in his room. Seth changed and took to the beach. The wind had picked up a bit more, but he ignored it and the occasional gusts of rain whipping in, and went for a run. Back in the shelter of his garden he did some sets of exercises. Expending energy lightened his mood, and after a shower he made a cuppa and perused a dive catalogue; his eyes drawn to a nice looking Cressi-Sub face-mask.

Bit bloody slow waking up today, he thought. Sure, he'd had a few beers and choofed on a couple of joints at Ross's party, but it wasn't even eleven when they'd left. Still, it had been a three-hour drive home, fully concentrating on the winding unlit backroads, while an out-of-it Hugh lay crashed out in the back seat snoring like a chainsaw in a tuba.

They'd had a joint when they got back and everything seemed cool until Seth mentioned Little Greg.

"He's alright for up here," said Hugh. "Be sweeping streets in Sydney though."

Yeah, thought Seth, sipping his tea – four hours sleep and a joint as a night-cap would give anyone the yawns.

When Hugh finally got himself up, emerging stunned and dishevelled, Seth made them both a decent breakfast. The guitarist wolfed it down, wordlessly dumped the plate in the sink and went for a shower. Seth regarded the bathroom door with bemused disbelief and irritation. Anyway, he consoled himself, I'm the best paid cook and bottlewasher in Cairns.

After his shower and a second coffee, Hugh wordlessly indicated the empty dope bowl.

"Mate, you just have to ask," said Seth.

Hugh opened a big notebook, its leather cover marked and stained, and stared at a blank page. Seth retrieved the dope from its hiding place outside and put a nice big head in the bowl. As he went to walk away, Hugh shot him an accusing look.

"What?" said Seth.

"You going to roll it?"

"No. No, I'm not."

"Aren't you getting paid enough?"

Seth's hand unconsciously became a fist. Hugh saw that and came out swinging.

"Yeah – right! Is that the answer to everything up here? Moronic machismo? You know, last night's gathering of Cro-Magnons must rank as one of the worst gigs of my entire life. Closely followed by that filthy sweatbox full of savages the other night. If this is what's on offer up here then I'm going to sit right here getting stoned until I'm allowed to return to civilization!"

Seth went outside and down onto the beach. With the wind playfully batting his face, he stood there for long minutes, and let the anger in his heart blow away.

OK, Hugh was going to drink coffee, smoke, watch TV, maybe write in his book. But not play guitar. Was he doing it to spite him? Now he remembered the call with Davey; the very important part at the end. It wasn't about him. The pressure was on Hugh to deliver songs, and he might well be freaking out that he couldn't. Poor bastard.

In the house, Hugh sat in a cloud of dope smoke reading an album sleeve. Feeling pity now, Seth left him to it.

The Weight of Love

Over on Scott Street a joyless spore infected the air. An exhausted looking Murri couple went past, clothes soaked with rain. From the next house up, a woman's voice rose in frustration. Rusting nail-heads bled down fibro walls. A fried flying-fox swung in the breeze above a creosote-streaked power pole. Seth felt dismay that he was now recognising the same bits of rubbish on the street.

He flicked through the radio dial, but after ten minutes of serious ABC talk, the horses and the dogs, much inane chatter, pop, oldies and country, he gave up. There were cassettes, but listening to music didn't appeal right now. He liked it while taking the Pig for a good run, but not if it attracted attention to him.

Some drama was provided in the third hour when a fat black cat appeared on the kerb outside Fuckinkev's and then ran out in front of a truck. No friend of felines, the driver put his foot down, and the cat, in a sudden blur, teleported itself to the other side of the road. It wasn't much, but it was better than watching The Sullivans.

After that, excitement levels flat-lined, and numbness of both a cerebral and posterior nature set in. He squirmed in the seat, time oozing by; then remembered a paperback amongst the camping gear; a filthy tale of fighting, fishing and fornicating that was taking many a camping trip to read. He considered digging it out, but reading in a car felt a bit weird. And he might just miss something.

So, he just sat there listening to the heavy-metal racket of the railyards and the patter of rain drops – then began flicking through cassettes. A Pat Metheny album, not too loud, took him far from there with its blissful sunny vibe.

When side two finished, he upped sticks and drove over to the main post office on Abbott Street where he bought a pre-stamped envelope.

He tore a page from his notebook and wrote to Sabbo, telling him that he was still on the case and making good progress – and that guardian demons had been secured to protect him inside. It was a short letter, but he took his time; finding the words and phrases that Sabbo would get, but no other bastard would.

After posting it, he drove home through wet and windy streets to see if Hugh had run off to spend his money. But no, the tight-arse was still smoking up a storm in front of the telly. Seth gave him a cheery wave and ate a mango, slurping it up over the sink. Not about to make lunch for anyone, he ate another mango and washed his hands. As he looked in the fridge and pantry cupboard for ideas for tea, the phone rang.

"Kelly? This is Wendy. I saw you the other day."

Saw me? More like pointed a rifle at my head, thought Seth. Over the line, a dining room rattled and chattered in the background.

"He'll talk to you."

"Yeah? Great. When and where?"

"Now. He's at Oak Beach, spearfishing on the northern end. On the rocks."

"Spearfishing at Oak Beach? Today?"

"He never cares about the weather."

It was wet and blowy, nothing too bad, but he didn't like it. Oak Beach was fifty kilometres up the coast; the remote beach two kilometres long, with a lane of beach houses at its southern end. White Cliffs, the rocky point at the northern end was even more isolated. This meeting smelt like a showdown. Surely Neary hadn't told the Macs?

Or maybe he just wanted to be a hard nut on an empty beach and see if this investigator fella had what it took to get him to change his story. Either way it felt suspect. But he had no choice; Neary might never talk to him again.

"Thank you, Wendy."

"Oh, I'm damn sure you're the start of more trouble for us. Tell him to leave Cairns."

Her directness was intoxicating.

"I'll do that," he said.

"He might even listen to you."

She hung up; the rest unsaid, but he reckoned he knew what she meant – he was a bloke after all.

After saluting a wilfully oblivious Hugh, he drove north along the Cook Highway; the traffic light to non-existent. Coming around Red Cliff Point, squally gusts buffeted the Pig. He looked at the southern end of Wangetti Beach and saw the sea busy with white-capped waves; the steel-plate sky awash with scuds of moving cloud.

The rifle range at Wangetti had drizzle and mist down in the trees around it. At Hartley's Creek, he crossed the bridge at the crocodile show joint, the creek there pulsing along through the mangroves.

Passing by the Rex Lookout, he glanced across the road at the expanse of grey-green ocean flecked with white waves, an incoming squall line blotting out the headlands to the south; the valleys on the slopes of Mount Mar and Mount Dug smoking with low cloud. It looked grand.

After another ten kays of cliffside curves, he turned off onto a single lane road by the ocean. The highway curved away, leaving Oak Beach and the headland of White Cliffs to poke out into the long sweep of Trinity Bay.

Driving down the sandy road, Seth eyed the dozen or so cottages and beach shacks on either side; some nearly hidden by stands of pandanus and hibiscus hedges. One of them belonged to Mr Rio, the singing star Peter Allen, and what better place for a hideaway than here; tucked in between the jungle range and the beach, far away from the magazine photographers and autograph-hunters.

Where the street ran out, a vehicle track went down to the beach next to Grant's Creek; the mangrove lagoon on the other side. Nosing onto the sand, Seth saw the creek-mouth was low-tide, but running nicely from all the rain. Crossing it was fine, but that wouldn't be the case a few hours from now.

The sand on the other side was firm, and he drove at a decent clip; the tree-spiked knob of White Cliffs ahead blurred by salt spray. The unbroken tree-line of she-oaks danced madly in the stiff wind, and the sea washed across the sand in great foaming sweeps.

Half-way along the beach Seth saw a vehicle parked by the whistling pines and palms in close to the rocky point. As he got nearer, he reduced speed then slowly drove up to a faded khaki Land Cruiser that was fully set-up for bush-bashing. He parked not far from it. There was no sign of Neary, and he sat there listening to wind gusts whistle around the Pig – and feeling very exposed.

Was there someone in the trees looking at him through

a rifle scope? Neary? Gordy Mac? Had he set himself to be knocked? After a minute he reckoned that wasn't the case.

He watched the point and the sea around it, seeing no spray of water being expelled from a snorkel. Back along Oak Beach, the long stretch of wind-pelted sand was deserted, above it the ancient rocky mass of Mt. Charlie brooding like a crocodile. A squall now came in, pouring over the peak and it vanished in cloud and rain.

Rescanning the sea Seth saw, almost around the point, a head and snorkel surface then go down. It was Neary playing at spearfishing. The invisible reefs and their fish were close; Garioch Reef less than a kilometre away; Yule not much further to the north, but there wouldn't be that much around here today.

He wasn't too crash-hot on waiting on the beach for the old criminal; it felt weak and he wanted to be in a position of strength. If this was some kind of challenge – he was going to rise to it, and he changed into shorts and got his Turnbull speargun, swim-fins and mask out.

Sitting in the frothing arcs at the tideline, he donned fins and went backwards past the wave break, spat into his mask and rinsed it. The speargun in the crook of his elbow, he fitted the mask, making sure it was comfy and tight. Satisfied, he submerged and began swimming out along the rocky point, keeping a little distance from it.

He felt the swell immediately, and saw the sand on the ocean floor shifting in great slow pulses. Maybe there was a low out in the Coral Sea; he hadn't been following the weather too closely. The runoff from the Macalister Range meant that visibility was nothing great; ten metres at best.

A few fish flitted; some dart and bream, and there on the bottom – the sudden spooked grey bulk of a guitarfish, bursting away in a cloud of sand. Wow, it was close to six foot long, thought Seth. What a lovely sea monster.

Encouraged by the sight of the shark-like ray, he chest-loaded the Turnbull and started searching for a big fish along the rocks of the point. Having a good catch when he met Neary would be a handy display of prowess.

As he hunted, he repeatedly turned from the headland, looking for the dark outline of a man's torso and limbs, or the quicksilver halo of a head breaking the surface. I'd like to see him first, he thought. Be real cool to get the drop on a canny old hand like him.

Now he flashed on a movie – Thunderball, and the underwater battle with the scene that always got a cheer at the Coral Drive-In; Bond tearing a loaded speargun off a baddie and ramming it spear-point first through his mask. Oh man, it had thrilled him as a teen.

Swimming on, he curved in around the point, the swell really pushing in now, the ocean like an invisible fullback shouldering him towards the rocks. Surfacing, looking for Neary, he was surprised at how fast he was being moved by the sea. Around him waves crested and broke, slapping his mask and clouding his vision. Right off the point, he stopped swimming for a moment and just rode the water.

The double tier of White Cliffs was close; the hardy trees and scrubs shuddering in gusts of wind. Big fists of pearly spray shot up as the ocean thudded into rock. A kilometre north, Pebbly Beach was rainy dim, the white flash of a car moving on the highway next to it.

The sea was moving him in towards the mass of rock. This is getting out of control, he thought. Underwater, the visibility had turned to shit; silt fouling the water, bits of seaweed on his mask. He started swimming again; full-speed away from the rocky point, but hard dark shapes began looming out of murky water.

Now rocks batted at his fins, and one punched his thigh like a foot-wide granite boxing glove. Tight in his fist, the Turnbull banged against rocks. A wave walloped his head, chrome-silver bubbles exploding across his vision. The bottom came up quick; black and tan, sand and granite; everything suddenly shallow. Sand rasped his knees, rocks rapped his elbows; the snorkel mouth-piece was torn from his teeth, the mask-strap twisting tight at his temples and hair – and he was flung onto a tiny beach submerged under half a metre of raging water.

The pull and push of the waves was a bastard, but with the help of the Turnbull, he got to his knees. Great bombs of water burst on knuckles of rock around him; the wind catching the spray and flinging it onto the surrounding cliffs.

Through his streaming face mask, Seth saw somebody standing motionless above him; an ominously powerful figure that made him think of that Greek god of the sea.

He scrambled to his feet and pulled his mask up. A few metres away, knee-deep in foam, was a bloke in paint-stained shorts. A diver's knife hung off a belt slung on his hips, and his mask and snorkel were pushed back, sitting on his head like a rubber and plexiglass crown. His cocked speargun was pointing at Seth's heart.

But – his face! It was ruined; a mass of red scar tissue with chunks missing from his eyebrows, nose and chin. Liam Mac had really gone to town on him.

The rest of him was as solid as a water buffalo; big-boned, thick corded biceps, chest hair going grey, dark nipples like thumbs. Though a man past his prime, he still looked fit and dangerous.

Seth threw up his hand in a futile gesture; the soft tissue and fragile bone of his hand wouldn't stop steel. Above the roar of the wind and sea, Pete Neary yelled at him.

"What you want? You wanna kill me?"

"No, no! This is about my mate – Gerry Sabbotini!"

They stood there, with the wind a high battle cry around them, waves grasping at their thighs and slapping at their shorts. Finally, the red-faced man lowered the speargun.

"We talk on the beach," he shouted. He pulled his mask down, and slid into the sea.

Get the drop on him? thought Seth. I might have to work up to that.

His thigh was sore, and he thought about climbing over the point to the beach, but the wet rock, big gusts of wind and the gear he'd have to carry in both hands put him off. It took ten minutes of solid swimming to get back around the point, the old crim far ahead of him the whole way.

On Oak Beach, Neary had reversed his truck into the shelter of some whistling pines and coconut trees. A table was set up behind it, flush to the windbreak of an open back door, and while Seth washed his gear in fresh water from the twenty-litre container in the Pig, Neary rolled a smoke and boiled a billy on a scratched primus stove.

Seth towelled off and put his dry clothes on. Getting a fold-up chair from the back of the Pig, he came and sat at the table. By the trees, and in the lee of Neary's truck, they were mostly sheltered from the wind and sporadic rain.

The old crim had put half a packet of Arnott's biscuits next to an opened tin of condensed milk and a jar of raw sugar. The boys from the bush loved their sweet stuff.

Neary landed two chipped enamel mugs of tea and sat down. His diving knife lay on the table, and Seth had a good idea that there might be a gun under the folded blanket just inside the vehicle's open back door.

Solemnly adding milk and sugar, they slowly drank tea and silently listened to the wind flog the coastline. Around them, palm fronds clattered and whistling pines whistled.

Seth kept silent. Frowning at the ground, Neary sipped his tea. Then he quickly tickled two Milk Arrowroots out of the packet and dunked them in his mug. Just as fast, they went into his mouth and his eyes went back to the sand. Ruminating on his treat, his scarred mouth moved slowly, savouring every soggy crumb. Seth looked away. Jeez, you wouldn't want to take his last one, he thought.

"You ever prospect? Gold? Tin? Stones?" said Neary.

"A couple of times."

Neary observed him now; his eyes hard smoky quartz. Seth wasn't about to tell any stories; he had nothing to prove. Neary slowly drank more of his tea. Then he began to talk, his words coming in gruff bursts, the pauses giving weight, maybe even emotion, to what he said.

"I was out near the Crystalbrook. Dropped off. No truck yet. Found some dirt with real promise. But bad country with ridgelines to the back of buggery. Gullies, loose rock, and dry. Dry as bones. Nearest water was a day away. I'm a young pup, I had over five gallons, so I reckoned I'd walk to it the next night."

Neary paused as Seth took an arrowroot biscuit. When it got dunked, he nodded approvingly and went on.

"The next day I buggered me ankle. Bad. Couldn't walk. Dragged myself and the water into a gully and chased the shade over big bastard boulders all day. Didn't sleep too well. Nor the next night. My rifle started looking at me. By the end of the third day, I was true-as done for. Then in the silence, that real silence – I hear voices. Women's voices. But there's no women out there, so I reckon it's angels. Confused. Looking for someone else."

Neary paused, his mind gone back through the years.

"It was three Black girls 'bout the same age as me. Out fossicking for banjo tin, gold. Barefoot in torn old dresses and army shorts. Strong and bloody fit. They had all they needed on their backs. They knew the country. Real tough gals. Saved my life."

The old crim stared into the past. A gust of wind wacked into the truck, and sheoaks whistled. Seth finished his tea and chucked the dregs onto the sand.

"Angels," Neary finally said. "What they did . . ."

His voice trailed off. Seth now got a sense of something wonderful that had marked this mean old bastard his whole life. Well, bully for him.

"You know about women," said Neary.

"Me? Ahhh, yeah. I suppose."

"I know about you. I know you do."

"I've done alright."

Where in hell is this going? thought Seth.

"You ever bash or threaten to bash a woman? To control her bloke?"

In that fractured mask of a face, his eyes were hunter-killer still. In spite of the terrible injuries, Seth could see the character of the man: he'd be either highly reliable, or highly dangerous – depending on what you meant to him.

"No."

Neary kept silent, his eyes drilling in. Then he gave Seth a tight nod of credence given.

"The Macs threaten Wendy?" said Seth.

Neary looked at his big hands.

"I couldn't do anything about it. I had to wear it and she's more important than me and my fucked-up life."

"They give you any money?"

The old crim snorted in disgust. "Not yet even half of it."

The tight scars around his eyes twitched as he moved things around on the table: lining up the teaspoon next to the diver's knife, putting his cigarette papers on top of his croc-leather baccy pouch. Sniffing hard, he put the tin of condensed milk back in his ice box.

"I spent years on the Cape and out bush all around here. Cairns used to be alright. Managed to mostly avoid those Mac bastards. I seem to recall you were mates with them."

"Mates?"

"Aw, don't go all to shit on me now."

Seth leaned forward in his chair.

"Let's forget about the past, hey? I'm here because of Gerry Sabbotini – the bloke who pulled Liam's sentence."

"Yeah, that's right – you're a good bloke, aren't you?"

"I am," said Seth. "But it's not helping my mate rotting in Stuart Creek because of your false fuckin' testimony."

Time to start pushing buttons.

Unfazed, Neary nodded sagely. Pragmatism had been knuckled into him his whole life. Things went wrong; you did your best.

"What do you want me to do about it now?" he said.

"Tell the truth in front of a lawyer, sign it, and then say it all again in court."

Neary sniffed again, his eyes distant but very clear. Seth waited, praying for a nod of agreement – and the darkness he'd kept squashed down resurfaced.

The Macs would get convicted, but they'd get even.

A wicked idea scuttled through his head. Right here was the perfect bloke to help him put the Macs in the ground. He had the motivation and . . . he'd knocked blokes before, hadn't he?

But the better angels of Seth's nature started in on him. It's the Macs, he pleaded. Makes no difference, said the bastards. You'll carry that mark on you forever.

Rejecting pitch-black temptation, he dropped the idea, expedient as it was, and refocused on the hard, old crim sitting there saying bugger all.

"Look, Neary," he said. "When this comes out, the last thing they'll want is to hang a perjury charge on you for lying at Sabbo's trial. This will trump that."

Something flickered in Neary's tight, red face.

"I couldn't care two shits about that."

His bravado didn't mask the uncertainty in his eyes.

I'll need to get the lowdown on this from Bob Loftus, thought Seth.

"So, you'll do it then?" he said.

"I didn't say that."

"Then what are we doing here?"

The skin of Neary's face crinkled in a heart-felt grimace. Emotions and feelings, and the words they engendered, were the enemies of hard bastards. The old crim was struggling for words; avoiding them too. It was like a mountain trying to speak.

Now Seth had a flash of why Neary had agreed to meet him. Problem was, it had nothing to do with getting Sabbo out of prison.

"They threatened to kill her, and worse," said Neary. "She works nine, ten hours a day, five days a week. There's usually six of them on a shift. I reckon that's pretty safe for daytime."

You're really worried for her, thought Seth, and that's commendable, but get her out of north Queensland and you'll never have to worry about any of this again.

"A bloke should protect his woman, right?" said Neary.

Here we go – a bloody heart to heart, thought Seth. I need to talk about what you did to Sabbo.

"Listen, there's money for you," he said. "Ten thousand dollars. With that and Wendy's savings, maybe a pay-out from a civil case down the track, you'll get a beaut place down there. Hunt rabbits, throw snowballs."

Neary stared at Seth, his eyes narrowing.

"You think you're a real smart bastard."

"Mate, can't you see your lady wants out of Cairns?"

In a flurry of movement Neary was up, his diver's knife unsheathed and pointed right at Seth's face.

Seth didn't move a muscle. Jesus, he thought, I pressed the wrong bloody button there.

Neary's eyes burned in his ruined face and Seth saw the conflict tearing him apart: the choice he'd been compelled to make between righteous revenge and the life of a young woman. He'd done the right thing and he was going to heaven for that, but it was unbearable where he was now; beaten and maimed with his face destroyed; a degrading emasculation almost impossible to take. Sticking around Cairns was about all the defiance he had left.

Taking a deep breath, Seth slowly stood and folded up his chair. All the while, Neary held out the knife as though keeping a wild beast at bay. Seth put the chair in the Pig and turned to the silent, incandescent man.

He wanted to tell him about Fuckinkev, and Bob Loftus the lawyer; an absolute bulldog ready to fight and win the appeal. And he could even have a go at the question the old crim wanted an answer to.

But Neary gestured with the pointed blade – piss off.

Seth shrugged, got into the Pig and started it. In the side mirror he saw Neary turn, yell in rage, and peg his knife deep into the trunk of a sheoak some metres away.

The southern end of the Oak Beach was lit by a moving ray of fuzzy sunshine and Seth followed his tyre tracks back towards it. He felt pissed off, and a bit rattled, but at least he didn't have six inches of marine cutlery buried in his chest.

Eternal Mystery

On the way back he made a detour into Trinity Beach. The wind and rain were easing a bit and he parked by the beach. He went up the side of the grassy hill, jogging up the long flight of wet concrete steps; a hundred and one of them they said. He needed a beer and at the top of the stairs he went into the concrete-block pub the locals called the Fountain on the Mountain.

The smell of old sweat, damp clothes, beer and muddy boots fought with a thick cloud of cigarette smoke. There was a stew of fellas in there, the pub packed with more than a few fishermen and other coastal jetsam. Some of the saltwater boys were true nutcases, known for a whole heap of crazy stunts, and with the addition of knocked-off workers, whackers and drifters, it was rough and loud.

Rock and roll blared from the juke-box, Acca Dacca and the Angels, and the energy level in the joint was high. Seth got a beer and listened to the conversations around him, most of them about great feats of physical strength, brute bloody luck and always coming out on top. Blokes in tank-tops and stinky cut-off shirts were outdoing themselves in topping every other bastard's story. Everybody competed to be a bona-fide bloody expert, even if volume replaced logic at times. Holding the floor amongst the ciggie butts and slops, these fellas knew something about everything.

Seth looked at his schooner, suddenly appalled. Blokes. Did they start bullshitting at birth or were they already doing it in the womb? This non-stop front, unrelenting show of hardness, and mastery of physical detail wearied him. How many cocksure, tough guys did the world need?

And how was the tough guy he'd just met at Oak Beach? Their rainy-day meeting had proven to be a real wash-out for him too. The Fossil had wanted an answer from a tough guy, but a tough guy hipped to the eternal mystery of women. Seth had fitted the bill.

The question was obvious. Can I live in peace after what those bastards did to me and still be a man? Seth knew that young Wendy had answered that question, but Neary needed to hear it from a bloke. You really are a fossil, he thought. Only her opinion matters.

But Neary wanted vindication; maybe absolution too, and it was as sad as bread without butter. Even if he had got his question out – Seth knew there was nothing he could say that would put out the inferno consuming him.

Now the thumping juke-box of the Fountain on the Mountain bashed into his thoughts, and drunken voices bawled a reply to the question The Angels were posing – "No way, get fucked, fuck off!"

Seth looked around at the beer-fogged eyes, the sweat-sheened biceps, and hard unshaven jaws. He sculled his beer and got the hell out of there.

At Machans he parked out the front of Sunny's place, glad to see her sitting there in the green nest of her plant-screened veranda with barnacle-spotted old bottles and bailer shells against the walls; pottery knick-knacks and fat crystals perched on exposed beams.

In her comfy-cushioned lawyer-cane chair, smoking a rollie, a sweating glass on the table, she looked solid and cosy with the wind gusting in around her.

As he stepped onto the veranda, Sunny got up, the smell of her an indescribable balm, and rattled the ice in her empty glass.

"Drink? White rum? Lime and soda?"

"Oooh, yeah, sounds great."

Sunny smiled indulgently and went inside. Except for a little tour of her cottage last year, Seth kept to the veranda when he visited. He sensed that she liked him doing that.

Around him pot-plant foliage danced and a hand-made mobile of bleached-out coral and pink and white seashells swung in the wind. A kid's drawing thumb-tacked up next to the front door fluttered. Looking at the pair of green thongs by the steps, he thought of Sunny's feet; so delicate yet so strong. She painted the nails sometimes and the colour always drew his eyes.

When she returned, they toasted each other, and with a husky chuckle of remembrance she re-lit her rollie.

"So, how's your friend going – the muso from Sydney?"

Seth laughed; instantly ashamed at the bitterness of the sound.

"Oops," said Sunny. "Scratch that."

"Yeah, I reckon," said Seth.

Sunny nodded kindly, her brow faintly wrinkling as she searched for a runaway shred of tobacco on her lips. Seth watched a small finger skim along the swell of her lips.

She looked up and there was that sexy little glint again. It felt good in a lazy grown-up way. You're one smart lady, thought Seth. Nice and slow is lots more fun.

"Think we'll get a cyclone this year?" said Sunny.

"Never know, hey. The weather station on Willis Island will give us a heads-up if there's one on its way. Maybe the frigate birds will fly in off the reef. The old blokes – the Murris and fishermen – reckon you can smell it coming."

"Ever been in one?"

Seth nodded. There had been a few – one a good deal worse than the other; a proper deadly nightmare actually.

"Yeah, when Judy came in, we were at Flying Fish Point staying at my mate's brother's place. We had this ginger-beer we'd made, right."

"Alcoholic?"

"Oh yeah, and it turned out to be like an early warning system. The corks started popping out of the bottles, and a bit later Judy crossed the coast. Atmospheric pressure, I reckon."

"Scary?"

"Nah. The Seymour Range blocked most of it. Bramston got a lick – trees down, sheds blown into the bush."

"You weren't here for Peter, were you?" she said.

Seth shook his head. The cyclone, two years ago, had made buying his place a little more affordable.

"The flooding was big where you are – Redden Island, and through the back here got evacuated. The northern beaches too – Holloways, Yorky's Knob, Smithfield. Army helicopters everywhere."

"Yeah, I heard about it."

Sunny suddenly laughed. "I'll show something from the paper about it."

She rose and went into the house and Seth sat in the snug nook of her veranda looking at the ocean barely ten metres away. Mother Nature was close at Machans.

Sunny, eyes twinkling, came back out and handed him a newspaper clipping. Some cheeky bastard at The Cairns Post had gone with - Yorky's Knob Cut Off.

It was ridiculous, but he had to laugh, Sunny laughing too. Then they drank in silence, quiet smiles on their faces. Eventually, Seth nodded seriously.

"Listen Sunny, if we get a real big one, I'll give you a hand to get your house sorted and put anything valuable in my truck. I can take you wherever."

"Wait it out with me?"

"Sure. Kerosene lanterns, joints, rum. Be fun."

"Sounds like a date."

"Well, that's up to Huey." Seth gestured at the sky.

A smile lit Sunny's face. "You're a good friend, Seth."

Maybe more than that, he thought. But before he could put a bit of that in his eyes, the phone began ringing in the cottage. Sunny sat up, startled.

"Oh shit, what's the time, Seth?"

He looked at his watch and told her. She jumped up.

"I gotta go."

"Yeah?" he said, wondering why.

"Yeah," said Sunny, reaching out for his empty glass.

Back at his joint, Hugh was smoking a cigarette and watching TV. The guitar cases were closed, but his writing book and a biro lay next to him on the couch.

Grabbing a stubbie, Seth knocked half of it off with two chugs then made himself a little joint, smoking it on the covered back porch. Rain began to lightly fall, the pip and pop on the tin-roof, and tap-tap-tapping on the leaves of plants creating a polyrhythmic soundscape.

Through the louvre-glass panes by the lounge, Seth saw puffs of smoke disappearing into the rain; sucked outside into the cooler air. It was Hugh finishing up a joint he'd rolled earlier. The rain pattered as Seth slowly drank his beer. After a bit, the TV went off. A few minutes went by. Seth turned his head to look into the house. Hugh was just sitting there – staring at his guitars.

Play, he willed him. It's why you're here. It's what you were born to do. Play.

Hugh got up, went over to the guitar cases and looked down. Seth held his breath. Then Hugh opened a case and took the Gibson Hummingbird out. Seth exhaled in glee.

Sitting back on the lounge again, Hugh's face softened, the haunted lines disappearing. His hands began to move on the guitar and sweet cascades of sound filled the room in a whimsical imitation of the rain. In ascending then descending cycles, the notes fell from the strings in liquid drops; their repetition conjuring up the eternal power of rain to rejuvenate and heal.

Seth turned his chair and listened, and time stood still, the grey green light of the dusk vibrating; his house like a sound-box floating by the Coral Sea. Self-consciousness flooded through him – he was staring at Hugh like a fan.

It didn't matter. The guitarist was utterly absorbed, his gaze on the gently falling rain outside, his fingers busy moving in graceful complexity along the fretboard. He found variations and sequences in repetition that subtly moved the music into different directions. Never lost for ideas, never bogged down by the obvious, his choices were inspired and unforced.

The immediacy of Hugh's playing, right here right now, was better than any album or crowded gig. Am I lucky or what? thought Seth.

The music stopped and he jumped up and went into the lounge, absolutely beaming at his mate finally playing. As he opened his mouth, Hugh threw up a stiff hand.

"I don't want to hear it."

"No seriously, Hugh, that was . . ."

"Shut up!"

Seth recoiled in shock, but pressed on.

"I just want to say how great that was."

"Is that right?" said Hugh with an awful show of mock enthusiasm. "And how the fuck would you know?"

That cut Seth to the bone. It locked him out.

"Oh, yeah, I know,' said Hugh. "You've seen me play lots of times."

Seth nodded. Yes, he had.

"Well, until you strap on a guitar and practise for ten fucking years you don't know what great is."

Hugh snapped the guitar away in its case and made for his room. At the door he turned, his smile like a brittle blade.

"You're just another groupie. No, I take that back — groupies fuck you at least. You're a paid servant and your opinion means nothing to me. So, keep it to yourself."

Then he closed the door with deliberate softness.

"Fuck you, man," mumbled Seth.

Peeved wasn't the word for it, so he got himself another beer, and out on the back porch tried hard to think about something nice. The phone rescued him. It was Dad.

"There you are. I got a call today from an old friend of Alex's. He wants to meet you at the Tradewinds Hotel for dinner, either tonight or tomorrow night around seven. Had no number to call back on, which is odd. I remember him as a bit of tearaway, but he asked about rates and availability, so it seems a genuine inquiry."

"Yeah, that's alright Dad. Who was it?"

"A Gordon MacIntyre. Do you remember him?"

Seth looked at the Submariner on his wrist.

"Yeah, I do. Thanks Dad, I'll go see what's the story."

They talked for another minute and Seth hung up.

Staring out at the garden he rubbed his jaw, his hand rasping along the stubble. Should be right, he thought. It's in public and I might learn something.

He shaved and showered, put on good aftershave and nice clothes. Then he knocked on Hugh's door.

"I'm going to see about some work," called Seth. "I'll be back in an hour, OK?"

The silence was like a padlock on the closed door.

Tornedos Rossini

The Outrigger was doing the business: a mix of tourists and business types staying there, plus a good wack of cashed-up locals, all getting amongst cocktails, ice-cold beer and fine wine – and of course, the food.

The Kamsler family owned the hotel the restaurant was in, The Tradewinds, and it was rated the best in the north, maybe in the whole state; the staff smooth as silk, the chefs world-class, and the rooms top-notch. During the marlin season, the hotel became Marlin Central, playing host to the international fishing charters and their guests.

In the bar, groovy young couples drank cocktails. Older blokes, likely on a holiday junket, guffawed and chortled, chilled lager glasses in hand. Freshly tanned women and men in their floral, once-a-year holiday wear, laughed and chatted, standing in couples or groups. As he passed the bar, a sharply-dressed bloke sitting there gave him a nod.

That's cool, thought Seth, nodding back. Nice to have my style recognised by someone who knows their stuff.

Pausing at the restaurant entrance, he felt trepidation.

I don't want to sit and yarn with this bastard, he thought. There's only one reason why he wants to see me – and it's spelt Sabbo. But there was no threat or bribe that was going to make him back down. He'd listen, admit nothing – then leave.

Still, he could have a drink. Sniffing the smells coming from the restaurant made saliva burst out into his mouth. As he re-lived the fully toothsome Tornedos Rossini he'd eaten the last time he was here, the maître d came up, the question in his welcoming smile. After explaining he was meeting a Mr MacIntyre, a young woman led him into the glorious din of the restaurant.

Man, he loved it; the blast of quality hospitality in full swing, the low-lit dining room abuzz with chatter and the clink of cutlery on china, and glittering with the starlight of glassware and jewellery. This was real living, a lively celebration of the best food, drink and company; everyone looking good, everyone feeling good, everyone luxuriating in the throes of grown-up pleasure.

Seth threaded through merry tables, smelling seafood and seared meat, mystery sauces, women's perfume and cigarettes. By a table, a flambe dish flared, illuminating the chef's smile and eliciting oohs and ahs. This culinary theatre put a smile on Seth's dial and set off an expectant grumble in his guts. The lovely hostess stopped and pulled back a chair from a four-seat table.

"Please," she said. "I'll send the drinks waiter over."

"Oh, that's fine," said Gordy Mac from his seat. "I've just ordered drinks for Mr Kelly and myself."

The young woman blessed them with a smile and glided

off. Gordy Mac, rattling the ice in his empty glass, grinned at Seth like the cat that had eaten . . . everything.

"No Liam tonight," he said. "He's down the Gold Coast for a few weeks, can you believe it? We're busy boys."

For a long second Seth considered putting Gordy on the spot, by not sitting down and telling him to get to it.

Gordy Mac kept grinning, and Seth noticed the nice tan coloured silk shirt he was wearing. And the gold Rolex on his wrist. His hair was nicely styled, not too short, not too long, his moustache and thick sideburns neatly trimmed. Gordy Mac had never been a scruff, but he looked like a newsreader on holiday right now.

"Sir?" A polite voice by Seth's elbow. "Your double Jack Daniels and cola."

He turned to see the waiter put two rocks glasses on the table, the ice cubes tinkling like happy laughter. Gordy nodded magnanimously to the waiter as he passed his empty glass to him then gestured at the seat in front of Seth.

"Mate – sit down. Please. If only to hoist one to that great blue that you, Liam and I had down the Barbary the other night. You have not lost your touch."

Seth looked around the room. No one was paying them the least attention. He looked at the drink again. It looked back. Ignoring Gordy, he sat, picked up the glass and took a big delightful pull on it. Looking over the rim, he saw on the next table a group of women talking and laughing.

One of the women was watching him. She looked kind of exotic, with a dark bob-cut and a sleeveless floral dress; her sharp eyes and bare brown arms very sexy. When he lowered his drink, her attention casually slid back to the conversation at her table.

"That was a beauty the other night, wasn't it?" Gordy Mac fired up a Silk Cut with a chunky gold lighter.

"I looked at us and thought – why aren't we doing this for money? Or for fun? Like we used to."

Because of what you two shits did to Sabbo, thought Seth. Because you and your brother are evil bastards.

"I miss Alex," said Gordy, his eyes tainted by emotion. "We were good together – the Macs and the Kellys. We were the first ones, hey."

Gordy winked, holding his cigarette like it was a joint.

"We planted the seeds, right? Now it's all over the front pages – in parliament too. Cairns, the drug capital of Australia. You see that? Now every bastard's doing it. I tell you mate, it's getting almost crowded out there."

Seth gauged his drink. Another thirty seconds and he'd tell this bastard to spit it out. Then he'd tell him to get stuffed. Twenty minutes after that – he'd be having a beer on his back porch.

"Think about the money we used to make and times it by ten," said Gordy. "Big money now. *Big* money. Forget sugarcane and tobacco – it's *the* cash-crop of the north."

A delirious smell filled Seth's nostrils. A voice purred at his ear. "Your Oysters Kilpatrick, sir."

"I ordered four dozen," said Gordy Mac.

Seth teetered on the edge as the entrée was laid before him. Stand up, he told himself. But those luscious, sizzling morsels held him to his seat, and he sculled his drink and got stuck in. As he ate, a new drink arrived.

"Keep 'em coming," murmured Gordy to the waiter.

As they polished off the first two dozen, the next round appeared, the rich perfume of bubbling sauce and grilled oysters a goad to Seth's appetite.

"You try the steak here?" said Gordy Mac.

With champing jaws, Seth flicked him a glance and briskly nodded. When the Kilpatrick were done, they sat back in the woven-cane peacock chairs, stifled burps with linen napkins, and looked around the dining room while they worked their drinks.

Gordy stroked his moustache and looked at Seth with speculative eyes. He knocked out a Silk Cut from his pack and lit up. Over his shoulder the pretty lady with the short hair was laughing, her earrings jiggling and bouncing.

The chatter of cutlery and the babble of voices was loud. Gordy leaned forward, putting his elbows on the table.

"Come in with us, mate. Like the old days. Five hundred a week. Guaranteed. Plus, a decent cut of the big scores."

Seth managed not to blink with surprise.

"We're doing really good. Made nearly twenty thousand dollars yesterday. Not too shabby, aye?"

Flustered, Seth picked up his glass and drank deeply. There was no way on earth he'd do it, but hearing this offer come out of Gordy's mouth was very strange; maybe the strangest thing he'd heard all year.

"We need you, mate, to help keep things in line. You're good at knocking heads and I heard about what you did out west last year. Impressive, mate, real impressive."

Seth's mind raced. How the hell did he know that? And The Fossil – a crim's enforcer, bashed by the Macs. For what? For not taking on enforcing work? Was he getting the same offer here? Surely Gordy didn't think he'd be up for it.

"It's a rough world out there now." Gordy Mac's voice was like filthy honey. "All the newcomers, and the you-know-whos, the cops too. And soooo much money to be made. You heard about what happened at Julatten hey?"

Seth had. Seven months ago, the charred bodies of a couple were found in their burnt-down, A-frame house. They'd been shot-gunned in their bed first. Seth couldn't say he knew them, but he'd met the bloke one time; a charismatic ex-Sydney-sider, a hippy but full-time grower and dealer. Yeah, the dope business was getting nasty.

"Shame about the wife," said Gordy Mac, smoothing the copper hair on his forearm. "You see, mate, I don't dump things like that in the open. Brings the cops like blowflies. Bad for business. I like to be discreet."

In a pig's arse you are, thought Seth. He felt spooked by the mention of those sad and evil deaths.

"You're discreet too," said Gordy Mac. "And trained. All those nights on the door, all those top-notch security boys you worked with in Sydney. You know how to keep a chain on it . . . until it needs to come off. Makes you dangerous, mate. And, well, Liam – he doesn't like the chain. Gets off it at times. Goes too far and gets everyone noticing. My brother can be very indiscreet."

Nah, I'm never going to work for you, thought Seth, and a smooth voice announced in his ear, "Tornedos Rossini with green peppercorn sauce and baked potato and sour cream, sir."

The Weight of Love

As the plate was placed in front of him, Seth knew he wouldn't get up; the silver-service buttered asparagus and beans the last straw. It was bloody weak of him, but damn, it was good.

Eating and drinking, taking his time, he only looked up to nod thanks to the waiter bringing the drinks. He knew Gordy was laughing at him like he was a little short-pants, but he was getting a top feed, and he concentrated on that.

The bastard had a good appetite too, and they finished around the same time. Seth wiped his mouth and eyed his drink. Time to go. This prick was playing with him.

Gordy Mac, as if aware of his thoughts, nodded, and his treacle drawl was now laced with venomous mirth.

"Look mate, if you're keen, you can start straight away. There's a bloke in Stuart Creek who's talking a lot of shit. Change his mind, shut him up – whatever you have to do."

Gordy Mac smirked. Seth tried not to jump across the table. The lady in the sleeveless dress was looking at him, a hint of concern on her face.

"Your drink, sir," said a voice and a man sat down next to him, putting drinks – one for himself and one for Seth, on the table. It was the sharp-looking bloke from the bar.

Gordy Mac threw his napkin on the table.

"Seriously, mate, I'm not pulling your chain. It's the big time now. You have a good think about it."

He got his lighter and smokes and stood up.

"Anyhow, this bloke's the real reason you're here. You'll do well out of this. I'll invoice you a finder's fee."

With a thumbs-up for the man who had just sat down, Gordy Mac deftly squeezed past crowded tables and left the restaurant. Seth watched him go, his attention caught by the nice leather shoes the bastard was wearing.

He needed that drink. Turning back, he was confronted with an outstretched hand and a massive smile. Ignoring them both, he grabbed his glass. The bloke removed the hand but kept working the smile. Seth took a big swallow and checked the cocky bastard out.

He looked fit, gymnasium or footy fit, and was dressed smooth, his long-sleeved shirt opened halfway, a good watch on his wrist. With a decent hair-cut just going to seed and a couple of rings on his knuckles – he looked like a player.

Cocky might be too short a word to describe his vibe though. Grinning like a pup in a pile of pig guts, the bloke's confidence was close to arrogance, and when he spoke, Seth just knew he was vintage trouble. Vigorous and well-modulated – it was the voice of an arch-trickster.

"I'm Andy, mate. Sorry if I've pissed you off, but Gordy suggested I meet you like this – off the cuff. But I see now you're not one for surprises."

Seth drank, eyeing the bastard over his glass.

"You're a private investigator," said Andy.

Seth shook his head. From his wallet Andy pulled out one of Seth's business cards.

"Kelly Investigations. Seth Kelly. That's not you?"

Crunching ice, Seth crushed irritation. How'd this joker get that? They didn't come in rice bubble boxes.

"I want you to help me," said Andy.

"What sort of help?"

"What you used to do. What you still might do."

Quality food and drink were supposed to relax a fella, thought Seth. Fat chance of that now.

"I want to get into gardening up here," said Andy with a wink. "Fifteen thousand for you to get the ball rolling. I want to learn how it's done. I want an education."

Seth half-heeded the pitch as his cerebral gears spun. Everybody knew he was out of the dope growing game. So why was Gordy Mac setting this southern spiv onto him? If he thought chucking mud at him would make him take his eye off Sabbo then he was dead wrong.

"Gordy seemed almost interested," said Andy. "Fifteen thousand dollars is fifteen thousand dollars – but I see a man juggling many things. He doesn't grow it, does he?"

Andy paused, awaiting confirmation of his insight. Seth stared at him. You look like you're used to juggling things, he thought.

"So, you're working as . . . what?" smiled Andy. "A private investigator chasing fiscal discrepancies, marital infidelities and relatives trying to stay missing. Pay well?"

Browned off, Seth stayed inscrutable. Why did every bastard have to run down what he did for a dollar?

"I thought so," said Andy. "Look, the fifteen thousand is just the beginning. I can give you a third of that now."

He splayed out a hand, making the number five.

"We can walk up the road to where I'm staying and I'll give it to you. Right now."

Andy's smile had gone supernova.

"You got the wrong person," said Seth.

"Oh, bullshit – I know about you."

No, you don't, thought Seth. All you know is what Gordy

Mac's told you. He stood and felt the booze heat his face.

"Listen, mate, I'm totally legit. I've got an investigator's licence and a squeaky-clean record. I pay my taxes and I iron my socks and undies too."

"So, what are you doing with Gordy then?"

"None of your bloody business."

He was too loud. Conversations stopped. Faces turned. Across the room, the roving maître d's eyes caught his. At the next table, the lovely laughing lady now wore a calm face that nearly hid her disappointment.

Seth formed a smile around his gritted teeth. My past follows me around like a hungry dog, he thought. Ignoring Andy, he chucked his napkin onto the table and left.

Outside, the warm air smelt wet, but there were no spits of rain as yet. A half-moon flickered behind low moving clouds and flying foxes bickered in the trees down Lake Street. Anger pushed his legs along. He got into the Pig and tried to reassemble his thoughts.

The money he'd just been offered was the first piece he got to. Five grand. Right now. Maybe he'd been too hasty. Maybe he'd give this joker a run-down. Maybe he . . .

Realisation knocked him on the head – neither he or Gordy had paid for the food and drink! That was way out of line. He got out and hurried back. Inside The Outrigger he went through the crowded bar towards the restaurant. Andy appeared at his side.

"Hey, Seth. Mate . . ."

"Hold your bloody horses." Seth made a bee-line for the cashier's desk.

"Slow down, I . . ."

Seth held up his hand and turned to speak to the man at the till; the maître d, his trained smile almost hiding his apprehension.

"Look, I'm very sorry," said Seth. "I walked out without paying. There was four dozen Kilpatrick, two Tournedos and . . . I'm not sure how many double Jack Daniels."

"It's fine, sir. Your friend paid."

"Friend?"

The maître d nodded at Andy; the smiley bastard giving the Cheshire Cat a run for its money.

"I tried to tell you," said Andy.

Seth pulled out his wallet.

"How much?"

"Gentlemen," said the maître d, indicating a couple now behind them waiting to pay. "Maybe . . . the bar?"

"That's a great idea," said Andy. "C'mon, let me buy you a drink." Seth bowed thanks to the maître d and followed Mr. Fifteen Thousand into the bar.

"Two double Jack Daniels and cola, thank you." Andy bathed the barmaid with his brilliant smile. Seth opened his wallet and finger-riffled the notes: three twenties, five tens and some ones. Andy watched with interest.

"What do I owe you?" said Seth.

"My shout."

"Nah, nah – how much?"

"You drive a hard bargain my friend. Ninety bucks."

Seth put the money on the bar. Andy ignored it.

"My sister's brother-in-law is a chef," he said. "Works bloody hard. It's good of you to come back and pay."

"I don't rip people off."

"That's what I heard."

Seth tried not to roll his eyes. The drinks arrived and Andy took a twenty from the money on the bar.

"And please, keep the change," he said.

"Really?" said the young woman. "These drinks are not even eight dollars."

"Please. You're working really hard. You deserve it."

"Ohhh, *thank* you, sir."

There was genuine pleasure in Andy's eyes. Well, that's cool, thought Seth. And so was paying the bill. Andy now bowed his head, collecting his thoughts, and when he looked up there was a shitload of sincerity in his eyes.

"Look, I'm really sorry, man. It's none of my business – you and Gordy. He gave me the impression you'd be up for my offer. Now I think he was having a lend of me. Let's forget about it and just have a friendly drink, yeah?"

Poker-faced and a bit pie-eyed now, Seth agreed with a nod, and Andy's smile cruised back onto his face. Without conversation, they slowly drank, casually checking out the people around them.

There were lots of suntanned laughing women to look at, but Seth watched the would-be grower from the corner of his eye. He looked relaxed; the hustle switched off; just a well-dressed, good-looking bloke sitting at the bar.

With an amused frown, Andy looked up above them at the speakers churning out some easy-listening rubbish.

"Neil Diamond. Not my first choice. Or last. I think I'd prefer two cats fighting in a piano."

Seth laughed.

"You like music?" said Andy.

"Yeah, I do."

"What do you go for?"

"Awww – rock'n'roll mainly. Some jazz. Bit of soul."

"Jazz? You like Al di Meola? Elegant Gypsy?"

"Sure. I've got that album."

A bomb of delight detonated across Andy's face, and he reached out and they clinked glasses. Seth had to smile. It wasn't just the clothes – the bloke had class.

The darling of a barmaid, busy making cocktails, heard the merry clink of glass and smiled at them.

"You heard the new live album?" said Seth.

"Live album?"

"Yeah, with John McLaughlin and Paco de Lucia."

Andy pulled a face of happy ignorance then burst into laughter, his voice drowning out the sickly-sweet plod of Sweet Caroline. Seth, happy-drunk at last, joined right in.

As the barmaid took cocktails to a hovering restaurant waiter, she zapped them with a radiant smile.

"I love to see good friends happy," she said.

And like good friends they drank easily, talking about music. Andy knew a bit, but soon he was speculating about people around them, spinning up tales about their dress-sense, jobs and sex lives. This brazen patter was bloody entertaining, making Seth crack up with laughter.

When they got onto fishing, Seth was feeling well-oiled. Declining another drink, he told Burns a bit more about the good spots up here then called time on the night.

Looking pretty pissed himself, Andy smiled in grandiose farewell. As they shook, Seth nodded seriously.

"Yeah," he said, the noise of the bar coming in waves.

"Yeah. Give us a ring."

Elation lit Andy's face; his eyes wide in gratitude – and something like audacity. He was stoked.

"Thank you, mate," he mouthed in the happy din.

Leaving him there, pretty sure he was going to try his luck with the barmaid later, Seth tacked back to the Pig. Feeling a tad full for the road, he sat and drank water. And thought about the fifteen grand and how it could very well be a plan B for next year.

Then Andy came out of The Tradewinds and started heading north on foot. Looks like he's off to spruce up his room for some company, thought Seth.

He waited for a minute, started the engine, and slowly tailed Andy to the Reef Hotel over on Sheridan Street; a double-story block of a thing in the three-star price range. Parked under a poinciana tree, he watched Andy cross the hotel's lawn to a wing of rooms, take a back stairwell up to the second floor, and then go into the room closest to the stairs.

Well, that's a bit bloody odd, thought Seth. This bloke can afford to pay for dinner, drinks and a good tip at The Tradewinds – but not stay there.

The fifteen grand started to wobble like a heat-mirage on a road out west.

The Funky Monkey

Next morning, Seth got up the same time as always and beat back a medium-strength hangover with orange juice and eggs, two pork sausages and a few slabs of toast.

The sun was almost out, and over a cuppa he thought a little more clearly about the bloke he'd met last night. Was the giant smile on legs for real? Did he have any money? Or was he just a southern con-job, that Gordy Mac in a spoiling move had flicked onto him like a ball of snot. Funny fella though.

And did Gordy really think he'd want to work for him? Or was it just more Mac head-fuckery? Yeah, the bastard was as slippery as a snake with a head on either end.

But he knew he'd been put on notice about Sabbo. The bonecrushers would be earning their money now.

Seth finished his cuppa and washed up. Noting the row of empties by the fridge, he saw his guest was averaging nine beers a day. And rum. It was time for a shop.

The lounge was a bit askew and he tidied up, emptying the overflowing ashtray and putting records back against the wall next to the stereo.

Sunlight streaming through the louvres hit an album at the front of a stack. On its cover: the bearded bespectacled artist with his arms crossed over his guitar; behind him a gorgeous flamenco dancer throwing a sultry stare. Seth began to frown, but he turned from the album as Hugh shuffled out of his room and went into the toilet.

"You can take a whizz in the garden," Seth called out. "Down the back where the neighbours can't see."

Hugh emerged, and made a beeline for the coffee.

"It means less cleaning for me. Your aim ain't so great, mate," said Seth.

"You're getting paid, aren't you?"

"Hey, Hugh," said Seth kindly, but digging deep. "Let's not go on like this, man. It's bullshit."

"Go on like what?" said Hugh over his shoulder.

Seth smiled like he was working the door of a club. Then quickly got dressed and went to work.

Once again, the EH Holden was conspicuous by its absence. For the same reason he didn't go sightseeing at the tip, Seth didn't break into the house and have a look around. Besides, there was nothing of importance that he didn't know about Fuckinkev . . . except where he was.

It was the act of doing something that appealed. This waiting and watching was pickling his brain.

After two hours of dreary inaction, he took solace in a chocolate milkshake at The Big Apple. A cool-looking lady in a sleeveless red top, sitting there reading a book, made him think he should read more. Accidentally finishing the milkshake with a shamefully loud slurp, he quietly took his leave and walked back to the Pig.

Scenic Scott Street sure wasn't calling, so he decided to go and bone-up on the wanna-be dope grower he'd got on the grog with last night.

At the Reef Hotel, he parked across the street in sight of the room Andy had entered last night. Taking a small pair of Tesco binoculars from the glovebox, he waited for a few pedestrians to pass then slid over into the back. Keeping a low profile, he took a proper squiz at the place.

The car park next to the street. A palmy reception area in the hotel's centre, the blue flash of a pool beyond it. Two double-story wings. A lawn and gardens between the carpark and the wing Andy's room was in. And that back stair-well. It looked easy enough.

Glassing the top floor, he saw that the room three down from Andy's was open: a housekeeping trolly next to the door. Panning back, he saw the man himself come out. Slumping down, Seth watched him go down the back-stairwell and come out onto the lawn.

Looking smooth in pressed black slacks, a white long-sleeved shirt and nice shoes, Andy was sporting that big smile – even though there was nobody around to see it. In the hotel carpark he got into a blue Ford Fiesta, checked himself out in the rear-view mirror then drove off in the direction of town.

OK, this might work, thought Seth. But as he reached under the dashboard, his fingers feeling for the catch, the housekeeper came out onto the walkway. Bugger.

Using the Tescos, he watched the housekeeper put dirty linen into a laundry bag. When she turned, her face now clear, Seth got a proper sexy thrill. He knew her, and more than that – they'd done the funky monkey together. Lots. It had been a while ago, but he sure liked the look of her now, tightly squeezed into her housekeeping dress.

Maybe she'd let me into Andy's room for a look around, he thought. Nah, bad idea. If there's trouble, she could end up wearing a good part of it and lose her job.

Still, it felt like a chance of finding out something, and she looked . . . fantastic. He locked up, went across the lawn and up the back stairwell. An ice machine on the landing crashed out a fresh load as he came out onto the walkway. Noting Andy's room was number twelve, he began undoing his shirt – for Miss Rosalie Lee.

They'd met at a rock'n'roll gig at The Pacific Hotel and had gone drink for drink all night; the end result being four or five months of frequent, energetic sex.

It had been wonderful, but she was a screamer – said it felt like shocks of electricity going through her. He'd felt some big zaps too.

Then for some reason lost in time, they'd stopped doing the do: their parting amicable, he remembered that.

"Psstt!" He aimed the loud whisper down the walkway.

She turned, a feather duster in her hand, a clip-board in the other.

"Heyyyyy, sexy woman!" Seth laid on the baritone, his shirt four buttons to the wind, and sashayed towards her like the original carnal man.

"Seth Kelly! My God! What are you doing here?"

Miss Lee was shocked – then delighted: a mad smile made her cheeks shine. As Seth came up, a wanton gleam lit her big brown eyes, and he openly admired her shape.

Gorgeous, strokable, succulently squeezable; she was a curvy cuddle-puss stacked, packed and without a scrap of shame. Memory opened his nostrils and made him shiver. Miss Rosalie, seeing just where that tingle was coming from, reddened, and her eyes swum with lust.

As though in one of her wettest fantasies, her hunky-chested spunk of an ex was blowing her workaday routine into sex-soaked pieces. She sure looked game, and Seth certainly was. Oooo yeah – it was on.

They fell back into the room. He quickly shut the door, took the clip-board from her hand, saw the work-sheet on top then dropped it with a rattle on the draining board of the kitchenette. The feather duster fell to the floor and they embraced, Seth leaning back to brace his feet against the opposite wall of the narrow space. She got stuck in to him, tongue-first. Oh, what a sex rocket she is! thought Seth deliriously.

Vibrating with lift-off, she moaned into his mouth and hitched herself up him, straddling his leg. Seth felt one of those zaps now as she squeezed in close, pashing him with real fervour. Breaking for air, she pushed hair away from her face, a single ring on a finger. Seth crushed regret and smoothly changed gears. With big hands he put her against the wall, put one arm down between her legs, and pressed it firm but nice against her. With wild-cat eyes she pressed back.

"Open your dress," he commanded.

"Ohhhh, my God!"

Hyperventilating with horny anticipation, Miss Rosalie frantically popped the buttons on her dress, while he gave her red-hot, sex vibes with his eyes. You are going to get it, baby. And good! Miss Rosalie squealed.

Seth slid a hand inside her dress and slowly ran it over her yummy curves. With a voluptuous groan, she started sliding along his forearm, pressing in on the down-stroke.

"Stop," he commanded her. Her hot pink mouth flew open and she froze. Reaching for her bra-clip, he did the quick in-out thing and released her breasts for his mouth. She just about fainted.

Putting his forearm back in place, he licked and sucked her lollies. Sliding a pre-emptive hand over her mouth, he felt her hot breath and the darting wet fish of her tongue. Head bent, he wallowed in her silky weight and warmth, her body-smell intoxicatingly divine.

Pulling his hand from her mouth, she began to gasp and squeak, and as these notes of frantic ecstasy became more frequent, the arm-sliding grew audibly faster. As she grew close, he gathered her in, picking her up, his forearm right there – and she went for it; one canvas shoe thumping against the wall, the other jumping in mid-air. Cramming her glowing face into his chest, she shuddered and cried out then sagged in his arms. When her breathing stopped racing, Seth kissed the top of her head and let her down, holding her until she could stand.

"Ohhhhhhh, my golly gosh. That was gooood."

"You didn't scream,"

"Yeah – I'm at work."

While Rosalie used the bathroom, Seth quickly read her work-sheet. Room twelve hosted a Mr Chris Burns. A blue biro number indicated it was the second week of his stay.

He put the clip-board back then washed his forearm in the sink. In the bathroom the toilet flushed. Seth went and took a peek out at the carpark, looking for Andy's car. He watched Sheridan Street until Rosalie came out in a jingle of keys. She was buttoned up and neat, her face absolutely radiant. What a woman, thought Seth.

She laid a hand on his chest. "What just happened?"

"You had a big comesy."

"Yeah, I know that, but why? I mean, what are you . . ."

"I saw you from the street and just thought . . . but hey, what time do you finish cleaning the rooms?"

"Three o'clock. Why?" Then her confusion blew up in a raucous yell of laughter. "Seth Kelly! You are too much."

"I am?"

Grinning happily, Rosalie picked up the feather duster and shook it at him like he was a horny devil that needed exorcising.

"Sorry babe, but I'm married now," she said. "Good job we didn't go too far."

"Never. You didn't scream."

Like before, they parted nice, their mad hushed laughter like naughty kids playing up in a romper room. That their reunion had included some hot sex in a downtown motel room was just too funny.

He blew her a kiss as he left, and as he walked to the stairwell, he looked at the lock of number twelve. He'd be back a bit later – when Mrs Rosalie Lee had finished.

A Fighting Town

He cruised around town looking for a red EH Holden, until his stomach started wondering if his throat had been cut. He popped into Frangipani's and got one of their truly ripper pies. Leaning against the Pig, happily scarfing the golden-brown marvel, he wondered why anybody would bother with Stigs.

Back at home, Hugh was sitting at the back porch table with his smokes and his notebook. From the little window in the kitchen behind the stove, Seth spied a single written line on the notebook's page. Break the block and play your guitar, he silently urged him. Relax and get into it, man.

But he didn't, and Seth went to the beach and ran four laps of it. After a cold shower and a quiet sandwich, he went back into town and sat in Scott Street watching until it hit three o'clock. After impatiently grinding out another half hour, he drove over to the Reef Hotel.

Parking under the poinciana again, he was pleased to see no blue Ford Fiesta in the carpark. He sat and watched for Rosalie or other staff. Coast clear, he got a Ziploc bag from the stash under the dashboard. Inside the bag, snug in the little pockets of a chamois wallet, was a beaut set of bumping keys made for the most popular Aussie brands of door-locks. There was also a pair of disposable latex medical gloves.

Pocketing these, he locked the Pig and casually strolled through the carpark and across the lawn. At the top of the stairwell he paused, looking around for staff or guests.

Seeing no one, he squatted down outside Andy's room, undoing the shoelace on one shoe as an easy-to-see alibi. Opening the little wallet on his knee, he tried the bumping keys, feeding each one gently into the lock, pausing before the last tumbler. Then the key got the bump – with a bit of rotational force thrown in at the same time.

The sixth key hit paydirt. The doorknob turned and the lock didn't have a scratch on it. Inside, he gently closed the door. With the bumping-keys back in his pocket, he re-tied his shoe-lace and slipped on the gloves.

Andy was a neat bastard: everything carefully squared away; jocks, socks, good slacks and shirts, loafers, canvas and dress shoes, all neat as. Seth stroked a couple of the shirts. Nice.

In the bedroom he lifted up the mattress, squeezed the pillows, ran his hands over the bed and looked under it. In the wardrobe, two spare pillows and a blanket snoozed. He checked them out, and then every drawer in the room; even looking under the Gideon Bible in the bedside table.

A hairdryer and a dead fly cohabitated in the bathroom cupboard. The toilet cistern contained nothing but water and the ball float, and in the fridge, a UHT milk carton huddled against left-over Chinese takeaway. The framed pictures were stuck to the walls, and the carpet edges were attached firmly to the floor. Aside from the clothes, shoes, and toiletries there was nothing to suggest anyone was staying here; no letters or scribbled notes, no rubbish in the bins. And no money either.

Down the bottom of the hall wardrobe, he took another look amongst all the shoes; taking his time, and he finally found a tiny scrap of greasy rag. Holding it to his nose, he got the sweet whiff of gun oil.

He'd gone over the joint like a drug squad detective but now he searched again in the unlikely places; behind the TV and phone, in the folds and rails of the curtains.

Reaching up to shake the blades of the ceiling fans, he saw a shadow between the roof and the fancy mounting of one of the two ceiling lights. A gap. Grabbing a chair, he took a look and saw something had been snuck in there.

Sticking his finger in, he hooked out a nicely weighted, transparent plastic bag. What was inside made him grunt appreciatively: a short-barrel Smith and Wesson Model 19 magnum revolver in a cool looking matte black finish. This bloke's a serious player, thought Seth. The fifteen grand now came back into focus.

Replacing the gun, he looked at his watch and saw that twenty minutes had passed. He went to the door, eased it open. Palm seeds rattled along the walkway roof in a gust of wind. Opening the door further, he stuck his head out. The hallway was clear, but now he saw a car pulling up in the carpark – a blue Ford Fiesta – with Andy looking up at him through the windscreen. Seth exited the room fast. Andy jumped out of the car and ran towards the wing.

Seth thundered down the stairs, balling the gloves into his pocket then burst out onto the lawn and ran for it. As Andy sprinted to cut him off, a tourist couple stopped to watch. In a major effort, Seth sped up. So did Andy, and with footy premiership precision he bored in and tackled Seth; both men hitting the wet grass hard.

Knocking clinging arms away, Seth rolled and jumped up. Andy, like that bugger of a brown fox, was already on his feet – and punching. Seth ducked, weaved; then with a double forearm blow knocked him away. But the bastard bounced right back like a coin off a drum – his fists flesh and bone comets. Seth parried fast, blocking blows then took a real cracker to the ribs.

On his periphery he saw onlookers, and a female voice implored them to stop. I'd love to darling, he thought, but this bloke's going all the way here. Ignoring the pain in his side, Seth fought to keep his attacker at bay.

It was a fight alright, but it began to turn weird. They were both pretty evenly matched, and like good fellas no-one kicked or used knees, but as their eyes met between deft, syncopated flurries of punches, Andy looked happy; like he didn't want this to stop. The bloke fought well, but without real intent. It felt like a bloody exhibition match.

I'm over this, thought Seth, and he made as if to run one way – then bolted the other. He wasn't quite fast enough and Andy grabbed him with strong arms. Now done with the gentleman bullshit, Seth smashed a hard knee into his groin. But the canny bastard twisted like an eel, avoiding the nutcracker blow, and his legs trapped Seth's leg like muscled snakes; his groin pressing in. Head-to-head, they grappled and wrestled, each one trying to trip and fling the other to the ground. Seth smelt shaving soap and felt Andy's breath on his cheek.

"What did you take?" grunted Andy.

"I called the police," yelled a masculine voice.

Seth strained to break free but Andy held on; the husky bastard intent on getting him on the ground.

"Stop it now!" The man's yell, right in their ears, made them jump apart. A hotel receptionist stood there, a biro in one shaking hand. "The police are here!"

"What did you take from my room?" said Andy, his eyes scanning Seth's pockets.

A white V8 Ford cop-car pulled up by the lawn and two cops jumped out; the older one shouting, "Move apart and stay right there!"

"You're a greedy fool," said Andy.

Seth stepped back, and the younger cop ran up to him, uncertainty in his eyes.

"You been drinking?" he said. "You gonna be trouble?"

Seth shook his head and brushed grass off his neck.

The questioning started; his answers mainly true, and of course, eyewitnesses had seen the man run across the lawn and pile into him like a New South Wales defender.

"So, this man here, a total stranger to you, just attacked you without explanation?" said the cop.

Seth nodded, happy to lie. With a handgun stashed in his room, Andy would be telling a couple too.

"Anything else?" said the cop. Seth shook his head, his eyes on the other cop.

Andy, standing close to the senior constable, was telling

him something. The cop was looking incredulous, but he was listening hard. Andy pulled out a small black wallet.

"Do you intend to press charges?" said the young cop.

Seth shook his head and watched Andy open the wallet. Something shiny in it made the senior constable's face darken. "You must be joking," he said.

The young cop watched them now.

"So, you were you arresting him?" said the senior cop. Shaking his head, Andy smiled ruefully as though he had wanted to, but lacked evidence.

You prick, thought Seth. You're a cop.

"Did you check in at the watchhouse on the esplanade?" The senior constable was looking more than a little sour.

"Yes, I did," said Andy. "Ten days ago."

"Yeah? Well, I don't know what it's like in Brisbane now days, but I'm damn sure you blokes don't brawl for fun out in public like this."

"That explains it," Seth said to the young policeman. "Your smart undercover fella must have got me mixed up with someone else."

The young cop, his eyes hard on Andy, grunted in what sounded like agreement. He put his hands on his hips and his gaze became a glare.

Seth shot forward and took a good look: in the wallet a silver badge with glints of enamelled red. With an amused side-long glance, Andy tucked it away. The young copper grabbed Seth's shoulder, redundantly saying 'stop.'

"What about him?" The senior cop stared at Seth.

"No, he's right. It's just a misunderstanding," said Andy and he gave everybody a lovely smile.

Silence fell and the small crowd waited. Andy winked at Seth then listened respectfully as the senior cop sternly rumbled in his ear. This cop business produced numerous smiles among the watching people.

Then the police dispersed the onlookers, and Andy or Burns, or whoever the hell he was, scrutinised Seth's belt and pockets. Seth ran his hands into his pockets, lifted his shirt and turned a three-sixty. The plain-clothed cop came in closer, his voice low.

"Were you trying to rip me off? Bloody stupid. I don't leave that kind of money lying about a motel."

"No. I just need to know who I'm dealing with."

As he said it, Seth looked the cop straight in the eye. The bastard stared back. Then he nodded, obviously satisfied with what he saw.

"Yeah, I heard you play straight," he said.

Seth snorted at this bullshit.

"You can fight, Kelly."

"Get fucked."

"Ah c'mon, that was a bit of fun, wasn't it?"

"Fun? You're out of your tree, mate."

The cop liked that.

This fella's a head-tripper, thought Seth, and an image of a fly wriggling on fly-paper flashed through his mind. He looked around and saw that everyone had gone – bar a teenage boy watching them with real interest. Seth gestured at him to clear off and he reluctantly did.

"You're undercover," said Seth.

"No, no."

"Bullshit – Mister Christopher Burns."

The cop raised his eyebrows in appreciation.

"No, like I told those boys – I checked in when I arrived. Think I'd do that if I was undercover?"

That sounded about right. Letting the local police in on the lurk was probably a good way to blow it.

"Gordy know about this?" said Seth.

The cop smirked and said nothing.

Seth laughed at him.

"Got friends on the force, has he?" said the cop.

Seth laughed at him some more.

"You got some I.D with your name on it?" he said.

"What for?"

"Let me see or I'm walking."

The cop pulled out a driver's licence.

"C'mon, mate," said Seth. "Don't piss me about."

With a smile, the plain-clothed cop took out the black leather wallet again and showed Seth a Queensland Police detective's photo I.D. card in the name of Christopher Burns.

"Chris," said the cop like they'd just met. The bloke was shameless.

"But you've worked undercover," said Seth.

"Sure."

"So that was all rubbish about growing a crop?"

"No, I mean it."

"You know that's illegal?"

Chris Burns laughed, rubbed his arm.

"Don't you worry about that," he said.

"You're kidding me – cops growing dope?"

"We want to suck in buyers of a certain level."

"Suck in?"

"Engage and arrest. The laws *they* break are real."

"So, it's not legal what you're doing?"

"I didn't say that. Look, we get the best and most up-to-date advice from our lawyers, OK. Look, I'm still serious about paying you to give me a hand. Fifteen thousand."

Seth looked at the muddy stains on their clothes. Unlike Burns, he was wearing old jeans and a t-shirt. The cop had ruined his nice gear.

"I think we deserve a beer," said Burns.

If there was a walk away time then this was it.

"Yeah, alright," said Seth.

Walking to the carpark, a shirtless bloke began clapping from the patio of a ground floor room. As they passed, he raised a stubbie in salute. "Top blue, boys! Top blue!"

Chris Burns waved back like he'd just won Wimbledon.

The Fiesta's smooth, but gutsy acceleration made Seth think the engine was not the original factory model. Yep, this bloke's a fully custom job himself, he thought.

At the bottle-shop by The Grand, Burns bought two cold longnecks of Cairns Draught. Up the mangrove end of the Esplanade, they leaned against the Ford's bonnet and drank them; looking across the mudflats and water to the range. Patchy cloud made rays of sunlight shine down onto the western slopes of the jungle-covered slopes – the Jesus light, Johnny Pep called it.

"Nice view," said Burns. "OK, listen, mate. You'll get the green light with me. No copper's gonna touch you while you're helping me. You're protected. But with any other dodgy business, you're on your own."

"I don't do dodgy business anymore."

Burns laughed. "Well, there you go! You're the perfect bloke. You've got the expertise, but not the exposure. And you even iron your socks and undies."

Seth smiled. It was a bit of a ball-stroker having a sharp detective wanting his help; a fella who could be a useful contact for Kelly Investigations in the future. But working for a cop? He was going to have to keep it real quiet. And who was the target of this sting? Seth felt the long shadow of consequences fall over him. It was a lot simpler when Burns had been Andy.

"You're not selling this dope up here, are you?" he said.

"The Macs want the first crop," said Burns.

Seth looked at the inlet, the D watching for his reaction. Is that so? he thought, feeling let off the hook now.

"The wet's coming now. Nothing's gonna happen until next year," he said.

Burns nodded and took a pull on his longneck. "I heard you and the MacIntyres have a bit of history. Some beef between you boys. Help me and you'll be getting a chance to put the boot into them."

A heron picked its way through hoops of mangrove on the muddy foreshore. Seth watched it while possibilities writhed in his head.

"This time next year they'll be banged up inside," said Burns. "Sound good to you?"

The Mac brothers busted was a champion idea, but Seth needed Sabbo out of jail before that happened. With those two evil bastards inside Stuart Creek, it would be open season on Sabbo – bonecrunchers or not.

The heron speared something with its long beak, and in a show of indifference, Seth blandly shrugged. Burns has heard some scuttlebutt on me and the Macs, he thought. But I'm not biting. He's a cop and he'll play me anyway he can, using anybody and anything as bait.

"You smoke dope?" said Seth.

"Sure. Working undercover you had to."

"Yeah, I guess so," said Seth. This is going to be a one-off, he thought. Burns won't need me after the first crop. I get the money, the Macs go to jail, and whoever he drops his sting on after that will have nothing to do with me.

"But I've smoked when I wasn't working," said Burns. "I'd get stoned and have a few beers with my betters and seniors at the bar. Sometimes the brass."

"Bullshit," said Seth, but he could see Burns was telling the truth. "How the hell did you get away with that?"

"A bit of Visine, a lot of balls. And they were pissed."

Seth blew up in laughter, and Burns joined in, pleased with the effect of his tale. When their mirth subsided, he spent a moment studying the view, before turning to Seth.

"So, you'll help me grow a crop?"

A breeze from the inlet made the mudflat stink strong. Seth watched the heron slowly disappear into the maze of mangrove roots – then he turned and gave the D the nod. The bloke's smile looked like it was going burst his head.

Burns now had a card in his hand and he handed it to Seth. Written on it in neat biro were two phone numbers – one in Cairns, the other in Brisbane. Seth put the card in his wallet, feeling almost sunburnt from the glow of the smile next to him.

"I'll be in and out of town, but after the wet I'll be here full time. North Queensland's a top priority for us. You've got the drug capital of Australia here," said Burns.

"Yeah, I heard that," said Seth.

"So, mate, we were talking about the fishing up here last night," said Burns, deftly moving it on. "But what's the hunting like?"

The D began quizzing Seth about wild pigs, and like last night, he was cool and funny; asking intelligent questions and listening to the answers with a serious ear.

It was a pity, thought Seth. Though no closer to trusting Burns, he couldn't help liking him – even if he was a cop. In different circumstances they might have been mates.

Burns saw that, and when he dropped Seth back at the Pig, he said, "You'll make a good friend in me."

Driving off, his rib aching from the hard punch that had bounced off it, Seth began whistling the bassline from Start! Heading back to work, he mulled over the man he'd just been fighting and drinking with.

Cairns had always been a fighting town, but getting into a punch-on in broad daylight at a downtown motel wasn't something Seth did for fun. Playing the rowdy in front of an audience was a mug's game. He'd seen enough of that nonsense working at concerts and pubs.

But Chris Burns had that sense of the show-off in him: the vibe of a stirrer and a joker; a cheeky cockatoo willing to push it a bit further – and all the while getting off on being the wild card in whatever situation he was in.

Memories shifted through Seth. He knew all about this kind of crazy-man front. He'd grown up with it.

The D also had the vibe that he was just playing, like it was all just a game, with his bullet-proof smile a constant challenge to call his bluff. Seth knew about that too.

Along Sheridan Street, fallen flowers from poinciana trees lined the edges of the grey bitumen with red-orange. Parked cars on the wide grass verges were speckled with the bright petals. Seth's whistling petered out.

Chris Burns was a capital city cop who might be good to know. Not only to make some money off, but as a contact for the business down the track. And he was a laugh.

The problem was – with his jokers-wild smile, reckless fisticuffs, defiant dope-smoking, and hidden firearm – he was probably a nutcase too.

Like Dolphins Frolicking

On Scott Street the day began to die while Seth waited for Fuckinkev. The bastard wasn't around in the daytime, that was for bloody sure. He'd have to come back at night and that didn't thrill him at all. Lurking around here after dark was the last thing he wanted to do.

Over waiting, he went shopping. At the Liquor Barn behind The Barrier Reef, he bought a couple of cartons of NQ Lager, five bottles of Australian red, a litre bottle each of Bundy rum and Jack Daniels, and some cola.

Out on the highway, he got fruit and veggies from the Fruit-Bat, and over at Stratford, Mr Marsh himself boxed up a nice chunk of rump, a whole eye-filet, a dozen lamb chops, beef and pork sausages – and two kilos of his spot-on bacon.

This was more like it. Spending Daddy Christie's money was way more fun than sitting in grubby old Scott Street.

Back home, a faded-pink Corolla two-door with milk-chocolate mud-sprays up its sides was parked out front. With a good collection of dings, it looked at least ten years old. In the back seat was a suitcase and a rolled-up swag.

From inside the house came the sound of two guitars. As Seth got the cartons of beer out, he listened, and what he heard made him smile like a kid with an icy-pole.

The players were smoothly cruising on a sweet island-style groove, chugging along on a lazy downstroke chop. As one guitar held the rhythm, tight but swinging with it, the other one picked out sparkling runs that sounded like dolphins frolicking in a glittering sea. Whoever this visitor was, they'd hit it off with the house guest.

In the lounge room he was absolutely stoked to find Jeffyman playing guitar with Hugh, both men side by side on the lounge. They looked up and the giant smile on his old mate's face lit up the room.

"Aaaaayyyy! Willya look at this one!" yelled Jeffyman.

Seth put down the beer and his mate jumped up. Hugh watched as they shuffled about, grinning like idiots. Then Jeffyman held the guitar away from him and they went in chest-to-chest.

Except it was more like face-to-chest, as Jeffyman was five foot four. As Seth hugged his nuggety little mate, he felt his energy light him up like an elemental force. It was like he had the sun glowing inside. No wonder the ladies liked him.

"You've grown," said Jeffyman as they stepped apart.

"But still no bloody smarter," finished Seth.

He checked his mate out. "You look different, man. Not exactly flash but . . . sorta respectable."

Jeffyman had worn his curly black hair in a rebel mop, sometimes with a red bandanna. Now it was short; styled even. And there were no leather bands on his wrist.

"That's what city living does to a fella," said Jeffyman. "A lot more cops down there too."

"You want a beer?"

"You serious? I'm on holidays."

Seth frowned at Hugh.

"Where's your manners, Hugh? You know there's beer in the fridge."

"Hugh, is it?" said Jeffyman.

"Yeah. So, what's your name, man? Nice lead playing there," said Hugh.

"Thanks, brother – I'm Jeffy," said Jeffyman and they shook hands.

"Aye? Didn't you fellas even say hello?" said Seth.

Jeffyman cackled. "I heard this one playing and I called out but get no answer. So, I come in and he's right into it; doesn't see me. I get the other guitar and start to play. He got one big shock alright, but he didn't stop playing!"

Seth laughed at that and opened two beers for Jeffyman and himself. Jeffyman took his and said to Hugh, "Don't you drink?"

"Well, yes I do," said Hugh, getting up. "But the butler forgets himself sometimes."

As he went to the fridge, Jeffyman raised questioning eyebrows. Seth made a I'll-tell-you-later motion with his hand. Jeffyman nodded and knocked back half his beer.

"I didn't know you've been stockin' up on guitarists," he said in his loud voice. "Good ones too."

Hugh came back, smiling at Jeffyman.

"Hugh, you wanna help me bring in the shopping first?" said Seth. Hugh sat down and lit a cigarette.

"Well, can you roll us a joint then?"

Hugh smoked away in imperial consideration then placed the cigarette in the ashtray. "Sure, why not."

Jeffyman up-ended his beer, finishing it. He let out a grand sigh of satisfaction and winked at Seth.

"I'll give you a hand, mate. Hugh can do the important stuff," he said.

Hugh smirked at the Tally-Ho packet in his hand. When Jeffyman said, "Here, roll up this," and dropped a nice head into the bowl, he smiled in triumph.

In the carport, Jeffyman came in close to Seth.

"What's up with him?"

"He's a bloody pain in the arse."

"Plays good guitar."

"But not enough. He's supposed to be writing songs, but I've only heard him play once since he got here."

"Where's he from?"

"He's a rich-kid from Sydney. I'm getting paid to baby-sit him, but he's not a happy camper."

"Rich and talented – I'd be cool with that."

"You're not wrong. Hey Jeffy, you remember Sabbo?"

Jeffyman's face went blank. "Ahhh – not really."

Seth searched for the words. It wasn't exactly advice he wanted; more like counsel. He and Jeffyman had grown a very profitable crop back in the day, and last year his mate had given him some very savvy counsel. He could be a cocky, headstrong bugger at times, but Seth valued his no-bullshit perspective on the world.

"Yeah, he's ended up in jail and . . ." began Seth.

"Brother, I don't want to know. Those days are over for

me. I'm graduating as an electrician next year and I'll be on good money after that."

Seth nodded, feeling a little put-out.

"I dig Brisbane, Seth. Everyone said it's a fast town, too fast for a boy from the north – but not this one! Found the nightclubs straight-up, good food, good bands too, and the other apprentices buy me beers, check on me and all. I'm their one and only Aboriginal mate, see."

It sounded pretty good and Seth felt ashamed.

"Yeah, sorry I haven't made it down to see you," he said. "I started a business since I last saw you."

"Old business or new business?"

Jeffyman's interrogative smirk irked him, and he dug out a business card from his wallet. Jeffyman read it then passed it back with an appreciative nod.

"Yeah, this is you. And without the headache of the old business."

"What was the old business?" said Hugh from the door.

Seth grabbed the box of Marsh's meat out of the Pig and passed it to Jeffyman.

"Growing dope?" said Hugh.

"Hey, Mr Guitar, you gonna stand there yapping, or you going to give me a hand?" said Jeffyman.

Hugh, loving it, readily took the box of meat.

When the food and grog were stowed away, they all got another beer and sat down in the lounge. Hugh presented Jeffyman with the joint he'd rolled and a lighter.

"You're a proper butler," said Jeffyman. He lit up and took two deep drags. Passing the joint to Hugh, he nodded at it and squawked, "Kranda."

"Kranda?" said Hugh.

"Yhhep, its grown there."

"So, how's your lady in Kuranda?" said Seth.

Jeffyman expelled a big plume of smoke.

"Howdja know that?"

"I'm an investigator, man."

"Don't give me that gammon. Who's telling on me?"

"Oh yeah, your Uncle Owen wants a word with you."

"Yeah, I seen him. Wants me to do some electrical work on his house, but I ain't legal yet."

"You've never been legal," stirred Seth.

"Nah, I'm super legal now days. Except for this." Jeffy pointed at the joint, "And I'm only smoking on holiday."

Hugh raised his beer in salute. Jeffyman clinked bottles with him and turned to Seth.

"Yeah, she's a lovely girl," he said. "But she's gone up to Cooktown for a wedding. I stayed last night at Maxie's. We had a good jam, but it's too bloody damp up there. You wake up with moss growing on you!"

As Seth got tea together, Jeffyman, always keen on food and cooking, hopped up and took charge of the meat. He lit the barbie, and cut and trimmed up three rump steaks; the stream of stories and quips issuing from his mouth interrupted only by big swigs of beer. Looking positively infatuated with the bloke, Hugh followed him around, laughing exuberantly and attempting quips of his own.

After making a big salad and an oil dressing for it, Seth put the jar of Auntie Grace's choko chutney, some French mustard, and the pepper grinder on the kitchen table. He found the linen napkins, folded but not too musty in the third drawer, and broke out a flash set of steak knives he'd never used.

Corn-on-the-cob and fat wedges of spiced-up potatoes were cooked on the barbie alongside the steaks, and soon they were in amongst it; Hugh lavishing compliments on the perfectly cooked steak; Seth readily agreeing. When they toasted the beaming chef, he heartily toasted them right back.

A good munch had been taken out of the first carton of NQ, and after dinner they started on nips of Bundy with their beers. Jeffyman rolled a joint, listening with smiling interest as Hugh coyly – can you believe it – got to tell his story.

"Countdown, yeah? The Tygers? True?" Jeffyman was delighted, but not overwhelmed hearing that Hugh was a rock-star: it was just stuff that happened when you were as cool as he was.

Expressing great pleasure that they'd jammed so well together, he slapped Hugh on the knee. Hugh grabbed his shoulder and loudly declaimed that Jeffyman was as good as any Sydney muso he'd played with. Whooping in self-congratulation, they toasted each other with more rum.

This is worth filming, thought Seth. Jeffyman, never short of confidence, had a manifest belief in himself and his capabilities that duller, slower people might unkindly call arrogance. In Hugh he'd found a twin brother.

Watching them raving away got Seth thinking; maybe Jeffyman could stay here for a couple of days and baby-sit Hugh? I could go and see Dad; then go full-bore on the appeal. And take a break from The King of Rock'n'Roll.

"Hey! Hey, Seth!"

The Danger Twins, shoulder-to-shoulder, were looking at him.

"You right?" said Jeffyman. "You spinning out?"

"No, I'm fine. What you doing the next couple of days?"

"Family, aye. Christmas next week. Why?"

"You wanna stay here? Lots of food, drink and smoke. You blokes can play music together."

Hugh shot Seth an odd, angry look. For crying out loud, thought Seth. What are you so up-tight about?

"Nah," said Jeffyman, "But I'll stay here tonight. I'm too out-of-it to drive now."

He pointed to the guitars. "Hey, Hugh, let's have a play. Show Seth here what we can do."

Hugh reached for a cigarette. "Um, yeah, that was fun before, but I don't really do that."

"What – play guitar?" said Jeffyman with incredulous amusement.

Hugh raised sad eyebrows as he lit up. The sulky grump doesn't want to jam because of me, thought Seth.

"Hey, no offense, Jeffy, but I'm a professional." Hugh's smile was consoling. "I'm writing songs at the moment, so that's where my head is. Don't want to dilute it y'know?"

"Bullshit," said Jeffyman.

Hugh nearly dropped his cigarette.

"You doing bugger-all here."

Hugh fired another angry look at Seth.

"Well, it's true," said Seth.

"You're real talented," said Jeffyman. "You got a good place and a good butler too. Don't waste your time, man."

"Thanks for your concern." Hugh bristled beneath his smile. "But I operate on a completely different level. You wouldn't understand. It's big money. Recording studios, TV appearances, tours. Give it a go sometime."

"You serious?"

"If you think you've got the talent."

"I might, but it won't be enough."

"It's all I've got."

"You also got that nice white skin, brother."

Hugh jerked in surprise then laughed.

"That's got nothing to do with it. It's the level of talent."

"Yeah? How many Aboriginal bands or players you seen on Countdown lately? Or hear on the radio? And don't say Marcia Hines or I'll give you a good slap."

Jeffyman, relaxed but very serious, showed no hostility or bitterness in his voice. Hugh stared at him.

"Nah, it's not about the level of talent," said Jeffyman. "You said before I'm as good as any player in Sydney. Or was that just bullshit?"

Jeez, where's the popcorn, thought Seth.

Outside, the tree frogs started up. Ash fell from Hugh's cigarette. Jeffyman waited.

"I never thought about that," said Hugh after a bit.

"Whitefellas never do," said Jeffyman. "Listen, you got opportunities I don't get. You *have* to go for it."

Hugh sat in silence. Then he began nodding slowly, and when he looked up with big penitent eyes, Jeffyman delivered a hearty slap to his knee

"Yeahhh, you got it now. C'mon, drink up!"

Looking as if he might cry, Hugh raised his beer. As he

toasted Jeffyman, his eyes flicked over to Seth. There was shame, maybe even apology in them, but best of all – the sharp realisation of who he was, where he was, and what he had to do.

Thank Christ, thought Seth. For the first time in days, he felt almost properly happy, and he laid a smile on the silly bugger. The silly bugger smiled back.

Jeffyman cracked up. "Look at you two – like an old married couple!"

After all that, they really got into it; Hugh and Jeffyman playing like wizards – for a bit, as they both really wanted to talk and laugh. Joints were blown, nips were quaffed, and the second carton got dented hard. The night ended, pre-dawn, with Seth and Jeffyman lugging an insensible Hugh to his bed.

Back in the loungeroom Seth drunkenly grabbed his mate by the arm. "Hey Jeffy. Thank you for that."

Jeffyman swayed. "He'll be right."

In the morning Seth surfaced like a log in a swamp; his head was foggy, his breath foul. He took a shower, brushed his choppers and put on the jug. Jeffyman had emerged bleary-eyed from his swag and was rolling it up. While he had a shower Seth made a good strong pot of tea and stared vacantly at the grey day outside.

They sat out on the back porch slowly drinking their cuppas, wordlessly contemplating the payback from their carousing.

"I never thought I'd say it, but you *can* party too much," said Jeffyman, "We must be grown-ups now."

Declining breakfast, Jeffyman got his swag together, and Seth walked out with him to the Corolla.

"Goes alright?" said Seth vaguely.

"Yeah, not too bad," said Jeffyman as he put his gear into the back. "It's Uncle Owen's old bomb. My nephews give it a good thrashing. Needs a service."

They both looked around as a car came down Cinderella Street. A blue Ford Fiesta.

Seth groaned; his hangover now doubly unwanted. Jeffyman shot him a look that he didn't answer. The car pulled up and Chris Burns hopped out, smiling like a sun-warmed crocodile.

"Morning, boys."

"Who you calling boy?" said Jeffyman.

Burns threw up his hands. "Mate, sorry! I didn't mean it like that. I have the utmost respect for your people."

"My people? Where do you know them from?"

"I'm screwing this up bad, aren't I?" Burns laughed as though embarrassed. "Respect, man. I mean respect."

Jeffyman turned to Seth. "You know this fella?"

"Yeah."

With a very suspect eye, Jeffyman looked the cop over. Seth knew he smelled a bullyman. Not just because he was Murri, which meant he'd been dogged by the bastards since he was a kid, but because he'd been a grower too. When he looked back at Seth, the flash of recrimination in his eyes stung. "You right then?" he said.

"Yep."

Jeffyman nodded coldly, got into the Corolla without a second glance, and drove off. Bugger, thought Seth.

"Feisty little fella," said Burns. "Old friend of yours?"

Seth frowned impatiently.

"Looks a bit like Sammy Davis Jr. Guess that makes you the Chairman of the Board, hey Frankie?"

Burns laughed. Seth's frown deepened.

"What are you doing here?" he said.

"Well, after you found me, I thought I'd find you. Keep things on an even footing."

"C'mon, Burns."

"Oh yeah, that's right. I want to up your money. My boss agrees with me that you're going to be a real asset. Wants to keep you sweet."

"Up my money?"

"Yeah. Twenty thousand dollars."

Seth kept frowning.

"Listen, the money's just the beginning. I can help you move things around here in Cairns."

"Move things around?"

"The MacIntyres." Burns gripped an imaginary throat. "I put them away and . . . you'd have more room. Room to bloom, mate."

Seth looked up the empty street – the sandy edges, a few pecking doves, the clumps of rustling pandanus, and the D's circus show felt a bit bloody loud.

"I don't give a stuff about them," he said.

Burns observed him with a bullshit intentness, his grin little more than a taunt. "Is that right?"

Seth yawned and scratched his head with both hands, and the cop's incredulous smirk smoothly turned into the bounteous smile of a department store Santa.

"Look, I'll give you five thousand right now. When you show us how to plant it, you get another five. After harvest and curing you get the rest. Sound alright?"

Twenty thousand bucks is a couple of years' worth of basic living expenses, thought Seth. And for maybe a week of work. It was easy money, but he kept mum.

"What? You want more?" Burns laughed delightedly.

He reached through the open passenger window of the Ford and pulled out a fat envelope. Opening the flap, he revealed the hundred-dollar notes stuffed inside. With his smile amping way up, Burns held the envelope out. The mango tree above them began to rustle with a coming gust of wind.

With some restraint, Seth said, "Nah. I think I'll wait until we start growing something first."

The gust strengthened and a hundred buck note peeled away from the envelope and flew across the road.

Watching it sail through the air, Seth yawned again.

Dust in Their Veins

Seth usually didn't talk to cops, especially not ones like Chris Burns, but he'd known a few – Uncle Don being one. Though not related by blood, he was a family friend of decades standing. He and Dad were close, and his wife Mary and Mum had been too.

With twenty-nine years of service across the state from Bamaga to Beerwah, Uncle Don had been a good rural copper – honest, awake and fair – and many a small town had been sad to see him posted on. He'd cared about all the people he served; rich and poor, black and white. Ever optimistic of making a real difference in the community, the corruption spawned by the money of the far northern marijuana business had turned his stomach.

In the last few years of his career, he tried to kick up a stink about it, but the bastards had prevailed. Sidelined, unpromoted, and probably threatened, he'd been glad to retire last year.

With Burns on his radar now, Seth reckoned a little chat with Uncle Don was in order. He rang the old cop and they arranged to meet at the Returned Services League club on the Esplanade around two. Uncle Don, like Dad and many blokes of their generation, had fought in the war, and the RSL was a quiet spot to have a beer with other fellas who'd gone through it back then.

After another cuppa, Seth went through the garden and ambled out to the mouth of the Barron. It was becoming overcast now, some rain on the way, and he turned from the sea and looked at the green sweep of mountain ranges running from False Cape to Mount Buchan. The immense view gave him raw solace. It was something that couldn't be knocked down, or blocked by multi-storey hotels. This country was going to be here forever.

Back at the house, Hugh had surfaced, and the pleasure Seth felt at seeing the bashful smile on the guitarist's face bloomed when he saw an open guitar case and the Phillips recorder set up. His mate had finally arrived.

While coffee was made, they had an amiably hung-over exchange about nothing in particular, Hugh courteously declining breakfast, at least not yet, and at the mention of Jeffyman, he fell into a reflective silence.

"Yeah, he's a good mate," said Seth. "He gave me some advice one time that probably saved my life."

Hugh looked up like he had a lot to say, but wasn't sure how to say it. Seth put a finger across his lips, smiling to show that he wasn't being a meanie, and he pointed at the guitar. "Say it with that, man."

Hugh stared at him. Then a pearler of a smile enveloped his face. He knew he was ready to do it now, so Seth gave him a number one smile and got the hell out of there.

He walked into Machans, barefoot and happy. Sunny wasn't home, so he went to the shop and bought the paper and a mango Weis bar. While kids fished with handlines off the bridge, he sat on the rock wall at Redden Creek and perused the news. A double page spread caught his eye.

With growing horror, he read about a proposed casino, hotel, and bloody everything else on the foreshore right next to Fogarty Park. Fifty-eight hectares? Three hundred million dollars? Two thousand luxury rooms? But when he got to the part about it being like a new Monte Carlo – the muddy inlet subbing for the French Riviera, he shook his head in disbelief. Somehow, he didn't see that coming off.

Then a story in the crime section made him laugh out loud. Last night, not thirty metres from the Cairns Police Station, some enterprising lads had broken into the Courthouse. They'd liberated the safe, containing nearly three grand, by using a wheelbarrow borrowed from the Mulgrave Shire Council office construction site next door. Tyre tracks on the courthouse's front lawn showed where a vehicle had been backed up to receive the prize. Seth chuckled. That sounded like the Cairns he knew.

He walked back up O'Shea Esplanade, just far enough to see Sunny's still empty driveway, before heading home.

Outside under the mango tree, he stood and listened to the Hummingbird inside being played with a delicacy that was sublime. It was a soundtrack to something dreamlike and beautiful, but floating on the ghost of a tough riff.

Unwilling to interrupt by going in, he went around and listened out the back, and it was just the coolest thing.

When the music stopped, he made cheese and spring-onion omelettes which they quietly ate; the sound of the Hummingbird still hanging in the air.

When they finished eating, Hugh dumped his plate in the sink. No thanks, either, but at least he's playing his guitar now, smiled Seth.

It was time to go see Uncle Don, and Seth dressed then collected his keys and wallet. As he waved goodbye, Hugh kept playing, grinning madly at him.

In town, Seth parked on the espy across from the RSL, and looked at the statue of the lone digger standing at ease atop the Great War memorial by the seawall. Flanking the big sandstone obelisk were a twenty-five-pounder field gun and a five-inch naval piece, their dark steely barrels saluting the Coral Sea.

Turning around, he reluctantly looked up at the huge concrete curve of a building going up next to the RSL. The site swarmed with construction workers and the ground resounded with the thud of piledrivers. Another bloody development, the Aquarius – sixteen stories of high-rise apartments, the tallest thing in Cairns by a long stretch. It was going to dwarf the diggers drinking next door.

Crossing the road, he went through the big white stucco archway into the cool air of the building. Only returned service personnel, or their guests could drink here, so Seth found his name in the guest book and signed in. Uncle Don was at the bar telling stories. He bought them both pots, and when Uncle Don finished nattering, they went over and sat by the double window.

They chewed the fat first, talking about Christmas. Dad,

Uncle Don and Auntie Mary were going to George and Bev Knuckey's for lunch and Seth was invited too. He said he'd keep it in mind.

Dad had told Uncle Don all about Michael Christie and his reckless rock and roller of a son, even alluding to the lucrative fee Kelly Investigations had secured. As an ex-copper, Uncle Don was as pleased as Punch when Seth got his investigator's licence. Now he was keen to hear more about these high-flying Sydney-siders.

Seth told him about Hugh; his amazing talent and fame, and the big terrace in Paddington where he lived. He also mentioned the non-disclosure part of the contract.

"What do you reckon he's done?" said Uncle Don.

"I don't know, but he can be a wild one alright. So, I'm baby-sitting him really. Make him meals, keep the fridge stocked with food and beer, pour the rum."

"Sounds like money for old rope."

"Yeah, sorta. There's a few twists in it though."

"Legal ones, I hope."

Uncle Don knew about his past.

"Musical twists. He's supposed to be writing songs but he's not, and I'm on his case about it. But listen Uncle Don, I was hoping you might help me."

"If I can – sure."

"I've been approached by a bloke reckons he's a copper from Brisbane. A detective."

"This to do with the rock and roll fella?"

"It could be," lied Seth. "But as you'll appreciate, I can't talk about it."

"You cheeky bastard."

"Name of Chris Burns, Uncle Don."

"Is that what he told you?"

"I saw his I.D. card and badge, but . . . I don't know Uncle Don. He doesn't quite seem the full quid. Can you help me find out what his story is?"

As he'd hoped, the hint of something suspect got the old bloke intrigued. Uncle Don was still steamed about how his career had ended. And the old bloke sort of owed him one. Last year Seth had handed him the biggest bust of his career. The ex-copper nodded and opened his wallet. "Got any shrapnel?"

They got some ten and twenty cent pieces together, and Uncle Don went to the pay phone down the hall.

Looking around the half-full room, Seth saw a group of blokes laughing appreciatively at a good yarn, and at the bar a knot of old blokes perched on stools; all wrinkled white legs and polished shoes, everyone listened to a truth being told; their heads bent in, almost touching.

Seth looked across the room at the old photographs of young men, the framed medals and weapons mounted up on the walls; mementos of guts-effort bravery and untold suffering. Yeah, it was hallowed ground in here. Probably the perfect place to ask to have a cop checked out.

As the beer foam dried on the sides of his pot glass, Seth wondered what Dad might think about Sabbo's appeal. It would be great to talk with him about it and get some advice, but his bent life had been hidden from his folks. It always felt wrong, and there'd been lots of lies. It wasn't always easy to maintain a double life, but Alex had thrived on the deception; like he was training for a spy mission.

While bullshitting Mum and Dad, he'd look Seth in the eye and chuck in barely-coded references to recent dope business or a chick he'd been with the night before, all the while smiling in rampant cheek, his eyes brimming with challenge. Life's a game, he used to say. Remember that when you play and you'll have nothing to lose.

It would be nice to think he could tell Dad anything, but revealing the world of Sabbo and the Macs to him wasn't going to happen. Straight almost five years, Seth had been happy for it all to become history. No such bloody luck now – it looked like he was making more of it.

When Uncle Don returned, he carried two pots. With a few cracks and a groan, the old bloke settled himself and had a good mouthful of beer. Seth, all ears, sipped his.

"You'll have to hold your horses, mate," said Uncle Don. "Coppers asking questions about coppers is a delicate art. I'll ring you when I hear something."

So Seth had a couple more with him and they picked over the footy, local politics and the weather. When a garrulous mucker of Uncle Don's, schooner in hand, came up to the table, Seth took his cue. As the mates slapped backs and loudly greeted each other, he squeezed Uncle Don's shoulder in thanks and left.

It was time to go and check out Scott Street again. Not expecting anything, he was more than bloody pleased to see the red Holden in the driveway. Mindful that the Macs could turn up, he parked down past Jubilee Street, and retrieved the two grand from the stash in the dash. After waiting for the traffic to dissipate, he strode quickly back up the street.

The Weight of Love

Eyeballing the house, he saw front curtains pulled tight and side-windows shut. There were no lights on, no radio or TV noise, no dishes clinking in the sink. It was a house of junkies alright, its denizens supine on beds or couches; the smacked-out creeps silently listening to the dust in their veins.

At the front steps he looked at the Holden. In the wheel arches and along the bottom of its scratched and dented sides was a fresh crust of red mud, evidence of some nasty road trip spent ripping-off and bashing blokes. Welcome home you bastard, thought Seth.

Raising his hand to knock, he decided to put Fuckinkev off balance, and go round and bang hard on the back door instead. With an evil smile he went down the side of the house. At the back door he looked around. The blank and sightless windows of neighbouring cottages looked back.

Quietly going up the wooden steps, he tried the door. It was unlocked, and when he cracked it – a breath of hell made him rear back.

He tried to anchor himself in the grey sky overhead, and in the growl of traffic on Bunda Street, as pure dread coursed through him. His whole being, like a cartoon cat with its hair on end, flinched from the door. But he had to know.

Pulling his t-shirt up over his nose, he started breathing through his mouth. Pre-vomit saliva spurted up under his tongue. He went inside and it was pure horrorshow.

The smell was like a living thing, the air thick and moist with decay. Bits of school biology lessons flittered through his head. Blowflies buzzed sluggishly about; others clung to the roof and walls, bloated and unmoving. He heard the squeaks of rats, saw their dark forms darting amongst the rubbish on the floor.

In the kitchen, he dry-retched as rats exploded from a slumped figure at the table, their nimble bodies thumping on the floorboards. Among dark cadaverine streaks on the table was a Bic lighter and a blackened teaspoon. Forcing himself closer, he saw a needle-tipped plastic syringe in one arm; on the wrist a gold chain bracelet. Fuckinkev.

Seth's knees wobbled. Around him the room hummed with death, and a hallucination of dreadful violence and despair grabbed him like a pinching skeletal hand.

the knife stop-starting then sliding between a held-down sailor's ribs. the working-girl with swollen purple mangosteen eyes, her front teeth bashed off at the gums. the dead man, swollen and blank-eyed in the long grass. the broken-down wharfie choking out alone.

Gut-punched with horror, Seth turned away from the corpse at the table.

This death house was conjuring up the stinking under-guts of sunny Cairns; the feral madness and infinite decay hidden behind the swaying palm trees, white sand beaches, and clear blue sea.

Beyond Fun-in-The-Sun festivals, stuffed cane-toads, hibiscus shirts, and seafood buffets, there was a hard-as-fuck world of underdogs; dispossessed and desperate, all fading day by day in the sunshine. Grog-rotted livers, grinding poverty, fever sweat and venereal disease; rape, murder and bone-deep dispossession – it all crowded into the little cottage on Scott Street.

The Weight of Love

Drunkenly weaving through the darkened living room, Seth was scarcely aware of the curtains crawling with flies and the rats bouncing off the skirting boards. Stumbling up the hallway, a new putrescine reek grew and a fresh clamour started. With freaky scrabbling and squeals of alarm, rats rushed out of the front bedroom and down the hall. Seth danced about, crying out as they ran across his boots and ankles. At the front door he made himself look into the room. Lying in a solid dark pool on a yellowing mattress was a second ravaged body; armies of blowflies and geckos doing battle on the low fibro roof above it.

As one hand scrabbled for the door knob, Seth bullied himself to scrutinize the naked corpse. Gagging badly now from the knock-out stink, he made out the blue scrawls of jail tattoos on the hands and saw the plastic barrel of a fit poking up from the groin. With the tolerance of a gorilla, Fuckinkev's mate Wessels had overdosed too.

Seth made it through the front door, rattled down the wooden stairs and vomited his breakfast onto the grass. A faint drizzle was falling now, and he relished the cool clean water dotting his neck and arms. Straightening up, he quickly checked out Scott Street. Seeing no one about, he walked briskly to the Pig.

Inside the truck, he grabbed his canteen and rinsed his mouth, spitting the deathly taste onto the ground. With a groan of revulsion, he flopped back in the seat.

He'd seen a few dead men before; a couple of them left to the full effects of the tropics, but the human carrion and awful vibe in that old cottage were a peek into absolute horror that he never ever wanted to see again.

Sabbo's voice sounded in his ear. *"I've never seen the Macs deal it, but they always have some for him. Keeps him on a nice short leash."*

Seth punched the door. He'd been well and truly played. The Holden had been returned last night or this morning. The men in the house had been dead for days.

Starting the Pig, he felt sick again, and this time in his head. What in the hell was he going to do now? His star witness had been artfully knocked off – self-injecting a hot-shot of heroin.

On the Beach

Driving home, the phone box near Tobruk Pool caught his eye. Still zinging like in a bad trip, he considered being a good citizen and calling the cops. But if he or the Pig had been noticed then a few days between an anonymous tip-off and today might well keep him from being hauled in. He spat mightily out of the car window and drove on.

At the house, Hugh wasn't inside, but his guitars were on the lounge by the Phillips recorder. Seth went out the back and saw the guitarist sitting on the beach looking out at the layers of grey sky, two empty stubbies in the sand next to him.

Seth went back in and took a good long shower, feeling grateful for his crisply painted bathroom with the stack of towels neatly folded and his toiletries all lined up. Drying himself, he looked at the painting he'd bought last year; Islander people sitting relaxed and still in a thatched hut. He shaved, patted talc on his pits and bits, and then clipped his finger-nails and finished them with a nail-file.

After hopping into a pair of nice clean shorts, he rolled a joint, popped the crowns on two beers, and went out to

Hugh. The guitarist had a packet of Stuyvesant red on the sand next to him, and when Seth sat down, he lit one up.

Seth gave him a beer, and tried not to notice the tragic smile he got in return. He lit the joint and smoked it for a bit. When he passed it to Hugh, he ignored the unspoken invitation to ask him about his misery.

They sat in silence, smoking and drinking, until Hugh could contain himself no longer.

"I feel so screwed up, man."

No, don't, thought Seth, happy to just be stoned now. Hugh looked dramatically distraught.

"Sydney is thousands of miles away. My career too. The world is turning – hope it don't turn away."

Seth cocked his head at Hugh.

"I need a crowd of people. But I can't face them day-to-day, and though my problems are meaningless, that don't make them go away."

"Aye?" Seth began to frown. Hugh gestured at a pair of scrawny looking seagulls flying by.

"Here I am living on the beach, but those seagulls . . ."

"Are you kidding me?"

"Oh, fuck it, man, I don't know!" Hugh jumped up and ran his fingers through his hair.

"I got so much music in my head I can't sleep!"

"But no lyrics, hey?"

"Yeah. I need to see and feel it, before the words come, Seth. Music flows in my blood but lyrics make me sweat."

Throwing his arms out, the sea and mountains a perfect movie backdrop behind him, Hugh worked the expression of tortured frustration on his face. It was silly really, but

Seth didn't mind – he was chuffed right now to be talking to Hugh about song writing and the process involved.

"Chasing the mystery, nailing down truth with words. It ain't easy, man," said Hugh.

"And you don't want to be writing 'baby, baby, baby' – all that teenybopper crap."

"Exactly! I'm twenty-seven. I want to *say* something."

Seth waited, but Hugh thumped back down on the sand and gave the view a whole lot of moodiness.

"So . . . what do you want to say?" said Seth.

"It's not about what *I* want to say. I want to write about real people, about their lives, their struggles and dreams. The everyday history that doesn't make the papers or TV."

Seth unsuccessfully suppressed a grin.

"What's so funny?" said Hugh.

Seeing hurt in his eyes, Seth reached out and grasped his shoulder. Hugh looked at him like a dog begging, but unsure of what it might get.

"Hugh . . . mate, you are about as far removed from real life as you can get. And it's great. Write some far-out lyrics and blow people's minds. You like Zappa, right?"

That didn't tickle the guitarist's fancy.

"It's a nice idea," added Seth. "Just not your thing."

"What do you mean – removed from real life?"

"C'mon, mate," Seth conned a quick grin onto his face. "The way you live. How you've always lived."

"The way I live? What's that mean?"

This was a turn off the track and Seth uneasily wrestled with evasion – then just went for it. But he kept it mellow; sympathetic even.

"Well, it's understandable – you've had a free-ride since you were a kid. Real people, like you were saying, struggle, and sometimes it is a bloody epic, but everything's always been laid on for you. You've had people picking up after you your entire life."

Hugh upper-lip drew back. Seth nodded sadly.

"With you, there's an expectation that it will all get done for you, all get provided for you, and that's fine on tour or recording, but in the real world . . . it makes you a bludger. From the smokes, drinks and food, to never pitching in to help, and not paying back money you've borrowed – you just help yourself. Truth be told, you're a user."

The guitarists' lips were a pursed white line.

"Mate, I'm being honest here, but you ever think of just doing something for someone just to help them? Make a little sacrifice now and then?"

OK, that's enough, thought Seth. Wind it up nice.

"And the unbelievable truth is – helping someone makes you feel good, man. True story!"

The ocean sounded like the faint roar of an audience. The lighter snicked and a cigarette crackled. Encouraged by what looked like concern on his face, Seth patted Hugh on the back.

"I'll get us some more beers."

Seth collected the empties, fingers in their necks, and walking up through the garden, he softly clinked them. Inside, he paused, hand on the fridge door, as Scott Street replayed in his skull. What a Godawful mess, he thought. But it wasn't my fault. Those bastards were walking dead men before I came along.

Fuckinkev must have opened his stupid yap and Gordy Mac would have put a reassuring hand on his shoulder, looked him in the eye and sincerely thanked him for his loyalty – then given his junkie flunky some super strong smack as a thank you.

Staring at a pineapple fridge magnet, Seth rubbed hard fingers across his mouth. With the favourite scratched, he had one name left on the card now – The Fossil.

But after getting a diving knife pointed at his face, not to mention a rifle aimed at his head, fronting up to Neary face-to-face right now looked unlikely to produce a payout. He needed a different approach. He needed a plan.

He got his note book, rang up Bob Loftus and a stupid bloody answering machine informed him that the lawyer was on Christmas break, and wouldn't be back until the fourth of January.

He didn't slam the receiver down, but he could have. Dial it down, mate, he told himself, you're going to have to wait. So will Sabbo, but at least it's not going to be seven years.

Pushing the grisly fiasco of the day out of his head, he got the beers. As he made for the door, the phone rang.

"Yeah, mate," said Uncle Don. "That policeman's real."

"You know what he's doing up here?" said Seth.

"What have you been up to, Seth?"

"Uncle Don, it's nothing to do with the old days."

The silence on the line was huge. Seth didn't want to say too much, but he owed the bloke a reply.

"I've got a mate in jail, Uncle Don. I'm trying to get him out. I've been talking to witnesses and I've got a lawyer working on an appeal. This policeman could help me.”

The old bloke made a noise. Seth hoped it was approval.

“Your mate’s innocent?”

“I’m sure of it, Uncle Don.”

There was no way Seth was going to mention the Macs. The ex-copper surely knew all about them, and Sabbo’s plight would get short bloody shrift.

“Alright, I believe you, son,” said Uncle Don. “So, here’s the drum. He’s in and out of the Esplanade; sends faxes, makes calls, doesn’t say boo to nobody and doesn’t hang about. He’s drug squad, probably doing the leg-work for an operation, and working solo for the moment.”

“Oh, that’s great, Uncle Don. Well, thanks for that.”

“Hang about – I’m a bit confused here. You reckon a Brisbane drug squad detective can help your mate?”

“Yeah, I reckon. Well, cheers, Uncle Don.”

“Is he one of your witnesses for this appeal?”

“Yeah, he could be.”

Seth listened as his lie was swallowed by silence.

“So, what about the rock and roll fella then? At the RSL you said –”

“He’s come good, Uncle Don! Settling down and writing some great music. It’s coming up roses.”

“Yeah? Well . . . OK then. Gee, that sounds bloody cosy, lounging around drinking rum and writing songs. Then going back to your house in Sydney. What a life, aye?”

“You’re not wrong,” said Seth, wishing it was his right now.

Happy Bloody Christmas

All over Australia, families were gathered around tinsel Christmas trees, maybe real ones if you were down south, opening up their presents and getting into the old festive cheer. Eskies and fridges were chockablock with beer and bubbles. Barbecues were being lit and ovens were heating up – ready for all the prawns, steaks, snags and turkeys.

At 23 Cinderella Street, Machans Beach, two shirtless men in shorts were drinking icy-cold beer and sharing a joint. There was some actual sunshine shining into the house, and Led Zep's 'Over the Hills and Faraway' was rocking out of the JBL speakers.

"Well, happy bloody Christmas," said Seth. "We might be a couple of orphans, but we've got enough beer, rum, food and choof for the whole family."

"If you hadn't told me it was Christmas, I wouldn't have known. I never do," said Hugh.

"You don't do Christmas with your family?"

"Not lately."

"There's no family do?"

"Oh, there's a do alright. Christie Chrissies are famous.

There's a big lunch spread with the whole family and their favourites and friends, plus a full cast of waiters, nannies and chefs. Eighty people usually."

"Is that right?"

"If the weather's good, it's out on the lawn in full view of the harbour with the bridge, the Opera House – all that shit."

Hugh took a big drag on the joint, passed it to Seth, and watched as a pelican passed overhead. Shaking his head in wonder, he exhaled.

"Man, my family are so different to me. Smoking dope, fucking three or four people in a night," he waved towards the stereo. "Page. They have no idea.

"My father hated the sixties and everything it meant. My sister pretended she understood, Mother didn't give a shit. I left school wanting to be Hendrix. I dug Gough and Brett Whitely; my father loathed them. Me having top-ten singles and being on TV wasn't an achievement to him – it was just confirmation of what a fuck-up I was."

"Awww, mate," said Seth, thinking of the money he was making reinforcing Christie Senior's viewpoint. Without too much guilt, he passed the joint back.

"Well, if it's any consolation, my folks didn't approve of my choices either," he said.

"Growing and selling dope?" Hugh took a big toke.

"No, they didn't know about that, but they knew I was fighting and rooting around Cairns, driving shit-hot cars and bikes, hanging out with rock'n'rollers, rev-heads and hippies. They wanted me to go to uni and have a family."

Hugh returned the spliff and caressed his chest.

"But they didn't know their son was an outlaw, a dope fiend, and a cocksman supreme," he said.

Seth rolled his eyes. "You're full of it, mate."

"So, who did you first have sex with?" said Hugh.

"Jesus, Hugh, I don't bloody remember. Besides, I don't talk out of school. Especially not to blokes."

"Oh, so if I was a woman, you'd tell me?"

"Turn it up, will ya?"

"You ever fuck two women at the same time?"

Seth stood up, prickled by a memory. The last time that happened had not been cool. Pretty sad actually.

"How's your beer?" he said.

"Well, this is unexpected – Seth Kelly, prude."

Trailing smoke from the joint in his mouth, Seth went to the fridge, grabbed two more stubbies and snagged the bottle of Bundy. Hugh bloody Christie, he thought. Super cool bloke one minute, total wanker the next. Ignoring the guitarist's combative grin, he put the bottle on the table and the roach in the ashtray. Going over to the stereo, he lifted the needle off the last track on the side. He didn't like it – never had.

"Don't you like James Brown?" said Hugh.

"Sure, but why did they have to put it on the album?"

"They just had to give the drummer some more."

"Big mistake. D'Yer Mak'er too."

"True. Should have left the song writing to the talent."

"The guitarist?"

"The guitarist."

"Is that how it's gone with The Tygers?"

"Basically."

Seth put on Waka/Jawaka and as the crazy jazzed-out vibe of Big Swifty filled the room, he grabbed a couple of tumblers and re-joined Hugh on the couch.

"Want a nip?"

"I think I do."

Seth poured them measures closer to chomps than nips, happy that Hugh had stopped stirring him.

With some Bundy onboard, they enthusiastically talked about what they really liked – music. After Zappa, the new Pretenders went on the Thorens turntable: Bad Boys Get Spanked cracking them up, Talk of The Town silencing them. For a minute.

Soon it was time for another joint, another chomp of rum and a beer. Going full-bore now, Hugh waved a finger at Seth, his voice loud. Seth nodded and yeah-yeah-yeah-ed – thinking about the next album to put on.

The track finished. As he got up, so did Hugh, still in full flight and unwilling to lose his attention. The cramped space between the lounge and coffee-table brought them together chest-to-chest.

What an uncoordinated drongo thought Seth. He began to step back, but Hugh threw his arms around him and kissed him full on the mouth; tongue and all. Seth froze in shock, caught between the fact that a bloke was pashing him, and drunken pride that Hugh liked him this much.

He pushed his mate away and Hugh stumbled back. Seth wiped his mouth. Yuck – he hated the taste of ciggies.

"Well, that's ruined Christmas," said Hugh defiantly. "Big strapping country boy finds out his mate from the city wants to fuck him."

Seth didn't like that. It was sleazy, not like a friendship at all. Hugh laughed unhappily.

"I always fancied you, man. Tried to get you upstairs a few times with the girls, but they thought you were scared of offending me or something. What a nice guy."

Blokes with blokes didn't worry Seth. It was none of his business. In Sydney, fellas had come on to him, usually with words, though he'd copped a few squeezes and bum-slaps. He took it as a compliment, but made it real clear to the persistent bastards exactly what was what. It sure made him think about the shit women put up with.

But what had him spinning a bit now was it being Hugh. It was unexpected and unwelcome. This was a paid job in his house, and, Christ, don't tell me he's been . . .

"No, I haven't been playing with myself over you in my room at night," said Hugh. He plonked down on a chair.

"That's why I'm here. I fucked the wrong man."

Seth needed a drink. He picked up the rum and took a good swig.

"He's a business partner and old school-friend of my father's," said Hugh.

Seth nearly spat rum. A balloon of crazy laughter burst out of him. Hugh fucking Christie!

"Oh, yeah, I really screwed up!" crowed Hugh.

Spurred on by Seth's incredulous mirth, he raced the words out, trying to beat the giggles.

"Down in the pool house at home! Father walked in!"

A great howl of laughter filled the room and they fell about in hysterics. When they finally settled, they sat back down and blinked away tears. Hugh sighed happily.

"Father was so, *so* angry. He had no idea, about me, or David, who's married with three kids. He *hates* poofters, with an absolute vengeance, and we seared an image onto his brain he'll never forget."

"Whoa! Stop," said Seth.

"Oh, that's right – you don't talk out of school, do you? Especially to blokes."

"Especially about blokes."

"What a gentleman," said Hugh. "Anyhow, Father blew his top and threatened to cut me off. I don't know how it went with David, but he's a tough man. How I like 'em."

What a story, thought Seth. Then he saw Hugh looking at him like they were best friends and the vibe was so good he looked right back at him, thinking – how is this, a great muso has become a mate. Then the bastard spoilt it.

"How do you know you don't like it?"

"Put a sock in it, Hugh."

Seth got up, finishing his beer, feeling frustrated, even a bit sad. Why can't we just be friends? he thought.

Hugh looked at him and his face melted with drunken profundity.

"No, no, no." He staggered to his feet. "Give me a hug, man. Seriously."

"Just – stop, OK?"

"No, no. Please. Give me a hug. All of that aside, I love you, man. You are a real, true friend and I know you care about me. I am very lucky."

Abashed, but bloody pleased at this acknowledgement, Seth beamed unsteadily at Hugh.

"Give me a hug, Seth. No bullshit. Like brothers."

With a slap on the back, Seth embraced his friend and it felt like a little Christmas miracle.

And what a great little miracle it continued to be. They kept drinking, feeding stubbies through the freezer to get them icy, having shots of rum and a joint here and there. Fried prawns, tomatoes and rice were cooked and eaten, and they drank a bottle of red with that. Albums were played while Hugh hilariously dissected songs and bands, explaining the dynamics and motivations behind them. Seth loved it. It was the best Christmas.

When the rain started, the volume of the Lumens amp went up to compete with the ocean of sound breaking on the tin-roof. It was too much to talk over and they just sat there, drinking and passing an unneeded joint back and forth.

When the downpour eased then ceased, the album on the turntable was done. Seth couldn't summon the energy to change the record. Neither could Hugh, and they sat in smashed silence.

Now the darkness welled up inside and Seth looked at Hugh. I wonder what you'd do about a mate stuck deep in the shit, he thought.

Though royally out-of-it, Hugh caught his look.

"What's wrong?"

"I've got this mate in jail," began Seth. "A good mate."

Hugh sat up. "Yeah?"

"Yeah. He was set-up."

"Wow. So, what happened?"

"Mate, it's a story."

"Worse than mine?"

Seth slowly nodded, his brow tightening at the thought of the battle he was now close to losing.

"Tell me, Seth."

Hugh's face swum with concern and Seth felt grateful. His friend could see the weight he was carrying.

So, he told Hugh about Sabbo, and as he spoke it tore him up deep that he was telling a story that might very well have an end now. If he couldn't get Neary to tell the truth – the final screwed-up scene would be his mate rotting away in prison.

Fair and Proportionate

Boxing Day went by sleepy and hungover, the heat and humidity fierce, and the fans in the house got a real work-out. They didn't talk much, but the vibe between them was nice and mellow. The next day Hugh got back to work, and as the days sweated by, the household evolved a routine.

Seth got up and exercised along the beach. When he got back Hugh would have showered and shaved. He'd have his papaya – as he insisted on calling it – toast, coffee and a joint then play guitar; using the Phillips as an audio note book, for nine, ten – even twelve hours a day.

In full creative flow he began working up songs, trying out guitar parts and bits of vocals – sometimes singing a single line over and over, or just humming the melody. He also spent time with his Koss earphones on, listening to what he'd recorded and playing along with it.

The work he was putting in was phenomenal, and Seth got a sense of this being make-or-break for the guitarist. If he used his will and his talent, he might escape The Tygers – and his father, and soar among the stars a free man.

Seth was rapt; wonderfully distracted too, and instead of thinking about Sabbo, he spent hours just listening to Hugh; sitting at the kitchen table with the pedestal fan playing over him, or on the back porch sipping an ice-cold beer. One wet afternoon, all this audio alchemy bore fabulous fruit.

With a gust of wind that rattled the canna lilies against the glass louvres, another rain squall arrived, drumming up a crescendo on the roof. The noise drowned out a great part Hugh was working on; a soaring chorus with a solid gold hook, and he stopped and lit a cigarette.

The downpour lasted five minutes, making the gutter pipes gurgle. When it stopped, Hugh picked up his guitar and played the part with real confidence; the tempo crisp, the selection of notes settled upon, each one's attack and delay precise. It was the sound of a musician satisfied with his choices, and as he came to the end, he smoothly segued into a two-part thing he'd come up with a few days ago. It sounded faultless – just meant to be. A song had been born.

Seth was blown away. I've just heard a piece of magic being made, he thought. Speechless, he just sat there, and when Hugh looked at him, all he could do was grin. Eyes lit with excitement; the guitarist grinned back.

He now ran through it all again, getting the tempo just as he wanted – then hit the record button on the Phillips. With the dripping roof and the ping-ping and werp-werp of frogs in the garden as an accompaniment, he made a first recording. Seth got goosebumps; the playing wasn't just note-perfect – it was inspired.

When Hugh hit stop on the cassette recorder and slowly laid down his guitar, his face shone with euphoria.

"Mate," breathed Seth.

New Year's Eve came and went; Hugh uninterested in going out, and Seth happy about that. On the fourth, he went and saw Bob Loftus, and the lawyer listened without comment as he told him about Fuckinkev.

"Bastards," said Loftus, when he'd finished.

Seth told him about Neary.

"I want to give him another go," he said. "With a letter first. A letter from you."

The lawyer nodded fervently. "Yes indeed, we can't stop now. Good idea, Seth. My letterhead, some legal lingo, and a clear plan of action will carry weight and show serious intent. If we show him what the doorway looks like, I think he'll walk right through it."

You could bottle this bloke's confidence, thought Seth.

"What about Neary lying at the trial?" he said. "I think he's a bit gun shy about that. Might be good to have all that spelt out for him in the letter."

"That shouldn't be too much of a problem considering the circumstances," mused Loftus, "But I'll make some calls and get some advice. Now Gerry's getting an appeal, no question, but I've got urgent clients to attend to, so I'll have the letter drafted up in two, maybe three days' time. I'll ring you to take a look before we send it to Neary."

Seth put a full manila envelope the size of a paperback on the lawyer's desk. Loftus raised his eyebrows.

"Twenty-seven thousand dollars," said Seth.

The lawyer sat back and nodded with firm approval, looking for a moment like Mrs. Sampson.

"Very good. Thirty-five thousand dollars carries a lot of weight. OK, he gets half when he makes a statement then he leaves Cairns with his girlfriend. When we fly him back for his day in court – he gets the balance."

"I'll go with that," said Seth.

"And I believe there's another thing that might spur his co-operation," said Bob Loftus. "I'll put it in the letter."

"What's that?" said Seth.

"The man who witnessed his beating is now dead. The carrot's got bigger, but so has the stick."

On the fifth, Michael Christie rang and Seth went for a walk. When he got back, Hugh looked both happy and sad. The stink in Sydney had just about blown over and a ticket home had been booked. In six days, he'd be gone.

The next day was nearly sunny and Seth had his second morning cuppa on the back porch. Inside the house, Hugh was into it – but agitated. He couldn't find the right place on a recording, and instead of using his headphones he was fast-forwarding and reversing it across the playback head. When the phone rang, Seth was happy to tell him to stop for a minute.

It was Dad with a phone number for some work – a Mr Henderson up the coast at Kewarra Beach. Seth rang and he sounded like an old duffer. He didn't say much, like most clients, he wanted to talk about his problem face-to-face. Seth wrote down his address and was told to pop around any time after three.

Hugh finally sorted out his hiccup and began playing. In his room, Seth lay on the bed half-listening and half-reading a fat blockbuster of a book about a Pommy sailor ship-wrecked in 17th century Japan.

He made basil, cheddar and beefsteak tomato jaffles for lunch, followed by mainly mango, but minted, fruit salad. After eating, Hugh made a praying gesture of thanks and got back to work. Seth returned to the land of the Shogun.

A Ninja bastard attacked the sailor, and when Seth next looked at the time, it was pushing three. He washed his face, put on a shirt, and went to see about the job.

A few kilometres north of Cairns, hidden from the Cook Highway by cane-fields, were a string of bayside hamlets known as the northern beaches. These villages nestled along the classic tropical coast of the post-cards – white-sand beaches, shady beach almonds and palm trees. Right behind all this beauty were mosquito and midge infested melaleuca swamps that fed into blood-warm, mangrove-edged creeks. In the deluge of a big wet, or a cyclone, the swamps and creeks flooded, and the access roads to the beaches would disappear, stranding residents.

Machans Beach was the first of these hamlets; Kewarra Beach four more up, and within twenty minutes he was motoring up Kewarra Street – the main drag that ran parallel to the beach. Overhead, the sky was a bright mess of off-white and vivid blue, and through his open window a stiff breeze brought the salt tang of the bay.

There wasn't a soul around; everyone at work or hiding from the humidity inside. Seth saw an occasional vehicle in a carport, or parked on the sandy roadside, none flash.

He passed a Landcruiser with a battered dinghy on its roof, and there were more boats in front yards dozing on trailers, or hidden under leaf-spattered tarps.

Almost every house was single story; built with Besser bricks, or fibro and timber; all with corrugated iron roofs. This was a sleepy northern beaches village alright, though village might be too grand a word.

He found the house, number 62, up towards the end of the street. Parking across from it, he heard a dog barking. Henderson's house, set back fifteen metres from the road, had a concrete path to the front door. A weather-beaten driveway, also concrete, went down the side of the house to a rusting open-sided carport.

There was no car and Seth speculated that Henderson's wife had gone out with it. Maybe he had something to say he didn't want her hearing.

He crossed the road and the barking dog, alerted by him arriving, kept on playing sentry; its yapping coming from the back of the closest neighbour's house.

Going up the path, Seth saw the lawn was unkempt and shaggy, and in fully overgrown flower beds, vivid pink and white blooms lolled in the breeze.

At the concrete front landing, enclosed by a knee-high breeze-block wall and a small tin roof, he saw no door mat or shoes: just leaves and dirt pushed into the corners in a bad attempt at a clean-up. Maybe Henderson had no wife or family. Maybe the poor bastard was alone in the world.

He went into the landing and something caught his eye. Leaning over on the side wall he saw a single fresh tyre track in the grass by the driveway. Puzzled, he reached out and knocked on the door beside him.

As he took his hand away, two percussive booms nearly blew his ear-drums out. Splinters and dust erupted as two holes appeared simultaneously in the front door at chest height; bloody big holes and punched out semi-automatic fast. Some bastard was firing a Colt .45 pistol at him.

Leaping the wall, he dashed towards the next house, his boots hissing through grass. Behind him, the front door banged open; the dog now going nuts. Up ahead he saw an old wooden pole fence, a veggie garden behind it.

Boom! Boom! Big bullets zipped past his skull. Glass smashed at the neighbour's and a ricochet whined. At the old fence now, Seth saw it was hollowed out with rot and he ran right through it, sending spongy wood and white-ant muck flying.

In the neighbour's garden, the grass was properly cut, the vegetable-beds neat and mulched. The owner must be a keen gardener – and here he was – a bearded old bastard holding up a hoe and shouting, "What's in God's name is going on!"

Seth threw a look behind and saw a man in a motorcycle helmet running past the house towards the back, a gun in one hand. Mr Henderson my arse, he thought.

"Go away!" yelled the gardener. Seth slowed right down and the silly bugger feinted at him with the hoe. "Get off my property! I'm calling the police!"

"Sorry, mate, sorry," said Seth, and he jogged across the garden towards Kewarra Street. He heard the cough of a trailbike starting up behind him, and as the sound became an evil yammering, he broke into an all-out run.

Furious adrenalin spiked through him as he heard the trailbike come from around the back of number 62. The shooter was going to cut off before he could get to The Pig.

Out on Kewarra Street now, he took off in the opposite direction, to where the road ended and thick scrub and swamp began. The bike kept putting on speed and so did he – rocketing along like a cassowary was about to stick a claw up his bum.

The road favoured the bike so he jinked into the garden of the last house on the street, hoping no hoe-wielding owner, or savage dog would attack him. Windows were shut, the carport empty, and he ran through it. Bang! – a fishing-buoy hanging from a beam disintegrated, glass fragments pattering and zinging off jerry-cans and gas-bottles. Seth couldn't believe this – the bastard was firing the gun while riding a bike!

Out of the carport, he jumped kid's plastic toys, dodged a sagging blue paddling pool and pelted towards the false cover of a line of drying washing. He madly tried to look over it, searching for a back fence, a sand dune – anything that might be a barrier to the motorbike.

The volume of the pursuing bike changed, the sound of the two-stroke motor bouncing off the house's concrete walls. It was right up his arse now – the gun aiming at the back of his head.

Seth ran into bras, jocks and dresses, getting a whiff of sun-warmed cotton – and right there, standing upright wedged between the ground and the thick braided-wire of the washing line, was a bamboo pole; the old-style way of pushing the washing up away from the ground.

Grabbing the pole as he flew past, he flung it sideways, and the clothes-laden line dropped a good metre. Three seconds later there was a big metallic twang, the sound of the bike stalling – then a thud, followed by clattering.

Seth snatched a look; saw the riderless trailbike on the deck, spinning along throwing up sand and dirt; shirts, socks and panties jumping madly from the shock of the collision.

Because the rider had a bloody big gun, Seth didn't stick around to see if he'd been knocked out. With a fast turn, he ran out onto the street again. Next door, the gardener was gone, probably calling the coppers like he said. Seth took another look behind.

Damn it – the rider was up already and running to his bike. I won't make it to the Pig in time, he thought. Even then, what's to stop him from driving alongside? A .45 round would go right through the door.

The scrub and melaleuca wetland, and the mangroves of Deep Creek where right there in front of him, but he might not make it out of the swamp alive. Getting caught knee-deep in the mangroves and mud, while wading the creek would get him shot in the back for sure.

He sprinted across the road and into Albatross Street, where a little creek ran parallel to the backyards of the houses on Kewarra Street. Getting off the gravel, he ran alongside the creek, and quickly identified the house up ahead that the Pig was parked outside of. He'd zip down the side of it and maybe affect an escape.

Behind him came the trailbike, its racket bawling down onto Albatross Street. The bastard had seen him.

Legs pumping, he got to the house and dived headfirst into the backyard a second before the bike roared into view. Jumping up, he used a small wooden boat sitting on ancient hardwood logs as cover, and ran across a tiny flower-edged lawn into the back of a fisherman's cottage.

The back of the house was a workshop, open-sided under a corrugated iron roof. The back wall was lined with jam-packed shelves, pieces of marine-ply, paint tins and oars. By the closed back door, next to flattened mud-crab traps, there was a busted old sofa and a rusty fridge.

He ran straight in and slid behind a small wooden dinghy leaning in a corner. It seemed unlikely he'd been spotted coming in here, but if he had; he was trapped, his back truly against the wall. Over the war-drum beat pounding in his chest, Seth listened to the approaching bike.

It slowed, stopped and idled – then came on, checking each backyard. The bastard must know his time's limited, thought Seth. Those big loud gunshots will have the cops here soon.

Now the bike was at the fisherman's shack and it came grumbling and chattering into the yard. Seth looked at the dirt floor and up at the cluttered shelves of the back wall for a weapon – something like his Turnbull speargun, or even a big bolt to throw.

With a rev of the engine, the bike turned away, and Seth listened as it went next door, and then to the house after. Inside the fisherman's cottage he now heard a man's voice speaking. Mate, don't come out now, he thought.

A minute later the bike returned, moving slowly, the

rider still on the look-out. When it got down the end of the houses, it turned back out into Albatross Street, and with a thwarted yowl, went full throttle onto Kewarra Street, and back out towards the highway.

Seth whistled softly and slowly came out from behind the dinghy. He looked at the back door. It was closed.

OK, he'd quietly nip down the side of the house onto the street, get in the Pig and casually drive away. Hopefully, no one would connect his vehicle to the gunfire.

"That's your Land Cruiser out front, hey boy?" said a gravelly old voice close-by. "I give the number plate to the police just now."

Seth looked around. No-one. He crouched and looked under the work bench then quickly ran his eyes over the tin roof and packed shelves.

"I saw you out there – running for your life," said the voice. "Sorry, son, but you need to talk to the police."

Seth stepped away from the back wall and looked at it. Amongst a hundred items on shelves or hanging up, there was a little open window into the house.

On its ledge was a good-sized golden cowrie and a few stainless-steel marine screws. Around the edge there were keep-sakes; a big, white sea eagle feather and a blurred black and white photo of dark-skinned young men, bare-chested and proud against the sea. There was a beautifully made bone dolphin on a leather cord – and a sepia-toned, spider-poo spotted drawing of the sexiest mermaid Seth had ever seen. In the middle of this frame of memories was a wrinkled, mahogany coloured face, with a pair of bright eyes that looked like they could see far beyond any horizon.

That scotched nipping off quietly, thought Seth, and he forced himself to smile at the old bloke. You couldn't blame him really; guns going off, trailbikes in back yards. It was a bit much.

"Haven't heard that sort of racket since Bougainville," said the old bloke. "Big gun, aye? You ever hear a Tommy gun going off?"

Seth nodded; last year a fella had used one to try and turn him into goanna food. The old bloke nodded back.

"Vietnam?" he said.

"Almost. I got my name picked but . . . it's a long story."

"By the look of you, they're all long stories."

That made Seth laugh, and the old bloke liked that.

"Well, if you're not running off, I'll come out," he said. Seth felt like he'd just passed some sort of test.

The cottage floorboards creaked, and the back door opened. A tabby kitten appeared, ran down the steps and started head-butting Seth's legs. The old bloke, small and wiry, stepped into the doorway. He looked savvy and tough, and his eyes looked over the big, blonde intruder on his property.

Seth held his hands so they could be seen. The old bloke nodded at that, and then came bare-foot down the worn back-steps. There was a jingle of bottles as he opened the rust-pocked fridge. "You wanna beer?"

Seth sure did, and they went and sat on the front steps, drinking in comfortable silence until the police arrived.

"You got the flash bullymen - the D-tectives," said the old bloke as the cops got out of their unmarked Falcon.

He wasn't wrong, the uniformed boys had been left in the sartorial dust by the two Ds in their shiny brown shoes and patterned ties that had been cool in 1973. Maybe. One D had sideburns, Dennis Lillee's moustache, and an infant beer-belly. The other one, pale as a maggot, was a skinny runt without hips, chest or arse.

Seth stifled a groan – he knew these pricks. They'd tried to squeeze him last year with threats, and he'd closed his front door on them.

"OK, who made the call?" said Sideburns as he walked up. The old bloke nodded like he was at an auction. The cop nodded back, looked at Seth and his eyebrows shot up in recognition. He hissed his discovery to his mate. The maggoty D stared at Seth then hurried back to the car and got on the radio. The old fisherman gave Seth a smile of weary sympathy then went inside and closed his door.

Sideburns had a really weird expression on his face – something like delight, even respect.

Though he didn't like them, Seth didn't instinctively hate cops like some of his mates did. Uncle Don had been one, and he'd had a couple of schoolmates who'd joined the force. Older cops were easier to handle; products of a less venal time, but most were as mean and bigoted as the new boys. Sure, there were many good cops; men whose sense of justice hadn't been amputated; men who'd resisted the depravities of power, and the pull of rancid opportunity. But if you spoke up, like Uncle Don, you were posted to oblivion, stonewalled, or hounded out.

Truth was, Queensland cops had the worst reputation in the country. Violent as any gang of crims, the bad boys enjoyed the unstinting support of the premier of the state and his rotten bunch of henchmen – no matter who they bashed, raped, ripped off, or murdered.

Growing up as a rebel, and a criminal by dint of dope, Seth had been unbelievably savvy. He'd been arrested just once; for beating a filthy rapist into a pulp. The boys at the station had been coldly appreciative; one old bastard intimating that if Seth had killed the grub it would have been more than fine by him.

And right now he was getting more of that good-on-ya-son vibe; this time from a mongrel cop who at their last meeting looked like he wanted to flog Seth with a piece of rusty mooring cable. The maggoty D came scampering back. "It's all good," he informed his partner.

Sideburns nodded, still grinning at Seth. The Maggot, unwilling to make that sort of commitment just yet, stared at Seth like he was a bottle of twelve-year-old scotch he'd found next to him in bed. It was horrible; the prelude to a leer or worse.

When Seth gave them a statement, describing exactly what had transpired – from the initial phone call from Dad, through to having a beer with the old bloke here – the Ds just nodded along, looking for all the world like two star-struck teenage girls. Seth felt ill.

Fortunately, they rallied and got back to it, and he gave them a reconstructive tour of the attempt on his life. After inspecting number 62, dusty and empty with a forced side window, they eyeballed the bullet holes in the door, and talked to the gardener next door. All brown teeth and white nose hair, the green-thumb angrily described how his peaceful afternoon had been shattered by gunplay.

Unprompted, but knowing it was coming, Seth gave his telephone number to the old bastard so he could pay for his rotten, broken fence.

Over at the clothes-line next door, the Ds made noises of appreciation as Seth told them about his move with the bamboo pole and wire washing line.

"Pity it didn't take his head off," said the Maggot.

"I would have stamped him when he came off the bike," said Sideburns.

"Yeah, that's a fair and proportionate response," said the Maggot.

"Fair and proportionate!" Sideburns' mo jumped like a shot crow. "It's not even halfway fair."

"Yeah, right," scrambled the Maggot. "Shooting him in the leg would be fair, I'd say."

When Seth answered the inevitable question as to who he thought his assailant was with a shake of his head, the Ds got seriously reflective as though racking their brains on his behalf. Seth almost laughed at this cop bullshit.

Back at the cars, the Maggot's tongue peeked from between bloodless lips as he took a statement from Seth. Sideburns then advised Seth that they'd catch up with him in the next few days with further questions; maybe an interview at the copshop on the Esplanade.

The business at hand seemed all done and the Ds now stared at Seth like he was a prize fish. Sideburns quickly looked around as though there might be someone on the empty street then came in close, his partner also hustling in, the anticipation on their faces like schoolboys about to open a Playboy.

"So, mate . . ." Sideburns began, and he quickly wiped his moustache a few times. The Maggot, now comfortable with it, smiled winsomely.

I'm gonna spew, thought Seth. For some reason these pricks are barring-up over me. I think I'd prefer a bashing.

"So . . . up at the Mitchell, hey?" said Sideburns. "You knocked him."

Now Seth got it. The Mitchell River had been at the guts of his previous encounter with these arseholes. What they didn't know then, but apparently knew now, was that he had killed a man out there – a stone-cold hardcase too.

And these sick bastards loved him for it.

Not because he'd taken a bad man down, like the rapist he'd smashed, no, these two clowns thought he was just like them – an aficionado of menace and violence, guns and death. They loved the macho drama and it didn't get much better than getting chummy with a brutal killer of other brutal killers.

"I don't know what you're on about," said Seth.

The two Ds hooted and cawed with delight. They hadn't expected anything less.

Chuckling, stinking of cigarettes, old sweat and beer, they milled around soaking up his mana, and Seth had to quickly step away before one of the grubs could slap him on the back.

Pulling into the carport at his place, a wave of weariness hit him – understandable really, as he'd nearly been sent off early with a couple of .45 slugs in his chest. At the open laundry door, he took a peek into the house.

In the lounge by the windows, Hugh was sitting with the Phillips recorder; headphones on as he listened to a playback. Seth turned away, trying hard to shut off the huge alarm bell ringing in his head.

He snuck back to the Pig and drove off, and on O'Shea Esplanade he pulled over at Sunny's place. The windows were all shut; no car in the driveway, and he sat there and tried to deal with the world of escalating madness he'd got himself into.

The man who'd tried to kill him had worn a full-face helmet, but Seth knew who he was. That trick of driving balls-out on a motor bike while firing a big pistol? He'd seen someone do that before – with Alex and Gordy Mac cheering him on.

I must be getting soft, he thought. Santa Claus isn't real and Liam Mac isn't on the Gold Coast either. I'm in deep now. This is war and it's going to go all the way.

He breathed deeply, knowing what must come next. It wasn't easy contemplating it.

Then with a spurt of relief, he saw Sunny's Honda Civic come down the esplanade. She waved at him as she pulled into her driveway.

He got out and walked over, tearing grim thoughts from his mind. Sunny was unlocking her front door as he came through the gate.

"Hey Seth, were you waiting for me?"

Seth smiled, but in his head, he heard the demonic roar of Liam's trail-bike eating up the ground behind him.

"Aww, yeah," he said, and her dear, sweet face and solid

presence filled him like desperate medicine. She watched him cross the veranda; suddenly alert, her eyes searching his. As he came up to her, Seth gave into emotion.

"Oh mate," he said, his voice suddenly near breaking. "I just had this thing happen and . . . give us a hug."

Without waiting for a reply, he put his arms around her and drew her in, gratefully surrendering to the sanctuary of her. Sunny tried to pull away, but he couldn't let go yet.

Sudden shocking agony destroyed the muscle power in his legs, and he slowly fell down and curled up like a bug. Footsteps ran and a door slammed. Sunny had driven her knee, good and hard, up into his groin.

Pain pinned him like heavy gravity to the wooden floor. He heard the key in the lock and then Sunny running to the back of the cottage. In a lonely miserable place, he fought the urge to empty his stomach onto the veranda. After an endless minute laying there, he sensed movement out on the street. Looking up, he saw a boy standing by the gate.

"What did you do?" said the kid in a fierce voice.

Seth groaned and slowly uncurled. It was a real effort.

"You did something!" yelled the kid.

Ignoring Inspector Midget, Seth got to his feet. Behind him the house was silent. Across the road, the sea was a giddy, moving mass. Leaning on a veranda post, he found his knees, and with equilibrium attained, tottered down the steps and out the gate, the kid watching him like a school prefect.

"What's wrong with you? Why you walking like that?"

I hope you never find out, thought Seth. Trying hard not

to lay down and curl up again, he hobbled away along the grass verge. "You did something wrong," shouted the kid.

Don't I know it, thought Seth.

In the Pig, he surfed waves of nausea, and as the sickly swell subsided, he began to sort through the anger, shame and anguish. Oh man, he'd really cocked it up with Sunny.

The nice vibe between them had come from a year or so of weekly, at times daily, contact: cheery waves from their cars in passing, laughter at the corner store, a couple of long conversations, and some short ones over cuppas, sometimes a joint. All this had created a real sense of cool intimacy; of adults just hanging out and not being hung up on getting it on. Now he'd blown it all away.

The potential for some sweet, naked loving had been there; he'd seen it in her eyes, and he could sure dig that happening, but what he'd really wanted, needed, just then was the blessed relief and the comfort of her. Holding her close, he could shut out the fear – if only for a moment.

But he'd become irresistible in the worst possible way, not letting her speak . . . and not letting her go.

Imagine how you'd feel, he thought. A bloke suddenly grabbing you in close, his arms tight across your back.

Yeah, that's right – you'd knee him in the balls.

A Bit More Class

Back home he waved at Hugh as cheerfully as he could, and the guitarist, still plugged into the Phillips, floated a smile back. In the shower, he saw that everything was still in the one piece and that was something. The pain would pass and he'd try very damn hard to make amends with Sunny, but right now he had a monster of a fish to fry. As sure as death, the Macs would come at him again.

After downing half a Vicodin and gratefully laying down on his bed, he thought about the next move. There were a few options, but he didn't like any of them.

He could take to the tall timber, but abandoning his home, his business, and the command of his own destiny would be an emasculating capitulation he couldn't wear. Now he felt Neary's rage at that diabolical helplessness — its poison killing by degrees.

Or he could roll over like a cowed dog, banish Sabbo from memory, and live with the Mac's advances.

No way, get fucked, fuck off.

Or he could go in hard and fast – gutting them before they got another chance.

Fury made him softly groan. He'd get Neary onboard now; they'd shoot the Macs' lights out and disappear their earthly remains. He should go over to Aeroglen right now, set the wheels in motion, take some cash . . .

But it wasn't just him on the battlefield. He had Hugh, and he wasn't just a job. He was a friend now, these last few weeks being proof of that. With four days left as a paid minder, his first task was to secure his charge. The Macs had lured him out of his home to put him offside, but they might not be so worried next time.

He gingerly got up, put on some footy shorts then casually went out the back. Crouched at his garden stash, he brushed away mulch, dirt and dead hibiscus flowers from the top of the waterproof pipe. Unscrewing the lid, he removed a sealed plastic bag.

Inside the waterproof bag was a Colt Python revolver, a speed-loader, and a half-full box of rounds. He checked the pistol; it was clean, oiled and unregistered – and the instrument of at least one death. He put the ammo back and resealed the stash. The speed-loader and gun were loaded; twelve .357, hollow-point magnum bullets in all, and he went and put them under a pillow on his bed. Then he took the phone on extension to the back porch and found Les' number in his address book.

His ex-army mate lived up near Kuranda on a big bush property. Hidden away there, Hugh could keep working on his music until it was time to go. And Les was a ballistics expert who kept a small arsenal of guns.

But Seth would have to tell him about the attempt on his life – he couldn't bullshit his mate.

After years of wartime service, Les avoided violence like the plague. He might agree, like a good mate, but asking him would put a good-sized dent in their friendship – maybe even begin its demise.

Other mates with bush properties came to mind before he had a fantastic idea. Why not hop on a plane to Sydney and hole up with Hugh in a nice hotel until the contract with Michael Christie expired? Rustling up the Yellow Pages, he phoned Ansett, who told him the first available flight was tomorrow afternoon. He booked tickets, getting an extra seat for Hugh's guitars.

Pleased with this shot of immediate action, Seth took the phone back in and listened to a rhythm part until the guitarist noticed him. Stopping mid-stroke, Hugh pulled the headphones up into his long hair.

"What's up, man?"

"Mate, can we talk for a moment?"

Hugh frowned and smiled at the same time.

"Can it wait a tick?" he said. "I'm *really* close here."

The bloke was just about pleading.

"Yeah, yeah, of course."

Knowing that a drink always helped a painkiller come on, Seth sat on the back porch with a beer and the frogs, and watched the light go.

Thankfully, the trip to Sydney kept his mind occupied. He'd have a great time checking out the clothes shops, and he'd catch up with Laidlaw and other good mates – maybe even meet a nice lady.

Around seven Seth made tea: lamb-chops, minted peas and carrots, baked potatoes and sour cream. When it was ready, Hugh came and sat down, grinning like a horse with a haybale. "So, what's cooking, Joe?"

"OK, listen, we're going to Sydney tomorrow. We'll get in around six. You can choose the hotel."

The guitarist stared at him. "Seriously?"

Seth nodded. Hugh looked over at the Phillips and his guitars, the view of the garden, and pouted mournfully.

"Do I have to pack up now?"

"No, no – keep going. Eight o'clock tomorrow night and you'll be all set up and writing songs again."

"Why?"

"Look . . . it's just better that I take you back a little earlier."

"This to do with your friend in jail?"

Seth nodded.

"Really?" Hugh looked thrilled. "You think something could happen here?"

"Pretty unlikely, but it's better we go. We'll find you a smoke when we get there and you can just keep working. Yeah?"

Hugh looked at him, his face fiercely contrite.

"Oh, yeah. I've got to keep working. I can't stop now. But you don't have to come. Unless you really want to."

"I'm coming."

Hugh looked chuffed.

"I signed a contract," said Seth.

The guitarist nodded seriously, and then looked around the house, his eyes lingering on the front door.

"Wow, this is like a movie."

Yeah, thought Seth, but with an ending you do not want to see.

After dinner, Hugh got back into it. Seth rang up Dad and told him about Sydney; spinning some bullshit about having to get Hugh to a sudden meeting with his record label. When he hung up, he let Hugh's playing dilute his shame. One day I won't have to lie to Dad, he promised himself.

He was packing a bag in his room, when he heard a car come down the street and pull up outside. Grabbing the gun from his bedroom, he checked that Hugh was still in headphones world, and then ducked out the back door. He quietly went up the side of the house and peeped around the corner.

In the diffused wash of light coming from the lounge, he saw a Ford Falcon with two men inside it talking; one smoking a cigarette.

It didn't look like they'd come to kill him, so he put the gun into the waist-band of his shorts at the small of his back and approached the car. Sudden torchlight blinded him.

"Get that off me!' he yelled.

The light went off and the Maggot giggled. Next to him the half-pissed voice of Sideburns rang out.

"Hey, there he is – bloody Magnum, P.I."

Seth became acutely aware of the Python's weight.

Sideburns got out and leaned on the roof of the Falcon. In the dim light Seth saw the glint of a 375 ml spirits bottle in one hand and the orange dot of the smoke in his mouth.

"Wanna drink?" said Sideburns.

"What do you want?" said Seth.

"Like we said this arvie – a few more questions."

"Here?"

"Yeah, the world is our office."

The Maggot grinned from the car like a truant kid.

Seth waited, thinking about the strength of the elastic in his shorts. Sideburns took a swig on the bottle.

"The motorbike was stolen. No witnesses, no prints, no skid-marks on the seat. Didn't find any of the five bullets fired at you either."

"We didn't look," said the Maggot.

"What for?" said Sideburns. "It's only a problem for us if normal people get hurt."

"Who's got it in for you?" said the Maggot.

"I told you blokes – I've got no idea. So, is that the only question?"

"What about those two drop-kicks at Scott Street?"

"Who?"

The Maggot's eyes bored in. Sideburns laughed.

"Me and Tim here have a theory," he said. "This known criminal associate of the MacIntyre brothers is discovered turning into fertiliser in beautiful downtown Cairns. Then this other criminal associate of theirs nearly gets a couple of extra arseholes put into him at Kewarra Beach today. Looks to us like the Macs are clearing some scrub."

"I'm no associate of theirs," said Seth.

"Who?"

"Get fucked."

The Ds chuckled. They were having fun.

"I'd be worried," said Sideburns like a smartarse.

"Real worried," said the Maggot.

"You wanna lend of a gun?" said Sideburns.

Gravity pulled on the Python.

"Or just tell us what's going on. We're not scared of the Macs. Mate, your future could be rosy with us onside."

Seth had to act, so he made with the jabbing indignant hands and gave them what for.

"No, bugger you! You bastards want to ask questions? I'll come down the Esplanade in broad daylight, alright? I'm not standing here in the dark listening to you pricks try to put your bullshit jig-saw puzzle together."

Still talking, he moved towards the front door, walking sideways as though about to turn away in disgust at any moment. In further decoy, this outrage was delivered with angry stabs of a finger. The two Ds grinned happily.

"Whatever you're cooking up to pour on me won't work. I'll see my lawyer tomorrow! I'll phone the ombudsman."

"Hoo-hoo – check this bloke out," said Sideburns.

Seth felt the door mat at his heels. Reaching behind, he found the doorknob and opened the front door.

"This is the second time you've come to my house trying to rev me up. Happens again and I'll kick up a big bloody stink. You just watch me!"

The gun fell, thumping loudly on the floorboards inside. Seth pretended to stumble backwards into front room, his heels banging on the wooden floor like the Python. The Maggot shrilled with laughter. Seth kept it up.

"It might be fun and games to you bastards, but aren't there murders and real police work to be done?"

Locating the gun with his foot he pushed it behind some swim-fins. It was time to wind it up now.

"You blokes have been warned. I'll be telling my lawyer about this. *Do not* come around here again!"

He closed the door and turned to go. Sideburn's liquor bottle smashed into it with an explosive bang and tinkle. Seth nipped over to the loungeroom door and looked in. Hugh, headphones in place, was nodding away. Seth went back to the front door and flung it open.

He smelt whiskey and heard a metallic click. Under the black cowl of the big mango tree and lit by the sepia light of the lounge, the Maggot was a nightmare child staring from the car window. Sideburns, his arms straight out on the car roof, was aiming his revolver at Seth.

The swamp smell of the river came in on a breeze. Further up the street a mob of curlews started screaming. As still as carved wooden statues, the three men watched each other.

Then Sideburns laughed, a raucous whooping that rose up from his chest in awe-filled recognition of the moment that had just passed. "Tell that to your lawyer," he said.

"You bastards don't scare me," said Seth.

Sideburns grinned, uncocked his gun and put it away. The Maggot pursed his little mouth and winked.

"You're a funny bastard," said Sideburns. "It was worth coming out here to see you spit the dummy."

"Well now you've had your jollies – piss off."

"Shouldn't look a gift horse in the mouth, mate."

Seth stared at them until Sideburns grunted.

"Fuck ya then."

The Maggot turned to face the windscreen; ready to go. Sideburns shook his head. "It's your funeral, mate."

Then to Seth's absolute relief, they pissed off.

In a daze, he quickly broomed the broken glass off his door-step onto a laid-out newspaper, then balled it up and binned it.

Inside, an oblivious Hugh was picking out a lead line. Seth put the pistol under his pillow, then got into Hugh's eye-line. The guitarist pulled the headphones up.

"What's up, Seth?"

"I'm knackered, hey. I'm gonna crash."

"Sleep well, man," said Hugh with a radiant smile.

As he went to his bedroom, Seth wondered if he'd ever had a day make a convenience of him quite like this one had.

It was just after dawn. The daylight was muted by an overcast sky, but everything outside shone with a dull, wet light. Heavy showers were coming in at intervals from the bay. They hadn't woken Seth up, because he hadn't slept.

A couple of times he'd even gone and stood under the little roof just outside his front door; the Python in his fist. Surrounded by warm night, the smell of whiskey strong, he'd listened carefully for the first wrong sound.

He got up, made the bed. Over a quiet cuppa, he leafed through his address book for 02 prefix numbers, thinking of who he might call in Sydney. Hugh appeared and made his coffee. After the first mouthful, he sighed with opulent pleasure and raised his mug at the bag of coffee on the Formica counter-top. "Oh Mareeba, I love you!"

"Take it with you. I can send you some as well."

Hugh nodded happily. "Will do, and yes please."

Using up the bacon, Seth made breakfast, and while he had another cuppa, Hugh made a final recording that was animated, precise, but beautifully spacious. Seth listened, standing where he could see both the back garden and the street outside.

Almost as soon as Hugh finished, it began to rain again.

"Well, how's that for timing?" he said, smiling out at the falling rain. He packed up the Phillips and put the guitars in their cases. Then he looked around at the loungeroom and blew it an affectionate kiss. "I've got to come back, man. I really do."

Seth didn't mind that, and he had a shower and shave, patted on some cologne then packed his toiletry bag. As he dressed, he admired the pistachio green silk shirt he'd spent thirty bucks on at Tom Hull's. Watch out Sydney, he thought, dredging up a winning smile for the mirror.

Hugh made another coffee, and Seth had a pot of tea to use up the milk. When the rain stopped, Seth reckoned a drive up the coast could be fun. With a few hours to kill, they could have lunch and a couple of beers at Ellis Beach on the way back, and then go straight to the airport from there.

While Hugh had a shower, Seth began locking up. From the street came the deep muttering of a big car, its wheels slowly popping on the gravel. Looking through the front room window he saw a nice bronze and white VJ Valiant two-door come to a halt. The engine was turned off, and in the silence a pigeon cooed.

Seth breathed deeply, his body tensing for a dash to the Python. The driver got out and looked over at the house, and the sight of her brought the biggest smile to Seth's face. If there was anyone on the planet that could raise his spirits right now – it was Stasia.

They'd had a thing: four wild months five years ago, a stack of great times in Sydney in '79, and a fair few spontaneous nights here and there. But beyond all that, she had to be one of the coolest people he'd ever met.

Stasia knew how to party, her laughter contagious, but she could stop fights and mind-games; often before they started. You'd never call her one of the boys, but she'd grown up with five tough brothers and comfortably stood as an equal with men. She could knowledgeably dominate a conversation; cars, drugs, footy, she knew a heap, or just cut through boasts and bullshit with insouciant ease.

Most blokes handled it well, pleased to be talking with Stasia, because not only was she on the money with what she said – she also looked better than great.

Seth followed his smile out to her, and like always, her pin-up curves zonked him good, her lusciousness set off by her cool sense of style; an effortless mix of hippy-gypsy witchery and revhead rock and roll. Kohl-eyed and be-ringed in black jeans and fine leather boots, she threw out her arms to him, making her antique lace top rise even further above her smooth sun-browned tummy.

"Nice car," said Seth. "When did you get that?"

"A few months ago, stranger. Hey, you're looking pretty swish there yourself."

"I'm flying to Sydney this arvie," said Seth as he came

up to her. Stasia, smelling of India or Asia, or something even more exotic, embraced him, smooching him on the cheek with a big breathy 'Mmmmh.'

Ohhh, let me die now, he thought.

Then Stasia leaned back against the Valiant and looked at him with odd appraisal. They hadn't seen each other for a while, but Seth could see this wasn't just a social visit.

"So, what have you been up to?" he said.

"I've been at Sunny's."

"Sunny? You're mates?"

"Yeah, we met in Northern Rivers a few years ago. Been friends ever since."

Seth rubbed his stomach and studied the grassy scrub across the road. Stasia followed his gaze, and waited. Seth sighed and looked sideways at her.

"I really mucked up, hey?"

Stasia nodded sadly.

"I know you like the ladies, Seth, but you used to have a bit more class. Grabbing her like that really scared her."

Feeling more than stupid, Seth turned to her.

"Look, the truth of it is – I wanted a hug. Hopping into bed with her would've been nice too, but I really needed a hug, and I just grabbed her and . . . I didn't let go."

"Like a mum hug?"

"Well . . . sorta."

"And then she . . . ow. It must have hurt."

"Don't be a bitch, mate."

Stasia searched his face with sly, dark eyes.

"Something happening? You having a hard time?"

"I reckon."

"Crims and cops again?"

He nodded glumly.

"Huh. You must really dig the excitement."

"Far bloody from it, Stasia – it's ruining my life."

Two crested pigeons bobbed and pecked not far from them, and they watched them for a bit.

"Sunny knows she overreacted," said Stasia.

"Great. Good for her. I'm sorry."

Stasia watched the birds some more.

"OK, you keep this to yourself, Seth, and use it wisely with her. The man she was with before she came here, used to bash her. Rape her too."

"Oh, no," said Seth, feeling a rush of anger and guilt.

"She was with him for three years. He did a real number on her, psyched her out, controlled her. She's still getting over it and that might take longer than three years."

"Oh, poor Sunny. I didn't know."

"Yeah, it's not something you talk about."

"Sometimes I feel ashamed being a bloke."

"That's understandable."

"I don't do things like that, Stasia."

"But you know a bloke or two who have."

Seth ran a hand through his hair. Memory lurked, dark and dangerous as a stingray in the surf. Stasia's charcoal eyes contemplated him.

"I lived in a shithole of a town whose name I now never mention," she said. "I knew a woman there who finally got jack of it. She killed him."

"Why?"

"You'd have to be her to really know, hey."

"He was a real bastard to her."

"Oh, yeah. But she got ten years."

"Ten years. Jesus. That doesn't seem right."

"Hey, what's happening?" Bare-chested in his crimson flares, wet hair slicked back, Hugh sauntered up, his eyes sticking like honey to Stasia.

"Hey, I know you!" said Stasia. "Aren't you . . ."

Hugh nodded, expertly grinning at her excitement.

". . . Marc Hunter? Wow! The under-age song!"

"I'm not him," said Hugh, miffed at the piss-take.

"Isn't he?" Stasia looked at Seth with mock-seriousness.

He shook his head gamely, suddenly tired of the future. Stasia, picking up the vibe, put a hand onto Seth's cheek, and an ineffable warmth flowed from it. A simple smile touched her lips, and she softly said, "It's easy to stop all that shit if you don't like doing it anymore."

Then she slid into the Valiant, pulled the seat-belt down with a strong tanned arm and clicked it home. Looking at her, Seth saw a future he should be considering. With bullet-hole eyes Stasia brought him back to earth.

"Boys outgrow things and leave them behind," she said. "Otherwise, they never become men."

She started the car, fully decked him with her best smile yet, and growled off up Cinderella Street.

Hugh, to his credit, knew something of substance had transpired and he quietly trailed Seth back inside. At the door of his room, his bags ready on the bed behind him, he asked almost in reverence, "Who was that?"

Seth grinned mirthlessly, Stasia's words glowing like coals in his head. "My conscience," he said.

Now a final sort of silence filled the house and the sense of an ending was strong. Twenty-five days had passed, and stuff had gone down and things would never be the same again. Music had been made, songs created, and lightning had been caught in the jar.

It began to rain, and when Hugh went into his room to finish dressing, Seth put the Python and the speed loader in the dashboard stash in the Pig. Better safe than sorry. And the airport's twenty-four-hour security meant they'd still be there – and ready to go, when he returned from Sydney.

He unplugged the Luxman amp and Thorens from the wall and covered them with batik cloth; a second piece going over the rows of albums. It was only going to be five days, but electrical storms, geckos and little bastard bugs were the enemies of the tropical audiophile.

The downpour passed as Seth methodically shut all the glass louvre windows in the house, snapping the metal latches flush to the frames.

When the phone rang, Seth went over, somehow hoping it was Sunny – but the voice on the line sent an electric shock of bad vibes through him. It was Mrs Sampson.

The Green Arena

"Mr Kelly? Mr Neary got taken away by two men."

"When?"

"Just this minute."

"What happened?"

"They dragged him out, half supporting him and there was rope around his wrists and his mouth was gagged and he looked half conscious. They stuffed him into the back of a car – roughly, poor man, and then drove off."

"What did the men look like?"

"I couldn't see faces. They wore bandannas. Caucasian, short hair, one average height, one bigger – both strong and fit like yourself. One wore shorts, the other jeans."

Mrs Sampson was channelling every TV detective she'd ever seen.

"And the car?" said Seth.

"A small orange thing with two doors."

The Datsun SSS he'd seen Liam with at the Barbary Coast that night.

"I called the police, Mr Kelly, but I didn't see the licence plate this time. I'm so sorry."

"No, no – you did good, Mrs Sampson. I better go."

"Well, if you find them before the police do, give those horrors a real flogging from me!"

Hanging up, he stood stock-still. Those bastards were going to knock Neary, he knew that, but they were going to have a little chat with him first to find out if he'd opened his mouth. In Cairns, the bush was always close, and they could be up a dirt track or next to a mangrove creek in the next half hour. After smashing the Fossil, the Macs would disappear like the evil spirits they were. He was going to have to be very smart – and very quick.

He turned. Hugh was right there, staring at him.

"Hey Hugh, I have to pop out. Back real soon."

"You're going to help Sabbo?"

"Yep."

"I'll come with you."

"Nope."

As Seth ran to the carport, his bladder twanged from all the cuppas he'd had. Damn it, he needed a slash, and fast. Dashing into the garden, he went for his fly, but a female voice from next door made him look up. A woman was coming towards the window; his neighbour Rod's current girlfriend, and he went further down into the garden. Out of sight, he impatiently stood for a long minute while his mind scrambled through the possibilities. Job done, he zipped up, and bolted for the Pig.

Neary's place at Aeroglen was ten minutes away. With the Python onboard, Seth drove fast but careful, his logic and intuition in overdrive, and he had a sudden flash that felt right on the money. He reckoned he knew where the

Macs taking Neary, and leaving cosmic coincidence aside – there was a bloody good chance he was right.

In the next few minutes, he would see the Datsun going north on the Cook Highway. If he put his foot on it that is. And he did, speeding along the rain-slick road, the empty cane fields rushing past, the green range ahead steaming with cloud, and lo and behold – the big Kahuna Buddha bloke gave it up in spades.

As he approached the highway, he saw in the northward bound traffic – the orange SSS Datsun coupe. Seth slowed down almost to a crawl; timing it, and when he turned onto the highway, he had a buffer of six vehicles between him and the Datsun.

Driving on to Smithfield, past the servo and the old but not very curious Olde Curiosity Shoppe, his confidence in his bush clairvoyance grew. Sure enough, at Clifton Beach the Datsun turned at a cracked and mould-streaked sign that said – Hannan's Tropical Orchid. Mangos, Lychees and More! Just like he'd thought: Pete Neary was being taken to Sabbo's old garage.

As Seth drove past, he saw that the muddy drive curved away out of sight. Nearly two hundred metres up the road was a gravelled pull-over area under a big old mango tree. He pulled in, the Pig's wheels popping mango seeds, and scanned the scrub until he saw what he needed – wheel ruts going into the bush. He could park down there out of sight of the highway. And witnesses.

He bumped down the rough track until he was out of view then turned off the engine. He got the speed-loader and the Python out of the stash, stuffed the speed-loader in his trouser pocket then held up the shiny revolver and looked at it.

Why have you parked here? he asked himself. Because you're going to have a go at knocking the Mac brothers. It would solve a few problems, and he might even get to see next Christmas. Yeah, it was kill or be killed time.

"Is that real?" said a voice and Seth spun around. In the back, amongst camping gear was Hugh bloody Christie.

"What the fuck!" roared Seth.

"I want to help you, man!" Hugh cried. "It's going to be heavy, isn't it?"

"Fucking oath! What do you think this is?" Seth roared louder, shaking the Python in the air.

The guitarist faltered as realisation began to sink in.

Seth forced himself to calm down. As ridiculous as it was, Hugh wanted to be his wing-man. Nice thought, but as useful as a chocolate teapot.

"Hugh, really seriously now – you stay here in the truck. You understand?"

Hugh stared at him; his expression unreadable.

"Actually, you can help," said Seth, now seeing a way to hedge his bets. God knows what might go down now at Hannan's Tropical Orchard – but this might save his arse.

"Just tell me what to do," said Hugh.

"Hang on a sec," said Seth. He started the engine and backed up the track while Hugh excitedly stared at him. On the highway he did a U-turn, drove up to the carpark by Bransford's tackle-shop and turned off the engine.

"Come up here," he said.

Hugh scrambled into the passenger seat and sat there,

big-eyed and all ears. Seth pointed to the public phone by the tackle shop.

"OK, call the cops and tell them it's about the bloke who just got kidnapped in Aeroglen. They know about that."

"Kidnapped?"

"Yep." Seth now pointed to the orchard sign back across the highway. "Then tell them to go to Hannan's orchard at Clifton Beach and head up to the sheds at the back. Tell them that the kidnappers are armed and dangerous."

"Armed and dangerous?"

"Yep. You tell them that I've gone in there too. Describe me, and what I'm wearing, but you *do not* mention this gun. You got all that?"

Reality overwrote Hugh's face with fear as he nodded. Yes, mate, thought Seth. Here's far north Queensland in all its filthy technicolour glory. Write a song about this.

It was lucky he was wearing a natural-coloured green shirt and that his pants were a simple tan brown, but he needed something to hide his blonde hair in there. He took his floppy army green bush hat out of the glove box and put it on. Getting out, he put the pistol into his waistband and pulled the shirt over it. Then he leaned in the window. "Hey, Hugh."

"Yeah?"

"Thanks, man."

He ran across the highway and jogged to the orchard's driveway. Where it met the road, a squashed cane toad rotted in a big stinky puddle. Skirting the edge, he dashed up the gravelled drive, anxious to turn the bend before someone came around it. Wet guinea grass lapped at his pants, the smell of the bush strong, and when he came around the corner into a massive clearing the sound of a million insects electrified the air.

Fifty metres away was a high-set wooden Queenslander up on poles, its cheerful sky-blue paint job cancerous with mould, and to Seth's relief, there were no vehicles parked beneath it. The driveway continued past the house, gently rising up to another bend that disappeared into a stand of trees.

To the right, a few hundred metres away, a spur rose up above the tree-line, its dense jungle slopes vanishing into low brooding cloud. On the left, row after row of fruit trees stretched away. Behind the orchards was another heavily forested ridge, rising up to the cloud-shrouded ramparts of the Macalister Range less than two kilometres away. Hannan's Orchard lay in a natural amphitheatre, like a vast green arena awaiting battle.

Watching the windows of the house, Seth ran across squelching grass towards it. Underneath, he stopped and listened for TV or radio or the creak of floor-boards, but the shrill insect hum continued uninterrupted. Across the clearing, where the wall of jungle green started, there was a flash of brown as a pheasant coucal broke from the grass and flew into the trees.

He left the house, ran up the drive and went around the bend. Overhead, trees blocked out the sky and a corpse-like smell filled the air – a dead dog tree in flower, and he avoided breathing through his nose as he passed.

The trees ahead lightened, their dripping leaves taking on the sullen glare of the sun above the low cloud, as the end of the bend approached. Seth took the Python out and checked it. Around him, the ear-piercing singing of insect legs rose and fell in waves.

Moving forward carefully, he looked up the driveway into another big clearing. There was a dab of orange at the far end – the Datsun SSS coupe, and closer to him, still a few hundred metres away; the corrugated-iron sheds of Sabbo's garage. Out front of the first one sat a baby-poo green Suzuki four-wheel drive; likely a getaway car.

From behind him came the oop-oop-oop-oop cry of a pheasant coucal. Seconds later a potential mate joined in, and their urgent spooky sound peaked and then stopped.

Although he'd come perhaps five hundred metres from the Pig, his shirt was soaked and sweat greased his skull. The breath of the jungle's lungs, heated by the invisible sun overhead and held in under the layer of cloud, filled the amphitheatre with a solid block of warm syrupy air.

Seth watched, but saw no movement at the garage. The doors of both sheds were closed, and by the furthest one, two poinciana trees glowed vivid and crimson against the close grey sky, their great mass of blooms like Chinese fireworks frozen mid-burst. Between their big grey torsos, a blue tarp had been strung up; its concave centre a dark clot of seedpods, twigs and leaves; beneath it a stubbie-strewn plastic table and some steel-frame chairs; a couple of them laying on their sides.

At the first shed, Seth tried the doors of the Suzuki then systematically punctured the tyres with his pocket-knife. Air hissed behind him as he examined the ground ahead. In the bush beyond the clearing's edge, he could see the impressively wide crown of a huge fig tree rising up above a group of other large figs.

With eyes on the far edge of the clearing, he raced from the first shed to the second one; taking cover behind one of the poincianas. Close to the shed, three vehicles rotted in a thicket of snaky looking grass. Seth recognised one of them as the Dodge truck criminal's mailbox.

Now some wind came through, the leading edge of a squally shower sweeping in from the bay. The dirty blue tarpaulin above him swelled and rattled, vegetate debris skittering about, and poinciana blossoms spiralled down like orange-red confetti. An empty stubbie clinked; rolling back and forth on the table.

Seth, his face against the poinciana, saw something just a few centimetres away enter his peripheral vision, and he sprung back. On the tree trunk, at head-height, a giant centipede was speeding along on dozens of quick legs. It was one of those foot-long, black and green striped bastards that stung like blue buggery; roused from its usual terrestrial haunts by the rain. That's all I need, he thought – some excruciating poison pumped into my face.

Moving to the cover of the next poinciana, he observed the Datsun SSS parked by the wall of bush, and saw no-one in the car or skulking near it.

A dull roaring noise came in on the wind. Seth looked back the way he'd come and saw trees disappearing into moving sheets of pale grey. The tarp began to rattle and jump as the rain raced across the clearing.

This was good. The loss of visibility might help hide his run across the clearing, and in the bush, the noise would help him move unheard. He sprinted towards the Datsun, his loafers sinking into juicy wet grass, and the rain hit, popping in his ears and flooding his eyes.

At the high green wall of bush, he crouched next to the car. As the rain drummed down on its orange skin, he did a number on its tyres with his knife. Checking the jungle edge by the car, he saw the mouth of a track – a dark notch leading in under the big trees.

Despite the shrouding rain, he'd be a moving silhouette at the path's entrance, so he got down and crawled into the darkness. Inside, he slid away from the bright opening and allowed his eyes to adjust. A vast space appeared, like an organic auditorium; its floor devoid of vegetation and scattered with drifts of tiny fig leaves. Fallen branches lay here and there; overhead, a high roof of massed branches.

The rain pelted down in a dull roar as he crept into the grove of figs; his eyes alert for movement. Crab-walking along, he came to the first of many aerial roots that grew down from the huge fig tree branches above. The root, nearly a metre wide, was made of many strands melded together like acid-inspired macramé.

Seth now saw that the fig trees were very old. A hippie Dutchwoman had told him that they were worshipped as gods in India. Looking at these ancient specimens, that didn't seem so very strange.

Then he felt a chill of horror; the natural wonder of this place suddenly despoiled. Up there in the towering mass of trees something huge appeared to stir and uncoil. Beneath his feet, the ground seemed to moan. There was murder in this place.

It wasn't just the Macs' activities here – there was also the evil echoes of whole families, dads, mums and kids, all rounded-up and slaughtered, their lives extinguished in the cold business of colonisation.

He swallowed painfully; tried to shake the dread, but it settled on his heart like a veil of flies. Wiping sweat and rain off his face, he moved towards the centre of the grove.

It wasn't easy to see how many fig trees there actually were. They'd been growing around and over and into each other for a long, long time, and the mass and mess of it was baffling.

Thick vertical branches grew from the horizontal ones into the ground, or fused into others. Solid ropes of aerial roots made impenetrable nets and screens. Two massive trunks slumped together, the twisted whiskers of yet more arboreal roots sprouting from their creased grey hides. Looking like molten animals – giant snakes and elephants frozen in battle, the grove of fig trees was an enormous maze.

Seth used the ragged curtains and columns of standing aerial roots as cover. Getting closer to the escarpment-like mass of the tree trunks, he ducked and froze – alerted by something moving up ahead.

A figure was ascending, rising up through space in the living cathedral of trees. About five or six metres above the ground, it came to a stop: a gagged and bound man gently swinging in the thick damp air. Suspended head-first from a rope around his ankles, Pete Neary looked like a beast ready for butchering.

Brothers

The rain slackened then came to a stop. From the dark roof above, unseen droplets fell, plopping and pattering onto the ground. Rivulets of water ran down trunks and root columns, evicting insects, and the humidity pressed in like a drunk mate.

Seth watched the buttress roots and tree trunk beneath the hanging man for movement as a minute ticked by. It looked like the Macs had hung The Fossil up to age a bit, softening him up for the gruesome grilling to come.

He looked down at the revolver in his hand. It was a powerful, accurate gun, but with a four-inch barrel he had to get close – at least ten metres close. Actually, make that as close as he bloody could, because Liam would have that Colt semi-auto from yesterday, and Gordy . . . well, best to assume he was armed too. It wasn't real good odds.

But they weren't expecting him, and the labyrinth of figs provided good cover. He had a real chance of ambushing the bastards – and gunning them down.

Taking a mental fix on the hanging figure of Neary, Seth began slowly moving towards the nearest fig tree, his mind gauging the best route to get in close without being seen. Sliding over the long thigh-high plate of a buttress root, the sole of his loafer slipped and he fell, thumping against the jumble of roots on the ground.

He suppressed an oath. Not only was that noisy – he'd dropped the fucking gun. Hopping up, he looked around. It took long frantic seconds to find it: fallen in a crevice between two big roots. He leaned right in, but the gun was out of reach. Panic sloshed in his belly. Keeping low to the ground and very alert, he looked about for a fallen branch of the right length and diameter. It took a minute or so, and he crept back to the crevice.

It wasn't easy, but after several attempts he began to get the hang of it. He'd get the pistol up to his waiting fingers on the next go.

There was a faint sound nearby. Seth spun around and caught a flash of movement through ropes of serpentine roots. Dropping the stick, he stepped away from the gun and listened hard. In the sound chamber of the vast grove, the noise came again – the faint scrunch of a boot on dry leaves. Seth raised his fists.

A sweetly hoarse voice said, "G'day mate."

Through a vertical gap in a great slab of fig tree trunk a few meters away, Gordy Mac was pointing a shotgun right at him. Seth kept very bloody still. From this distance he'd get turned into pet mince.

Then Gordy vanished, and Seth made to run, but the bastard darted around the trunk very fast; the shottie snapping back to his shoulder as he came to a stop. With ice now filling his guts, Seth settled back on his heels.

Gordy Mac studied him with narrowed eyes, his ginger moustache twitching as he moved his tongue inside his mouth. Without dropping his gaze, he spat past his trigger hand onto the ground. "Cheap bloody steak."

Seth waited, wondering – where the hell was Liam?

"Move over there will ya, mate?" said Gordy, using a jerk of the shotgun barrel to indicate a spot next to some hanging roots. Seth moved over nice and slow; Gordy Mac turning like a well-oiled wheel to keep the gun on him.

That's a Remington shotgun with at least four shells up the tube, thought Seth. Gordy's a crack-shot. Growing up on farms out west, he'd have shot hundreds of pigs and dingos – and a few blokes. Shooting was second-nature to him, and that made him far more lethal than any tooled-up local crim or gun thug in Kings Cross. Always, the boys from the bush were the ones to watch.

He stopped at Gordy's nod, and saw the clever bastard's eyes flickering over the ground around him; mapping out its unevenness in preparation for whatever came next.

A burst of electricity lit Seth up. Sprint forward, go low and dive hard, he thought. Get under the shotgun barrel and spring up under the ear-shattering blast.

Gordy Mac's eyes snapped back onto him like fucking Lee Van Cleef, his red knuckle in the Remington's trigger guard looking more than ready to squeeze. They stared at each other for a bit, neither even close to underestimating the other. Then Gordy nodded in approval.

"Nice shirt, mate. You wanna lose the hat, though."

Up your arse, thought Seth. Out beyond the grove of fig trees, the pheasant coucals called.

"So, Sabbo's been in your ear," said Gordy. "And you've been getting in old mate Pete's ear, and poor old Kev too. Stirring this up hasn't helped anybody, has it?"

And you want to know who else's ear, thought Seth. When Liam comes back, you'll get to finding that out. His guts filled with ice. It might get very bloody painful soon – then end.

He flashed on Hugh now; his mate must have rung the cops, and although there weren't any cop-shops up on the northern beaches, Mrs. Sampson's call would have got the ball rolling. He had to draw this out a bit longer.

"I just want Sabbo out of Stuart Creek," he said.

"That's not gonna happen, mate. He's in there because he's in there because he's in there. You've a better chance turning back the tide."

"You never know until you have a go."

"There's nothing to go for. It's done and dusted."

"Nah. See, Sabbo's got a big family and half of Innisfail put in a word for him in court. And there's others who are onto this; ex-cops, lawyers – even a Brisbane detective. If Neary and I don't make it back for tea tonight – there's some serious blokes who'll want to know why."

Gordy Mac laughed.

"Brisbane detective? You mean Burns? He doesn't give a piss-fart about Sabbo. He'll tell you anything you want to hear. He told you he was going to bust me, right?"

Gordy chuckled at Seth's desperately impassive face.

"Burns is full of it, but he'll pay good. Looks like I'll be doing a bit of business with him after all. I had to string him along to push up the price, and you helped. Thanks."

Gordy Mac took the shotgun from his shoulder, held it across his chest, and let a winning smile crease his face.

"Look, mate, let's be reasonable. What say we walk over there, you knock Neary as a sign of good faith then come in with us and be the man we know you are."

Seth shook his head.

"Oho – the tough kid, hey?' said Gordy. "I remember when you . . ."

The Remington flew back up into position, now aimed slightly to the left of Seth's head. Something had caught Gordy Mac's eye; something beyond Seth.

Keeping his body very still, Seth slowly turned his head to look over his shoulder. There was a silhouette moving at the entrance of the track into the grove. As it came in under the big canopy, Seth's date squirmed. Liam.

"Who's that?" muttered Gordy Mac and relief washed through Seth. It wasn't Liam – the first cop was here.

"Go stand over there," hissed Gordy, gesturing with the shotgun towards the big buttress root of a nearby tree. "Keep your yap shut or I'll blow it off."

As Seth went towards the root, his eyes looked beyond it to another buttress root then on to the trunk of the next giant fig, its girth sinuously curving away in a gloomy web of aerial roots. Near the waist-high wall of the root, he stopped. Though pretty much boxed in, he could easily see over the buttress root, and he turned to look at the approaching figure. In the low light he made out long hair, and his heart sank like a stone. It was Hugh.

"Shhh," murmured Gordy, and they watched in silence as the figure got closer and closer. Seth wanted to yell out, but Gordy would kill him. Then he and Liam would hunt the King of Rock and Roll down like a mongrel dog.

With his city-boy eyes and brain, Hugh was just a few metres away before he saw Gordy pointing the shotgun at him. He stopped and yelled in shock.

"Ohhhh, man," said Seth, making Hugh turn to him. He gave his stupid, stupid friend an intense look that said – did you call them? Hugh, blinking in shock, managed a nod. Then he stumbled forward and yelled at Gordy Mac, his voice cracking with fear.

"Don't shoot him! Aim that at me, man."

Gordy frowned – he *was* aiming at the long-haired fool.

"Who's this?" said Gordy.

"Don't worry about him – he's nobody," said Seth.

"I wouldn't say that," said Hugh.

"Shut up, Hugh."

"Hugh beauty," said Gordy. "Hugh nobody."

"You ever watch Countdown or listen to rock music?" Hugh's eyes glittered with emotion.

"Nah, music's for poofs and girls."

Somewhat shocked, Hugh shut up.

Where's Liam? thought Seth, looking around.

Gordy Mac showed him a line of good teeth.

"He'll be back in a sec – don't you worry. Bloody cheap steak gave him the runs. Then you're gonna tell us what's true . . . and what's bullshit."

"This is bullshit," said Seth. "Hugh's from Sydney and he really is famous. Put us in the ground and his very well-connected family won't stop until you're locked up. Like I said, there's people who'll want to know what happened to us. There's a shit-hot lawyer, and my Uncle Don, who's a decorated ex-copper with a footy team's worth of mates still on the force. Killing a few dumbo crims is one thing, but you're playing with fire if you knock us."

Gordy Mac allowed himself a frown.

"This is a big pile of shit you're walking into, Gordy, one you'll never get out of. Face the facts, mate. Liam's got to own-up to bashing Neary. He's got to do the time."

Gordy Mac's face contorted in rage.

"Get fucked!" He jabbed the Remington at Seth. "What sort of a dog ya think I am? Shop my own brother?"

The knuckle whitened. Gordy was going to shoot him, but no – the bastard had a whole lot more to say.

"You think you know us but you don't! We've done stuff that would uncurl your pubes. We've fronted blokes so hard you'd break axes on them. Sorted out the bastards five *and* six at a time – shit that would make the Barbary Coast the other night look like dancing lessons! We've twisted bent coppers around our fingers and drop-kicked crims back over the border, and we always backed each other up. Always! You think I'd shop in my own brother? Would you have done that to Alex? Hey? Hey?"

Seth felt unbearable longing and sadness. Alex? I need you now, mate. It was too hard – loving someone who was gone, and his brother had been gone five years now.

Driving back down from Auntie Grace's on the winding Gillies Highway in a thunderstorm, Alex had come off the road and tumbled fifty metres into a gully. Seth had seen his ute – a twisted metal coffin covered in flies.

Mum had been in that ute. She'd died too.

The pain was manageable now, but the guilt sometimes floored him. If only he'd had the guts that day.

"Answer me!" yelled Gordy. "Would you have shopped Alex to the cops?"

What a stupid-arse question, thought Seth. Though he could be a real bastard, Alex would never have bashed a bloke nearly to death; then made somebody else take the punishment. Kellys and MacIntyres? Two different beasts entirely.

"Would never have happened," said Seth. "Alex had the guts to front-up for whatever he did. So, you gonna kill us because of your brother's stupid temper?"

"Yeah, why not? We'll make it the double. You won't be the first Kelly boy we've put in the ground."

Under the shadowed roof of dripping figs, falling water-drops slowed and stopped; tiny balls of silver suspended in mid-air. The patter and rustle of dripping water clicked off. This complete stillness was a deep inhalation – the calm before the howling noise that filled Seth's head.

It was as if Gordy Mac had punched his brain clear out of his skull. Something huge shifted inside him, slipping and grating like giant bone cogs out of sync; then locking in with an immense sub-sonic thud. He had shifted into a gear he never knew existed.

Gordy Mac laughed. "How about that, aye?"

Seth was silent.

"Alex was so stupid. And we were become mates again. Nicking twenty pounds of our dope then trying to sell it to mates of ours? C'mon. We hid in their tractor shed and when he was done unloading it, we jumped him. But the clever bastard got to his ute and took off. The rain was fierce that day and we finally gave up looking for him and went down the Gillies in a storm.

"And guess who was there in front of us? Your stupid brother. Liam just piled into him and rammed him right off the road. I'd have been happy just giving him a good flogging. Yeah, sorry about your mum."

"I'm not," said Liam, coming around the flank of a fig tree. He was empty handed and bare-chested, a green t-shirt tucked into his shorts.

"What . . . what!" In shock, Hugh looked back and forth from Liam to Gordy – then beseeched Seth with bugged-out eyes. "Did he just say his brother killed your brother and your mother?"

"Who the fuck is this?" said Liam.

"Who the fuck are you?" Hugh yelled hysterically.

"I'm Liam."

Hugh goggled at him, making bleating noises. Then he sank down, hyperventilating madly, onto his haunches. Liam came over like a shark, circled around Hugh and then stood over him. Looking very pleased, he gave Seth a horrible knowing smile.

Iceberg cold now; his heart numb, his brain crystalline; Seth quickly clarified what he'd just seen in the waistband of Liam's shorts – a piece of steel pipe, not the Colt pistol.

Gordy Mac spat again and cleared his throat.

"OK, let's get to it, aye? What did you tell Burns about Sabbo? And who's this lawyer?"

Seth said nothing.

"Oi!" yelled Gordy Mac, "You listening to me?"

"I think we broke him," crowed Liam. "From rooster to feather duster – just like that."

In celebration, he gave Hugh a swift kick in the ribs, and the crouching guitarist squealed in pain.

"Ha! He's like his poofter mate here," said Liam. "Too scared to speak."

Seth laughed.

"What the fuck are you laughing at?" said Liam.

"Calling *us* poofs," said Seth. "That's real cheeky. See, a lot of the blokes wonder why you're never with women, let alone a girlfriend. They all reckon you're into blokes and I think they're right."

Liam shot Gordy a wild questioning glance.

"Yeah, check with big brother first," said Seth. "Does he have to hold your prick when you take a piss?"

"I'm gonna make you scream for your mum," said Liam, reaching down to his waist. Metal pipe time, thought Seth, taking his first, and maybe last, steps forwards.

"Liam," said Gordy Mac. "Liam!"

Seth kept chucking shit like a monkey at the zoo.

"You're piss-weak, mate, a real mental midget. You're nothing without your brother – everybody says so."

"Shut up!" bellowed Gordy, shaking the shotgun muzzle at Seth "Get the fuck back!"

An ear-splitting scream shocked them all. It was Hugh; a wild-haired apparition springing up, his head aimed at the underside of Liam's jaw. There was no way he could miss, and as Seth saw the shotgun jerk towards Hugh, he spun around and went from zero to a hundred – the muscles in his legs exploding with power and energy.

He ran at the buttress root and dived over it. From behind him came the clack of teeth, a big grunt, and the sound of the metal pipe bouncing off roots. Then the Remington boomed.

It felt very wrong leaving Hugh, but an American mate had explained it to him one time. As a teenage lifeguard in California, he'd been trained to go in if someone fell off a pier. In rough seas the person in distress would be used as a buffer against the shell-encrusted concrete pylons of the pier; the brutal logic being – if you don't keep the rescuer safe, you now have two victims.

Seth slammed onto the ground, taking most of the force on his shoulder and mashing his left ear hard. Rolling, he felt the hard ridges of roots chop into his ribs. Gasping from the pummelling, he used the roll's energy to leap up and swing up over the next buttress root wall. Boom! The edge of the root exploded in a spray of pulped pith by his elbow, the living wood shuddering in his hands. Gordy was unbelievably quick – but he'd missed.

Behind the buttress, Seth landed hard then scrambled madly on all fours along the curve of the fig tree.

"You idiot! C'mon! He's running for it!" shouted Gordy. Liam screamed weirdly. His brother swore.

Keeping lizard low, Seth went around the fig and on to the one beyond. Out of sight now, Gordy's voice fading, he stood up and ran, jumping over the ankle-twisting mess underfoot, dodging the vertical branches and roots; going flat-out like a winger with the ball and the try-line in sight.

Adrenalin was electrifying him, but he forced himself to take cover behind a tree trunk for a moment. He had to be real damn smart in his choice of direction here. This maze of figs was full of dead-ends; living cages he'd get caught and shot dead in. As he looked for the way ahead, his ears listened for the sounds of pursuit.

In the dripping silence he touched his mashed ear; saw blood on his fingers. He'd lost his floppy hat, his ribs had been pummelled, and – damn, his silk shirt was ripped right across the back. It was ruined! He tore it off in anger then took a deep breath to clear the bullshit from his head. OK, he thought. I need the Python pronto.

There'd be short-cuts here that only a kid who'd played in these trees would know. Seth shivered. It didn't feel like kids had ever played here. More like died here.

Ditching his socks and ruined loafers, he slid up the fat fig trunk and carefully peeped back at the way he'd come.

A figure was moving with canny silent steps through the snaking roots and branches towards him – Liam, and the prick had found his hat and was wearing it. Blood ran from his chin, streaking the t-shirt he'd put back on. He paused, opened his mouth and painfully stuck out his tongue. Seth felt savage glee at what he saw. The bastard had bitten half of it off. Shivering with the shock of his injury, Liam moaned then closed his mouth.

A faint crack of a branch breaking underfoot sounded. Liam ignored it and Seth knew that Gordy was coming fast from around the other side of the stand of figs. The bastards were encircling him. Molasses slow, he pulled his head back. The only way now was up.

Using lateral rootlets sprouting from its trunk as hand-holds, he quietly climbed the tree; toes splayed for grip, his biceps swollen with effort. The roots bit into his hands and he slipped back a couple of times, but got himself six metres up onto a big, thick branch.

Long and oval, it was a metre wide in parts, with stinky wet fissures and rotted hollows along its length. Laying on the sweeping limb, Seth listened. Nothing moved, but he could feel Liam listening right back.

Up here he had a better sense of direction. He carefully looked around at the fig trees, trying to spot a route along the branches. Getting to the Python was going to require some Tarzan-style leaping and climbing.

Crawling along the ponderous living log, glad it couldn't sway or move under him, he sensed movement below and stopped. Drifting his head towards the edge, he looked obliquely over it, and saw Liam creeping along on all fours towards the fig tree's trunk. Seth had a bad feeling he was going to climb up it.

As he lay there, something moved under his neck and in a ticklish rush of movement, one of those big poisonous centipedes came running up onto his face. Grimacing in disgust, he shut his eyes and locked his body against the spasm of reaction. Happy as Larry, the creature trailed mindlessly across his face then stopped in his hair – its stinger right by his eye. For crying out loud, thought Seth.

A few long heartbeats went by before the unholy thing began to move again, its length rustling along his skull, its feet busy in his hair. At his mashed ear it paused. Then started nibbling. The old locking the body against spasms business began to falter. It was too mind-bendingly itchy for him to take.

Starting slowly, then speeding up, he tilted his head and felt the centipede's weight move under the tug of gravity. As it began squirming, trying to hang on, Seth jerked his head and flicked the centipede off onto the wide branch – where it would hopefully piss off. Looking tightly over his shoulder, he saw the big insect scrabbling to stay on the branch – then vanish into space.

From not far below came a grunt; the falling centipede startling Liam. Now the bastard had to be looking up, just knowing he was lying there on the branch.

Sure enough, a loud ragged cry rang out to summon his brother. Seth hopped up and took off. At the sight of him, Liam howled like a dog, his eyes drilling up were insane with rage and pain. Beyond feral, he looked rabid.

It was piss chilling alright, and with his hands grabbing at aerial roots for balance – Seth ran for his life. Liam followed, moaning and grunting as he leapt around the fig tree's great sprawling base.

A long limb from the next fig appeared through leaves, and Seth went for it; monkey-climbing up a long twist of cable sized roots. Close to the branch, his palms, wet and gritty, slipped. As he fell, he hooked an arm around the roots, taking some bark-burn arresting his fall. Hanging there, he flung his other arm up and grabbed tight. With groping feet he found solid purchase on the root rope.

Up he went, but as he got to the branch, the wet roots slipped through his hands again, and he pulled a move to make Nadia Comaneci proud. Swinging his legs sideways onto the branch, he jack-knifed the rest of himself up onto it. It wasn't a perfect ten, but it would do.

Laying on the branch, he stared up into the canopy and listened as the big tree's crown rippled and stirred in the wind. Thank you, Kahuna Buddha person, he thought.

He carefully got up and began to navigate the long limb, the trunk and branches of this new tree now hiding him from Liam.

Then he remembered Gordy was coming the other way. He was in plain sight up here – a big blonde possum ready to be shot to pieces. He quickly got back down again and started crawling along the hard, wet skin of the fig.

Halfway across, a noise below made him stop. Sneaking a look, he saw Gordy Mac taking cover behind the fat slump of arboreal root, the Remington swinging up into firing position. Knowing his pale face in the dark canopy was screamingly obvious, Seth began to inch his head back – praying that the bastard wouldn't look up.

But the bastard was busy looking down the barrel of the shotgun; concentration etched on his face. Then he fired. Something good-sized flopped onto the ground, there was a faint liquid sound, then silence.

Gordy jerked the shotgun down. His mouth flew open. He walked forward, the gun slack by his side, and called out in a shivery child-like voice, "Liam? Liam?"

Seth quickly stood – and jumped, falling through the air like a V8 engine block, his knees aimed at Gordy's head and back. It was a vertical tackle from the Devil's team; Seth willing death into him; projecting total killing force, his whole intent to batter through muscle and bone and rupture and burst internal organs.

As they hit the deck, Seth expended the energy of his

fall into Gordy Mac and fell sideways, his eyes finding the Remington as it clattered onto roots. It took a moment to get to his feet, and he snatched up the shotgun, pumped in a fresh cartridge and aimed it at Gordy Mac's head.

His first instinct was to shoot, but the man didn't move. Snapping the shotgun up to his cheek, he swept it in an arc – praying for Liam to appear in the gloom. Adrenaline fizzed through his blood; murderous wrath buzzed in his head. Like a berserk warrior, he shivered with fury.

Then he saw about five metres away, a tangle of freshly torn aerial roots at head-height, standing out white and sappy – and someone laying beneath it. Liam.

He lowered the shotgun and walked over. A chunk of Liam's head was missing. By his body lay the green floppy hat, oozing with viscous grey and bright fresh red.

Oh yeah, thought Seth. The boys from the bush sure knew how to shoot.

Killing the Dragon

The sight of Liam punched a steel pin of pain and regret right through him. He'd wanted hands-on revenge, but he wasn't going to get it now. Going back to Gordy Mac, he put the shotgun to his head. You'll do, he thought. And I'll be doing the world a real favour.

The dismal drone of insects rose and fell. His battered ribs throbbed and sweat ran into his eyes.

"Don't do it, Seth!" came a frenzied cry.

He turned and saw a man waving his hands in the air like a crazed messiah in the desert. Hugh.

Joy flooded through him like cool fresh water. He took his finger off the trigger and he went to his friend. Hugh's clothes were a mess and he was shivering with shock, but thank Christ – he was unhurt. In elation they hugged, and Seth felt profound relief.

"What you did," he said softly in Hugh's ear. "Mate."

They drew apart, Hugh beaming with stunned pride, and Seth looked over at Gordy. He was motionless, blood bubbling at the corners of his mouth. You'll keep for a few minutes, thought Seth.

Hugh had noticed Liam now, and before he could get a good look, Seth led him to where Pete Neary was. Untying the rope, they lowered him as gently as they could onto the ground. Seth cut the bonds, helped Neary remove the gag, and after a few choice oaths and a great hawk of a spit, the old crim looked up at Hugh.

· "Looks like you saved our arses, boy," he said.

"I knew if Seth got a chance, we'd all have a chance," said Hugh and he furiously rubbed the top of his head.

"I think I broke his jaw!" His voice jerked and jumped. "I got behind him and ran for it! I was really good at the hundred metres in school! If I hadn't started playing the guitar – well who knows?"

Neary stared at Hugh.

"Hey, I got a shotgun fired at me!" yelled Hugh happily.

Neary shook his head, then grumbled to his feet.

"Where are those bastards?" he said.

"I'll show you," said Seth.

He made a 'stay put' gesture at Hugh, picked up the shotgun and took Neary to the brothers. The scarred crim stood over Liam; his red face impassive as he took in the damage Gordy had done. Then he spat on the ground next to the corpse.

"No tears for you, mate," he said.

"The cops are coming now," said Seth. "We got to work out our stories."

"Yeah, you do," said Neary, looking at the Remington in Seth's hand. He pursed scarred lips, his brain going over what he'd heard before the third shot. Seth waited for the question, but Neary just gestured for the shotgun.

Seth gave it to him and he went over to Gordy Mac. Taking his t-shirt off, he wiped down the gun with it. Then using the shirt as a glove, he carefully pressed Gordy's fingers onto the trigger, pump and stock of the shotgun; using each hand accordingly. Holding the Remington by the end of its barrel, Neary laid it down a little distance from the unconscious man.

"Don't want the wrong story," he said.

"Yep," said Seth. "So, we'll tell the cops the truth? The whole story. Why they grabbed you and how it was Liam who bashed you last year."

Neary pulled his t-shirt back on and regarded Seth for a long moment. "You came for me. I won't forget that."

It wasn't even close to springing Sabbo from prison, but Seth let it be for the moment.

With two lengths cut from the rope, they bound Gordy Mac's wrists and ankles. Testing the knots, Seth looked at his face and felt a bilious stew of emotions in his gut; satisfaction being the least of them.

"Listen," said Neary. "What you did for me . . ."

"Help me get my mate out of Stuart and we're square."

"That's what I was thinking. I wanna do it. Tell the truth in court. Stick it up Gordy and his brother – may he burn in hell."

Seth could have hugged the bastard, but he put out his hand instead. The Fossil shook it firmly with a rough paw. It was a deal and it was done.

They walked back to Hugh, who was now puffing on a

Stuyvie. "How you doing?" Seth asked him.

"OK, I guess. I'm . . . wow." Hugh looked happily dazed.

Seth now remembered the Python. It was a crime scene here, though it felt like it had been one for a hundred years, and the cops would have a good poke around.

"Wait here a sec," he said. Stray waterdrops fell on his back and chest as he went over and located the gun. Using the branch from before, he inched the Python up until he could grab it. Too good to chuck away, he stuck it in his pocket, and then went back to Hugh and Neary.

"Let's go wait for the cops out there," said Seth.

"Yeah, this place is bad news," said Neary.

As they walked under the trees towards the light, Seth stopped and listened. While Hugh and Neary moved on, he went back to the bodies lying in the gloom. Gordy Mac was conscious now, moaning in pain, and Seth stood over him in silence.

Finally, Gordy noticed him. His eyes flickered in agony; foamy blood and saliva plastered his moustache and ran off his chin. Looking dumbly up, he forced out words, the low growl of his voice now a desiccated croak.

'Ohhh – my back, my chest. I'm real fucked up, mate."

His eyes darted about.

"Liam? Liam! What did I do?"

Gordy began to cry, his smashed-up body shaking with painful ragged sobbing. Seth stared at him. Just like that, hey, he thought.

Seeing a man he'd been afraid of since he was sixteen, now in pieces: physically, mentally and emotionally, was very strange. A shitload of stuff just flew off him then, like sheets of corrugated iron in a big blow, and a seemingly life-long load left him.

Crystal bloody clear now, he saw how the driving fists and evil smiles, and all that menace made of spilt blood and violent death would one day come to its inevitable end. It went from A to fucking B.

Stories Dad had told him and Alex as kids now flashed through his head: Beowulf & Grendel, Theseus and the Minotaur, St. George and the Dragon. The beast was dead but he didn't feel like a hero.

"Seth, mate. Where's Liam? Where's my brother?"

Seth's eyes flicked over to Liam's body. Gordy saw that, and he madly tried to look, frantically fighting against the roots under him, rocking and twisting; first husking out shouts of pain then panting in misery.

Seth watched him gasp down mouthfuls of air as he finally turned himself over. His head moved – then froze. Through a gap in the root columns, he beheld his brother, and a primitive keening wail burst out of him. He raged and shook as if in a fit, his boots jumping and knocking against roots.

Some blokes reckoned wreaking revenge was the best feeling, but Seth didn't feel it. Instead, he was gripped by an awful truth. As he watched the power of Gordy Mac and all those bastards like him turn to dust, he saw not just Gordy there – but Alex too.

Devastated, he turned and vacantly walked along the track out into the light. By the orange car, Neary shot him a look devoid of judgment. Hugh stared with fearful eyes.

"He saw his brother," said Seth.

Hugh let out a big breath. Neary snorted.

"I'm going down to the garage for a minute," said Seth, and he jogged over to the sheds.

Under the lee of a dripping roof, he fossicked through a forty-four-gallon drum and found some plastic bags and an oily rag. After wiping the Python clean, he wrapped it with the speed loader in the rag, and then the plastic; securing it all with a bit of wire. Then he walked into the nearby bush and hooked the package up on a branch. When the dust settled, he'd return for it.

Walking back, he felt totally drained of energy; bereft of thought or feeling. His body throbbed like a bastard too.

He sat on the bonnet of the Datsun while Neary silently smoked a rollie. Hugh paced about on the squishy grass, smoking too; occasionally throwing glances at Seth.

Ten or fifteen minutes went by before a white police Land Cruiser appeared at the far end of the clearing. In an explosion of nervous energy, Hugh yelled at it, waving his arms in the air. Seth got off the Datsun, and he and Neary stood with their hands in full view.

Bumping and skidding over the grass, the vehicle pulled up and two edgy-looking cops got out; hands hovering at their gun holsters. Neary sneered contemptuously.

The cops relaxed a bit as Seth gave them the bare-bones of it. Then he took them into the grove of figs where Gordy Mac now lay silent; his eyes tightly closed.

After grimacing at Liam's head, the cops identified the brothers from their wallets, and Seth helped them carry Gordy Mac out to the clearing. The junior cop radioed it in, and at the mention of the victim and suspect's names, the fella at the Esplanade, gruffly incredulous over the crackle, made him go through it all again.

"Twenty to twenty-five minutes they reckon," reported Junior when he was done. "Well, that caused a big stir. Who the hell are these MacIntyres, anyway?"

"Criminal scum," said his boss, looking straight at Seth and Neary. You can take your tarbrush and stick it up your arse, thought Seth.

The cops questioned Hugh and Neary, but neither had much to say. After that, they all waited in tense silence until the homicide detectives arrived, closely followed by the ambulance.

It was a small town alright: the two Ds were Sideburns and the Maggot, and they looked impatiently at Seth and Gordy Mac while the senior copper gave them his report. Sideburns instructed the uniformed boys to watch Neary and Hugh, then gestured for Seth to lead on.

As they moved out of earshot, the two Ds bubbled over.

"Fuck me! Liam Mac." said Sideburns.

"You shot him, didn't you?" said the Maggot.

"Nah," said Seth with a definitive shake of his head.

The two Ds laughed in hearty disbelief.

"You're a machine, Kelly – you really are."

"He's gonna put us out of a job, Barry – I swear he is."

Under the dark roof of fig trees, the two cops chortled like kids on an Easter-egg hunt, fairly wetting themselves at the sight of Liam Mac. Gazing down at the body, they fell silent, wallowing in tabloid-headline emotions. They were living the dream.

"Well, how about that," said Sideburns finally. "Liam

bloody MacIntyre. A few crims will sleep easier tonight."

"I sure will," tittered the Maggot.

Getting right to it, Seth told them what had gone down. He knew he was going to have to tell this story again and again, and already he was tired of it.

"What's with the long face, mate? Buggerlugs here," Sideburns punted his shoe into the dead man's ribs, "Was going to put you in the ground. I thought you'd be a bit more pleased."

Yeah, so did I, thought Seth. But stranger still, was the surge of anger he felt at the cop kicking Liam.

The Weight of Love

When Sabbo came out the entrance of Her Majesty's Prison Stuart Creek, sniffing the air like it was freshly baked bread, he saw a huge smile in the driver's window of a Toyota FJ 55. He walked over, the owner of the smile got out, and they had a bloody good hug. Some idiot in a parked car wolf-whistled but Sabbo didn't care. No bloke ever had a mate like Seth Kelly.

Even his family thought that now. Dad and Vinnie had been keen to pick him up and take him to Innisfail, but they'd understood; he wanted to see the bloke who'd got him out of jail first.

Jeez, what a big lump of muscle thought Sabbo. He let go and the two men beamed at each other. Then, bugger it – Sabbo hugged him again.

"Woah," said Seth. "Let's go find you a lady first thing, aye?"

They got in the Pig and grinned at each other.

"What do you want to do first?" said Seth. "I'll drive you to the Gold Coast if you like."

Sabbo laughed like the free man he was.

"You know what – let's get out of here quick-smart and stop in at Cardwell for some toasted crab sangas."

"Nice. Then we'll have a couple of beers at the pub."

"Genius there, Kelly, genius."

Driving north, they raved about cars, the footy, fishing, music, and just about everything else – except for the story of Sabbo's emancipation. That was for when they were having a beer.

At the Seaview, a McCafferty's coach was pulling out. Inside it was empty of customers, the tables being cleared by two young women in t-shirts and shorts, and Sabbo smiled softly, grateful for their presence.

At the counter, a sweaty-faced but genial lady took their order; toasted mud-crab sandwiches, three each please, and a couple of nice cold Bundaberg ginger beers they'd grabbed from the drink fridge.

They sat at the open side of the café. On the sidewalk a teen loitered on a rust-specked chopper bicycle, looking damn serious about something. Seth and Sabbo quietly grinned at the little tough-guy, and then they idly looked across the deserted two-lane highway to where palm trees framed the view of the islands in Rockingham Bay. Nice.

Their food came and while they hoed in, multi-coloured lorikeets fed noisily in a flowering tree by the road. Soon just crumbs remained on their plates, and they went for a walk down along the seashore and blew a joint that Seth had thoughtfully brought.

Then they moseyed up to the pub and had a few beers, and while they drank, Seth filled his mate in on the whole story. Sabbo couldn't believe half it, crying out things like, "No way! The lead-guitarist of The Tygers?" and "Gordy said that?"

When Seth got to that day at Clifton Beach – with Neary hanging from a tree, Hugh's desperate attack, and Gordy killing Liam – Sabbo fell silent. Seth didn't tell him about Mum and Alex. Even Dad wouldn't know about that.

Sabbo basically knew the rest; the appeal clinched with Neary's testimony, which was pro bono too, and Gordy Mac finally admitting that his brother had bashed Neary. I guess it's not dobbing if he's dead, thought Seth.

Gordy Mac had a slew of offences; manslaughter being one, and what with the drugs, money and illegal guns found on the property he'd just bought; the bastard wasn't getting out until the 21st century.

In court, Seth tried to catch his eye, but Gordy looked drugged-up; as though on strong painkillers. Seeing that Seth had broken his shoulder, four ribs, a few other bones, and collapsed a lung – that seemed pretty likely.

And a beer with Robbie the Bomb confirmed what Seth pretty much knew. Totally busted and broke, and without his evil brother, Gordy Mac was finished as a force in the criminal world of the north. The only thing likely to make Seth watch his back now were magpies with chicks in the nest.

"Who'd believe it?" said Sabbo, when Seth finished. "If it hadn't happened to us, I'd be calling bullshit for sure."

Seth nodded and drank his cold beer. There'd also been something else happen that day that he wasn't going to tell Sabbo about.

When he'd got to the watchhouse in Cairns, Sideburns had left him in an interview room; a bright, windowless box stinking of paranoid sweat, old ciggie smoke and stale farts. Time had gone by slowly.

Sitting with his back to the door, he didn't turn when it opened. It was Sideburns, back to start the interview. But as the footsteps came up, Seth heard the metallic click of a revolver being cocked behind his head.

Bad things could happen to a bloke inside a Queensland copshop; threats and verballing the least of it; bashings and 'accidental' deaths the worst. Sideburns knew all that. The bastard was trying to put a scare into him.

"This is from Gordy Mac," said an unfamiliar voice.

Seth's heart skipped. Then familiar laughter rang out and he turned to see Chris Burns cracking up, his eyes wide with glee. His hands were empty, but the unclipped holster on his belt wasn't. Seth felt like hitting the idiot.

"So, you got him," said Burns. "And with two witnesses who'll say otherwise. Very sharp, mate, very sharp."

Seth flatly shook his head. The cop stared at him – then nodded. "I bet you wish you had," he said.

Seth shook his head again, but he couldn't quite hide the lie in his eyes. Burns had loved that.

"You right there, Seth?" Sabbo was looking at him with concern. Seth nodded and finished his beer.

"I'd have been freaked-out too, seeing Liam like that," said Sabbo. "Rotten bastard that he was. Let's talk about something else, aye?"

They did, and after a couple more beers they piled into the Pig and began heading north again.

Seth flicked on the Marantz. It was on radio and playing a top track – Rio de Camero by The Masters Apprentices – and they grooved on that until the ads came on.

Seth turned the radio down and cast a speculative eye at the cassettes in the middle console. What would Sabbo like? He began reeling off titles. Sabbo happily shrugged.

"All of them, mate," he said. "But listen, I wanna give you some money. For what you did for me."

"Nah, just pay me what I spent – five hundred bucks."

"No, I want to give you more."

"No way, man. You've got a garage to get going."

"No listen, Seth, I . . ."

"Look, get me out of prison if the time comes. But only if I'm innocent, okay?"

Sabbo laughed and the over-excited voices on the radio came to an end. A song began, its guitar intro and chiming chords very familiar. Seth boosted the volume as the bass, drums and keyboards kicked in. Sabbo beamed like a kid and nodded in approval. Seth racked his brains. This song – he knew it. Then the vocals came in.

up the back of Clifton Beach
where Sabbo's garage used to be
some everyday history went down
beneath a man hanging from a tree

"What the hell!" yelled Sabbo.

"Shhh! Shhh!" yelled Seth.

He pulled over in a screech of rubber, killed the engine and they stared open-mouthed at each other.

It was a showdown many years foretold
and somebody there, well he never got old

a shotgun in a brother's hand
broke out of jail an innocent man
The guitar dirtied right up as the pre-chorus started.
when you run with the hardest boys in town
you learn your lessons wherever they are found
With a hook that was pure gold, the winner of a chorus soared. Tears pricked Seth's eyes, and damn it, if Sabbo wasn't looking like a bloody puppy too.

> *you gotta love your brother even if he doesn't care*
> *you gotta love your brother even if he isn't there*
> *if you wanna be free and live without hurtin'*
> *then you gotta be strong and carry the burden*
> *of the weight of love*

Seth turned to the window, not wanting to look like a big sook. He didn't want to look at Sabbo being one either.

Outside, the sunset soaked the landscape; the Kirrama Range crowned with a mass of white and purple cloud, the hills beneath a deep dark green. Ten metres away, some big storks were foraging in the scrub.

As he listened, marvelling at the song and its execution, Seth thought of Alex. Letting go wasn't easy, but he felt he was just about there. And he thought of Sabbo and Vinnie. And Gordy and Liam Mac too. What a life, aye?

The music stopped and the chiming guitar of the intro came back in as a haunting coda. A semi-trailer roared by, rocking the Pig in its wake and the song ended. Silence. Then the announcer hurriedly came back on.

"Wow! First time we've played that - and what a song! The Tyger's lead guitarist Hugh Christie has struck out on his own and that's his first single – The Weight of Love.

It's a new entry on the charts at number nine with a bullet, but I'm calling it right now folks – that's a number one!"

The Land Cruiser was the only vehicle on the highway now, and over Rockingham Bay more rain was coming in. In the scrub by the road, the feeding storks looked up, alerted by strange sounds; mad whoops and yells coming from the two-tone truck.

A bit of everyday history had gone down.

Author's Note

Far North Queensland is full of characters. Over the years I've been lucky enough to meet a few of them. So, this is where I tell you that the 'resemblance to anyone living or deceased in this book is entirely coincidental.'

The Weight of Love is the second novel in a trilogy featuring Seth Kelly, set in Far North Queensland, and taking place in the 1970s and 1980s.

A soundtrack to The Weight of Love

Here is some of the music from the book, plus some complimentary tracks that speak of the place and era – the times, latitude and attitude.

Berserk Warriors – Mental as Anything
Hard Head (Live) – Renée Geyer
I Like It Both Ways – Supernaut
Never Say Never – Romeo Void
Big Swifty – Frank Zappa
Rio de Camero – The Master's Apprentices
The Weight of Love – The Black Keys
On The Beach – Neil Young
Bad Reputation – Joan Jett
Cold Blood – Peter Tosh
No Holding Back (Ryan Theme) – John Scott
Heavy Voodoo – Lee Scratch Perry ft. Keith Richards
Sueño Con Mexico – Pat Metheny
I Got You – Split Enz

Acknowledgements

A huge acknowledgement and thank you
to my Alpha and Beta readers for their invaluable
feedback. You know who you are.

A mighty thank you to Michael 'Gonzo' Gompert
for his editorial diligence, crucial logic,
and technical knowledge.

And big love and eternal gratitude to
my best friend Jan Brown for her
savvy advice, continuing support, and
keen eye for both facts and emotions.